Praise for *Wings of a*

"*Wings of a Dream* is a sweetly told story of lost and recaptured hope. Set during a time of turbulence yet drenched in simplicity, the story transports the reader to another era. This is a perfect sit-back-and-put-your-feet-up story. Enjoy."

—Kim Vogel Sawyer,
bestselling author of *My Heart Remembers*

"Anne Mateer has crafted an unforgettable tale filled with characters who will remain in your heart long after the last page has been turned."

—Kathleen Y'Barbo,
author of *The Confidential Life of Eugenia Cooper*

". . . *Wings of a Dream* is a heartwarming story of an ordinary woman caught in the middle of extraordinary events. Anne Mateer made me laugh, she made me cry and—most of all— she made me care deeply about Rebekah and her friends and family. Readers searching for an engaging story with themes that resonate in the twenty-first century need look no further than Anne Mateer's delightful debut, *Wings of a Dream*."

—Amanda Cabot,
author of *Tomorrow's Garden*

"Mateer has written a poignant love story set amid the turbulent and often forgotten Influenza Epidemic of the early 1900s, expertly blending history and Biblical truths with warm, unforgettable characters."

—Maureen Lang,
author of *Whisper on the Wind*

WINGS *of a* DREAM

WINGS *of a* DREAM

ANNE MATEER

BETHANY HOUSE PUBLISHERS
a division of Baker Publishing Group
Minneapolis, Minnesota

© 2011 by Anne Mateer

Cover design by Dan Thornberg, Design Source Creative Services

Published by Bethany House Publishers
11400 Hampshire Avenue South
Bloomington, Minnesota 55438
www.bethanyhouse.com

Bethany House Publishers is a division of
Baker Publishing Group, Grand Rapids, Michigan

Printed in the United States of America

Library of Congress Cataloging-in-Publication Data
Mateer, Anne.
    Wings of a dream / Anne Mateer.
        p.   cm.
    ISBN 978-0-7642-0903-1 (pbk.)
    1. Young women—Fiction. 2. Farm life—Fiction. 3. Air pilots—Fiction.
4. Soldiers—Fiction. 5. Influenza Epidemic, 1918–1919—Fiction. 6. Life
change events—Fiction. I. Title.
PS3613.A824W56 2011
813'.6—dc23   2011025209

Scripture quotations are from the King James Version of the Bible.

11   12   13   14   15   16   17   7   6   5   4   3   2   1

To my Lord and Savior,

the One who gives and refines my desires and my dreams

and makes my heart willing to follow wherever they may lead.

I am humbled and amazed.

CHAPTER
1

October 1918

*R*ebekah Grace, if you don't hurry we'll be late for the lecture." Mama refrained from shouting, though her voice carried easily up the stairs and into my bedroom. Ladies didn't raise their voices, after all.

"Coming, Mama." I pinned my wide-brimmed hat over my light brown hair before turning my head from side to side, trying to get the whole view in the small looking glass mounted on the wall. The hat wasn't the latest style, but it would do. At least for Downington, Oklahoma.

Thankful that Mama had relented to skirts above my ankles, I raced down the stairs, hopping over the final step, then stopped to catch my breath before heading outside to meet Mama and Daddy. In spite of my excitement, I forced my feet to carry me with the slow dignity Mama expected of a young woman just turned nineteen.

Climbing into the back seat of the buggy, I cast a glance back at the crude shed that housed my brother's Tin Lizzie and heaved a sigh. "We could take Will's car, Mama. Arrive in style like Mrs. Thacker."

Mama harrumphed her disapproval, even though I knew in her mind Mrs. Thacker had the last word on everything of value in culture and society. "Her husband insists she ride in that thing, but she'd prefer a quiet, dependable conveyance."

I pressed my lips together to hold back a comment as Daddy signaled the horse and we jerked forward. I didn't believe Mrs. Thacker held the reservations Mama attributed to her. Mrs. Thacker had lived in the modern world, far beyond the farmlands of Oklahoma. If it hadn't been for her husband taking over the bank in town, she wouldn't have chosen to settle in Downington, I felt sure.

"I expect your help tonight, Rebekah Grace. Others will be here to improve their minds. We Downington Women's Forum members have as our duty to facilitate that effort."

"Yes, ma'am." I rummaged through my handbag, trying to hide the smile tugging at my lips. Mama might be concerned with everyone's intellect, but my intentions weren't quite so noble. Tonight I intended to make sure Arthur Samson understood my desire to get out of this town and see the world. With him.

Daddy let us off at the front door of the schoolhouse. Light shone from every window, keeping the growing darkness at bay. A large automobile idled nearby, but I couldn't see who sat behind the wheel, Arthur or Mr. Thacker, so I followed Mama inside.

"Thank heavens you're here, Margaret." Mrs. Thacker sailed toward Mama, gloved hands meeting Mama's shoulders for a moment as their cheeks almost touched. Then Mrs. Thacker pulled away. "People will begin arriving shortly."

Mama set her handbag in a seat on the front row. "What should I do to help?"

"Nothing at the moment. We'll greet people as they arrive, maybe help them find a seat. Of course I'll introduce Dr. Whitmire."

My attention wandered from their conversation. I couldn't muster the same enthusiasm for hearing a theology professor's lecture.

The door opened again. The two potted ferns he carried hid his face, but I knew it was Arthur. No one else in Downington these days wore the tall boots and brown uniform of a soldier.

"Put those up front," Mrs. Thacker told her nephew. "One on either side of the podium."

My gaze followed Arthur up the aisle, admiring his purposeful stride, his strong arms. He set down the plants as directed.

"That's fine," Mrs. Thacker said. "Now come say hello to Mrs. Hendricks and Rebekah."

He turned toward us, removing his hat as his lips rose in a lazy grin. White teeth glistened against sun-darkened skin, as did his closely cropped hair, the color of sunshine.

"So nice to see you again, Mrs. Hendricks. Miss Rebekah."

I stood straighter and grinned right back. Voices beyond the door drew Mama and Mrs. Thacker toward the entrance. The three other members of the Women's Forum bustled inside and exchanged greetings as Arthur came to stand beside me. My insides melted like butter on hot biscuits as he gazed into my eyes.

It had been the same since the first moment we'd met, nearly three weeks ago, when he'd come to Downingtown to visit his aunt and uncle. He wasn't like other boys I'd known. He didn't trudge along in dirty fields. He soared above them.

A college graduate. An aspiring aviator. A man of the world.

The fact that he paid attention to a country bumpkin like me set my head spinning and my heart pounding.

His eyes never left mine, though people filed into the room around us. I didn't want to let the moment go. Not yet. I laced my fingers together and took note of listening ears. Leaning toward him, I asked, "Do you have a seat yet, Mr. Samson?"

He leaned in, too, and winked. "I'd hoped to forego this pleasure altogether." He looked toward the door and then back at me, his invitation clear.

I bit my bottom lip and glanced at Mama. She stood on one side of the entrance, Mrs. Thacker opposite, while the other ladies flitted around, leading people to empty seats. No one took notice of us.

Arthur put his hand on my elbow and urged me toward the back corner of the room. Ensconced in shadow, his smooth voice wrapped around me like the silk shawl my aunt Adabelle had sent for my high school graduation.

"What about you?" His voice was low, in tone and volume. "Are you pining to hear a lecture this evening?"

I bit down a nervous giggle as Arthur's lips curved into another grin. His voice dropped to a whisper. "Sit with me on the front steps. It's our last chance to talk. I leave for Texas in the morning."

At that moment, Mrs. Thacker swept toward the front of the room, Mama following close behind. Before Mrs. Thacker could turn to face the gathered crowd, Arthur and I slipped out the door and into the twilight.

I settled on the middle of the three steps, straightened my skirt, and tucked my shoes up under the hem as Arthur walked into the schoolyard and lit a cigarette. The rumble of voices slipped across the still air. A smatter of clapping. By the time the droning began, Arthur had ground his glowing stub into the dirt and lounged beside me, leaning back on his elbows.

"This time next week I should be up in a plane." His head tipped back as if he could see himself up in the sky now. "First over Texas, then over France. Or Germany."

I followed his gaze to the heavens, thinking of the many times I had, as a child, wished upon the first star of evening. Now I believed God directed my path, but I prayed that path included Arthur.

"I wish I could fly up there with you."

"Do you?" Arthur sat up a little, his laughing eyes roving over my face. "Wouldn't you be afraid?"

I shook my head, remembering hours, days, years of yearning to be free from housework and gardens and livestock. Free from Mama's scorching looks and sharp tongue. Ever since I'd graduated high school, I'd dreamed of leaving this tiny, boring town behind. "I want to go places, do things. I want a life full of more than planting and harvesting and chores. A life worth living."

"I could teach you to fly an airplane," he said.

The stars winked at me from above. I cocked my head and tried to imagine soaring above the ground all on my own. My stomach somersaulted. "Maybe you could teach me to drive a motorcar before I attempt a plane."

Our laughter mingled together like honey in hot tea. And tasted just as sweet.

He leaned toward me. "We could do exciting things, Rebekah. You and me."

I pressed my hands to my middle. Did he mean it? Would he be my wings to fly beyond Downington?

His usually languid voice turned intense. "You aren't like any girl I've ever met. You dream big. I like that."

My arms wrapped all the way around my middle now. Did he mean what I thought he meant?

He gathered my hands in his. "After I take care of the Huns, I'll come back to get you. We'll live in Dallas or New York or maybe somewhere in Europe. I can look around while I'm there."

I sucked in the night air, closed my eyes, and for a moment envisioned all my dreams coming true. "You'll be a celebrated war ace. I'll be a clubwoman with my name and picture in the newspaper every week." Tears pushed at the back of my eyes, but I refused to cry even happy tears.

My eyes flew open again as his fingers intertwined with mine. "Tell me you aren't teasing me, Arthur. Tell me this is real."

With a finger beneath my chin, he tipped my face up toward his. "I wouldn't say it if I didn't mean it, Rebekah."

He leaned closer. I swallowed hard, his face now inches from mine, his breath caressing my cheek. My eyes fluttered shut. His hands landed on my waist before the fire of his lips shot through me. It was like nothing I'd imagined or experienced before. Seconds passed—or was it minutes? It seemed ages, yet a mere flash of time. When he pulled away, I reminded myself to breathe.

He draped one arm across my shoulders as if it had been there a hundred times. I shivered once and nestled my head on his chest, beneath his chin. We sat there, silently spinning our dreams until applause burst from the schoolroom.

Arthur helped me to my feet. We tiptoed into the back of the room and clapped along with the others. Just as we'd suspected, no one imagined we hadn't been there the entire time.

Arthur and I helped Mama and Mrs. Thacker put the room to rights after the crowd had gone.

"Rebekah Grace?" Mama called from the other side of the room as she slipped her handbag over her arm.

"I think we're leaving." The whispered words scratched my throat as I turned to Arthur.

He squeezed my hand, then let it go. "Don't forget to write to me." His breath tickled my ear.

Mama stopped near us, her company smile in place. "I hear you are leaving us, Mr. Samson."

"Yes, ma'am."

"Well, you be careful over there." Her gaze held his. "I expect you'll come see us again when you can?"

The grin he threw in my direction tingled me from head to toe. "That's my intention, Mrs. Hendricks."

Mama's eyes remained on him, though she spoke to me. "Say good-bye now, Rebekah." She offered a curt nod before charging out the door as if we hadn't a moment to spare. Would she forever treat me like a child?

"Good-bye, Mrs. Thacker, Mr. Samson." I gave them each a shy curtsy before my eyes held a lingering farewell with Arthur's. Then I hurried down the steps and scrambled into the waiting buggy. Daddy slapped the reins. We jolted forward.

I leaned out the buggy to look behind us, one last farewell. But Arthur was nowhere in sight. And already my heart ached with missing him.

CHAPTER 2

*T*wo days after the train carried Arthur to Camp Dick in Texas, a sweet yeasty smell from the kitchen tickled my nose. I pulled my shawl closer around me, debating whether to help Mama bake or remain brooding in the parlor. I sighed and looked at my hands. Mama said busy hands helped pass the time. But what did she know, really? She'd met Daddy here in Downington, where she lived but a short buggy ride away until the day they married. Still, I had to do something to occupy my mind or I'd go mad thinking about Arthur.

Before I made it to the kitchen, a knock rattled the side door. I stopped in the hall.

"Why, Mr. Graves." Mama used her syrupy voice, the one reserved for my potential suitors.

Barney Graves's deep mumble replied. His heavy steps resounded on the floor. Then a hollow thud. Mama's box of groceries from his store.

The oven door creaked open. Now the scent of cinnamon overwhelmed me, but it couldn't lure me in. Not with him there.

A shudder passed over me as I pictured Barney's pasty face behind bushy whiskers. He had to be thirty, at least. Why in the world did Mama think him a catch?

"Rebekah Grace?" Mama's voice sent me flying into the parlor. I flattened myself against the wall and prayed she wouldn't search for me. But Mama knew me too well. Before I'd finished petitioning the Almighty, she appeared. "There you are. Come walk Mr. Graves to his car."

My shoulders sagged. Mama leaned close, her voice barely above a whisper. "I know you're pining after Mr. Samson, but my advice in finding a man is the same as for baking a cake: it's best to have the ingredients on hand for two, in case the first one falls flat."

She had a point, though I didn't doubt Arthur. Hadn't his promises been as good as an engagement? After this horrible war ended, he and I would marry and head off on all kinds of adventures. Still, there was no use fighting Mama. I fixed a smile on my face and followed, determined to endure.

"Mama said you were leaving, Mr. Graves." I crooked my fingers around his elbow and led him across the yard. What could I talk to him about? "You must be so proud to see your name up there with your father's now. Graves and Son Dry Goods Store. It sounds quite prestigious." Truthfully, I thought Graves an unfortunate last name, and not one I'd spread across my place of business.

His shy eyes lit with hope as I stared up at him. "Yes, Miss Rebekah. I'm right pleased."

"Well, you should be. Quite an accomplishment for a young man like you." I batted my lashes as he stammered an answer I didn't really catch.

He climbed inside his new Model T, and the engine roared to life. I stepped back as the automobile chugged away, splaying a trail of dust behind. I felt a bit guilty after he motored out of sight. As my gaze drifted above the gritty spray and fixed on the expanse of clear blue sky, I prayed again for a life that stretched out into the unknown rather than one that trudged along in Oklahoma dust.

The old swing hanging from the massive oak creaked in the breeze. I sat on the smooth wooden seat and pushed with my feet, as I had so many times as a child. It was too early for Arthur's first letter, but I figured it wouldn't be too many more days before it arrived. Would he write words of love or simply tell me about his training? I leaned my head against the weather-worn rope. If only I knew how much longer until we could be together.

"Rebekah Grace?" Mama's voice sounded as if she didn't realize Mr. Graves had gone on his way.

"Yes, Mama?" I stopped the motion of the swing as she stepped onto the porch. Her gaze roved this way and that, looking for an automobile still lingering at the roadside.

"Come help with dinner." A clipped tone now.

"Yes, Mama." I trudged through a carpet of dry leaves, once again yearning to be free of the old routines—cooking, cleaning, collecting eggs day after day. The heat of the kitchen closed around me as I stepped inside, stifling as a wool blanket on a summer day. Mama wiped her forehead with the sleeve of her simple, old-fashioned dress.

"I'll do this. You catch a breath of air," I said. She nodded and stepped outside.

An hour later, Daddy sat down at the old trestle table in the kitchen to eat his fried chicken. As much as Mama tried to make us out as some kind of landed gentry, we were just plain farmers. The chicken had come from our overflowing henhouse. She'd wrung its neck herself that morning. We might own a farm that produced more than most, or one that looked as if a bevy of old-time slaves kept every nook and cranny spotless, but really Mama and Daddy's hard work kept it all going.

Daddy bit into his chicken and closed his eyes, as if he'd somehow made it to heaven in that moment. And I think he had.

Meatless Tuesdays always made him grumpy, in spite of his support for Hooverizing to help the war effort. After he swallowed down that first bite, he leaned back in his chair as if to relive the experience in his memory before chancing another in real life.

"Did I see Barney Graves earlier?" His eyes twinkled at me, and I tried to twinkle back.

"He was by for a minute. Seeing Rebekah Grace." Mama's smugness irritated me, like a bad case of poison oak.

I laid down my chicken leg and wiped greasy fingers on my napkin. "He delivered Mama's order from the store."

"He stayed a bit, didn't he? That was for you." Mama turned her attention back to Daddy. "I invited him for dinner after church on Sunday."

Daddy looked at me, his eyes asking if I consented. I bolted for the stove. "More green beans, Daddy? They sure are good."

As I returned to the table, Daddy passed a sly glance to Mama. She acted like she didn't see, or didn't understand. I sat back down, my fork spearing one green bean at a time, lifting them to my mouth in an even cadence.

Only the clink of our forks against the old tin dishes broke the silence in the room. Then Mama jumped from her chair and hurried to the window. "I do believe someone's coming up the road." She peered through the glass before she straightened and smiled. "Mr. Graves is back, Rebekah. You better run right out and see what he wants."

"Yes, Mama." I went out there all right, but not in any hurry. I figured he wanted to invite me to a house dance or share some tidbit of gossip. But that wasn't it at all. He just handed me a telegram and said to give it to my daddy.

Did Barney tip his hat and take his leave? I didn't notice. I held that slip of paper between my fingers, my legs shaking like a newborn calf's.

Everyone knew a telegram meant death.

CHAPTER
3

$\mathcal{I}$ wobbled back into the kitchen, anxious to steady myself before I heard the worst.

What if it was Arthur, his death ending all our dreams? I imagined myself crying at his funeral, pictured my resigned walk down the aisle to meet Barney Graves.

Mama met me at the door. "Why didn't you invite him in?" Her neck craned to see past me.

I held out the telegram in reply. Mama's flushed face drained white as she snatched it from me and looked to Daddy. Then I thought of Will. My brother lived every moment in danger on the Western front. I sat hard in the nearest chair.

Mama didn't sit. And she didn't say a word. She pulled a hairpin from the tight knot of pecan-colored hair at the back of her head and slipped it beneath the flap of the envelope. I winced, the tearing of the paper ripping through my heart. But Mama remained unruffled. I admired her strength in that moment. Determining to show the same fortitude, I sat up straight, waiting for the words I felt sure would shatter me.

Mama let out her breath, never taking her eyes from the paper. "It's my sister, Adabelle. She's ill." Her lips curled into a frown.

My whole body relaxed. Aunt Adabelle. She'd sent a short note and the shawl at my graduation last year, but I'd only seen her twice in my whole life. The first time I'd been seven or eight years old. I remembered a soft hug and a wide smile, green eyes, and smooth skin. She skipped with me, hand in hand, to the chicken coop to gather eggs, asking questions all along the way. Did I like school? Who was my best friend? Was Will a good big brother? Did I like to play with dolls or climb trees?

And when I answered, she listened.

We found twelve eggs that day. She cradled each one before setting it in the basket. I wondered if she knew how much Mama hated when I broke the eggs before they made it to the kitchen.

But when she and Mama came together, Aunt Adabelle changed. The laughter in her voice stilled, and the sparkle in her eyes vanished. She and Mama spoke in short, awkward sentences. I didn't understand the distance between them. I only knew Mama disapproved of her sister. And Mama's disapproval was nothing to be trifled with.

Yet something in me had always cottoned to those memories of my aunt. It gave me the courage to ask, "What should we do, Mama?"

"Do?" The spark of scorn in that one word could've started a prairie fire.

I glanced at Daddy. He wiped his mouth with his napkin and pushed back his chair. It scraped across the kitchen floor, almost as a command to listen to the words that followed. "She's all alone in the world, Margaret. Except for us."

Mama plunged her hands into the water-filled tub. I watched her scrub a pot, rinse it, and scour it again.

Daddy stood, his presence filling the small room. "I expect

you'll do right by her. She's your kin." Three steps and the screen door slapped shut behind him.

Mama's hands stilled. I held my breath, reveling in Arthur's safety—and Will's, too. My face warmed as I realized a telegram about Arthur wouldn't have come to us anyway. It would have gone to his mama.

The clank and splatter of Mama's dishwashing began again. "I guess you could go."

At first I wasn't sure I heard the words at all. Maybe they were in my head, the words I wanted her to say. Even if I was nineteen now, Mama wouldn't like the idea of me traveling alone. I stared at her stiff shoulders. Her hands never abandoned their activity. Yes, I must have imagined the words. I reached across the table to pick up Daddy's plate.

"Could you do that, Rebekah?"

My attention jerked back to Mama. "Do what?"

Her shoulders curved in an uncharacteristic slump as she wiped dripping hands on her apron. "Go to Texas and take care of your aunt."

Texas. Where Arthur zipped across the endless skies. My breath stuck in my chest. Only the Lord could make Mama willing to send me to Texas, to Arthur, right now. Arthur was my God-ordained future. This could mean nothing else.

"By myself?" My voice squeaked a bit, but whether from excitement or nerves, I couldn't quite tell.

Mama leaned against the Wilson cabinet and folded her arms across her chest. "Yes."

I wanted to shout and dance my acquiescence, but I didn't think she'd appreciate that. "I'd do my best, Mama."

Her lips lifted in a small smile, as if she approved of my answer, but she seemed to consider me for a long time afterward. I didn't look away. I wanted her to know I was old enough and mature enough to go to Texas. I longed to take on the challenge and a change of scenery, just as my brother had. And if such an adventure took me a closer to Arthur, all the better.

✦

By evening, my suitcase and handbag stood at the door, ready for our pre-sunrise departure for the train station. Mama had spouted off more instructions for the journey than I could hope to remember, but I knew my stop was Prater's Junction, Texas. Mama figured someone there would be able to direct me to Aunt Adabelle's place.

I had no idea of the distance between Prater's Junction and Dallas, but trains went everywhere these days, didn't they? Maybe Arthur could hire a team and buggy, or even an automobile, and come to me. We'd manage it somehow, I felt sure.

Long after the lights were extinguished, I crept downstairs, avoiding the squeaky place on the fifth stair and along the well-trod hall. In the parlor, I fumbled to ignite the wick of the smallest lamp. It finally glowed a tiny circle of light.

The October air seeped through my nightdress as I sat at the writing desk, the pen's nib poised over the blank page. A tiny prick of black escaped, blemishing the pristine paper and overcoming my inhibitions.

> *I'm coming to you, my darling Arthur. Tomorrow night*
> *I will be in Prater's Junction, Texas, at the home of my*
> *aunt, Adabelle Williams. Please address your letters to me*
> *there. I wait with great anticipation to see your face again.*
>
> > *Your forever love,*
> >
> > *Rebekah Grace Hendricks*

I rubbed warmth into my chilly fingers before addressing the envelope. Stamp affixed, I extinguished the lamp, groped my way

23

to the kitchen, and slipped the letter into my handbag. I'd mail it tomorrow, along the way. Then I would wait. Arthur would find me soon, by letter or in person.

With careful steps I crept back to my bedroom, but I didn't sleep. Instead, I spent the night at my window, my chin resting on the low sill, my gaze following the moon's journey across the star-pocked sky.

The Lord finally had seen fit to deliver me from Downington. Arthur wasn't the only one spreading new wings.

CHAPTER
4

$\mathcal{T}$he train slowed and the conductor called out the stop at Prater's Junction just after bare fields blazed orange with the waning sun. The whistle screeched our arrival into the station. I wondered if Mama would be relieved that no strange man had tried to strike up a conversation with me or be disappointed that I didn't get to heed her advice and freeze him with a silent stare. Not that I would have done that, exactly. It might have been interesting to converse with a stranger who would walk off the train and out of my life. But the opportunity never presented itself.

Black smoke streamed in through open windows. I coughed until I made it to the open air of the platform. For the first time in my life, I'd left Downington—home—far, far away. My lips curved upward, my feet itching to dance a jig. Instead, they jumped when the whistle screamed and the train strained forward. A cinder landed on the skirt of my traveling suit. I brushed it away and lifted my chin, ready to meet my adventure.

But where to begin?

No one lingered near the empty tracks. Had anyone else disembarked? I didn't recall. The heels of my laced boots clomped loud on the flat planks. I reached the small building at the back of the platform and peered through the windows. An empty waiting room opposite an empty office.

I turned to look beyond the station. In spite of the dimming day, I recognized that Prater's Junction had even less to recommend it than Downington. But no matter. I'd get Aunt Adabelle back on her feet, and she'd help me find a way to Dallas, to Arthur. Then my life would really begin.

Two steps down and I stood in the rutted road that crossed the train tracks. A horse whinnied near my ear. I dropped my suitcase and jumped back with a squeal as hooves danced behind the hitching post. An empty buggy jiggled behind the startled animal. I stretched my hand toward the velvet nose.

"There now, pretty boy." I stroked him until he calmed.

Voices murmured in the distance. I strained to see the people talking, but the depot building obscured my view. Surely one of them owned this horse and buggy. But as the shadows lengthened, the voices fell silent, leaving only the chirp of cicadas and an occasional lowing of faraway cattle.

A bit of tinny music sounded from one of the storefronts that lined the main street of town. Beyond that, faint squares of yellow broke into the gray of evening. The thought of walking up to a strange front door to ask directions filled me with horror, so I decided I'd wait for someone to claim the horse and buggy.

The coming night cooled the heat of day, and while I welcomed it, I still shivered as I picked up my suitcase and headed back up onto the platform. My foot hit something solid. I stumbled forward, the weight of my suitcase pulling me toward the floorboards. My ankle bent sideways, and I cried out in pain.

Strong hands caught my arms, held me aloft.

"Whoa, Nellie!" The man's hat darkened his face.

"Thank you, sir." I took a step back, wincing at the pain in my ankle. I lifted my sore foot until only the toe of my boot touched the ground and tried to balance myself with dignity.

"Are you injured?" The man pushed back the rim of his hat before cradling my elbow in one hand.

"No, sir. I'll manage."

He studied me now, seemed to realize he didn't know my face. "Welcome to Prater's Junction, Miss—?"

I raised my eyebrows and tried to look down my nose at him, but Mama's face wouldn't work on me. I burst out laughing. He joined in. "I'm Rebekah Hendricks. And you?"

"Henry Jeffries, sheriff." He doffed his hat and tipped his head.

"The sheriff? Quite a welcoming committee, I do declare." Did I spy a blush creep over his face? "I wonder if you could help me find my mother's sister, Adabelle Williams. I've come to take care of her for a while."

The jovial expression softened a bit, but if from the fading light or from something else, I couldn't make out. "I'll take you to her. Do you have any other luggage?" He glanced over his shoulder before lifting my suitcase and heading toward the road.

"No, just that." I tried to follow, but as I took a step, dull pain throbbed in my ankle. I let out a tiny yelp.

"Forgive me." The sheriff came back and helped me wobble down the steps. "Wait here." He rushed past the horse and buggy and disappeared behind a building in the distance.

An engine sputtered to life out of sight. Then an old-model automobile chugged toward the platform. Sheriff Jeffries jumped out, stowed my suitcase in the back, and held the door open as I climbed into the car.

We lurched forward into the twilight, one of my hands clutching my bag, the other holding my hat on my head. Thin beams of light moved before us on the road.

I'd ridden with Barney Graves in his Model T once. With

other passengers, of course. What would Mama think of me riding alone with a man she didn't know? On second thought, maybe I wouldn't tell her about this.

The jostling settled some. I removed my hand from my hat and glanced sideways at my companion. A well-made suit, though Mama would sniff at its rumpled state. Large, smooth hands gripping the steering wheel. His gaze pinned to the road.

We hit a rut. I bounced from my seat, the roof above me crushing the crown of my hat. I must have let out a whoop, because Sheriff Jeffries slowed the car.

"Are you all right?"

"Perfectly." My cheeks hurt from grinning.

The car gained speed again. I couldn't see the dust collecting on my white blouse, but I knew it was. I'd have to brush it clean at my aunt's house. For now, I wanted to enjoy the ride.

"Do you know my aunt very well?" I asked.

Sheriff Jeffries hesitated. "Fairly well."

Something in his voice pricked my interest. "What's she like?"

He turned his head for a moment, his eyebrows slanting toward his nose. "Don't you know her?"

"I've met her. But she and my mother don't . . ." How did I say it without speaking ill of my mother or her sister?

He whistled long and low. "Wondered why I'd never heard of you before."

It comforted me to know Aunt Adabelle hadn't told our business about town. I didn't want anyone to know about the argument I'd heard between Mama and her sister during Adabelle's second and final visit to our home.

"I don't see why you won't just move back here, Adabelle," Mama had scolded, as if Adabelle were no more than my own eleven years.

Mama thought I was helping Daddy and Will in the south

28

field, but I'd come back for lemonade, heard the voices, and slipped beneath the porch. I lay in the cool dirt, listening.

"I've lived on my own for over ten years now, Margaret. I like it. I like not having anyone tell me what to do."

"Except your employers, of course."

"I mean with my life. I get to make my own decisions; they just direct my duties within their households."

"But a woman living alone is unseemly."

"Why? I'm a widow, Margaret. How can you find fault with me for that?"

"If you hadn't run away with that boy—sixteen was far too young."

"I loved him. I still do." Aunt Adabelle's voice sounded sad.

She went away again without saying hello or good-bye. And Mama never mentioned the visit. Ever.

Had Aunt Adabelle loved her husband the way I loved Arthur? I hoped so. In fact, I was counting on it. I squinted into the darkness as I spoke to the sheriff. "Has Aunt Adabelle been feeling poorly for long?"

"No . . ." He drew out the word, almost as if he thought I should know the answer to my own question. Then he slid another look my way.

"Is she confined to bed?" I watched his eyes narrow as if he were trying to see something far away. I peered through the windscreen. All I saw was road.

"Seen any of the influenza up your way?"

I hadn't heard of any particular outbreak of flu around our town, but I hadn't paid much attention to the goings-on in anyone's life but my own lately. Still, relief swept through me. I'd had the flu before. A week or so in bed and Aunt Adabelle would be up and around again, wouldn't she? After that, I could figure out a way to get to Arthur.

Silence hung between us, awkward as a crooked picture. "Is that what she has?" I asked. "Influenza?"

"Yes, but . . . " His lips puckered shut.

"But what?"

The car slowed. A two-story farmhouse loomed against the darkening horizon. "Is that her house?"

"Yes." A long, unsure word.

That same uneasy feeling I'd had when I held the telegram in my fingers returned now, pushing at my chest in a way I didn't understand. Why did his manner disturb me so?

Light spilled from a downstairs window. I brushed aside my concern. Sheriff Jeffries probably didn't know the whole situation. He probably imagined my aunt's illness to be worse than it was.

We motored past the low picket fence that closed in the house yard and stopped near the back gate. I lowered my throbbing foot to the ground and stood. The pain made me wince, but I could bear it. I held the sheriff's arm for support as he led me to a door—the kitchen, I felt sure. We stepped inside the dark room, the smell of stale food hovering over the shadowy dishes that littered the kitchen table.

"This way." The sheriff hurried me along to the lit room across from the kitchen. A thousand questions started and died on my lips before a towheaded girl appeared. Her dirty dress hung limp. Her bare toes hugged the cold floor.

I stepped back. A child tended my aunt?

"Ollie Elizabeth"—Sheriff Jeffries put a hand on her head and tipped it back so he could see her face—"this is Miss Ada's niece. She's come to help."

The girl's large eyes turned in my direction, then looked back at the man she obviously knew. She pushed her unruly hair from her face before whispering into the stillness. "I told Miss Ada that Mr. Doc would come."

"And I'm sure he's doing his best to get here. Don't you worry."

The serious-faced girl nodded. Then she tilted her head and eyed me once more. "If you're going to stay, you can use my room." She tiptoed past us, toward the dark staircase.

The sheriff motioned for me to follow. For now, I saw no other choice.

CHAPTER
5

Ollie Elizabeth led me up a narrow staircase. The pain in my ankle dulled a little with each step. And my boot didn't pinch, so it must not have swollen much. When we reached the top, she pushed open the first of two doors. Its hinges creaked like an old man's knees.

The night air squeezed between the window sash and sill, the smell of woodsmoke on its edges. I shivered, but more from the heaviness of this place than from the cool bite of the air. A thin strip of moonlight through the glass lit the room enough for me to discern a bed against one wall, a dresser against the opposite one. The simplicity reminded me of home. I relaxed, chiding myself for taking on Sheriff Jeffries's foreboding.

Ollie remained with her back against the open door.

"Is this your room?" I asked her.

She lifted one shoulder. "I slept in here before, but with Daddy gone, James likes us all together." She nodded toward the room next door and again brushed aside the lock of hair that fell across her eyes.

Before? Daddy? James? What didn't I know about Aunt Adabelle's life? I gritted my teeth, not sure how much to ask this child. Instead I laid my hand on her thin shoulder and knelt down, my eyes even with hers. "I'm here now, honey. Everything's going to be fine."

One corner of her mouth turned down. Didn't she believe me? "You go on to bed. I'll take care of things for a while."

Her mouth opened, as if to protest, then shut again before she scurried like a scared rabbit into the next room. I slid my suitcase next to the dresser and stared at the wall dividing one bedroom from the other.

Aunt Adabelle obviously needed help. I knew I could keep house and make the meals, but I'd never had sole responsibility for a child before. In fact, I'd rarely had any contact with children, except for the younger students in school. But Ollie seemed quite capable. She'd obviously been taking care of things until now.

Stepping back into the dark hall, I let my fingertips graze the wall and guide me back to the staircase and down again. I needed to ask the sheriff some questions before he left. Errant curls tickled my face as my shoes thudded unevenly toward the lit room. I stood blinking into the brightness.

"Here she is, Adabelle." The sheriff's voice held a tenderness that surprised me.

My eyes adjusted to the light, my nose to the overwhelming scent of camphor and mint. Sheriff Jeffries stood beside the bed holding my aunt's small hand. I studied the face staring at me from under a mound of quilts. It didn't hold any resemblance to my memory of Aunt Adabelle. No rosy cheeks or shiny eyes. Her skin looked taut against her bones, not soft and full as I remembered. I tried to hold back a gasp, but it half-escaped into the quietness of the room.

Sheriff Jeffries's head jerked up. He stared at me as if my panicked thoughts had run loose into the room. Then he softened again, signaling that I should take the chair next to the bed. I did as he bade, but I'm sure my eyes resembled lily pads on a pond when I looked back at him. Mama had always kept me out of the sickroom. She nursed Will and Daddy and me all on her own.

I would ask the sheriff to stay.

But he couldn't stay. Not all night. Not without a chaperone in the house.

His gaze locked on mine. "You're in good hands now, Adabelle."

I gave my head a slight shake. My hands weren't good. They were young, inexperienced, immature. And this didn't look like the flu symptoms I'd seen. Aunt Adabelle appeared seriously ill, with her sunken, dark eyes and pale face. I didn't know how to take care of someone so sick.

Sheriff Jeffries only nodded. "Doc Risinger will come again as soon as he can."

"Thank you . . ." came the croak from the bed. A rasping intake of breath followed before the word "Sheriff" found its way out of her mouth.

He stood. I did the same, following him to the door.

"Water's in the basin," he said to me. "Keep cool rags on her skin."

"Who—" I swallowed down the lump in my throat. "Who is Ollie? Am I to care for her, too?"

He rubbed a hand down his face. "Adabelle's been caring for Ollie Elizabeth and her brothers and sister since their mother passed. With their daddy off fighting the Germans, they needed someone."

I tried to comprehend his meaning. Brothers? Sister? Did they have no one else?

"I'll be back tomorrow, okay?" He settled his hat on his head and left before I could find my voice to protest. Watching the room empty of him was like watching the rope slither down the water well into oblivion, only the plunk of the bucket indicating the bottom had been reached.

My plunk came in the form of another rattling breath from the bed beside me. I forced myself to smile into my aunt's face. Remembering the rags and cool water, I dipped a dry square of cloth in the basin, then wrung out the water before dabbing it on my aunt's forehead.

"I expect you don't recognize me, Aunt Adabelle. I'm Rebekah. My mama—your sister—sent me to look after you." Hearing my own voice calmed my nerves.

A spasm of coughing shook her. I stepped back from the bed, the rag limp in my hands, until the coughing quieted.

She held out her hand to me. I returned to her bedside, my stomach boiling with panic.

"Beautiful," she whispered.

What did she mean?

"Won't be long now." Slow words. Tired words.

"Don't worry, Aunt Adabelle." I pulled the cool cloth down her hot cheeks. "I'm here now. You'll be up and around in no time. I promise."

My voice sounded far more confident than I felt.

I dozed in the chair, startling awake at intervals—sometimes to silence, sometimes to my aunt's moans. Each time, I'd rub the sleep from my face and reach for another rag to baptize her feverish head in cool water.

Aunt Adabelle's skin appeared darker near morning. Or perhaps the light waned, instead. I peered at the kerosene lamp on the bedside table, but its clear bowl showed plenty of fuel, and its flame blazed on a trimmed wick. I touched another wet rag to her face. My fingertips warmed as if I touched bread fresh from

35

the oven. If only Mama had let me watch her healing hands at work over those she loved. But she hadn't. So I carried on with only the sheriff's meager instructions as my guide.

He'd promised the doctor would come. But when? With shaking hands, I gathered my unruly hair, trying to pin the wildest strands into their proper places. Then I attempted to smooth the front of my skirt, the fabric now as wrinkled as an old woman's hands.

As the outside darkness muted to gray, dark spots, almost purple, streaked my aunt's ashen cheeks. Was that normal with a fever? Then a crimson line trickled from her mouth to her chin. It touched the white edge of the top quilt and spread into a blood-red stain.

My heart nearly stopped. I jumped from my chair and wiped her chin clear before inching away from the bed and the blood. As uninformed as I was, I knew this did not portend good. My back hit the solid wall. I slid toward the floor, gathering my knees to my chest.

Rattling, gasping breaths filled the room, filled my ears. I longed to run away, to listen instead to the rustle of the wind through the trees or the ripple of water over a cluster of stones. I hadn't anticipated this. I'd only focused on escaping the farm and finding an adventure.

Sometime after dawn, Ollie stood at my side, blond hair matted, eyes swimming with tears that didn't fall. She reached her thin arms around my neck and laid her cheek on my head. Relief tumbled over me as I closed my arms around her.

We held each other for only a moment before I stood on tingling legs and took Ollie's hand in mine. We moved back to the chair near the bed. I pulled Ollie onto my lap. She reached for Aunt Adabelle's hand and held it between her two small ones. I dabbed a damp cloth against the blood now coating my aunt's chin.

Aunt Adabelle moaned, long and low, a weak cough shaking her whole body and spilling more bright blood onto her covering, this time streaming from her nose, too. Ollie didn't flinch as I reached across to clean my aunt's face. She only brought the waxen hand to her small lips, kissed it, and tucked it back beneath the quilt's edge.

Muted thumps sounded overhead. I looked up, as if I could see through the ceiling. I ran my tongue over my dry lips.

Ollie slid from my lap. "I'll get them." She straightened her shoulders. "I put the oats in to soak last night. My mama taught me to make the oatmeal before she . . . before Janie." Her small body bent slightly downward, like a sapling in a moderate wind, as she left the room without another word.

What was I doing here? Someone else should be in charge. Mama. The doctor. The sheriff. Not me.

"Help me, Lord." My whispered words fluttered the stillness. Words I didn't want Ollie to hear but needed in my own ears.

Aunt Adabelle tried to breathe, her head turning toward me. "The . . . children . . . please." Blood gurgled from her mouth around the words.

One red spot dripped onto my hand. I stared at the crimson splotch. My aunt's blood on my hand, the same blood running beneath our skin. Mama had long ago abandoned her sister. I couldn't do the same.

Pushing back sweat-slick hair near her temple, I leaned close, breathing out my words near her ear. "I'll take care of them, Aunt Adabelle. I promise."

My aunt fought to pull in another breath. "There's no one else." She coughed out another flow of blood as my eyes filled with tears.

"I don't know if I—"

"God sent you." Her words rattled out with a heave as her spirit pushed free of her body and unabated silence covered the room.

CHAPTER
6

The rain started between the time I closed Aunt Adabelle's eyes and the moment I arrived in the kitchen. It was appropriate, I guessed, the sky raining down the tears Ollie Elizabeth did not cry. I could tell she knew, even though I didn't say the words aloud. Watching her determination to be strong made me think of Mama, and made me want to weep along with the sky.

Two little boys looked up at me, too, their eager faces already smeared with breakfast. Ollie placed another bowl on the table, this one in front of a chair on the end, the place I assumed my aunt had occupied. I should have taken over the breakfasting, but I sensed the girl's need to keep at it, so I sat. The boys stared at me with wide eyes as their spoons traveled from mouth to bowl and back again. Ollie dribbled molasses on top of the colorless blob in my bowl.

"Thank you." I managed to pick up my spoon and stir in the thick sweetener. I wouldn't slight her for the world, yet I had no desire for food of any kind. Aunt Adabelle lay dead in the other room. And I had no idea what to do next.

Ollie remained beside my chair. I shoved a spoonful of oatmeal into my mouth and forced it down my throat.

"That's James and Dan." She nodded at the boys, her brothers. "James just turned six. Dan turned four last summer."

"It's nice to meet you," I said, feeling ridiculous.

They looked at each other. I could almost see the thoughts flying between them, requiring no words to be understood.

"This is—" Ollie stopped short, staring at me.

"Rebekah," I finished for her.

A wail pierced the air. The wail of a baby. My heart leapt into my throat. How young of a baby? Could it eat? Walk? Talk?

Ollie scurried up the stairs while James scowled. Dan copied his brother's face.

I had no idea what to say to them. I hadn't had many conversations with little boys. Especially those bereft of both their mother and the one who had stepped in to fill her place. How would I tell them their Miss Ada was dead? Even now, did they really understand what "dead" meant?

Cold prickled my skin. I pressed my hands to my face and suggested more fuel for the stove. James and Dan both scrambled off the bench seat.

"You get two pieces. I'll carry three," James said.

"I can carry three." Dan hurried after his brother, his face fixed in determination.

When they reappeared, small logs overflowed their arms. A wood stove? We used coal at home, but how different could it be? James shoved the fuel into the side of the stove, then shut the grate again as I crossed the floor.

My anxiety quickly turned to pleasure, at least on this front. Six burners and a teapot or coffeepot warming stand in back. A warming shelf above and a hot water reservoir, too. A larger and newer range than Mama's. I could manage this, even with the different heat source. Maybe I'd like it so much I would ask Arthur to buy one for our home.

Ollie returned carrying a round-faced, golden-haired baby.

"Oh!" I folded the cherub-like child—seven or eight months old in my estimation—into my arms. The baby grabbed my finger and pulled it toward her pink mouth. "And who is this little darling?"

"Janie."

I bounced the dimpled girl up and down. She giggled and clapped her hands. I pulled her cheek to mine, inhaling her cotton-warmed-by-the-sun scent. The next moment she turned outstretched arms to her sister, aware, suddenly, that I wasn't someone she knew.

"Does she eat oatmeal, too?" I asked.

Ollie cocked her head at me. "Of course."

My cheeks warmed. I should have known. "I'll fix hers."

"Not too much." Ollie pulled the high chair close to the table and plunked her sister inside its confines. "And no molasses, just a dab of milk."

I nodded and went to work, but when I pulled a pitcher of milk from the evaporative cooler in the corner, I stopped.

Milk. From a cow.

I tried to keep the wariness from my voice. "Ollie, honey, do y'all have a cow?"

"Yes'm. Ol' Bob." She took the bowl from my hand and began to feed her baby sister.

"Bob?" Maybe she'd misunderstood my question.

"James named her that when he was just little. He didn't know milk cows were girls."

"I see." I rubbed away the wrinkles I felt on my forehead. Was this my aunt's home or the children's? Had Aunt Adabelle taken them in or come to stay? I really needed some answers. Pulling a large shawl from the row of hooks on the wall by the door, I flung it over my head and shoulders. The only thing I could be certain of now was that cows had to be milked. Every day. Twice a day. I assumed someone else had been tending to that task, but if they knew I'd arrived, the job would likely be left to me. I readied myself to plunge into the muddy yard.

"Can we come, too?" James's eager eyes slammed into mine.

"Miss Ada always lets us help." Dan nodded along beside his brother.

How could I resist? They didn't know yet that Miss Ada had flown to heaven.

"Ollie, take care of Janie." I opened the folds of the heavy shawl and gathered the boys around my legs before we plunged into the curtain of rain. We splashed past the gate and the garden, moving as fast as their legs would carry them. Ol' Bob's bawling grew louder. I swooped Dan under my arm and carried him the last little way.

By the time we pulled open the barn doors, our clothes hung heavy with water. The agonized plea of the cow spurred me onward. I knew how to do this. I'd been milking since I wasn't much older than Ollie. I grabbed a pail from the wall and found a stool near the stall.

Ol' Bob gazed at me with grateful eyes as I pulled her teats in a steady rhythm. With each stream that hit the bucket, questions swirled in my head. What connected my aunt to this family? How had the children's mother died? When would their father return?

Finally, I stripped the last of Ol' Bob's milk, patted her rump, and stood. A large, empty barn met my gaze. Several stalls. Empty stalls. And double doors at the opposite end.

A whinny cut through the air.

"What's out there?"

James and Dan stopped their game of tag, cheeks red and chests heaving. James managed to push out his words. "Tom and Huck. They're our mules."

"And Dandy," added Dan.

"That's Daddy's horse."

Daddy's horse. "So this is your daddy's farm, then?"

James nodded. Dan joined him.

One question answered. A thousand more to go.

41

Thunder rumbled outside. I led the mules and horse into empty stalls and gathered my shawl again for the return trip through the rain. The boys' clothes still dripped from our first excursion. Oh, well. No harm done going back through the rain, then.

I let them run ahead, though I didn't linger far behind. "Stop on the porch," I called as they bolted through the gate and up the back walkway. Then I spied a blanketed horse tied to a fence post.

I left the milk bucket on the porch and sprinted past the boys. "Strip off your wet clothes and run upstairs for dry ones," I called as my wet shawl slapped against the board floor of the porch. I followed watery footprints exactly where I knew they'd lead—Aunt Adabelle's bedroom.

A man in a dark suit stood over the bed. Ollie watched from behind him, Janie quiet in her arms. I took the baby from her as the man—the doctor, I assumed from the black bag he carried—turned. Ollie threw herself at his middle. His heavy gray moustache twitched as the girl's sobs broke the unnatural quiet.

I blinked back tears. Tears of grief and relief. The doctor looked at me from under scruffy brows before he turned his attention back to Ollie.

"Hush now, child." He knelt down. Her head moved to his shoulder, her arms stealing around his neck. "Miss Ada isn't sick anymore. Ye didn't want her to be sick, remember?" His r's rolled slightly, hinting of a homeland beyond American shores.

Ollie shook her head as he lifted her. I hushed a whimpering Janie. His gaze moved past me, to the doorway. I whipped around. James and Dan stood naked and unashamed, their eyes big in bloodless faces.

My cheeks warmed. "Clothes on, boys." I shooed them from the room, blocking the doorway with my body. They ran up the stairs. I bit my lip and turned back to the old man.

He returned Ollie to the floor. "If ye'll see to the little ones," he said to her, "we'll tend to things here."

She nodded and took Janie from me. I stepped aside. After one long look at the still figure on the bed, Ollie retreated to the chaos upstairs.

The man nodded at me after Ollie disappeared. "Sheriff told me ye'd come."

"Yes, but not soon enough." I glanced at Aunt Adabelle's waxen face, a face that resembled the doll Daddy bought me for my tenth birthday.

"T'wasn't much to be done. The Spanish flu hits hard and quick. But at least ye can care for the children."

"The children." I felt my whole face crinkle with a frown. "I understand this is their daddy's farm?"

He lifted one of Aunt Adabelle's cold hands, laid it gently across her chest. "Frank Gresham. His wife, Clara, didn't make it through her last birthing."

"Janie." My whisper faded amidst the thumping overhead.

"Frank'd already been shipped to France. Adabelle moved in. She's been helping out around here since they were babes, all three. Took to them as her family, seeing as she had no one else."

My face crumpled with sadness instead of confusion. My aunt had no one else because Mama refused to speak to her. How could Mama have let it come to this?

The thumping from upstairs calmed a bit, the quiet silencing my questions.

"Ye'll want to dress her, I think." The doctor's words broke through my musings and stole all moisture from my mouth. Did he think I knew how to do what he asked of me? Weren't there women in this town—Aunt Adabelle's friends—who would be better suited to such tasks?

He walked from the room. I followed, shutting the door behind me. "Ye won't have time for laying her out. We need to get her buried. Likely there'll be few who can leave their own to attend."

I didn't know which disturbed me more: his reading my mind or his intimation that Aunt Adabelle wasn't the only fatality. I knew influenza could take the old and the young and the ones already sick with other ailments, but my aunt didn't fit those descriptions.

"Will someone come for her?" croaked from my throat.

The doctor scratched behind his ear, agitating a tuft of hair that afterward refused to lie flat again. "Tomorrow morning. Early. Can ye have everyone ready?"

"Yes." But could I really ready a woman for burial? Then a more terrible thought struck. Could I prepare these children to witness it?

"I guess the children have to be there." I ventured the words past my fear, hoping for a tiny reprieve.

He answered in a grunt I interpreted as agreement. "No one else to care for them. Everyone around here has their own to tend." Did I read fear in his face, too?

My fingers curled around one another as I gathered my courage. "We'll be ready."

His eyes turned stern before he spoke again. "And there's to be no church or school until ye hear further. Don't want this spreading any more than it has."

His words sank deep and heavy, like a boulder dropped in a pond. He opened the back door to leave.

"Wait." I followed him out onto the porch, the boys' wet clothes tangling my feet. "Will you please send a telegram to my mother? Margaret Hendricks in Downington, Oklahoma. Could you tell her . . . what happened?"

His shoulders sagged as if I'd handed him a fifty-pound sack of flour to carry along with his regular load. But he didn't falter as he jotted the information onto a pad of paper, then climbed into his buggy. I stood in the yard, arms across my chest.

In the morning we would bury my mother's sister. By tomorrow evening, I hoped to hear from Mama. She'd tell me what to do next.

CHAPTER 7

The next morning didn't proceed as I'd imagined. But how could it? Four children clustered about me, eager for adult attention, while the weight of my aunt's unattended body hovered over all.

"Can't we see Miss Ada?" James pestered.

"Not now."

Dan turned the doorknob of the bedroom.

"No!" I flew to him, frightening Janie to tears, dragging Dan away as his feet kicked air. James's wide, solemn stare poked holes in my resolve to be strong.

"Ollie, spoon out the oatmeal. Boys, sit down and eat." I set Dan on the bench and scooted him close to the table. They all complied, eventually. Just as they scraped the last bits of breakfast from their bowls, heavy footsteps paraded across the back porch.

I pulled off my apron and wiped Janie's face. "Ollie, take everyone upstairs."

As soon as the stomping quieted, I opened the kitchen door. Water dripped from the brim of one man's hat. Two others stood behind him, a coffin on its end between them. Older men. I guessed the younger ones were all off at war.

"You're here for . . . her." The words stuck in my throat like a spoon in overcooked oatmeal.

The man nodded. "Mr. Crenshaw said to tell you he'd come for y'all in his automobile."

"Mr. Crenshaw?"

"Owns the store over t'town. Don't know if that new-fangled car of his will make it through this mud, though."

I let out the breath I hadn't realized I'd been holding. Mr. Crenshaw with a car. We wouldn't have to ride with Aunt Adabelle's body.

The men stepped inside. I couldn't bear to see the coffin enter the house empty and leave full, so I hurried upstairs and helped dress the children in their Sunday best, all the while listening to the bumps and stomps of men shouldering their sad load through the house and out the back door.

A little while later, the jangle and squeak of horse harnesses called me to the window. I watched the wagon pull away, the plain box filling the bed, the horses splashing mud and water with every step.

"Mr. Crenshaw will be here soon." I spoke more to fill the silence than to inform the children. "In his automobile."

A spark lit in the boys' eyes, grief over Miss Ada momentarily forgotten. They hurried down the stairs and planted themselves at the front window in the parlor, next door to the room where their caretaker had lain. Thankfully, the men had closed the door when they had taken her from the house for the last time.

When the *ah-ooga* of a horn shouted Mr. Crenshaw's arrival, James and Dan beat us outside. Ollie, Janie, and I arrived on the front porch to find a scarecrow of a man holding a boy in each lanky arm. An umbrella teetered over his head, keeping them dry and clean. For the moment, at least.

"Mr. Crenshaw?"

"Yes, miss." He turned and stalked down the front walk, his long legs needing only a few strides to reach the car. Ollie dashed between raindrops and climbed into the back seat with the boys. The baby and I settled in the front beside Mr. Crenshaw.

The tires spun in the deepening mud, but they soon took hold and we jumped forward. I stared straight ahead, wondering where the cemetery was located, who would be there, and if Mr. Crenshaw would bring us home again. And I worried about the children. Janie, I knew, sat blissfully ignorant while Ollie remained painfully aware. She'd explained to her brothers about Miss Ada yesterday. At least, she'd said she had. I waited for their questions about heaven and death and funerals, but none came. How much did they understand? Their mother had left them less than a year ago. But did James and Dan really understand that Miss Ada wasn't coming back?

The car slipped and slid down the muddy road. I gripped the edge of the seat with one hand and Janie with the other. Finally, we passed the train depot and turned onto the main street. Had it been just over a day since I'd arrived in this place? The girl who stepped off the train that evening seemed far away from me now.

I noticed more than when I had arrived, albeit through a curtain of rain. One large sign over a storefront read Crenshaw's Dry Goods. Other businesses flanked our silent driver's establishment, but I didn't take the time to read the name of each one. A few houses straggled within sight of the meager storefronts. Then the town gave way to empty space, to pristine land broken by a white-steepled church, its stone-dotted cemetery huddled to one side.

Mr. Crenshaw parked close to the white pickets edging holy ground and silenced the engine. He handed me an umbrella and took one himself. The drizzle picked up its pace, as if it dared us to race it to the newly dug grave. Dan and James tried to oblige the challenge. Ollie and I held them by their shirt collars in an attempt to keep them beneath the umbrellas.

A man stood beside the hole in the ground. His face reminded me of Daddy's droopy-jowled hound dog. He held a black book I assumed to be a Bible. Beside him, the fresh-cut boards of the coffin were already smeared brown. I tried to imagine Aunt Adabelle resting peacefully inside—clean and dry. Not the Aunt Adabelle I'd seen on her deathbed. The one I remembered from my childhood. The one with soft curves and laughing eyes.

Ollie must have been thinking the same thing. She slipped her hand into mine. "My mama always said rainy days were the best ones for sleeping."

I squeezed her hand and managed to give her a tight smile, but from the edge of my vision I noticed James at the lip of the hole, peering downward. Dan inched forward to join his brother. Both of them stood out of my umbrella's reach now, hair plastered to their faces, clothes clinging to their small frames. I plopped the baby into Ollie's arms and stepped toward the boys. Black mud captured my boot, oozing over the ankle-high top. I managed to yank it loose as I reached for Dan's hand and led it to my skirt. He grasped the fabric in his chubby fingers, as I'd intended. Then I rested my hand on James's shoulder, keeping him near me, both boys half under the shelter of my umbrella.

I didn't hear the preacher's words. Instead, my eyes wandered to the little ones now in my charge. I thought of their soldier father. Missing his daughter's birth and his wife's final breath. And now the trusted friend who cared for his children had left them in my inexperienced hands. And me a perfect stranger to them all. I would write to him. Set him at ease over the state of his family and his home.

The church bell pealed. My head turned toward the sound, scraping a gaze across three other muddied mounds. For a moment, I couldn't breathe. In a town this small, with many of its men off at war, four deaths this close together would be a devastating thing.

James whipped around, his small fingers cupped beneath his freckled nose. Liquid red dripped through his pale fingers. It took me a moment to register it as blood.

Blood.

Bile rose in my throat as I pulled a handkerchief from my sleeve and tried to mop up the mess. But it kept coming.

Ollie thrust Janie into my arms. I juggled the baby and the umbrella as I pushed down into an awkward squat, cringing over the remaining soreness in my ankle. Dan pulled on my skirt, his weight almost knocking me backward onto the soggy ground.

"It's okay, James." Ollie calmly lifted the skirt of her white dress and pinched the tip of his nose.

"He ain't sick, is he?"

My head jerked toward one of the men who'd come with the wagon. He spit into the rain.

"No." I hoped the snap in my voice smacked him as firmly as an open palm, but his words stirred my insecurities.

"His nose bleeds sometimes," Ollie told us, finding a clean spot on her dress and pinching again.

Dan started to cry, hiding his head in my skirts as I forced myself to stand.

Over and over and over again Ollie sullied her dress with her brother's blood. Her crisp, white dress wilted with rain and mud and blood. The dress, she'd told me, that Miss Ada had finished just before the influenza forced her into bed.

The preacher said amen. James's nose stopped bleeding. I blew out a long breath, anxious to get the children back home without further mishap.

The men threaded two ropes beneath the coffin, one on each end, readying it to lower into the ground. Straining at each rope-end, the four men held on with gloved hands, letting the thickness slide through in small intervals as rain waterfalled over the brims of their hats. But wet took its toll, whether on gloves or rope or wood. Someone, something, lost its grip. The wooden box tumbled from its rope cradle, landing at the bottom of the hole with a squishy thud.

Dan stepped forward, peering into Miss Ada's grave. "Uh-oh," he said. "It fell down."

I closed my eyes, praying I wouldn't let loose the scream in my head. "Yes, dear." What else could I say?

Ollie pulled her brothers away from the edge, afraid, I think, that they would pitch in headlong, as well. I thanked the preacher and the other men, as Mama would have expected, while Ollie herded the boys to the car. No matter about umbrellas now. Maybe the rain would wash some of the muck from our clothes. With Janie in my arms, I stood graveside another moment. Shovelfuls of mud dropped with jarring splats on the wood below. I hurried away, wishing I could cover my ears with my hands.

Then I recognized James's small voice through the clatter. "Miss Ada's gone to heaven to be with Mama, right, Ollie?"

"Yes, James. Mama and Miss Ada are in heaven and Daddy's in France. But Daddy'll come home soon. And I'll take care of you until then. Don't worry."

James spied me, his smile quivering. I tried to put on a brave face, but as the thick mud sucked at my boots, I thought of my aunt at the bottom of that hole. And I thanked God that the rain hid my tears from the children.

CHAPTER
8

I half-expected Mama to come marching into the house after the last train whistle blew that evening. But she didn't. And no one delivered a telegram from her, either. Soon, an empty Sunday stretched before us.

My whole body ached. A hundred times that morning I felt my cheeks, my forehead, the back of my neck, checking for fever. But though my fingers tingled cold on my skin, no unnatural heat warmed them.

We needed a quiet, peaceful activity. "Do you have any books we could read?" I asked. Ollie nodded and scampered to a shelf in the corner while I lit the kindling in the parlor fireplace.

I figured they owned a Bible for sure, which would be quite appropriate for the day, but I hoped she'd return with a story that would capture their attention for a length of time.

The little flame caught, then blazed to lick at the larger logs. I warmed my hands for a few minutes before establishing myself on the sofa. The children scooted close. Ollie handed me a book, a piece of red silk jutting from the pages about a third of the way through.

"Miss Ada was reading this to us," she said. "Before."

Before. So much in that one word. Before Miss Ada got sick. Before Miss Ada went to heaven. Before. Sometimes it was good to go back to before.

I ran my fingers over the gold-embossed letters stamped on the front and smiled. *Heidi.* "My mama read this to me when I was about your age." I lifted James's chin. "And to my brother, as well."

"Where's your brother?" he asked, suddenly interested.

"In France, like your daddy."

"He knows Daddy?" Dan said.

"No, I don't think so." But I smiled, imagining these children's father—Frank, was it?—crossing paths with my brother, Will. What if they met? Became friends?

"Hush now and let Bekah read." Ollie tapped the book before poking Janie's thumb between the baby's rosebud lips.

The fire crackled, warming the room. Janie fell asleep in a bundle on the floor while Heidi's world stole all thoughts of grief from the rest of us. The fire died a bit. We read on until my stomach rumbled loudly.

James sat up. "I'm hungry, too."

A soft knock at the back door destroyed the last vestige of our peaceful tableau.

James raced from the room. I followed, stepping over sleeping Janie at my feet.

"Why're you here, Sheriff? Nobody did nothin' wrong." James's little-boy swagger carried from the kitchen.

I arrived as Sheriff Jeffries ruffled the wispy curls on top of James's head. "I'm glad to hear it, son." But when the sheriff raised his gaze to me, his eyes lost their twinkle. "How are you?"

"Fine." His simple question stirred a nervous twitter in my belly.

He glanced down at James, and I breathed in relief. Of course.

He'd have heard about the nosebleed yesterday and come to check on us. Mr. Crenshaw had said someone would.

"We're fine. Really we are." I watched his hat spin beneath his fingers. "May I pour you some coffee?"

The sheriff nodded and threw one leg over the bench at the kitchen table, his hat slapping the flat surface. He pushed back his damp hair and rested his head in his hands. Another tingle of uncertainty sailed through me. I had enough on my hands with the children. I didn't need a melancholy sheriff, as well.

The coffeepot sat on the warming shelf at the back of the stove, but little heat radiated from the dying fire, and the remaining coffee had thickened since morning. Dared I throw it out? Mama always said waste was a sin. I swirled the sludge at the bottom of the pot and shrugged. From the look of things, Sheriff Jeffries probably wouldn't notice anyway. The thick liquid dribbled from the spout into the cup, and I carried it to the table.

He didn't look up, just lifted the cup to his lips and sipped the tepid drink without complaint. "We never thought it would come here." He cradled the cup in his hands, even though I knew no warmth seeped into his fingers.

"Didn't think what would come?" I glanced at James, then leaned down to whisper in his ear. "Scoot, now. Let me talk to Sheriff Jeffries."

James hurried from the room. I pulled out the chair at the head of the table and sat.

"Never seen anythin' like this flu before." He pulled a newspaper from his coat pocket and slid it across the table to me. "Got your mail out of the box. Didn't figure you had time to think of it yesterday."

The *Dallas Morning News.* My heart danced. Dallas had to be nearby if they received its newspaper. I tried to keep the excitement from my voice. "Does this come every day?"

He nodded, drained the last of his coffee. "Frank liked to keep up with things beyond the *Junction Sentinel.*" He clanked the cup back on the table. "I guess I'd best be going."

He stood, as did I, but I kept one eye on the newspaper, greedy to drink in the words of the place I longed to be, the place Arthur lived.

"I'll come check on y'all as often as I can," he said.

"Thank you." I patted the newspaper, as if to assure myself it would still be there when I returned from seeing the sheriff to the door.

His boots clomped across the floor, his hat twirling in his hands. I felt sorry for him, though I wasn't sure why. A wail rose from inside the house.

"I have to—" I gestured toward the sound.

"I understand." He jammed his hat on his head and hurried across the yard.

"Wait!" I ran outside, heedless of cold or rain or mud. "Can you tell me if the doctor sent a telegram to my mother?"

He rested one foot on the tire of his automobile and gazed at me across its top. "I don't know. I'll find out." He cranked the engine and drove away while the high-pitched cry called me back inside.

"Dan sat on her." Ollie bounced the screeching baby in her arms.

"Sat on her?" I looked at Dan.

"I wanted to see if she was squishy like the sofa."

I slapped a hand across my mouth, but laughter bubbled up anyway, coming out as a snort. I pressed my lips together. Tight. Not speaking until I regained my composure. I shoved my hands to my hips, hoping to mimic Mama's sternness. "You shouldn't sit on your sister."

Dan hung his head and shuffled away. James followed.

"I'll get Janie a tea biscuit. She'll be fine." Ollie carried her sister from the room.

I plopped down on the nearest chair, my legs and arms splayed out, weariness consuming me. I'd thought being in Prater's Junction would afford me a few weeks to concoct a plan to get to Dallas, to Arthur, to a whole new life. And I'd hoped I'd have my aunt's help in that. Things certainly hadn't proceeded as I'd expected. But I still believed God had sent me here for a reason.

Of course, the only lasting reason I could imagine was Arthur.

Dan wiggled his way into my lap, tucking his head beneath my chin and pulling his knees to his chest. My arms circled his warm body as I sighed. I wasn't sure how long I'd be in Prater's Junction with the children, but I was certain my time here would not be dull.

Exhaustion claimed the children early that evening. I carried three of the four up the stairs to bed, their bodies slack with sleep. Only Ollie managed to climb the stairs on her own—barely.

My body longed for rest, as well, but my mind refused to be still. Embers from the afternoon blaze glowed in the fireplace, lighting my way to the ornate parlor lamp on the table in the center of the room.

A circle of light grew wide as I turned the lamp key, illuminating not only the room but the painted lilacs on the lamp's globe—and the newspaper on the table. I snatched the paper into my hands and settled into the upholstered chair closest to the table to scan page after page. War news. Agricultural news. Local events. Then I reached the short blurbs about the Spanish flu.

More cases cropping up in Dallas. Be diligent to prevent becoming ill. Hospital beds filling. Death notices rising. And Camp Dick under quarantine.

I bolted upright, my heart thudding like a horse's hooves on hard ground. I had to write Arthur. I had to know he wasn't ill. My gaze searched the square room. No desk that would house pen and paper. Lighting a smaller lamp, I carried it to the kitchen and searched the drawers in the tall Wilson cabinet. Still nothing.

Back in the hall, I stood before the closed door of the downstairs bedroom, Aunt Adabelle's bedroom. Perhaps it had been her sanctuary from the scurry of little feet, her refuge in the long evenings. From here, she might have written letters to the children's father or read his letters to them. But the feel of tucking my aunt's cold arms into her best dress, fastening shoes on her stilled feet haunted me. Did a whisper of her remain there? Did I dare intrude?

In spite of my hesitation, my worry over Arthur demanded an outlet. I placed my hand on the doorknob, then sucked in air and paused. Closing my eyes, I pushed the door open, releasing my breath at the same time. It took a moment before I found the courage to look. Brightness seeped from the small lamp in my hand, dispelling the darkness.

A sharp wind careened through windows left open to air out the room. The chill set me shaking as I placed the lamp on the side table. The room burst into full view. The bed, stripped clean, ready to be remade. The empty porcelain basin on the washstand. The rocking chair, moved to the other side of the bed now, near the chest of drawers. And shoved into one corner, a combination bookcase, one half composed of shelves closed behind a glassed door, the other half a fold-down writing desk and drawers.

Window sashes fought against meeting their sills, but I eventually managed to lock the wind outside. Still shivering, I pulled out the straight-backed chair tucked in beside the bookcase, lowered the desk, and rummaged through pigeonholes and drawers.

Writing paper. Envelopes. Pen and ink. I gathered them to the desktop as greedily as if they were Arthur himself instead of my means of communication with him. Then I spied a bundle of envelopes crammed into a lower slot. I eased the letters into my hands, leaving the other accoutrements forgotten. I swallowed hard, unable to tear my gaze from the bold scrawl across the top envelope. *Adabelle Williams, Prater's Junction, Texas, United States of America.*

From Frank Gresham? My stomach roiled as I glanced back at the open door. But there was no one here to care whether I read the words not meant for me. I needed to know what these letters contained. This man would come home a widower, four small children and a farm left solely to his care.

If he returned at all.

Perhaps he'd been injured. Perhaps he'd already boarded a ship for home. Should I read the first letter—or the last? I let the letters slide to the desktop, fanning out like stepping stones across a shallow creek.

I picked up one from the middle and removed the single sheet of paper within.

My eyes zipped over its contents. It didn't go on for any length, but it was a nice letter, just the same. One of profuse thankfulness to my aunt for stepping in. Instructions to his children, but few endearments. A letter like I imagined my daddy would write.

Remembering my urge to write to Frank, I pushed aside the envelopes and pulled a blank sheet near.

> *Dear Mr. Gresham,*
>
> *My name is Rebekah Hendricks. I am Adabelle Williams's niece. I regret that I must be the one to inform you of the illness and untimely death of my aunt two days ago. Just before her passing, she sent for my help. I didn't know of her keeping your children, but I promised her I would stay with them, at least until other arrangements could be made. Would you have any instructions for us on that point?*
>
> *Again, I am so sorry to be the bearer of bad news.*

*I understand you've had quite a lot of that since your
arrival in France.*

Sincerely,

Rebekah Grace Hendricks

I folded the letter into an envelope and copied the address from
the corner of his letter to my aunt. After I set it aside, I wrote
to Mama, letting her know I'd stay with the Gresham children
until I heard from her or their father—or Arthur.

Then my hand finally took up its original task.

A smile curled my lips as I imagined the letters I'd receive in
the coming months, rambling missives that would still my heart,
I felt sure. And when the fighting ended, Arthur and I would fly
together into the wild unknown, living in Dallas or New York or
maybe Europe. Entire scenes stretched before me like a moving
picture show, complete with tinny piano music.

My pen scratched against the paper. Frantic words imploring
Arthur to stay well. Heavy words concerning Aunt Adabelle's
death and burial. Laughter-tinged descriptions of the children.
Adorations of my beloved.

Come to me soon, I urged again and again. I signed my name
with a flourish.

By the time I folded my thoughts into the envelope and waved
the ink of his address dry, my mind longed for sleep to capture and
hold me. I climbed the stairs with heavy feet, telling myself that
Mama would reply soon, by letter or telegram. Once she knew
the circumstances, she'd come to help. And once I'd convinced
her and Arthur that the Lord had brought me to Texas to speed
our plans for the future, Arthur and I would embark on the life
God intended us to live, in a world so much larger than the one
Mama and Aunt Adabelle had chosen to inhabit.

CHAPTER
9

The children and I hurried across the mushy ground as the sun peeked out from behind the clouds the next morning. We milked Ol' Bob, fed the chickens, and turned the mules and horse into the corral after filling their troughs with feed. But we didn't stay long in the barn. Too much sunshine to be enjoyed. And I'd decided it was time to do laundry.

I filled one tin tub with shirts and pants and skirts and dresses. Our clothing swam beneath browning water as I pushed up the sleeves of an old calico workday dress I'd stuffed in the bottom of my suitcase for just such a chore. Beneath the heavy kettle in the fire pit, I lit the kindling, adding in the newspaper from last night until the larger logs caught the flame. We took turns filling the pot with buckets of water from the cistern.

The sun toasted my neck and shoulders as I scrubbed cloth against washboard and fed each piece through the wringer. Squeals of laughter filled the air. I stretched my back and gazed into the expanse above my head.

Did the quarantine mean Arthur didn't fly? Or was he in the sky this very minute? I'd read a newspaper story about an airplane that crash-landed in someone's yard. As the boys in the plane brushed themselves off, the family invited them in for dinner.

What if Arthur fell out of the sky? Would he survive with just a few bumps and bruises? A hawk soared a lazy circle high above my head, and I prayed the wings of Arthur's planes held as sure. And that if he came crashing down in anyone's yard, it would be mine.

When the sun stopped high overhead, I doused the children's mud-caked feet with water, then wiped an arm across my damp forehead. Wet clothes remained to be hung on the line. Heavy work I didn't think could be accomplished while keeping a close eye on the children. "I think y'all need naps this afternoon."

Groans answered me from all except Janie. She clapped her hands and wrinkled her nose in an ear-to-ear grin. I didn't imagine she'd understood what I'd said, but it helped all the same.

I rushed our cornbread and molasses lunch, noting that I must explore the cellar later and find us something different to eat. After sending the children to bed, I lifted wet fabric from basket to line until my shoulders ached and our clothing flapped. Yet in spite of my weariness, my hands and feet moved with the nervous energy of a horse before a race.

All my life I'd watched shining bays and dappled grays run the crude track outside of Downington on the Fourth of July. I watched them dance at the starting line, eager to be off. Watched them surge forward at the sound of the starting shot and run until they reached the finish line. My starting line stretched before me now—the coming of Mama's telegram or Arthur's letter calling me to him would be the gunshots that would send me running toward my destination. A track filled with tasks more magnificent than mucking out stalls, scrubbing laundry, or weeding a family-sized garden. But I'd keep my promise and take care of things here until then.

With the last clothespin in place, I explored the kitchen. I found middle-full sacks of flour and sugar as well as a few canned goods behind the cabinet doors. And of course the full sack of cornmeal. I'd glimpsed the empty garden just beyond the house. I hoped to find vegetables crowding the cellar shelves, ready for winter consumption. Should that be the case, we'd have plenty of variety in the coming days.

I lit a small lantern and tugged on the heavy wooden door leading into the belly of the earth. Truth be told, I hated cellars. Except during a twister, of course. The big door fell back and smacked the ground. Lantern held aloft, I descended the steps. Crude shelves lined the walls. I held the light higher and peered into the first bushel basket. Green beans. A barrel beside the shelf brimmed with potatoes. Squash. Onions. Turnips. Some peas and ears of corn. Bundled herbs hung from the wooden rafters.

I grabbed handfuls of green beans and potatoes, gathering my apron skirt into a kind of sack for my treasures. Back in the sunshine, I blew out the lantern. The thought of green beans and potatoes cooked with the salt pork I'd noticed in the kitchen stirred my appetite and sent me racing for the kitchen.

Then a high-pitched beeping caught my attention. Sheriff Jeffries's car bounced along the grass at the side of the house. My heart leapt. Never had I thought the arrival of a sheriff would thrill my soul, but I was starting to look forward to Sheriff Jeffries's visits. I raised my hand to wave before remembering the load I carried. Beans and potatoes spilled onto the back porch. I brushed dirt from my apron and met the sheriff in the yard.

"Where are the kids?"

"Sleeping. At least I hope they are."

His mouth turned down for a moment as he plucked something from his pocket. "This is for you." He handed me a telegram. My heart pumped wild with joy, until I read the ticker-tape words on the page.

Mama's sick. Stay put. Letter coming soon.

Love, Daddy.

My feet paced as I read the words again. Mama sick? How sick? Spanish flu sick? I sat hard on the edge of the porch and leaned my head against the pillar holding the roof above my head. I forced the words in front of my eyes once more.

"What's wrong?" The sheriff's Adam's apple bobbed as his hat began its familiar dance in his hands.

"My mama's sick." Saying the words out loud made it so much more real. Tears stung behind my eyes. I couldn't look into his face.

"What are you saying?"

My gaze met his. "I'm worried about her."

His eyes narrowed. "Won't your daddy take care of her?"

"Of course he will. But I might—" I looked back at the black letters on white paper. Daddy'd said to stay here. But didn't Mama need me?

"You're not going to leave these kids, are you? Isn't that why you came here?"

My head jerked in his direction. "I didn't even know about them when I came here. I thought Aunt Adabelle would be better quickly. I thought—" I waved my hand and squeezed my eyes shut. "It doesn't matter what I thought."

"But you will stay, won't you?" A rising voice, a slackened face. Panic, clear as crystal.

I captured my tilting emotions, returning them to solid and upright once more. "Can't someone around here care for the children until their father comes home?"

The sheriff shook his head. Back and forth. Back and forth. Like a swing pushed into motion with no one to still it. "I don't think so. Everyone around here has more than their share of burdens right now, what with the war and the influenza. And what about Frank's livestock? You can't just walk off and leave."

"This isn't my responsibility." I pulled in a deep breath and stood as tall as I could. Still I had to tilt my head back to see his face.

He slapped his hat against his thigh. "I expected any kin of Adabelle's to do as she would do—her Christian duty."

I flinched. How dare he imply I was less of a Christian than my aunt? My fist clenched tight as my lips pressed into one another. With a toss of my head, I forced my body to relax as if I hadn't a care in the world.

"Of course I'll stay and take care of the children—at least until their father says otherwise." Or until Daddy says to come home. Or Arthur asks me to be his bride.

I swept up the porch steps, ignoring the beans and potatoes scattered at my feet. "Now if you'll excuse me, I must put supper on the table for these precious children."

The sheriff jammed his hat on his head, his face red all the way to his ears. "I'll be back when I can, but almost every house has the influenza now. Doc's bleary-eyed. I'm trying to help out."

I noticed Ollie Elizabeth then, stealing along the side porch, finally sitting at the corner. Sheriff Jeffries's expression gentled. He reached into his pocket—this time extracting four peppermint sticks.

"Share with the others." He handed them to Ollie before stalking to his car and puttering away.

Frustration tempted me to stomp and scream. But I refrained. Even so, I had no intention of staying in this place for months on end. I refused to get stuck on yet another farm. I was nineteen years old now. Wasn't I entitled to make my own decisions? To live the life I desired?

I peered down the road that led to the train station. My dreams hovered close, like a dust cloud approaching from the horizon. If Arthur couldn't come to me, I'd go to him. Prater's Junction was far closer to him than Downington, no matter the circumstances.

My attention returned to Ollie. She stared in my direction, her head cocked, her eyes narrowed.

"Did you sleep?" I asked.

She didn't answer.

"Are the others awake?"

"Not yet." Ollie licked her candy. "Miss Ada and Mama wouldn't have made me lie down with the little kids."

"Is that so?" I gathered the beans and potatoes into my apron skirt again.

Ollie sucked her sweet for a little while before she answered. "Yes."

The defiance in her tone irritated me. I opened my mouth to answer back, but forced the words to stay locked behind my lips.

Nine. She's only nine, I reminded myself. I sat down beside her. She scooted to the farthest edge of the step. I wondered how much she'd heard of my conversation with the sheriff.

Little feet pattered the porch behind us. James had even managed to drag Janie down with him. I didn't want to know how. Ollie handed them each a peppermint stick. Grins erupted as quickly as a rainbow after a storm.

As I carried the vegetables inside and scrubbed them free of dirt, I thought about Mama. I should have known something was wrong. Mama would have answered a telegram right away. And what about Arthur? He must have received that first letter I sent, the one I mailed on the train ride to Texas. Wouldn't he, too, have answered immediately if he was able?

After a glance at the children still on the porch, I ran to the mailbox outside the front gate. I hadn't heard anyone arrive or leave, except Sheriff Jeffries, but I'd been in the cellar for a little while.

My letter to Arthur had disappeared. In its place were the *Dallas Morning News* and a farming magazine. I peered into the empty box for more. Nothing.

"Can I take those inside?" James asked with outstretched hands.

I gave him the newspaper and magazine. He bounded up the stairs and into the house, the screen door slapping shut behind him.

A hand yanked at my skirt. "I'm hungry, Bekah." Dan's sticky face stared up at me.

I sighed and led him inside. Until God sent me elsewhere, I would do my best by these children.

CHAPTER
10

On Wednesday, I began to think I might lose my mind with worry. There'd been no mail in our box. Not even the newspaper. Nor did anyone venture into our isolation. Were we the only ones left alive in this place?

We finished breakfast and morning chores. I knew I ought to clean the house, but instead I paced while the children played hide-and-seek in the yard. We could use a few things from the store. Oatmeal, for instance. But where would I get the money to purchase anything?

My search of the kitchen hadn't turned up any cash. Would my aunt have kept some in the bedroom? I tore through the desk, the dresser. Still nothing. Then I spied a handbag on a hook behind the door. Whether Aunt Adabelle's or Clara Gresham's, it didn't much matter.

But my rummaging turned up only a wadded handkerchief. Might as well throw that in the wash. I shook it out. A folded bill fluttered to the floor. I stooped to pick it up, smoothing it out straight.

Five dollars!

Thank you, Lord. I held it to my chest for one brief second before lifting the window and sticking my head into the open air.

"Let's go to town," I called.

James and Dan hollered and whooped.

When Ollie and I met in the kitchen, she looked askance. "You hitchin' Dandy to the buggy?"

"I could." Hitching up the horse was usually Daddy or Will's job, but I knew how to do it. I stopped to consider; I needed this trip to fill the whole afternoon. "But it's such a pretty day. Why don't we walk, instead?"

Her eyebrows rose. She looked at Janie in her arms, then back at me.

"I'll carry her; don't worry." But really I had forgotten about the baby. Would I ever think through a plan before I spoke it?

We ate a quick dinner before noon. After cleaning up, I led my little brood down the dirt road toward town. Though the air held a chill as delicate as the lace circling my underskirt, the sun warmed our backs and our heads as we walked. The boys raced to this tree or that rock. Janie clapped her hands as a bird swooped near our heads. Ollie tried to carry her sister, but that didn't last long, in spite of her determination, and she reluctantly passed her to me. Janie twisted and turned, kicking her chubby legs, wanting so badly to run with the others.

My arms drooped and my back grew stiff. When the train platform came into view, relief as refreshing as Saturday night bathwater flowed over me. My steps quickened, as did the children's.

A trickle of perspiration slid down the side of my face. "Almost there, baby girl."

Janie giggled at me with a toothless grin. I planted a kiss on her pug nose. Yes, everything would be fine.

The boys charged up the wooden steps to Mr. Crenshaw's

store. James pulled at the door, but it stayed shut. He turned to me, eyes wide. He yanked again, cheeks puffing out with effort. The door didn't budge.

Ollie shook her head. "I've never known Mr. Crenshaw to close, except on Sundays. Are you sure it's not Sunday?"

"Of course I'm sure." In my head, I played back the days since Aunt Adabelle's burial. This was definitely not Sunday. But the town did seem to be deserted. I knew most farmers wouldn't be in town on a weekday, but no one? That didn't seem right, either, even in a place as small as Prater's Junction.

"He probably went out on a delivery. I'm sure he'll be back in a minute." I sat on the top step, Janie in my lap, and studied the town I'd only glanced at twice. False-front buildings, their siding weathered gray, flanked the dirt road. A board sidewalk ran along the length of each side. I squinted into the sun, reading the signs above the doors across the street.

A brick bank building anchored the corner. Beside it, the *Junction Sentinel* office, the sheriff's office, and what looked like Attorney-at-Law stenciled on the next large window. I stood to see what resided near Mr. Crenshaw's store. The post office, a barbershop, and was that a saloon farther down?

The road veered north at the end of the buildings. Along the cross street, the houses I'd noticed on our way to the churchyard sat quiet and still. No laundry flapping on the clotheslines. No babies crying or children shouting in play. I returned to sit near Mr. Crenshaw's establishment. Ollie joined me while the boys kicked up dust in front of the quiet storefronts.

My heart inched toward the pit of my stomach. Where was everyone?

"May I help you?" A vaguely familiar voice came from behind me.

I jumped to my feet, pressing Janie close to my chest. The preacher, his hangdog face even sadder than I remembered, stared at me through red-rimmed eyes.

I moistened my lips. "We came to . . ." What had we come to do? "I wanted to get some things from Mr. Crenshaw."

His mouth smiled, but his eyes remained distant. "He's out helping Doc tend the sick." His gaze roved over the five of us. "Any of you sick?"

"No, sir." I watched the children's heads shake in reply. "I'm expecting a letter. Or two. Nothing came in our box yesterday. I thought I'd check at the post office." I glanced back at the post office, door shut, shades pulled.

"Mr. Jamison runs the post office, but he's down with the influenza. Mrs. Crenshaw's been helping out. I imagine she's at home."

Ollie grabbed my hand and pulled me in the direction of the first small house beyond the dry goods store. "It's my friend Mildred's house." A rare smile lit the girl's face.

"Thank you," I called as the preacher plodded away in the opposite direction. A moment later we stood at the Crenshaws' door. Ollie knocked. I knocked. The boys made no end of little-boy racket. Yet no one appeared. Just as I determined to go wait in front of the store again, the door creaked open. A woman appeared, hair disheveled, face white.

"Yes?" That one word seemed to steal every breath from her body.

I stepped back, pulling Ollie with me, glad that something in the yard had captured the boys' attention. "Please, ma'am, we're looking for Mrs. Crenshaw."

She nodded once.

My breath came in quick gasps. "I'm Rebekah Hendricks, Adabelle Williams's niece. I'm expecting a letter. From my daddy." *And Arthur*, I said in my head.

Mrs. Crenshaw leaned her head against the doorframe, her body sinking toward the floor. I handed Janie to wide-eyed Ollie just as the sick woman crumpled in a heap.

"Ollie." I held my voice steady instead of letting my panic spew. "Take the others and wait for me at Mr. Crenshaw's store."

"But—"

I clenched my teeth. "Just go."

With a huff, she marched toward her brothers. "Come on."

I should have scolded her for barking at them like that, but maneuvering Mrs. Crenshaw to her feet occupied my full attention. Already tears pushed at my eyes as Mrs. Crenshaw fought for breath. I hadn't known enough to be frightened around Aunt Adabelle. But now I did. I didn't want this woman's fever to jump into my body, but neither could I leave her where she lay.

Easing the woman's arm around my neck, I pulled her up with me, securing her with my arm about her waist. A little girl in a nightgown appeared, flush-cheeked and barefooted. Mildred, I assumed.

"Go back to bed, honey. I'm putting your mama back to bed, too." The girl obeyed. I practically carried her mother to the bedroom, laid her down, and covered her with a quilt. Her eyes spoke gratitude.

"I'll wait for your husband at the store. He should be back soon."

She closed her eyes. I crept from the room and ran from the house. Halfway to the store, I stopped. The newspaper article I'd read encouraged washing your hands often and staying away from those with flu-like symptoms. I rounded the corner of town wondering if I dared allow the children around me now. What if one of them fell ill? Yet they'd all been with Aunt Adabelle. As had I. Maybe God would keep us well.

Mr. Crenshaw stepped outside his store.

I pushed ahead of the little ones. "Your wife . . ." I glanced over my shoulder and rubbed my hands against my skirt. "Your wife is very ill. I put her in bed. I didn't know what else to do."

Janie reached for me. Dan clung to my skirts. Mr. Crenshaw

put a hand on my shoulder and opened his mouth, but nothing came out. He ducked his head for a moment before his watery gaze met mine. His chest rose as if drawing in a wagonload of air. His arm dropped to his side, his gaze fixed on his house.

"Go home, Miss Hendricks. It's the best place for y'all to be." He closed the door to his store before he plodded down the steps and across the road toward his home.

My chest ached from holding back the full force of my fears. Reading about the scourge in the newspaper had been one thing. Seeing the Spanish Lady take its toll on an entire town made my knees weak. I practically dragged the children to keep up with me on the walk home.

When I glimpsed the mailbox in front of the house, I ran. My greedy hands searched inside. My fingers brushed paper. Mail. On top of the newspaper I'd come to expect, a letter from home.

But that would have to wait. Hot water was needed. And lye soap. I wouldn't take any chances with this influenza. I scrubbed my hands three times and made the children wash, too. Then I shut myself in Aunt Adabelle's bedroom, again shoving aside the memories of her lifeless body. I needed a place where no one would intrude, and I felt certain Ollie wouldn't set foot in here. Not yet.

I sat on the still-naked mattress and slit open Daddy's letter with my hairpin. I'd never known Daddy to write anything. Mama took care of the correspondence.

Rebekah,

Your mother is gravely ill.

I dropped the letter to my lap, unsettled as much by the shaky hand as by the words I'd hoped not to hear. Would God take Mama as He'd taken Aunt Adabelle? Wiping my cheek, I forced my runny eyes back to Daddy's words.

She took the news about Adabelle hard, but I think she was glad you were with her at the end. Pray for your mama, girl. Keep yourself and those children as far from this illness as possible.

I love you,

Daddy

I walked to the window and leaned my forehead on a cool pane of glass. Would Mama be as ill if I'd have been there? Maybe Mama had hidden her illness from Daddy for too long. That would be like her. But I would have seen it. I could have told her—

No, I couldn't have told her anything. Mama was Mama. She wouldn't take advice from me.

And I couldn't help her now. I could only help these children and myself. I threw open the sash, hands gripping the windowsill. "Please make Mama well," I prayed. "Keep Will safe. Show me a way to get to Arthur. Give me strength."

The words stopped. I had nothing left to say. Did God really hear such simple pleas?

From the window, I watched Dan and James line up at the far fence.

"Go!" James dashed ahead of his brother, both of them headed for the porch. James reached it first.

Dan threw himself into the dying grass and melted into hysterical sobs.

"Heavens to Betsy." In a flash, I was out the door, lifting Dan from the ground. He refused to put weight on his feet as tears chased each other down his wind-chapped cheeks.

"Let's go." My voice held the same tightness I often heard in Mama's voice. I tried to shake it away, but I wasn't in the mood to coddle children. I plunked Dan on the bench beside the kitchen table, ready to scold. He hiccupped down another sob and brushed his sleeve beneath his nose.

Then my heart melted. This child had lost his mother and his Miss Ada—and might not even remember his daddy. I slid my hand down the side of his face, sweat and tears and dirt mingling on my hand. "I'm sorry you lost the race." I stroked his face again before folding him into my arms.

"You should've whipped him good. Daddy would have." Ollie's cold eyes stared at me. I stared right back. Her gaze finally wavered, slipping to the floor in defeat.

My voice dropped to a whisper. "Why don't you cut us all some cornbread and spread it with molasses?"

Her back stiffened again, but before she could defy me, Dan wriggled free from my grasp, his mourning turning to dancing, so to speak.

"You makin' me somethin' to eat, Ollie?" He shoved his thumb in his mouth.

Ollie pulled it out again and held him close. The look of a jealous woman flashed across her face. "Of course I am, Danny."

Ollie Elizabeth stayed up later than the others that night. A stifling quiet descended between us, magnifying the night noises outside the slightly open window. She'd lost her mother, and she resented me. I understood that. But while part of me wanted to comfort her, another part of me, the part raised in Mama's house, wanted to send her to bed without supper. What did she need more—a mother or a friend? If only someone would tell me what I was supposed to do.

I searched for something to say. "Perhaps school will start again soon. Would you like that?"

Ollie shrugged and twirled a lock of hair that fell near her chin.

"Do you enjoy school?"

She squirmed on the sofa.

I took a deep breath, needing to make some kind of connection with this girl who'd been carrying a woman's burden. "I know you must miss your daddy a lot right now. I know I miss mine."

She pulled her knees up to her chest, stuck the end of her hair into her mouth and chewed on it a minute. Then she flicked the strand of hair behind her shoulder. "Don't you miss your mama?"

My throat tightened. "Yes. My daddy sent word that she's sick right now. I wish I could help her."

"Does she have the influenza?"

"I think so." I moved to sit beside her. "What did you and your mama do in the evenings when you missed your daddy? After he went to France?"

She paused, her gaze rounding the room. "Sometimes Mama'd read to me from books or the newspaper. And she'd tell me stories about Daddy and her, when they were young. And we'd read Daddy's letters. Miss Ada read us Daddy's letters, too. But I don't think one's come in a while now."

I chewed the nail on my thumb and crossed to the fireplace mantel, where the carved clock that tolled out the hour stood guard over the dying flames. "Maybe we can do some of those other things, too. You could even tell me the stories your mama told you—so you don't forget."

She shrugged, pulled her knees closer to her chest. I sat beside her again, folding my hands in my lap, trying to smile but fearing it came across as a grimace instead. "We're both worried, aren't we? You about your daddy. Me about my mama—and my brother over in France. Maybe we can help each other."

She went quiet again. Then her eyes brightened. "We can pray for them."

"Yes, Ollie Elizabeth, we can certainly do that." Shame stirred my stomach. I should have been the one to suggest that. The clock clanged nine times, freeing me from my guilty thoughts. "Why don't you run on up to bed, honey?"

Ollie inched from the sofa. I turned her shoulders toward the hall. "It's getting chilly. Don't want you to catch your dea—" I bit off the word and gave her behind a playful swat. "Scoot now. I'll see you in the morning."

She hesitated, then reached up and pressed her lips to my cheek before scurrying away.

I touched the place on my skin, still warm with her breath. Every time I thought nothing more could surprise me, something did.

CHAPTER
11

A screech jarred me awaked. A thud followed. No morning dawn seeped through my window. I pressed my hand against my palpitating heart. Another screech, then sobs. I bounded from my bed.

James met me just outside the children's bedroom door, rubbing sleep from watery eyes. I picked him up, pressed his head against my shoulder before peeking through the dark at the others. Shadows stirred. Ollie even sat up and blinked. I shushed them and slid to the floor, cradling the six-year-old like a baby. Another nightmare. His third since we'd buried his Miss Ada.

Of all the children, James seemed to be having the hardest time, but with Miss Ada's passing or his own mama's death, I couldn't quite determine. Oh, he'd romp and play with his brother—and forget. But then he'd remember. And his grief would come so hard and fast that he couldn't hold it inside. Like now.

"I'm here, James. Bekah's here." Rocking back and forth, I imagined myself a child without mother or father to comfort and console. And it wasn't such a foreign feeling, with Mama so ill and Daddy far away. I stroked James's hair. I could manage for myself, but what could I do for this little one who dreamed of falling into a dark hole like Miss Ada?

"'Rock of Ages, cleft for me . . .'" It started as a hum, the words finally coming clear in my mind and whiling their way out my mouth. "'Let me hide myself in Thee.'"

James's chin drooped toward his chest. I sensed he'd never been fully awake. His weight sank into me. I closed my eyes and rested my head against the wall, as if it were indeed the Rock of Ages holding me upright.

Night air seeped through my flannel gown and prickled my flesh. "Let's go, little man," I whispered. "We both need some sleep."

I made it to my feet and stumbled into the next room, where I laid my little-boy bundle on the bed. Then I crawled in beside him, wrapped my arms around his small body, and prayed neither of us would dream of dark, muddy holes in the earth.

A few hours later, I again scrubbed my hands over the wash-basin in the kitchen. My skin burned, but ever since I'd walked into the Crenshaws' house, the newspaper articles assaulted my mind with searing clarity. Stay away from crowds. Stay away from those who have the disease. Cover your mouth. Wash your hands.

I'd been careless to take us into town. But there'd be no more taking chances. I'd protect these children from the enemy influenza as surely as their father protected them from the evil Huns. I would care for them and this house and this farm in Aunt Adabelle's stead. Frank would come home, and I'd have the satisfaction of a duty done well when I headed off into my new life.

We finished breakfast and chores. Then I sat down to think through our days. We needed a plan. Ollie and James gathered close around me. Dan wandered to the corner to stack wooden blocks while Janie sat at my feet, mesmerized by a rag doll. I drew a line down an empty page, forming two columns: OUTSIDE and INSIDE.

"Let's see. There's Ol' Bob." *Cow—milk morning and night,* I wrote under OUTSIDE. "And the chickens." *Feed hens and gather eggs.*

I tapped the pencil against my lips. "There's a slop barrel, but no pig."

"Pig's loose in the woods until butcherin' time," Ollie said.

"Daddy said she eats acorns out there." James put his elbows on the table next to my paper and rested his chin in his hands.

"How'll we get him back?" I asked.

Two blank looks and raised shoulders answered me. I sighed and moved on. "The horse and mules must be fed and their stalls mucked out. And the garden needs to be readied for winter."

"Sounds right." The look of concentration on Ollie's face reminded me of Mama. I shot up a prayer for her healing before returning to my list.

"Inside, we have laundry and housecleaning. The fires must be kept banked. Fill the lamps, trim their wicks. Air and make the beds. And we must keep the linen around the evaporative cooler wet or our milk will get hot and spoil."

"And bring in wood and water," James added. "That's my job." He pulled himself up straight.

"And me," Dan chimed in from his place on the floor.

"And take care of the baby and bake and cook dinner and—" Ollie tilted her head in my direction. "Bekah, you ever done all this before?"

"Of course I have." But never all at once, without any help. And never with children underfoot, either. "Don't you worry, I know just what to do."

"Miss Ada never had to make herself a list like that." Ollie pointed to my dark words on the white paper. "Mama, either."

I chewed the inside of my bottom lip. I needed Ollie's help. I needed her to believe in me, to be on my side. I forced aside my uncertainty. "I made this list for y'all," I said. "I wanted to make sure you knew what we needed to do every day."

Ollie scrunched her nose at me, as if she saw straight through my bluff.

My gaze wavered, wandering to the window, wishing for more confidence. Perhaps a large dose of fresh air would restore my confidence. "If we're going to take care of this farm, I need to see something more than the barnyard. Who wants to show me?"

A chorus of shouts answered.

I laughed, really laughed, for the first time since I'd arrived. And it felt good. More like me. I picked up Janie and headed for the door, the children gamboling about my feet like lambs in springtime.

We romped through sparse woods and along a slow-moving creek.

"Daddy lets me pick cotton sometimes." James puffed out his small chest.

"Me, too," Dan added. James scowled in his direction while Ollie sniffed like a disapproving old woman.

I looked over bare fields and remembered the thick mud that had clung to our shoes during that last bout of rain. And although I recognized the empty cotton bolls and knew the crop had been harvested before I arrived, I had no idea what came next in the process. "Does your daddy plant mostly cotton?"

Ollie answered this time. "Of course. Cotton's the cash crop. Over there"—she pointed to a field more familiar to my eye—"he grows some corn. But that's to feed us and the animals." Her voice dropped to a whisper. "At least that's what Mama always said."

I caught her small hand in mine and squeezed, hoping that one small act conveyed the words of sympathy I couldn't trust myself to speak. My gaze roved over the fields. I didn't know much about cotton farming. A few around Downington planted cotton, but my daddy and the others I knew grew mostly corn. Row upon row upon row of green stalks producing fat, yellow ears.

Then it occurred to me to wonder how in the world Aunt Adabelle had gotten both the corn and cotton crops out of the fields and to the mill and the gin on her own, four little ones in tow. Did she hire help? Did she take to the fields herself? I quaked at the thought. Mama would have a fit if she thought she'd sent me to a place where a lady would stand in the blistering sun and pull cotton from the bur by hand.

From our place in the far corner of the fallow field, I spied a small house in the distance, smoke puffing through a pipe in the roof. "Who lives there?" I asked.

"That's the Lathams' house. Brother Latham is the preacher."

The hound-dog-looking man. At least we had neighbors. That gave some comfort—until a familiar horse and buggy pulled into view and stopped at the small house. The scruffy-faced doctor almost ran inside. I turned away, fear and compassion warring within me. Did they have the influenza there, too? I shuddered.

"Let's get back to the house." I herded the children in the direction we'd come. They complied, their mouths rambling on and on as we walked. But I didn't hear their words. I kept looking over my shoulder and remembering that the Spanish flu hovered nearby.

CHAPTER
12

I dawdled over breakfast on Saturday morning, my nerves stretched as thin as cotton thread on a spinning wheel. I'd still had no word from Arthur. Was he ill?

"Listen, Bekah." Dan's head jutted from his neck as he strained to hear a sound.

"I don't hear—"

"Someone's comin'!" James raced into the kitchen and out again. The rest of us stumbled after him like shipwreck survivors catching sight of a passing ship.

Sheriff Jeffries's Model T stopped close to the fence, its engine sputtering into quiet. The sheriff climbed out of the car, shook the dust from his coat. "Thought you might like some help around here."

The children raced down the porch steps. Sheriff Jeffries swung Dan up in the air, but his eyes never left my face. I bit my lip and concentrated on Janie as she painted the shoulder of my clean blouse with her half-gnawed teacake. I sighed. Maybe I could make myself a bigger apron.

I switched Janie from one hip to the other. In spite of my worry over Arthur and Mama, the sight of the sheriff set me in a more playful mood. "Do we need help?" I hollered. "Well, let me see. I don't know as we have any lawbreakers to be hauled off to jail. You boys seen any outlaws?"

Dan and James giggled, and the sheriff grinned as he swiped his hat from his head and twirled it round and round his fingers. "Figured you might like a break from farm chores. I don't imagine it's easy for a slip of a girl like you to take care of it all."

I pulled my shoulders back and lifted my chin, my good humor retreating a bit. "I do just fine, thank you."

He held up his hands. "I didn't mean to imply otherwise. Just bein' neighborly."

I studied his eager eyes, trying to decide if I should be offended or flattered. But unlike Mama, I never could stay offended long. I threw him a grin. "You do the rest of my barnyard work, and I promise a filling dinner in return."

"My pleasure." He bowed at the waist and slapped his hat on his head.

Now it was my turn to blush. Help sounded wonderful, as did company, but did I sense something more in his manner? I ought to turn the conversation to Arthur during dinner. That would make it clear that my future was spoken for.

Janie screeched for my attention.

"I'll clean her up." Ollie took the baby while I brushed mush from my sleeve. Until my fingers froze in horror. What had I been thinking? I'd invited a single man to dine with me without a chaperone. Not just a conversation, but sharing a meal. Yes, the children would be with us, but what if Arthur chanced to hear of it? Or Mama?

My cheeks blazed now. I covered the heat with my hands. I couldn't rescind the invitation. My gaze roamed wildly over the barren yard. Then an idea surfaced. A picnic. I could spread a quilt here, in the front yard. In full view of the road. Yes, that would be more proper. And quite an adventure. I'd never attempted a picnic in October.

"Ollie?"

She answered from the kitchen.

I met her there, plunged my hands into the wash water, and scrubbed them hard. "Ollie, we're going to have a picnic for dinner. Under the big oak in the front yard."

She wrinkled her nose. "Picnics are for summertime, out by the creek."

"Well, we're having an autumn picnic, here at home. I'll need your help."

Ollie dried Janie's face with a dish towel, her muttered words indistinct.

A storm gathered in my chest, readying to spew its fearful fury. "What did you say?"

"Nothing." Ollie cast a sullen glance in my direction, picked up her sister, and left the room.

⚜

Saturday's Hooverizing sacrifice was pork, so I couldn't cook up the bit of salt pork we had left. Yet the thought of killing and plucking and cooking a chicken made me tired. On meatless days, Mama often baked vegetables into a pie, so I did the same. And with the last of the figs I'd found in the cellar, a pudding for dessert.

By midafternoon, I sat back against the tree, my own plate empty while the sheriff forked seconds, then thirds, into his mouth. Although vegetable pie wasn't typical picnic fare, he didn't seem to mind.

The children chased each other in a game of tag, their laughter ringing in the air. Only Janie sat on the blanket with us, trying to crawl past my reach.

83

"So tell me, Sheriff. What does a lawman do with his time in a sleepy town like this?"

He wiped his mouth with his napkin and set aside his empty plate. "Lots more than you think, Miss Hendricks."

"Please call me Rebekah." I smiled at him.

"Rebekah." He nodded and took a long drink of sweet tea. "The young people around here have kept me busy of late."

"Young people?"

"Those old enough to know better but still young enough to act out anyway. Just mischief, mostly."

I pulled Janie onto my lap, letting her clap my hands together. "Like what?"

He chuckled. Janie copied him. He laughed harder, shook his head as he found his voice. "Can't laugh about it with most, but they went on a spree moving outhouses to barn roofs, for one."

My eyebrows shot up and my mouth dropped open. "Can that really be done?"

"They found a way."

I giggled as I pictured it. "What else?"

He sobered a bit. "Painted Mr. Duggan's cow with black and white stripes. Sounds harmless, but the cow got real sick. The boys' parents made them work for the money to pay Doc Risinger for the medicine to make her well again."

"Oh, my! I never imagined."

Silence fell between us, though the shrieks and laughter of the children echoed all around.

"So, do you plan to live out your days with a star on your chest, keeping Prater's Junction safe from vandals?"

He shifted around, rustling the dead leaves beneath our blanket. He didn't look at me. Instead, he stared off down the road that ran in front of the house.

"I guess." His shoulders rose and fell with his resigned sigh.

Did the sheriff have dreams beyond this tiny town? Would he

and I have that in common? I cleared my throat as Janie leaned over my legs and pulled fistfuls of brown grass from the yard. "What would you rather do?"

His eyes met mine for only a moment. "Be a Texas Ranger."

I sensed he'd never said that to anyone else. Maybe he wished he hadn't said it to me. He turned his attention to my charges with a wistful smile. "Clara loved watching them play like this. So did Adabelle. She and Clara were so different, but they both loved these kids."

Now came my turn to squirm a bit. I'd said I'd care for them. But could I love them? "Tell me, Sheriff, how far away is Dallas?"

His cheeks puffed out as he blew out a long breath. "More than an hour by car. A bit less by train, even with all the stops. Why? You figuring on taking a trip?" His eyes narrowed.

James, Dan, and Ollie flopped breathless onto the blanket. James and Dan grabbed the last of the cornbread and shoved it into their mouths.

"I have a friend in Dallas, so I was wondering is all."

"What friend, Bekah?" Cornbread spewed from James's mouth as he spoke.

"Finish chewing before you talk, James." My lips pursed, and I cringed. I sounded like Mama.

With an obvious swallow, James cleared his mouth. He wiped the crumbs from his lips with his sleeve. "Do I know her?"

When I laughed, Dan nestled beside me. I tickled him, letting his cackle give me time to think. I studied the top of his head while I spoke. "No. My friend's an aviator. Or at least training to be one."

From beneath my lowered lashes, I watched the sheriff's eyebrows shoot upward but quickly resume their normal place. "Camp Dick?" he asked.

"That's right." I looked him full in the face now. "I'm expecting a letter any day. We're—making plans."

"I see." He pushed to his feet, stretched his lanky legs, and set his hat atop his head once again. "Thank you for dinner. It was quite a treat."

I nudged Dan aside, set Janie on the blanket, and stood, brushing a stray leaf from my skirt. "Thank you for all your help today, Sheriff."

James jumped from the ground, his little legs churning toward the gate. Ollie and I shook our heads at each other. You never could tell what got into James's head.

He raised himself on tiptoe, gazed over the low fence, and bounced up and down. "He's here. He's here."

My heart lurched. "Who's here?" Could Arthur have found me?

I picked up a startled, crying Janie and held her over my pounding heart, my mouth dry with anticipation. "Who, James? Who's here?"

I reached the gate out of breath. A strand of hair fell from its pinned place into my line of vision as I handed the baby to James and tamed the unruly curl. I didn't figure I needed to pinch any color into my cheeks. I felt sure they'd pinked enough in my excitement. Covering my middle with my hands, I breathed deep, determined to be the ladylike young woman Arthur had fallen in love with.

A cloud of dust moved our way, accompanied by the dull thud of hooves against the hard earth before a horse pulled up in front of the gate.

"Howdy-do, miss." A barrel-chested man peered down, nodding to each of us in turn. When his attentions reached the sheriff, he belted out a roaring laugh that shook the bag slung across his shoulders. "So that's why you didn't mind delivering the mail out this way all week."

Sheriff Jeffries turned red as a ripe tomato. My eyebrows rose this time.

The sheriff swooped his hat from his head. It twirled fast in his hands as he gulped air. "I happened to be out this way earlier in the week, checkin' on the Lathams. I knew I'd pass by here and save you some time."

The big man shifted on his saddleless horse, unable to hide the mirth on his round, flushed face. "Sam Culpepper, miss. Brought your mail." He handed me a folded newspaper. I took it, my mind still trying to comprehend that though Arthur hadn't come to me, Sheriff Jeffries had. Sometimes without my knowing it.

Mr. Culpepper tipped his hat. "Sure am glad for the sheriff's help this week. Doesn't do for the mail to get held up, but so many're sick or nursing the sick. I'm mighty late today. I do beg your pardon."

"Of course," I stammered. "I understand."

The mail carrier tugged the leather straps attached to the bit in the horse's mouth. I contemplated the newspaper in my hand, my most consistent contact with the world outside this farm.

"Is it still bad—in town, I mean?" I gave the sheriff a sideways glance. He hadn't volunteered such information. But neither had I asked.

"It ain't good, that's for sure as shootin'. Buried three more yesterday." He glanced at the children and lowered his voice. "Took a boy and his father within hours of each other."

I let out a deep breath and felt a sudden urge to wash my hands again.

His large head shook. "Some say it's the judgment of God. Some claim it's the Germans attempting to kill us all in our beds. Either way, not much to do but pray."

I nodded, thinking of Mama and Mrs. Crenshaw.

"I need to get on now. Still more deliveries to make before dark."

Suddenly my eyes went wet, and my fingers itched to fling the newspaper, let the pages fly to every corner of the yard. I wanted this scourge to end, wanted Mama to get well and Arthur to send for me. I wanted Frank to come home to his children so I could get on with my life.

"Are you well, miss?"

I pulled my distracted thoughts back to the moment. "Yes, I'm well." But I didn't believe my own words. "Thank you, Mr. Culpepper."

I stepped inside the fence. "And thank you again, Sheriff, for your help."

"My pleasure." But the sheriff didn't sound as if he'd found any pleasure in the day after all. He waited until Mr. Culpepper's horse trotted away before cranking his car's engine to life. I hated hurting Sheriff Jeffries's feelings, but I didn't want to him to misunderstand. My destiny lay far beyond this or any other pokey town. With Arthur.

He eased his car into gear and sputtered away. I turned back toward the house. Dan clutched my skirt, begging to be held. Janie laughed in James's arms as her sister played peek-a-boo. And my world righted. I couldn't fall apart. I didn't have a choice. These children needed me. They had no one else.

I unfolded the newspaper. An envelope tucked inside bore the familiar slant that quickened my heart. Arthur hadn't come in person, but he'd arrived all the same.

CHAPTER
13

I woke up chilled. Winter had come to our part of Texas, though I knew the warm weather was by no means over for the year. I put off dressing and instead crept downstairs with clothes in hand, the bare floor cold beneath my feet. And I couldn't endure cold feet.

I rummaged through the chest of drawers in the downstairs bedroom. Who did the clothes belong to—my aunt or Frank's wife? A shiver ran down my back, and I decided it didn't matter. I pulled out a pair of knitted socks and slipped them over my icy feet. Then I tiptoed into the kitchen, stirred the embers in the stove, and added a few sticks of fresh wood before setting the oatmeal to cook.

Another empty Sabbath stretched before me. No possibility of mail. And likely no visitors. Arthur had written of the quarantine at Camp Dick, though, to my great relief, he declared himself well. But he wouldn't be able to come to me for a while.

The children would need something to fill the hours. Something fun but in keeping with the focus of the day. I remembered the Bible I'd found on the shelf in the parlor. We could read about Jonah and the whale and Daniel in the lions' den and act them out together. A grin spread across my face, then vanished.

Mama would be mortified at the thought of play-acting on Sunday. But it would be Bible stories, after all. Surely God would understand and approve, even if Mama didn't.

I took a sip of coffee and thought of Mama. Was she better or worse? I hated not knowing. As much as I chafed against her tight rein, I didn't want her to die. If only she'd let Daddy put a telephone in the house. Then I could get word. But then again, that would require this house to have one, as well. No use pining over what couldn't be. So I again begged God not to take Mama as He'd taken her sister.

A sizzle from the stove interrupted my prayer. I looked up as oatmeal poured over the edges of the pot. Jumping to my feet, I lifted the pot from the burner, groaned, and set it on the worktable. A harness jangled outside the window. I flung the door open and ran out onto the porch.

Then I remembered my nightdress.

"Morning." The preacher nodded once and averted his eyes.

With a shriek, I ran back inside and slammed the door, barring it with my body as breath pushed hard and fast against my chest. I couldn't decide if I wanted to laugh or cry as I listened for the buggy to roll from the yard. Instead, footsteps faded around to the front porch.

I charged up the stairs, two at a time, threw off my nightclothes, wriggled into my work-a-day dress, and pulled on my boots, lacing only the top to keep them from flapping like agitated chickens.

Ollie appeared, rubbing the sleep from her eyes.

"Get dressed, dear," I said. "It seems we have company."

"Who?"

"The preacher." I swept past her and fairly flew down the stairs again. With my hand on the front doorknob, I stopped.

My hair. I ran my fingers down my braid, separating it into one long mass. Knotting it at the back of my neck, I tucked the ends through and hoped it would stay in place without the usual pins—at least for a little while. Maybe now that I was on my own I'd get it bobbed. . . .

I pulled in a deep breath. The odor of strong coffee and burnt oatmeal wrinkled my nose. Be dignified, I told myself. You are a woman, not a child. I opened the front door and peeked around. But no preacher waited.

A horse whinnied nearby, so I gathered he hadn't left. With a huff, I returned to the kitchen to clean up my mess. By the time a new batch of oatmeal simmered on the stove and a full pot of coffee sat on the warming shelf, the jowly preacher knocked at the kitchen door and handed me a brimming pail of milk.

I passed it to Ollie. "Coffee?" I offered.

He shook his head, eyes shifting back and forth. "Could we visit out front?"

I followed him out the door. His stout legs made quick work of the porch that wrapped around the east side of the house. His black coat flapped in the breeze as he removed his matching hat and acknowledged my more respectable presence with a slow nod. Then fear shot through me like a bolt of lightning in a night sky. Had he come bearing tragic news? I reached for the back of the rocking chair.

"Is there a problem?" I tried to erase the tremble in my voice.

"I'm Brother Latham." He stuck out a work-worn hand to accompany his shy smile. "I'm sorry I startled you this morning. I wanted to make some visits since we aren't having services today. Yours is the closest house to mine."

I exhaled as I shook his hand. At least he didn't seem to consider me less of a Christian after the nightgown incident. I motioned to the other rocker. He sat.

"I'm Rebekah Hendricks—" I looked down at my hands,

embarrassed at my awkwardness—"although I expect you know that."

He nodded.

"I'm sorry I wasn't more sociable in town the other day." I winced, thinking of the scathing look Mama would have given my inattentiveness, even in such a trying situation.

He waved my words away. "Think nothing of it, child."

I remembered seeing the doctor's buggy at the preacher's house on our walk around the farm. Should I ask after his family? What if it wasn't good news?

Brother Latham leaned forward, resting his elbows on his knees. The calloused hands and weathered face said he wasn't solely a preacher. He also farmed. Two jobs rolled into one, with sickness adding to the workload on both ends.

"You won't have heard, of course, how many have been taken ill in these parts." He sighed. "That's for the best."

I almost interjected what I knew, but before I could draw breath, he continued on. "Our small congregation has already lost several members, including some from its founding families. Your aunt will be most sorely missed. She was a good friend to all. And we are praying for Frank, too, as he absorbs this unexpected news."

I nodded, my gaze intent on my hands.

"I can't imagine how he must feel knowing his children are all alone."

My head jerked up.

"I mean, well . . ." Brother Latham allowed his words to drift away, his droopy eyes staring at me with apparent concern.

"It's very kind of you to trouble yourself about us, Brother Latham." I folded my hands in my lap, as prim and proper as you please, and counted my fingers. Then I inhaled a deep breath. "I'll be staying on and caring for the children awhile." I looked up, sure my discomfort stood naked before him. "I promised my aunt I would."

He gave a curt nod, as if he approved of my plan, but his eyes seemed to concede that he accepted this only because he saw no other option. "Do you have everything you need?"

"I believe so." My confidence grew with each word. "We have vegetables from the garden and milk from Ol' Bob, as well as eggs from a few chickens, and the cistern is full from all the rain. I found flour and sugar and a good bit of cornmeal, as well. I'm sure we can manage until . . ."

Until what? Until Mama got well? Until the children's father came home? Until Arthur married me?

The preacher slapped his meaty hands against his knees and rose to his full height.

I stood, too. "Thanks for stopping by."

His head bobbed, jiggling the flesh beneath his chin. "Any other chores I can help with today?"

The question startled me. "Don't you need to get on to your other visits?"

"What good would I be if I just visited and left without offering a hand of help to those in need? Kind of like saying, 'Go, be filled,' instead of giving a hungry man a piece of bread."

His words made sense, but I couldn't imagine Reverend Huddleston, back at home, rolling up his sleeves and milking a cow or mucking out a stall, no matter how great the need. He seemed better at sitting in a parlor with a delicate china teacup in his hand.

I thought to protest, to assure him I could take care of things myself, but when I noticed my unlaced boots, my resolve melted. "Your help this morning has been greatly appreciated. I promise I'll send for you should we need anything more."

The children gathered at the front door now, their faces peering through the screen.

"My wife will be over when the sickness abates. She's helping nurse some of the others, as well as a few of our own. But Ollie and James know the way to our house should you need us before then." He looked at the two oldest children. Solemn nods spoke their reply.

He strode around to his buggy and hefted himself onto the seat. "Frank has been good about sending his pay to Adabelle, so open any letters that come from him."

I exhaled my relief. Army pay. I hadn't thought of that. But how long until the next batch came?

CHAPTER
14

On Friday morning, I picked my way across the dew-damp yard after giving Ollie instructions to watch the little ones. I did some of my best thinking with my cheek pressed against a cow's warm flank, the milk plinking into the tin pail.

Ol' Bob swished her tail at me. I rubbed my hand down her nose before pulling the stool close. My fingers pulled at Bob's teats, the rhythmic motion as familiar to me as frying a chicken or sweeping a floor, leaving my mind free to roam.

We'd need a few supplies soon. I'd rummaged through Frank's letters in the desk yesterday looking for money. I found nothing.

But I read through letter after letter as I searched. Mostly stilted words of a grieving man, one who didn't quite know how to talk to his children. And yet, in one old letter addressed to Clara and written before he'd boarded the ship for France, his tender expressions of joy at the coming birth of his child ripped at my heart.

Would Daddy's or Will's—or Arthur's—letters sound like Frank's, given a similar situation? I couldn't imagine. I told myself Frank's character wasn't really any of my concern. What I needed most at this moment was Arthur's assurance that my life wouldn't keep plodding along on this predictable line, like a mule plowing a furrow over an unending strip of sod.

The bucket brimmed with the foam of warm milk. I cooed to the cow and forked fresh straw her way. The smell of the barn drew me back to the remembrance of home. How I wished Mama were here. She'd know exactly what to do next.

I trudged back indoors no more peaceful than when I'd left the house. James sidled close, his small fingers slipping into mine. Ollie wiped a towel across the last clean plate. Then she coughed.

Not a big cough, but enough. I shuddered at the memory of Aunt Adabelle's purpling face. And the blood. I led James to the wash bucket and called the others there, as well, plunging grimy hands into the water and scouring them with soap over and over again.

Whatever else happened, I would keep us all well.

Thunder rumbled less than an hour later. Rain drummed against the window, echoing in my ears, reminding me again of Aunt Adabelle's muddy grave. Would Mama suffer the same fate?

Dan tromped into the kitchen, water dripping from his hair and his clothes, puddling on my clean floor. "It's raining," he announced.

I picked up a dry rag. "Go change, young man."

He scampered off while I dropped to my knees, mopping up his trail.

Crash. Tumble. Bump. Scream.

I ran into the hall. Dan lay at the bottom of the stairs amid a jumble of wooden blocks, blood oozing from his head.

"Heavens to Betsy!" I nearly fainted as my stomach threatened to spill its contents. "Ollie!"

She already stood beside me.

"Wet a towel and bring it here."

She dashed away as I knelt beside the screaming child.

James stood over him, too, tears streaming down his face. "I just wanted him to hurry."

I brushed him aside as Ollie arrived, the towel dripping a river behind her. I wrung water onto the floor, then held the limp flour sacking to the gash. Blood seeped toward the edges of the cloth. "Get me another." I kept my voice low, trying to calm the situation, though I felt anything but calm.

Three towels later, the bleeding slowed. Dan only sniffled now. James's tears dried and Janie crawled into the hall to add to the commotion. I leaned my head against the wall, my clean dress now streaked red. If I closed my eyes, would it all disappear?

I squeezed my eyelids shut until the darkness seemed complete. But when I opened them again, everything remained. I leaned over Dan. "Let me look, honey."

He screamed as I pushed the hair away from the wound. I wished I could scream, too. Scream or vomit, I wasn't sure which. Did the gash need a doctor's care? Mama would know.

I cradled Dan's knees over one of my arms and supported his head with the other as I carried him to the kitchen. "Ollie, get a quilt and lay it on the floor near the stove." My arms sagged as I waited. Finally, I laid him down. Ollie pressed the rag to the oozing spot on his head.

A horse and buggy stood in the barn, but how long would it take my uncertain fingers to hitch one to the other? And even if we made it to town, to the doctor's house, would he be home? I knew he continued to care for those ill with influenza. Maybe he wouldn't have time to deal with this.

Tears streamed down my face now. I wanted to yell at Aunt Adabelle for dying, at Mama for being sick, at Arthur for being quarantined. Most of all, I wanted to yell at Frank—Dan's father—for being out of reach, across the ocean.

I put my head in my hands. Even God had abandoned us, I was sure. But the thought of lowering that feisty little boy into a muddy, gaping hole in the ground spurred me forward as surely as a cowboy kicking his horse into a gallop.

"I'm going to get help. Keep towels on Dan's head. Give Janie some warm milk and have James lie down with her so she'll nap. I'll be back as soon as I can."

I flung open the door and burst through the downpour before any of them could protest. One step beyond the gate, my boot sank deep in the black mud. I wrenched it free and took the next step. And the next. Brother Latham's offer of help came to mind, but I felt sure Dan needed a doctor. So I trudged on toward town.

By the time I reached Doc Risinger's house and pounded on his door, my whole body shook like a high branch in a spring storm. But along the way I'd come to a decision: someone else could take care of these children. Once Dan had the care he needed, I would pack my bags and head to Dallas, to Arthur. I could use the money I'd found in the handbag. Arthur could pay back Frank Gresham later. I'd hire a room, wait for Arthur to be free of the quarantine, and beg him to marry me. Now. My mind was made up, my heart relieved.

Until Doc Risinger opened the door.

"Go away, child," the doctor rasped, purple-shadowed eyes sunk into his thin face. "I can't do ye any good now."

CHAPTER
15

I stuck my foot between the door and the doorframe. "What do you mean?" I could only see a sliver of his tortured face.

"Just what I said, child. The fever's got hold of me. Go on. Do the best ye can."

"But I haven't come about the flu. Dan's fallen down the stairs and cut his head. It's bleeding."

His head moved back and forth, but barely. "Wash it good. Sew it up if ye need to." A heavy sigh. "Wait here and I'll give ye some iodine to smear on it, too."

He pushed the door until it inched my foot back and clicked shut. I paced the small porch. I had to get back to Dan. I'd already been gone too long. The sky still cried its steady tears, but at least I could see beyond the curtain of rain now.

The door cracked open. Unsteady fingers thrust a small bottle into my hands. The door shut before I could voice any apprehension or appreciation.

I plunged back into the muddy track that ran out of town. Slipping, sliding, sinking. Covered in mud, I reached the yard, then the kitchen door, calling for a blanket and a change of clothes. The blanket came first.

"The bleeding stopped just after you left," Ollie told me. "And I put the towels in there to soak." She pointed to a bucket on the porch.

"You did good, honey. Now watch over the boys while I get changed." I moved around to the side porch.

Only the downstairs bedroom window had a view of me here. The empty room with the door that remained shut. Huddling near the house, I peeled my dress and underclothes from my body and wrapped the clean blanket under my arms. In spite of the chill, it felt good to be dry.

I leaned over a bit, gathered my hair in my hands, and squeezed. Water splattered against the boards of the porch.

"Beautiful day, ain't it?" Mr. Culpepper's rumbly laugh followed.

I pressed myself flat against the side of the house, heaving for breath as I cinched the blanket more tightly across my chest. One bare foot tried to cover the other. My naked arms had nowhere to hide. How long had he been there? What had he seen? I groaned, refusing to even glance toward the road.

The mailman's good-natured chortle faded into the distance. I'd been seen wearing nothing but an old blanket. And Dan's head still needed mending. But then I realized what Mr. Culpepper's presence meant: we had mail. Tears snaked down my face as I shook with laughter I couldn't hold inside.

"You okay?" Ollie handed me clean underclothes, as well as what must have been one of her mother's calico work dresses.

"I'm fine." I giggled out more laughter as I dressed. It didn't matter how hard I tried. I'd never be the lady Mama desired me to be.

I checked Dan's head again. The gash didn't look as horrific now. "James, why don't you run out and get our mail? And for heaven's sake, carry an umbrella."

100

He darted for the door. I had no illusions that he'd come back dry. I just needed him out of the way while I doused Dan's gash with iodine.

"Hold Ollie's hand, Dan. Squeeze as hard as you want. This won't hurt—much."

I held my breath as I dabbed the medicine on top of the gash. Dan howled like a tomcat with his tail stuck beneath a wagon wheel. I looked up for a split second as James skidded to a stop just inside the kitchen, his face void of all color. Envelopes fell from his hand as he bolted from the house.

"James!" My voice followed him, but my legs couldn't. Not until I'd finished with Dan.

Dan whimpered. I dried my hands, wiped Dan's tears, and started out the door to find James. Then my foot rustled one of the letters. I stooped down to pick it up. My hand trembled as I scurried to find the others that had scattered. My treasure hunt produced two more. I fanned them out like playing cards. One from Daddy. One from Frank. And one from Arthur.

"Hold these." I handed them to Ollie.

"One from Daddy!" Her squeal followed me as I dashed out the door, careful to lift my clean skirt above the mud and keep the umbrella directly over my head. If I knew James at all by now, he'd have buried himself in a haystack, probably with his hind end sticking out. I whistled my way into the barn, my nose wrinkling at the smell of moist hay and manure.

"Come out, come out wherever you are," I sang out as if we played a game of hide-and-seek. Sure enough, a chubby leg disappeared into a wall of hay. I reached in and pulled out my little man, his dirty face streaked with tears.

"Is he dead?" he asked, his bottom lip trembling.

I wrapped my arms around him and placed his arms around my waist. Not that he required much encouragement to cling to me. "He's all better now, James."

"I'm so glad I didn't kill him." His wail filled the barn, starting Ol' Bob and the mules to bellowing, too.

A chuckle escaped me as I tipped his head back. "You come and see just how fine he is."

He blinked up at me, as if weighing the truth of my words. A slow grin lit his face. I gave his behind a pat. He didn't need any other encouragement. His little legs plowed through mud as deep as his knees until he reached the house.

"Now, Rebekah. Read it now." Ollie pulled me toward the parlor, James jumping up and down beside her, Dan limping along behind, as if it were his leg hurt, not his head.

"Hush. You'll wake the baby." I let go of Ollie's hand and picked up Dan instead. Not until I had him nestled in the corner of the sofa did I slit the envelope and pull out the letter.

Something plopped to the floor. Ollie stooped to pick it up.

"Look! It's Daddy!" She held a photograph between her fingers.

"Let me see!" James tried to yank it away. Ollie held it out of reach and climbed up beside me. Dan leaned in. James hoisted himself over the back of the sofa, his hands on my shoulders for balance.

A blurry photograph. Three uniformed men beside a bridge, their faces too far from the camera to make out clearly. But they all looked young. More like Will's age than Barney Graves's.

My heart pounded in my ears. "Which one's your daddy?"

Ollie pointed. The middle one. The one with his arms draped over the shoulders of the other two. The one with the solemn face.

"You sure, Ollie?" James climbed over my shoulder and squeezed in next to his sister, eyes scrunched as if trying to remember the man who stared up at him from the picture. Dan blinked in confusion.

I unfolded the sheet of paper and took a deep breath. The children quieted. I skimmed past his greeting to my aunt.

> *"Ollie Elizabeth, be good for Miss Ada. I expect you to help her and not to boss your brothers around. Take care of Janie, too. I'm praying that you will grow into as fine a woman as your mama was.*
>
> *James, don't try to split the wood by yourself. You scared Miss Ada near to death. Let someone else do that for now. Others will help out. A real man knows when to let others help.*
>
> *Dan, I'm counting on you to grow big and strong so you can help plant in the spring. I'll need you and your brother both when I get home.*
>
> *My Janie, I can't wait to meet you. How you must be growing up already! But please don't get too big for your daddy to hold you."*

I heard Ollie sniffle, felt her head heavy on my knee. I smoothed back her hair but couldn't look at her. My own tears lurked too close to the surface. Instead, I slid the picture and letter back into the envelope and cleared the bottled tears from my throat.

"Let's go on to bed. It's been a long day."

No one protested. Not even a whine. And their silent grief unnerved me. With each shadowed step up the stairs after them, I pondered this man, his words so often short and stiff, yet these moments of tenderness, too. His sweet notes to his children, even the daughter he didn't yet know.

I needed to understand Frank Gresham, the father of these children. I needed to know what would happen to them after Arthur whisked me away.

In the middle of the night I crept back down the stairs. I couldn't sleep after reading my letters. Not with Daddy's words burning in my head. *She's out of danger, but the doctor says the influenza has weakened her. She might not ever be quite the same.*

What did Daddy mean, exactly, by "weakened"? Never had I known such a word to describe my mother. I couldn't imagine Mama as anything other than, well, Mama.

I eased open the bedroom door, touched the match to the lamp's wick, and spread the letters of the day on the desk before me. I skimmed Daddy's again. *Do you intend to stay with the children until their father arrives home?*

Anger and guilt tangled up inside me. I believed God had sent me here. Aunt Adabelle had said it, too. And I'd promised her I'd care for the children. I even told the sheriff and the preacher that I would stay. But I wanted to go. I wanted to be with Arthur. I wanted a more adventurous, more exciting life.

My fingers traced Arthur's signature, the flourish beneath in the form of an airplane. He hadn't asked me to come to him. Hadn't mentioned seeing me at all. Just detailed his boredom with the quarantine.

Frank might not come home for months or years. Or what if he never made it back? I held Frank's letter toward the bit of lamplight. *October 11* was scripted at the top.

Three weeks ago, on a day my aunt still walked the earth, he wrote these words. Surely he had the news of my aunt's death by now. He'd write to someone he knew and ask him or her to step in and care for his children. Wouldn't he?

I dipped pen into ink and bled my heart onto a clean page. *I need you, Arthur. I'm desperate to see your face.*

On and on the words flowed. Desperate words. Aching words. I wrote until they stopped. Then I pulled the lamp closer and read over my letter. In one motion, I swept the paper into my hand, wadded it into a ball, and tossed it on the floor. I drew out a clean sheet. But the right words wouldn't come. Only petty, empty words that sounded like a spoiled child.

Maybe I oughtn't write to Arthur yet. As soon as they lifted the quarantine at Camp Dick, he would come in person. I felt sure of it. He didn't mention it so as not to raise my hopes. Or perhaps he intended to surprise me with a visit.

But if I couldn't write to Arthur, I had to write to someone. Almost of its own accord, my pen addressed a letter to Frank Gresham. I poured out the stories of Aunt Adabelle's funeral, Dan's head injury, James's nightmares. I asked what to do with the fields and the livestock and the garden for winter. I assured him of his children's health. Finally, I folded the letter into an envelope. But it wouldn't reach the mail train until tomorrow. Crossing the ocean would take weeks. What if Arthur came for me before Frank replied?

I imagined one situation after another, but no matter which way I thought things out, I knew I couldn't leave the children without knowing their father hovered close at hand.

CHAPTER
16

$\mathcal{T}$wo days after my letter to Frank disappeared from the mailbox, I splurged with the white flour and baking powder, my rolling pin slamming into the slab of biscuit dough. Thud, roll. Thud, roll. Again and again.

Every frustration pounded the dough flat.

Then a knock rattled the kitchen door. My hand jumped to my chest as I huffed out air. Mama'd done that same thing ten thousand times when we burst into the kitchen and startled her from her task.

A stout woman opened the door and chuckled as she lifted a gingham-covered basket into the air. "I thought y'all might like some sweets we had sitting by."

I wiped my hands on my apron before reaching out to accept the stranger's offering. "Thank you very much."

"I'm Irene Latham. I expect you met my husband."

"Oh, yes, ma'am. He said you'd been helping out with the sick." I stepped backward, anxious to put some distance between us.

She shrugged. "I've done what I could. For many, that wasn't enough. Took some so quick, like your aunt." Her eyes went misty. "I'll miss Adabelle. She was a good friend. But at least I have the comfort of knowing I'll see her again." Her gaze lifted toward heaven. It seemed a sincere gesture of friendship, not a showy display of piety.

I liked this woman immediately, and in that moment, I wished I would have had more time to get to know Adabelle. I believed we would have been friends, not just family.

"Please, sit down." I pulled a golden-crusted pie from the basket before positioning the coffeepot on the burner.

"Where're the children?" Mrs. Latham glanced about her.

"Ollie's giving a tea party in the barn. And Janie's napping." I gave her a guilty smile. "I needed a little peace and quiet."

"Of course you did." Her laughter trilled through the room as she patted my hand. "A young thing like you isn't used to the chaos of children at her skirts all day long." Her eyes danced as a grin stretched her full lips. "Though by your age, I had two myself. But at least you haven't wanted for company. I hear our sheriff has been quite attentive."

My face burned as I turned to pour our coffee. Just like in Downington, everyone knew everyone else's business around here. But did they know I was plotting my way out of this town?

I set cups of coffee on the table, deciding to ignore her insinuation. "When I came to take care of Aunt Adabelle, I had no idea she had charge of four children. I haven't had much experience with children before now. Seems like we've had a crisis every day I've been here." I plopped onto the bench at the table.

"Tell me what's happened." Mrs. Latham lifted her cup to her lips, eyes full of concern.

So I told her about Dan's cut head and Mr. Culpepper coming by while I was dressing on the porch and even her husband catching me in my nightclothes.

When I finished my tales, Mrs. Latham blinked twice. Her lips twitched, and then she threw back her head and howled laughter.

I stared into my cup, uncertain, at first, how to respond. But after a moment my mouth curved upward, and I found myself laughing with her. And oh, how good it felt. Not just to laugh. To laugh with someone. Arthur had made me laugh. I missed that.

"Those boys are quite a handful." Mrs. Latham wiped tears from her eyes as she shook her head. "But at least Ollie Elizabeth's a help. I told your aunt she had the patience of a saint with them."

I wasn't sure I quite agreed with her about Ollie not being a handful, but I pushed that thought aside, greedy for information about these kids and this place. "Can you tell me a little about their mother?"

The humor left Mrs. Latham's face. She sipped her coffee, her eyes staring holes into the table.

"I'm sorry. I shouldn't—"

Mrs. Latham reached out and clasped my fingers in hers. "Yes, you should. It's just been such a trying time. For everyone. So much loss. So much grief." She squeezed my hand and let it go before pushing her empty cup my way.

"More?" I asked.

"Please."

Thankful for a task to do, I didn't hurry. By the time I returned a full cup to her, she seemed ready to talk again.

"Clara was a sickly thing. Honestly, I'm surprised she made it through three deliveries. They weren't small ones, those kids. But she didn't mind. She loved her children, wanted as many as she could have. Adabelle came to help out not long after Ollie arrived. Clara didn't have the strength to manage the cooking and housework and a baby all at once."

My breath had caught while she spoke. Now it streamed out again. Aunt Adabelle had been around long before these children's mama died. Had that made bearing her death harder for them?

Mrs. Latham smiled at me again, a bit of joy wrinkling the corners of her eyes. "Adabelle loved this place as much as she did those kids. She's the one that put in the flowers and tended them. And the garden. On top of taking care of the house and the children—and Clara."

I opened my mouth to ask about Frank, but the children burst through the door. James threw himself at Mrs. Latham with such vigor I felt a jealous prick at my heart. It surprised me. I ought to have been happy knowing he could find affection for another woman, but it gnawed at me all the same.

She gathered each child to her, looking into upturned faces, tweaking a nose, kissing a cheek. Their easy smiles told me they knew her well, but my hands still fidgeted unaccountably in my lap as my stomach jumped and lurched like an old bull with a cowboy on its back.

"Y'all giving Miss Rebekah much trouble?"

James toed the floor. Ollie averted her eyes.

Only Dan piped up with an answer. "See my head?" He pulled back the hair from his scab. "It's mostly better now."

Mrs. Latham laughed again. "I should hope so." She drank down the last of her coffee and pushed from the bench.

"Must you go already?" I heard my own desperation, the pleading whine of a child, but I didn't care. In spite of my twinge of jealousy over the children's easy way with her, I realized I'd missed having a woman to talk to.

She picked up her empty basket. "Too many chores piled up at home for me to visit anymore today. But I'll come around again soon. I promise."

The whoosh and whinny of a horse outside caught my ear.

"My husband. Always right on time." Mrs. Latham swept out the door more gracefully than I imagined so substantial a woman could move.

I followed. Brother Latham stood at the porch. He took his

109

wife's hand and led her down the steps as if she were royalty. After her feet reached the ground, he turned to me.

"The danger seems to have passed. No new cases in almost a week, Doc says."

"How is the doc?" I asked.

Brother Latham's mouth turned down at one corner. "Whether it's influenza or exhaustion that has him down, we don't know for sure." Brother Latham helped his wife into the buggy before climbing in himself. "We'll meet for church tomorrow. And school will open again on Monday."

Mrs. Latham peered around her husband. "How about we come by for you in the morning, around ten?"

Church. And school. Finally, something normal.

❦

Oh, what a glorious thing to be back among the people of God. Even with the graveyard hugging the side of the small building, the fear that marauded the entire town seemed to melt away as we sang hymns and listened to Brother Latham preach on heaven. I figured his sermon encompassed all he'd wanted to say at all the quick funerals but didn't have the chance. He described us as being sojourners in this world and true citizens of the New Jerusalem. He talked of mansions built on streets of gold and of eyes wiped dry. I tried to picture my aunt there, singing with the angels, a smile fixed on her face as she beheld the throne of God.

But as pretty and peaceful a picture as he painted, it still didn't make me want to go there anytime soon. I had my life to live first. My life with Arthur. I hugged the thought to myself as we bowed our heads to pray, asking God to be with Mama and Will and to bring Arthur to me soon.

❦

The women spread dinner on the grounds between services. I hated that Mrs. Latham hadn't told me to bring something. She just patted my hand and laughed, told me there would be plenty more times I could help.

Once the children and the men had eaten their fill, the women settled down around a plank table, enjoying the warm afternoon sun. Voices buzzed up and down the table, among young women and old. Obviously they'd all missed contact with their friends during the battle with influenza.

"Tell me more about yourself," Mrs. Latham said. She seemed truly interested. So I told her about Mama's illness and Daddy's farm. About Downington and my soldier brother.

Then her eyes took on a merry look. "What about your beau? Is he back home or 'over there'?"

"Not back home." I ducked my head like a shy schoolgirl.

She coaxed Arthur from me with more questions. I recounted his dreams of flying and living in a big city, but also the corn silk hair that waved above jovial blue eyes, the face that beamed with pleasure at most everything. I stopped before I told her about his lips, how they had pressed into mine. How I relived the warmth of them every night before I fell asleep. But I think she knew anyway. When she raised her eyebrows and laughed, I looked away, sure she could read my mind.

So I changed the subject to Frank Gresham. "Why did he go off to fight? Surely his age could have kept him here. Especially with a sickly wife and small children."

She motioned me to follow her from the table, which I did. We sorted her dishes into a pile for her boys to load back in their wagon. "He's not as old as you might expect," she said as we worked. "He and Clara came here mighty young—and already married. Besides—"

A throat cleared behind us. We both turned. Sheriff Jeffries's fingers fidgeted with his hat. He nodded at Mrs. Latham, and then his gaze locked on me. "Would you care to take a walk before the evening service, Rebekah?"

I looked past him, toward the group of children playing tag, then to the babies, Janie included, asleep on a blanket in the shade under the watchful eye of a gray-haired lady. "I think I'd better stay near. For the children."

"Of course. The children." A faint blush spread across his cheeks, as if he'd forgotten my purpose here. "Another time, then." He settled his hat back on his head and strode away without giving me a chance to reply.

I glanced at Mrs. Latham. My face heated at the merriment in her eyes.

"Mrs. Latham, I—"

She patted my hand. "Call me Irene, honey. You're plenty old enough, and we're friends, aren't we?"

I pressed my hand to my chest as tears filled my eyes. Friends. I really had a friend here—and an older friend at that. It made me feel grown up, even more than caring for the children did. "Thank you . . . Irene."

CHAPTER
17

Stop it, Dan. I told you not to scratch." Ollie's voice from the kitchen met me as I toted an armload of laundry down the stairs Monday morning. Dan's head showed all the signs of healing, but keeping his grimy hands away from the spot proved difficult.

"You can't tell me what to do!" Dan yelled back.

A shuffle of bodies. A scream.

"No! Let him go!" James had apparently joined the fray.

"If you don't listen to me, God will send you to the bad place, with the devil."

I charged into the kitchen, dropping the dirty clothes and grabbing Ollie's arm. "You are not his mother."

James stuck out his tongue at her. I reached out and snagged James with my free hand and marched them both up the stairs, their howls filling the house. I sent Ollie into the children's room to put on her school dress while I left James writhing on my freshly made bed. Then I returned to the woeful Dan, coddling him and Janie until their tears melted into smiles.

When Ollie finally raced from the house, braids flying, eager to be off to school, relief and sadness tugged at either side of my heart. Had Mama felt this way when she put me on the train nearly three weeks ago? I suspected she did. Probably more so, for I wouldn't return later that afternoon to sit at the table, drink a glass of milk, and tell her about my day.

I didn't have time to ponder the strange motherly feelings. A full day of chores awaited. I scooped the laundry back into my arms and followed the boys outside.

When I pulled the envelope from the mailbox that afternoon, Frank's familiar handwriting stared up at me, but it was the address that stopped me cold.

Miss Rebekah Hendricks, Prater's Junction, Texas.

My mouth dropped open. I turned the envelope over and stared at the flap. Thankful that Ollie hadn't arrived home from school yet, I slit the envelope with my hairpin. The paper shook as I drew it out. I leaned against the thick trunk of the half-bare oak tree.

Miss Hendricks,

I received word of Adabelle Williams's passing on to glory and of you staying on with my children. I know they are not your responsibility, but from what I hear, you weren't given much choice. Thank you for your Christian kindness in helping those in need.

Tell Ollie Elizabeth I'm depending on her. Keep the boys in line with a switch if you have to. Please let me know how they are doing. It seems so unfair for them to lose both their mother and their Miss Ada without their father to comfort them. Yet I must believe God knows best even if it seems a hard thing.

I don't know how long you intend to stay, but if it could be until I return home, that would be greatly appreciated. If you need anything at all, ask George and Irene Latham.

Sincerely,

Frank Gresham

I blew out a long breath as I read over the words again. To my relief, he seemed to care, both about his children and about my being here. And how could I refuse his request? Arthur had not yet given me assurance that he would marry me before he left for Europe. If I stayed here, perhaps I could at least see him again before he shipped out. And being on my own and in charge was better than going back to my old life in Downington.

❧❦❧

Ollie meandered into the yard as I finished hanging the clothes on the line. The other children napped upstairs, and I intended to keep it that way.

"Will you lay those towels and cloths to dry on the hedge bushes for me?" I said.

She dragged the basket over to the side fence. With careful concentration, she stretched each cloth until it lay fully exposed to the air, if not the sun. I shook out the skirt of my gingham work dress and pinned it to the clothesline before crossing the yard to help her.

"My mama used to let me do this. Miss Ada, too." Ollie draped and stretched the last kitchen towel on the prickly green leaves. "I helped Miss Ada help Mama before she had Janie." She smoothed the edges of each towel, making them line up with each other. I let the silence linger between us.

"When Miss Ada got sick, she told me I'd have to grow up right quick. I didn't go to school for a few days. I thought it was fun being in charge." When she turned to me, fear peeked out from behind her serious eyes. A tear slipped down her cheek. She didn't bother to wipe it away.

A fist seemed to close around my heart, wringing from its depths a compassion I didn't know it contained. "Oh, baby, I'm so sorry."

She threw herself at me, her thin arms circling my waist, her shoulders heaving with sobs. "I'm sorry I made Dan mad. I'm sorry I couldn't keep Mama and Miss Ada alive."

I held her cheeks in my hands. "It's not your fault. Do you hear me, Ollie Elizabeth? It's not your fault your mama died. Or Miss Ada. It was . . . Well, it was just meant to be, that's all."

She buried her head in my body and wept some more. I wanted to join her. Who was I to offer platitudes when my mama remained in this world, even if Daddy's letter had hinted she had one foot in the next?

Help me, Lord. I knelt in front of the girl, wiped the tears from her face, and prayed for the words to say. "Death comes to us all, Ollie. Miss Ada knew that. So did your mama. Your daddy knows it, too. He probably sees it every day. But God is always here, watching us, helping us. I know it."

"How? Can you see God?"

Staring far off over her shoulder, I pondered how to express what I knew to be true. I thought of Irene, of the light in her eyes in spite of all the death she'd seen in her congregation, her community. The words rose up from somewhere deep inside of me. "I know it because the sun comes up every morning, no matter what. And the rain falls on the crops. And babies are born. I know it because even when death comes, we go on living."

The words slashed against my heart like barbed wire tearing flesh. Could I live out my own words if Mama died? Or Arthur? Or Will? Could Ollie endure it if death came for her father, too?

Both of us, our lives stretching out along an unknown road, would have to trust the Lord to work out our futures. Until then, I prayed we could find some comfort in each other.

Later that week, a short note arrived from Arthur. Talk of peace had him discouraged. He wanted to challenge the German aces in the air. But I hugged the information close, believing that the war might soon end, Frank would come home, and Arthur and I could begin our life together.

Irene missed church on Sunday. "Down in her back," I heard from her eldest, Nola Jean. And Sheriff Jeffries's undivided attention all day rubbed me wrong. Like sitting with Barney Graves in the parlor. A nice man, but one who seemed to want more from me than I was able to give.

The following Monday the back door burst open. Irene's round face glowed red as a hot stove, her breath coming in chugs, like a steam engine. A newspaper waved in her hand.

"It's over!" She wheezed out the words as I led her to a chair in the parlor. "It's over. Early this morning."

Could it be? I grabbed the paper from her hand. The moment I saw the headline of the special edition *Junction Sentinel,* I let out a holler. "The war's over!" I danced a small jig before throwing my arms around my new friend.

She shook with laughter. "Praise Jesus! Praise Jesus!"

Janie grabbed at my skirt, a panicked look on her little face. I swung her into the air.

"It's over, Janie." I brought her down and danced her around the room. "The war is over. Our boys are coming home!"

Dan and James bounded in, yelling over each other, wanting to know what had happened.

"The war's over."

It only took a second for their eyes to light with understanding.

"Daddy's coming home! Daddy's coming home!" They grabbed hands, continuing their chant and spinning in a circle until they had to sit down.

Arthur would be through with his commitment, never having to leave American soil. And Frank would begin his journey home, as would my brother.

No more rationing. No more casualty lists. No more boys buried in faraway graves.

A knock at the door turned all our heads.

"Mind if I join in your celebration?" Sheriff Jeffries grinned, his hat doing its customary dance in his hands. His hair had been slicked back and smelled of tonic.

I held up the newspaper. "Why don't we all celebrate together? Come to supper. I'll wring some chicken necks, like we did to the Kaiser and his army."

"Are you sure about that?" Irene pushed to her feet, her breathing finally normal again.

"Positive." I twirled a circle before setting Janie on the floor and skipping off toward the henhouse.

The sheriff's voice trailed behind me. "That girl sure is full of life."

The smell of baking chicken wafted into the corners of the house, adding to the festive feeling. The chicken and cornbread and squash fed our bodies while our souls reveled in the news of armistice. Voices bounced off the corners of the rooms as everyone tried to talk over each other, each wanting to tell what they'd heard.

The sheriff sat across the table from me. He did have nice eyes. And a not-hard-to-look-at face. He'd make some girl a very respectable husband. And he'd be a good father to her children. I sensed that as I watched him bring James and Dan into the excited banter.

His gaze met mine. I smiled at him, hoping my gratitude showed but praying he didn't read into the expression more than I intended. My heart belonged to Arthur.

By the time the Lathams and the sheriff took their leave, my back ached and every dish and pot and pan in the kitchen sat dirty on the table or in the washtub. Irene and her girls had offered to help, but I'd recognized the tired in my friend's eyes. And I wanted to prove—to myself, if nothing else—that I could handle the household tasks.

I did let the older Latham boys haul in water before they left. The dishes could soak overnight. It wasn't like we had pressing tasks to do in the morning, anyway. Just another day of chores, each the same as the last, only now in a world suddenly stilled with the peace of armistice. And what this new world held for me, I couldn't wait to discover.

CHAPTER
18

𝒯he thought of peace drove me happily from my bed early the next morning. I forced myself to clean a tubful of dishes and set another batch in water before I allowed myself even one sip of coffee. Finally I settled on the porch with my warm mug to enjoy the pleasure of yesterday's newspaper beyond the front-page stories.

The cool breeze rippled my unbound hair as I scanned the pages. Then a headline leapt from page thirteen.

Wednesday, Dallas Day at Love Field: Arrangements Completed for Caring for Large Crowd at "Flyin' Frolic."

I bolted upright, sloshing hot coffee onto my skirt, and read on. A day of aerial demonstrations and pageantry for the public, combined with a celebration of the armistice. Special streetcars would run to Highland Park, with short-haul jitneys carrying spectators from there to Love Field.

Surely the aviators from Camp Dick would all attend, wouldn't they? But it would cost money to take the train to Dallas. There'd also be the conveyance to Love Field, plus the price of admission.

And food. I'd have to buy food. Or would Arthur treat me to dinner?

Plans crowded my head—clothes, train schedules, someone to care for the children. I ought to telegraph Arthur and let him know how to find me. Or should I take my chances and surprise him?

Never mind. I had the whole day to figure things out. I gulped down my cooling coffee. I needed to get caught up on all the chores and then bathe and wash my hair. A smile ached my cheeks, and my toes almost didn't hit the ground on my way inside. If I could have squealed without waking the children, I would have done that, too.

But my self-control mattered little. Before I made it to the kitchen for a second cup of coffee, three pairs of feet pattered down the stairs.

Arranging my adventure would have to wait.

In the gray light of dawn I tiptoed down the stairs. My mouth stretched in a yawn, body and mind rebelling at the early hour, in spite of my excitement. My plans had come together quite well, although there hadn't been time to go to town and send a telegram to Arthur. I'd just have to trust I could find him at the air show. I'd pray for it. God had shown me that Arthur was His plan for my life, so I felt sure He'd answer.

After all, He'd already smoothed the way by making Irene agreeable to keeping the kids for me for the day, even though her eyes had asked questions I had no desire to answer. I needed her to be my friend, not my mother. She'd given me a wary smile, but a smile nonetheless, and told me to go on and enjoy myself.

The trust in her face opened the door to guilt. I doubted she approved of me going to Dallas by myself. But I'd made my decision, and I intended to see it through.

As I opened the door to Aunt Adabelle's bedroom, the mirror over the washstand beckoned me. A bottle of French perfume on the washstand caught my attention. Had Frank sent it to his wife before he knew she'd passed? After only a moment's hesitation, I pulled the stopper from the heavy glass. The room filled with the sweetness of a thousand flowers at once.

I dabbed the fragrance on the skin behind my ears as I stared into the mirror. Brown eyes blinked back at me, lighter brown hair just visible beneath my hat. A couple of pinches on each cheek and they colored nicely. A turn from side to side returned a verdict of presentable. I clasped my hands beneath my chin, wanting to both laugh and cry. Today I'd see Arthur. But first I had to get to that train station on time.

I hurried back into the hall, peeked out the front door. Nola Jean Latham sauntered across the yard at that moment, spindly legs and arms shooting out from her too-small dress.

She spied me and came on a bit faster. "Mama sent me." She hopped up on the porch. "I'll take the little ones back to my house. Ollie can walk to school with the rest of us."

My toes bounced against the porch floor, eager to be off. "That sounds fine, Nola Jean. Tell your mother I said thank you."

She nodded, plodded into the house, up the stairs, and out of sight. I scurried to the kitchen, wrapped a piece of leftover corn-bread in a clean cloth, and tucked it into my handbag. It would do for a bite to eat until I arrived at the Flyin' Frolic.

James and Ollie shuffled into the kitchen. James rubbed his eyes, then blinked up at me from his bench seat at the table as he sniffed the air. "Mmm. You smell like Mama, Bekah." His eyes and nose scrunched in confusion as he stared at me. "Where're you goin'?"

Ollie's head jerked my direction. Dan sauntered to the table, more awake than his brother. "Nola Jean got Janie up, too."

"Yes, I know. Remember, James? I told you last night that I had to go to Dallas today."

Ollie's eyes narrowed to slits.

"I forgot," James said, laying his head on the table. "Is Nola Jean goin' to get my breakfast?"

"Yes, she is."

The girl walked in that minute, Janie content on her hip.

"Be good for Nola Jean and Mrs. Latham, now."

James's bottom lip trembled. Dan nodded and stuck his thumb in his mouth. I laid a hand on each boy's cheek.

James leaned into my hand. "When are you coming back?"

My throat tightened. Janie stretched her arms to me. I avoided her reach, kissed her head, and started for the door.

Janie screamed and wriggled until Nola Jean let her down. Still wailing, she crawled after me, red-faced but without tears. She gulped air, screaming, then breathing, and screaming again.

Ollie followed Janie onto the porch. I hurried toward the gate. Part of me wanted to run back and sweep that sweet baby into my arms. To hold on tight. But the greater part of me wanted to go. Now.

I glanced up the road. Then I looked back at Ollie and Janie—and James and Dan, who now stood on the porch, as well, their expressions of bewilderment jabbing my already tortured soul.

If I could take care of them, anybody could, I told myself. Nola Jean would do just fine. I forced myself forward. Janie shrieked again. I closed my eyes and ran.

❦

As the train pulled away from the station, my heart twisted in my chest like a wet skirt beneath my hands. How could I have left Janie in such a state? I covered my eyes. James's face, full of longing and fear, haunted that darkness. But this little trip was for the best. The children didn't need to become any more attached to me. They needed to be ready to welcome whoever would care for them when I left. Irene. Or Mrs. Crenshaw. Or maybe even Frank's new wife. It wouldn't be unusual for him to take one right away.

My head lolled against the window as a yawn stretched my lips. The gentle sway of the train rocked my aching eyelids closed.

I dreamt Arthur and I sat together in his airplane, high above all I knew. The world looked different from there. Small. Insignificant. And it bothered me that it felt that way. When a commotion woke me, I felt dissatisfied, as if my dream trip wasn't exactly what I'd hoped it would be. Yet it was exactly the adventure I longed to take.

The train emptied, mostly, at Union Station in Dallas. A huge building, several train lines coming and going. People whizzed past, hardly a face that didn't carry a broad smile and a quick laugh. The war was over. And today Dallas would celebrate. Swept up in the festive crowd, I forgot all about the farm, the children, and their father. I even forgot Daddy's words about Mama's recovery, or lack of it.

Finding Arthur filled my thoughts. But how to get to the Frolic? Out of the corner of my eye, I spied a man in uniform. I'd given up on Mama's instructions not to talk to strange men, so I walked right up to the soldier, bold as you please.

"Excuse me. Would you know where I could catch the conveyance to Love Field? For the Flyin' Frolic."

His eyes raked over me, from my feet to my head. I took a step backward, pulling my coat more tightly around my body.

"I'm on my way there, too, pretty lady. Perhaps we could go together?"

"I . . ." My heart pumped faster, and I swallowed hard. "I don't know . . . sir."

He reached for my hand and laid it in the crook of his arm.

"Captain Denton, miss. Let me escort you there. Wouldn't do to have you wandering the streets of Dallas alone, now, would it?" His toothy grin didn't ease my concern, but I allowed him to lead me to a ticket counter anyway.

"Oh! I thought the trains weren't running out there. Don't we need a streetcar?"

Captain Denton shook his head. "They got a special train ready to go to Love Field for today. Forty-three cents for the round trip."

I looked at the man behind the counter. He nodded in agreement.

"Well, then. That sounds just fine." And it did. Much more familiar—and safe.

I handed my money to the ticket agent—money I felt sure Frank had sent home for his family. But I couldn't worry about that now. Besides, it wasn't as if I'd spent the entire five dollars. The ticket clerk directed us to a booth where I could also purchase my admission ticket to the Frolic. Fifty cents more. I bit my lip and prayed the remainder would be enough to get the children and me through until Frank came home.

Captain Denton led me to the platform. Hundreds of others waited with us, or so it seemed. When the train whistle sounded, the crowd swarmed ahead, everyone wanting to be the first aboard. Captain Denton held my arm, guiding me through the throng, securing a seat for me by the window and one on the aisle for himself.

He whistled low. "This is something, isn't it? I never imagined so many people would be coming out to watch the show."

A nervous smile played on my lips. "No, I never imagined."

He leaned back in his seat and crossed one leg over the other. "Are you from Dallas, Miss . . . ?"

My fingers gripped my handbag. "Hendricks. And no, I'm not from Dallas. I'm from Oklahoma, but I'm staying . . . nearby." My tongue slid across my dry lips. "I came out to find my . . .

my beau. He's stationed at Camp Dick." I clamped my lips shut, wondering if I'd given the man too much information.

"I know most everyone at the camp. Who is this beau of yours?"

I clicked the clasp on my handbag as I studied Captain Denton's face. His blond hair and brown eyes appeared warm and inviting now, more friendly.

"Arthur. Arthur Samson. From Tyler."

His eyebrows arched.

"What?" I laid my hand on his arm. "What do you know? Please, tell me. I beg you."

His face rearranged, all smiles now. He patted my hand. "Don't you worry. I'm sure he'll be thrilled to see you."

I leaned against the back of the seat in relief. Arthur would be glad to see me. Of course he would. That's why I'd come.

CHAPTER
19

I had thought Union Station crowded, but the airfield teemed
thicker with humanity.

Captain Denton ushered me inside the gates. I unbuttoned my
coat, fearful I'd faint before I found Arthur. Between the crush of
people and the rising sun, I welcomed the refreshing November
breeze closer to my skin.

We picked our way through the crowd, my head turning left
and right as I gripped my handbag more tightly. So many uni-
forms. So many faces. What if I couldn't find Arthur?

"Don't worry. I'll find him for you." Captain Denton's voice
carried over the din.

"I've never seen so many people in one place in my life!" I
stood on my tiptoes, trying to get a better look.

Captain Denton chuckled as he led me to the bleachers. "You
sit here and enjoy the show. I'll find your Mr. Samson." He found
me a seat before striding off in the opposite direction.

It didn't take long for me to remove the coat completely and
lay it across my lap. My skin tingled with anticipation. Arthur

would be with me soon. I'd see his face, hear his voice. Of course, we wouldn't be able to embrace. Not in public. But our eyes would hold each other. And when he spoke, his words would wrap around me as securely as if they were his arms.

Airplanes thundered overhead, drowning out my daydreams.

A man in front of me leaned toward his wife. "Jennies. They're called jennies."

I raised my eyes to the sky, oohing and aahing with the rest of the crowd as the aviators piloted their planes through loops and rolls, sometimes flying upside down, other times heading in a straight line for the earth before suddenly lifting back up into the air. My hand covered my thumping heart. Never had I imagined the aerial feats I watched that morning. Did Arthur do such things?

The acrobatics continued for a while longer. My stomach rumbled as the show drew to a close and my worries crept back in. What if Captain Denton couldn't find Arthur? And what if he never came back to find me?

I craned my neck for sight of a familiar face. Of course there were only two possibilities—Captain Denton and Arthur. And I didn't see either one. The stands around me began to empty, talk of the buffet dinner on everyone's lips. I sat nearly alone now, chewing a fingernail.

Then a hand raised in the distance. I stood, eager to see the face. The crowd parted. Sheriff Jeffries's broad grin met my gaze. I sat back down on the wooden seat. What would he think of me for leaving the children and traveling on my own to Dallas? My head turned this way and that, seeking escape. Then he stood before me and I had no choice but to acknowledge him.

"Imagine meeting you here." I tapped my foot on the plank beneath my feet.

"Great, isn't it?" He lifted his face to the sky until his neck stretched long. "Amazing what those boys can do."

As I nodded, two men in uniform closed the distance behind him. Two familiar men. My heart seemed to stand still.

Arthur.

His uniform accentuated his leanness. Had he lost weight since he'd arrived here? Had he been ill and not told me? I searched his face for any signs of weariness, but he looked as hale and hearty as always. I popped up from my seat, my coat and purse filling my hands, my feet stumbling out of the stands until I stood on solid ground.

He stopped just beyond my reach. I wanted to throw myself in his arms, but in spite of all my bold actions of the day, I couldn't quite forget myself to that extent.

"Rebekah." Arthur's eyes didn't light on mine. His gaze darted to the ground, the sky, beside me, behind me, refusing to land on anything for more than an instant.

I stepped forward. "Arthur, darling."

Sheriff Jeffries's mouth hung open. And of course his hat twirled around and around and around in his fingers.

Arthur glanced at Captain Denton.

"Ah. I guess we'd better be going now." Captain Denton turned to the sheriff. "Let me show you the electric lights that will come on after dark."

Captain Denton dragged the sheriff away—but not before Sheriff Jeffries gave Arthur a long, hard look. Then we were alone. Or almost alone. A few others still mingled about the grandstands.

He moved closer. "What are you doing here?" His hushed voice sounded accusatory.

"I . . . I . . . " Those weren't the words he was supposed to say.

He rolled his eyes and looked away. Grabbing my arm, he led me behind the bleachers, away from the stragglers.

"Darling." I put my hand up to caress his cheek. "I was worried." He pulled back as if I'd slapped him.

"Look." He swiped back the lock of straw-colored hair that tipped over his forehead. "I don't know how to tell you, so I'll just say it straight." He took a deep breath and finally looked me in the eye. "I'm engaged."

My lips curled. "I know. To me."

Then I realized he wasn't talking about me. We weren't actually engaged. Not yet. My chest refused to draw air.

His hand shook as he lit a cigarette and placed it between his lips. I stared at the bright red tip, the smoke dissipating around us. The eyes that had spoken volumes avoided me now.

"Lily's a nurse. She was around a lot during the quarantine." He puffed a few more times, then tossed down his cigarette and ground it into the dirt beneath his feet. "I'm sorry, Rebekah. I never meant to hurt you. I thought you'd forget about me."

"Forget?" I devoured air now, filling my chest to spew the anger that roiled there like storm clouds in the spring. "How could I forget those days in Downington? How could I forget your promises? And the letters you wrote me? Forget! You told my mother you intended to come back for me. You promised."

His expression never wavered, almost as if he didn't remember the conversations I'd recited to myself a hundred times or more.

I took a step back, rage rolling like thunder inside me. "You, you . . ."

I didn't know any words terrible enough to call him. Humiliation stole over me, burning my face. He didn't want me. Perhaps he never had. All my hopes for the future lay buried in an instant.

My legs threatened not to hold me upright a moment longer.

"Everything okay here?" Sheriff Jeffries again.

I bit the inside of my cheek, refusing to let my tears flow as I fumbled to don my coat. The sheriff reached around and held it for me.

I looked at a spot in the sky, above and to the right of the sheriff's head. "If you would direct me to the train, Sheriff Jeffries, I'd like to return to Union Station."

I assumed he nodded, for he began to walk. I followed him to the gate where I'd entered with Captain Denton, Arthur tagging along behind. We stood together on the platform, the three of us, Arthur's guilt clear on his boyish face.

It felt like hours before a train screeched to a stop and emptied of its jubilant passengers. I climbed into the railcar, jerking my elbow away from Arthur's helping hand. The sheriff led me to a seat, but my eyes remained forward as the train gained speed. Just a short ride and I'd be back in Union Station. From there, I could return to Prater's Junction.

But what I really wanted was home. I wanted Mama to hold me while I cried out my story. But I couldn't go home. And Mama, still recovering, couldn't come to me, either.

In spite of feeling so grown up these past few weeks, I suddenly wanted to be a child again. Yet I knew that to be impossible. I'd said I would care for Frank and Clara Gresham's children. Frank was counting on me to keep my word.

"Rebekah?" The sheriff's voice, kind but unwanted.

I pressed my lips together, determined not to cry. Not here. Not yet. For I feared that once I started, I'd never stop.

We waited three hours for the train that would carry us back to Prater's Junction. "Don't you want something to eat?" Sheriff Jeffries asked.

One glance into his face and I had to look away. Too much pity there. I shook my head. He sighed before his shoes clomped across the floor to find food for himself.

He returned and sat next to me.

131

"Please, Sheriff. Go on back to the Frolic." I looked in his direction, but not at him. "I can get back by myself."

He wiped a handkerchief across his mouth. "I've had enough for the day. I'll see you back home. I don't mind."

I opened my mouth to protest again, for Prater's Junction was not my home. Would never be my home. But what was the use? So we sat in silence, as I reviewed the details of my romance with Arthur over and over again. What had I done wrong? When had I misunderstood his intentions? Nothing in my life had prepared me for this pain of loss.

Yes, Aunt Adabelle's death had been sudden and shocking, but she'd been ill. Besides, it wasn't like I hadn't known anyone who'd died before. I remembered Amy Jones from my first years of school. We'd played together at recess. Her sleek black braids mesmerized me, as did her dancing black eyes, and her laugh that sounded like bits of glass raining down on each other.

Amy'd been swept away in the creek when she went to fetch water. She was nine years old. And there was John, more Will's friend than mine, kicked in the head by an old mule. And, of course, the boys killed in the war.

Death didn't surprise me. It didn't surprise anyone I knew. But I couldn't comprehend this betrayal. All the men in my life kept their word. Arthur had said he loved me. Hadn't he? My mind pictured each of the letters in my possession. Well, at least he'd asked me to wait for him. And he signed his letters "with all my love." Or had that been my closing line?

Anguish rose from my toes, through my legs, my stomach, my chest, like rainwater filling the cistern a few drops at a time. Soon the grief would choke me, and I'd have to let it out. But not yet. Not yet.

The day had drawn to a close when the train let us off at Prater's Junction.

Sheriff Jeffries touched me gently on the arm. "Let me drive you home, Rebekah."

I forced myself to look him in the eyes. "I so appreciate your friendship today. I really do. But I need to walk. I need some time alone."

He nodded with a frown but stepped aside. I swept past him into the dusky haze of twilight. It reminded me of the first evening I'd walked into what I'd thought was my aunt's house. That night I couldn't have anticipated the tragedy that awaited me.

Now I had no care if dangers lurked in the shadows. What did it matter if anything happened to me? Arthur was out of reach, flown away to a future where I had no place. He'd done more than kill my dreams of romance and adventure. He'd stranded me here, in a life I had no desire to lead.

Tears stole down my cheeks. I didn't give in to them, the excess simply overflowed without restraint. I hooked my handbag around my arm and watched the shadow of it swing as the moon played hide-and-seek among the clouds. Nearly two whole dollars of Frank's money—money meant for his family—gone. Spent on a fool's errand. I figured Daddy would send money if I asked. But how would I explain what I'd done?

And what about Mama? How would she take the news about Arthur? Of course, in her mind, Barney Graves still waited, like those extra ingredients in case the first cake fell flat.

I pulled my coat around me, the day's warmth having left with the light. The road turned. I looked up, expecting a dark and gloomy house. Instead, light glowed through the parlor window. My stomach clutched. I didn't want to see anyone now. Maybe I could sleep in the barn, avoid any conversation until morning. As if in answer, a swift breeze rolled out of the north and reminded me that the calendar said November. In spite of my coat, sleeping outside the house wouldn't be a pleasant experience.

My feet carried me through the gate, up the walk and the porch steps, and around to the back. The heels of my shoes echoed on the planks, but no one met me at the kitchen door. I set my handbag on the table before following the trail of light to the parlor. My steps slowed. I picked up an umbrella from the brass holder in the hall and held it in front of me, its point my protection.

Whoever resided within must have heard my shoes rattling the floor, maybe even my heart beating against my chest. I rounded the corner and stepped into the brightness. Ollie lay on the sofa wrapped in a quilt, her big eyes blinking back at me. I lowered the umbrella.

"What are you doing up? Where's Nola Jean?" Exasperation, fear, and longing collided, leaving my words harsh and condemning.

She sat up. "Nola Jean wanted to go home after she milked Ol' Bob. Said she hated walking alone in the dark."

What had that girl been thinking, leaving four little children alone like that? I'd have some words for her tomorrow.

Ollie scooted off the sofa but didn't move toward me. "I told her you'd be home soon. Besides, Janie cried most all day long."

No wonder Nola Jean wanted to leave. I didn't blame her. I wanted to melt into a puddle on the floor myself. Already I felt more tears spilling over onto my cheeks. I avoided Ollie's gaze, straightened the lace doily on the small table beside the sofa. "I'm home now, honey. Get on to bed."

She hesitated, seeming to need something more from me, but I had nothing left to give. I needed time to think. Time and quiet. And I imagined I wouldn't get much of either come daybreak.

I snuffed the lamp and followed her up the stairs. My teeth chattered as I slithered into my flannel gown and huddled beneath the quilts. But even as my body grew warm, I wondered if the children had enough to cover them. Sometimes Dan kicked off the blankets as he slept. My bare feet hit the chilly floor. I sucked in a sharp breath before hurrying into the next bedroom.

Sure enough, Dan's leg hung off the bed, out of the reach of any scrap of fabric, as if his feet needed a head start to hit the floor when he woke. I pushed him closer to his brother. He turned on his side, his leg disappearing under the covers. I tucked the quilt beneath the mattress.

Pushing back the mass of blond hair on his head, I could see the place where I'd clipped it short around his wound. I needed to check that in the morning, make sure his scalp was healing as it should. And perhaps I should cut the rest of his hair to match. I'd been here almost a month; both boys needed a trim.

My feet tingled on their way to numb. I tiptoed back to my bed and climbed in. None of my earlier warmth remained. I stretched the quilts over my head and crunched my knees to my chest. Just as well. Cold fit my feelings. It reminded me that I had no hope of someone to warm my heart or my bed.

CHAPTER
20

Opening my eyes the next morning was like prying open the cellar door in a stiff wind. I pulled the covers over my head and turned to the wall. I couldn't continue as if my heart weren't battered and bruised.

Yet I did. I grit my teeth and managed the morning chores, even if it did feel like moving through a dense fog. Sick and dying, Aunt Adabelle had cared for these children until she couldn't lift her head from the pillow. I had only a broken heart and dead dreams. Could I do any less, even if my future seemed as lifeless as the bare branches of the old oak tree in the front yard?

On Saturday morning, a wagon rumbled up the road. Before I could rouse myself to see who'd come, Irene stood beside me at the stove.

"We thought you'd enjoy a trip to town," she said, unwinding a scarf from her apple-cheeked face.

The older children hurrahed while Janie clapped her chubby hands and wrinkled her nose. Irene took the dish towel from me. "Hurry now. I'll help the children get ready."

I flew to my room, thankful for clean clothes and the fact that I'd done all the chores at daybreak. It wasn't until I grabbed my handbag and made for the door that I remembered the letters I'd penned that week. One to Daddy. One to Frank.

My insides jittered as I thought of the words I'd written to this man whose wife rested peacefully in the churchyard while a girl he didn't know cared for his children. I couldn't tell him of my broken heart, of course, but I assured him we were all well, that his children longed for his homecoming, that I would remain until he arrived.

Shoving the letters in my handbag, I climbed into the back of the already crowded wagon.

"Up here." Irene scooted closer to her husband and patted the space beside her on the buckboard. Beulah, her youngest, sat content on her lap.

I picked my way through the crowded wagon bed as if I were barefoot in a briar patch. It wouldn't do to stomp on little fingers or toes.

"Did you have fun in Dallas, Rebekah?" Nola Jean's wistful question quieted the commotion.

"Tell us about it." Another of the Latham children.

I lumbered over the seat, trilling what I hoped sounded like laughter. "There were more people there than I've ever seen in one place in my whole life."

"I wanna hear 'bout the airplanes." A younger Latham boy.

Irene touched her husband's arm. He clicked his tongue, and the horses lurched forward, jerking me off balance. I grabbed the side of the seat. The children tittered from the back. Irene hooked her arm around mine.

"I'll hold you in. I've got too much substance for these horses to throw my weight around." Irene laughed as her older children snickered from the back. Even Brother Latham's mouth rose with mirth. Irene kissed the neck of the little girl in her lap, whose giggle sounded like a miniature version of her mother's full-grown one.

I looked off into the bare fields and thanked the Lord that He'd given Irene such a gift for putting everyone at ease.

The horses slowed as they passed the row of businesses that had become familiar to me now. I spied Mrs. Crenshaw in a rocker on her porch, her hand raised in greeting. That simple gesture revived my spirits a bit. But when the white steeple rose into view and I glimpsed the graveyard that rested beneath its shadow, an ache started in my chest and moved into my throat. My heartache amounted to little in the face of what others had lost.

Brother Latham's horses danced to a stop. Children emptied from the wagon bed as he wrapped the reins around a hitching post and extended his steadying hand to me. When he turned to his wife, he first took Beulah from her and then wrapped his free arm about her waist and lifted her down. They gazed into each other's eyes for a long moment, the love so intense I had to look away.

My chest felt as if it would cave in on itself. What were my chances of finding a love like that? They seemed very slim to me now.

I lifted my face to the sun's weak heat. I'd thought Arthur the answer to my prayers. I'd thought God had made a way for us to be together. Now what? Surely God had more in mind for me than caring for four motherless children in a backwater Texas town. I hugged my arms around myself and took a deep breath. The smell of dying grass filled my nose.

"I expect you have errands to do," Irene prodded.

"Yes, ma'am." I patted my handbag. "The store. The post office. And I'd like to check in at the bank, I think."

"Good idea." She set Beulah's feet on the ground. The child toddled to Nola Jean's outstretched hands. Irene watched her baby with a wistful expression as she directed her words to me. "I'll leave you to your own things, then, unless you need my help."

"I'll be fine."

She turned that loving look on me now. "Of course you will." Her words seemed meant for far more than a day of shopping.

"Meet back here around noon. I brought a picnic lunch for all of us," she said, waving me away.

Children's voices drifted along the chilling wind. I craned my neck to see Ollie, James, Dan, and Janie, but I couldn't find them. Irene nodded toward the square building beyond the church. "They're on the playground in the schoolyard. Nola Jean will watch them."

I breathed deep and long, drinking in the freedom of the moment. The board sidewalk creaked as I stepped up, my shoes clapping the same hollow tone as at home. The sound reminded me of shopping with Mama or walking with Arthur, and moisture blurred my vision a bit. I missed Arthur, and perhaps even more, I missed the anticipation of all my dreams coming true.

I entered the dry goods store first, walking straight to the glass jar filled with peppermint sticks. I'd buy some for all the children for the ride home. A small way to repay the Latham family for their kindness.

Mr. Crenshaw met me there, his face less haggard than the last time I'd seen him.

We stood in silence, my gaze roaming the store until I cleared my throat and plunked my meager coins on the counter. "I need a dozen peppermint sticks, please." As he filled a brown paper bag, I realized we probably needed other things, too, but I hadn't made a list and had little cash left to spend.

I gathered my small purchase and walked next door to the post office, its walls lined with slots for mail to be sorted and carried out to the rural routes, as well as the houses in town.

"I need to mail these," I said to the man behind the counter. He looked over my letters before nodding. Then he pulled a bundle from a slot and handed it to me. "You're lucky Mr. Culpepper hasn't been by yet today. You've quite a batch of things to take with you, even if your newspaper hasn't arrived yet."

I stared at the magazine he put in my hand. *"Better Homes and Gardens,"* I read aloud.

"Yep. Miz Williams took great pride in that subscription."

I ran my hand over the cover. Mama took this magazine, too. She loved the "homes" part. I had a funny feeling Aunt Adabelle loved the "gardens." They were like that, I'd begun to realize. Two ends of a seesaw. One went up, the other down. Riding the same board, but on the same plane for only an instant of time.

"And here're your letters."

I tore my gaze from the magazine and took the envelopes. My heart seemed to stop midbeat. One addressed in Mama's copperplate script. A bit shaky but still recognizable. The other in Arthur's unmistakable hand.

My stomach clenched. I stumbled out the door and plopped on a bench at the end of the sidewalk. Laying the magazine in my lap, I slipped Arthur's dispatch inside the pages. I couldn't read that letter in the midst of town. I needed someplace familiar and private. Only my aunt's house fit that description.

I opened Mama's correspondence instead. But before I could get beyond her familiar greeting, a voice shouted in the street.

"Pa! Hurry, Pa! James fell down the old well."

James? My James? I lifted my skirts, even though they already stopped well above the ground, and ran after the others headed toward the schoolyard. With every thump of my feet on the hard ground, I prayed it wasn't my James. I needed to see my little man, to know he was okay. My heart feared the worst.

I ran past the churchyard, trying not to feel Clara's or Aunt Adabelle's scorn for not keeping better watch on the child. Out of breath, I arrived at the gathering crowd. I pushed through to the center. Brother Latham lay stretched on the ground, peering down into a hole.

"He's in there all right. Wedged in. Not too far down. Get a rope." When he looked back, his eyes met mine.

I fell to my knees at the edge of the broken boards that covered the opening of the old well shaft. "James! It's me, Rebekah!"

"I'm sorry," came the whimpered reply.

I leaned farther over the edge. "I'm here, baby. Don't worry. Brother Latham will get you out."

I heard other crying now, from behind me. I turned, knees still grinding into the hard ground. Ollie held Dan close to her, as if she feared he'd leap into the hole to save his brother. But something was missing. I couldn't think what.

Then I knew.

"Where's the baby?" I shrieked. My whole body quaked as I clawed my way up from my knees. I grabbed Ollie's shoulders and shook her. "Where's Janie?"

Her mouth quivered. Tears streaked down her dirty face. "Where's—"

A hand rested on my shoulder. "She's here, Rebekah. Nola Jean has her." Irene's face remained serene, as if she didn't understand we were trying to rescue a small boy from a dark hole.

A dark hole. I crawled back to the lip of the well, Ollie's whimpers stirring my guilt into a dizzying whirlpool. I'd talk with her later. I had to focus on James now.

My head dipped into the darkness. "I won't leave you, little man. I promise."

Only his keening wail replied.

CHAPTER
21

Sheriff Jeffries took charge of the rescue, his face nearly blood-less, his eyes only occasionally glancing my way. When the men finally raised James from the earth's depths, dinnertime had passed, but supper remained distant. It seemed like he'd been in that hole for hours. In reality he'd been too big to fall far. A cheer rose from the gathered crowd when his head emerged into the sunlight. I let go of Ollie and Dan and took James into my arms.

"Oh, baby." I laid my cheek against his. "Are you all right? Where do you hurt?" I burst into tears, though I'd thought I'd cried my eyes dry as that old well.

Someone extracted the boy from my grasp. The sheriff. He held James in his arms while frail Doc Risinger examined the scraped and bruised arms and legs, checked his head and his eyes. Then the sheriff returned James to my embrace with a sympathetic smile.

James's head drifted to my shoulder, his breath hot on my neck. "It was dark down there."

"Yes, baby." I rubbed my hand on his back. "I'm sure it was. You were a brave boy."

"And kinda cold."

I tightened my arms around him, trying to warm his clammy skin.

His head rose, and he looked me in the eye. His grimy fingers stroked the edge of my face. "It was real interesting, but I'm glad you got me out." He snuggled into my shoulder again.

A rush of tears threatened to burst from me again—until I caught Irene's nod. She put an arm around one of her children and walked toward the wagon. I figured we should do the same. I turned to Ollie and Dan, Janie confined between them.

"Let's go home." I clutched James in one arm while Janie curled into the other. I'd have gathered up Ollie and Dan, too, if I'd had as many arms as a spider has legs. But Sheriff Jeffries did that in my stead, walking silently beside me, helping us into the Lathams' wagon.

I stayed in the back this time. Janie snuggled into my lap; James curled at my side. Dan stood behind me, his four-year-old arms draped around my neck, while Ollie sat with her skirt overlapping mine. I mouthed a thank-you to the sheriff as we pulled away.

By the time we reached the front gate, my body felt as stiff and sore as if I'd been washing quilts the whole day long. I climbed down, stretched my back, and readied to take Janie. James screamed for me to hold his hand. I shifted Janie to my hip and reached for the boy.

Irene leaned around her husband. "All safe and sound."

I hoped my weak smile conveyed a smidgen of my gratitude, which rose as big as a harvest moon. They drove away as we trudged into the house. We needed baths, but I couldn't make myself drag out the tub and heat the water and dirty up several towels on top everything else.

I laid my handbag on the table, amazed that it remained in my possession. Then I remembered my letter from Mama—and the one from Arthur.

"Where're my letters?"

Ollie's eyes grew big. "I didn't see any letters."

I tore through my purse, screeching out my fear. "Where are those letters? I have to have those letters!" They weren't there. Neither one of them.

Ollie stepped away from me. James inched closer to my side. I rubbed my forehead. Where had I put them? I'd sat down, then run to the schoolyard. Eyes squeezed shut, teeth clamped tight, I commanded myself to remember. But nothing came. Only images of James in the dark depths.

I collapsed into the nearest chair, nearly bumping James's head with mine. Then I saw the magazine on the bench. A deep breath moderated my voice. "Where did you get the magazine, Ollie?"

Her face twisted. Concentration? Confusion? I didn't have any strength left to figure it out.

"I don't know." A frantic shaking of her head accompanied the words. "I don't remember. Someone handed it to me as we were leaving. I don't know." She crumpled to the floor in tears. I wanted to do the same.

Help me, help me, help me ran through my head as I tried to regain my composure. Those letters had to be somewhere. If someone thought to pick up the magazine, they'd have thought to get the letters, too. Unless, of course, they'd blown away when no one was watching.

I felt a scream rising to my lips. Mama would've slapped my face to calm me, but Mama wasn't here. Like it or not, I was in charge. My jaw tightened as I tried to hold back the tornado of feelings twisting inside me.

James's bottom lip jutted out, trembling just a bit. I pulled him onto my lap, crushing him to me until he squirmed to get free. Ollie still lay crying on the floor. Janie joined the chorus. Dan, I feared, wasn't far behind.

I shoved Aunt Adabelle's treasured magazine. It slid across

the bench, then fell, skimming across the bare floor, flopping to a stop when it rammed into the wall.

Ollie gasped. "Rebekah! Look!"

Two envelopes spilled from between the pages of the magazine. Dropping to my knees, I gathered them up like precious jewels, suddenly remembering I'd stashed them there.

"God found them," James squeaked from behind me.

"What?"

"God found them. I prayed and God found them."

I stared at him. "You prayed?"

Ollie stood beside her brother now, her arm around his shoulders. "Like our mama taught us. Nothing is too big or too little to pray about. Mama and Miss Ada prayed about everything."

My mouth opened, then shut again. *If you have the faith of a child* came to mind. But did I?

I stood, clutching the letters to my breast. "We'd all better get to bed."

Ollie looked up at me with surprised eyes. Her wailing turned to a whine. "But we haven't had any supper yet."

I pinched the bridge of my nose and squeezed my eyes shut. I didn't howl, as I wanted to. I answered calmly, but my words held no sweetening forgiveness. "You'll have to get your own, then. I'm going to bed."

I stormed upstairs with my letters, half guilty that I'd left a nine-year-old with such a task and half relieved that none of them followed.

CHAPTER
22

*T*he next morning I burned Arthur's letter. No part of his pathetic explanation soothed my pain. Mama's letter, on the other hand, I read over again in the light of day.

She told me she felt much better now. *A lot of fuss over nothing,* she wrote. She'd be up and around and back to her old self again very soon. And didn't I think I should come on home and leave those children to someone else's care? Barney Graves had mentioned he missed seeing me.

It sounded like Mama, all right. But I'd told Adabelle and Frank and Sheriff Jeffries that I'd care for the children, and no matter how Mama prodded, I wouldn't break my word.

I looked at the letter again. Shaky handwriting. Stray drops of ink at the edges of the page. Not Mama's usual pristine letter. Maybe Daddy hadn't overreacted after all.

I slid Mama's letter into the drawer with my clothes. I'd answer it later, let her know, firmly but kindly, that I could make my own decisions now and that I intended to do my duty toward these children. But I wouldn't tell her about Arthur. Not yet.

A few evenings later, I chewed the end of my pencil, trying to make a list of what we'd need to see us through the winter. Cornbread didn't seem as monotonous now that I'd found the churn and made butter. I'd even pressed the creamy white lump into a mold carved with intricate curlicues surrounding a fancy G.

But we needed stamps. And the children wanted to make a Christmas box for their father. I hated to spend the last bit of cash, but I figured we could manage to purchase some trinkets for Frank—a comb, toothpaste, gum, Hershey's bars, shaving cream, shoelaces. And yet, Thanksgiving would be upon us soon. And Christmas on the horizon after that. I'd need more money before then or there wouldn't be presents for the children.

Thump. Bump. A chorus of screams.

I dropped my pencil and charged up the stairs two at a time, heart pumping faster than a steam engine, throat aching to release a wail of my own. But it wasn't James having a nightmare. Two beady eyes stared back at me in the moonlight. Two beady eyes attached to a hissing possum.

A branch from a big cedar elm waved near the open window, letting in the breeze on this warm evening. Just a short jump for a cunning creature. And the clucking from the barnyard told me we were not this rascal's first stop for the evening.

Ollie huddled the children on the far edge of the bed, next to the wall, the fear in her eyes naked in the pale wash of moonbeams. Dan's screams filled the air, his eyes squeezed shut, mouth open wide. My anger flared, protective as a mama bird with helpless babies in the nest. I wouldn't let them down.

I wanted to say the word I'd heard Will say when Daddy's wagon rolled across his toes, but I dared not. Instead I did what Mama—and the children—had taught me. I prayed.

"Keep that nasty creature away from these children, Lord. And from our chickens, too." I hissed the words toward the spitting possum, hoping it would frighten him away. It didn't. He stood his ground.

We stared at each other, both wondering who would make the first move. I decided it had to be me. I hopped up on the bed. The possum turned its head to stare at me. I leapt toward a cane-seated chair, grabbed it up, and jabbed the legs at the overgrown rat the same way I'd seen the lion tamer do when the circus pitched its tent outside of Downington a few years ago.

"Get away." I thrust the chair again. The possum backed toward the door. I poked again. He hissed and squirmed but kept scooting toward the hall.

When we reached the top of the stairs that mean old thing decided to make one last stand. He lunged toward me. Ollie screamed from the doorway of the bedroom. I pushed one leg of the chair into the possum's chest.

Can a possum look surprised? This one did as he tumbled backward down the stairs. I followed his path as he rolled to the front door, scampered into the dining room, then through to the kitchen. I ran after him, picking up the broom and swatting him out the kitchen door before he could get his legs fully underneath him. Of course, by then I think he was glad to go. I slammed the door shut, barely missing the tip of his hairless tail.

The children swarmed around me, arms circling my legs and my waist, Ollie's moist eyes staring up at me in the dim light.

"You saved our lives," she said.

I chuckled, trying to diffuse her fear, but my knees shook like warm jelly as I ran my hand down the braided rope of hair that fell to the middle of her back. The lamp still shone in the parlor, dimming the darkness of the kitchen like a faraway star on a moonless night.

"Why don't we all camp out in there?" I nodded my head toward the parlor.

Ollie's head bobbed with such force I worried it would fall off her neck. We gathered quilts from the bedrooms. I wedged Janie between the back of the sofa and Ollie's body before pulling and tucking the quilts around the rest of us on the floor. I didn't even bother to extinguish the lamp.

Dan stirred first the next morning, bounding from atop the pile like a puppy ready for play. I raised my stiff neck and put a finger to my lips, but trying to keep a four-year-old quiet was, well, nigh impossible.

James's head popped up, his eyes blinking at the light and the unfamiliar room. Then his face brightened. After he disentangled his foot from my ribs, I could actually draw breath again. He ran to the kitchen. "Let's see if that ol' possum is still hangin' around, Dan."

Dan followed, of course, as eager as his brother to see the creature that had scared him senseless in the night. Ollie groaned as I got up. She put her arms around Janie and they cuddled together.

Rubbing my neck, I stumbled into the hall. James was under my feet almost before I knew it.

"I bet I could get him with Daddy's gun." He looked up at me with the most serious expression I'd ever seen. As if he were fifteen, not six. My mouth twitched, but I determined not to laugh.

"You know you're not allowed to touch Daddy's gun," Ollie's half-asleep voice called from the parlor.

I put on my stern face. "Yes. I'm sure you know that, James."

His whole body sagged in defeat as he turned and stomped away. "She said no," I heard him say from the kitchen. A smile twitched at my lips.

"Rats," came the younger voice, followed by the muffled thud of two bottoms hitting the floor.

A giggle escaped me. I imagined their little faces full of disappointment over not getting to take their daddy's gun after the nasty creature. I clamped my hand over my mouth until my stomach hurt from holding it in. I fled up the stairs and screamed my laughter into a plump feather pillow, tears streaming down my face. It felt as good as a hot bath on a cold day and made the adventure of the night worthwhile. I climbed into clothes as fresh as my attitude and hurried downstairs to rejoin the children.

"Would you like me to take care of the milkin' this morning?" Sheriff Jeffries's baritone carried through the screen door.

Now I could hear Ol' Bob bawling. "Yes, thank you."

I stood at the door and watched him go, his boots crunching across the yard. Why couldn't I have feelings for a man who always seemed to show up at the right time and say the right things? Mama would declare me a fool not to keep his ingredients in my pantry, so to speak. In fact, she might even put him ahead of Mr. Graves now.

But I couldn't dwell on such things today. I returned to the kitchen. Ollie scrubbed her face and hands at the washbasin as I started breakfast. I'd had my fill of oatmeal, so I fried up some corn cakes to drizzle with molasses, wondering if I could make the leftovers do for both dinner and supper.

A clatter of voices rose in the yard. I glanced out the door. James and Dan sat on the porch, deep in conversation with the sheriff. The possum had grown in the retelling. It had nearly bitten off the baby's hand, according to Dan. James had run it off, according to James. The sheriff nodded at each interjection, his face as serious as if they relayed the price of cotton.

He spied me and straightened, holding out the milk pail as his cheeks brightened.

"Would you care to breakfast with us?" I didn't figure it mattered much anymore whether we had a chaperone or not.

"I'd be glad to."

I held open the screen door. All three tromped inside. For the first time in a long while, breakfast seemed like the beginning of a good day.

CHAPTER
23

*I*n spite of our dwindling supplies, I invited the ten Lathams and Sheriff Jeffries to spend Thanksgiving with us. I wanted a festive atmosphere, with company around the table. Like the day we'd heard news of the armistice. I relished the work, the exhaustion. It gave me less time to think.

On the Wednesday before our feast, I rolled piecrusts and peeled and cooked the pumpkins. Even though the air outside hinted of winter, the kitchen burned like summertime.

"I need more wood for the stove," I called out the door while I wiped my arm across my forehead. "And would someone open the window for me, too?"

James staggered through the kitchen door and opened his arms. Chunks of wood crashed to the floor.

Squeezing my eyes shut, I determined not to scold him for the racket. "Thank you."

Dan came up behind, a piece of wood in each hand. He tossed them on top of James's pile. "Some 'uns coming."

I threw the wood in the stove before glancing out the window.

Far off down the road walked a slender man, a suitcase swinging in his hand. It couldn't be Frank. Not yet. But if not Frank, then, who? Fear and excitement, anger and relief jumbled together like berries in a cobbler until I couldn't separate one from the other. Had Arthur changed his mind? Come to apologize in person? Did I want him to?

"Ollie, watch the pies." I ran outside and stepped into the road, my heart fluttering and my stomach in knots.

The man waved an arm above his head. "Little sister!"

All my anxiety melted into astonishment. "Will!" I raced down the road and threw my arms around my big brother's neck.

"Ho, there." He stumbled backward. "Don't cry."

"It's you. It's really you." My tears wet his neck as his hand rubbed a circle on my back. When I finally pulled away to study his face, he appeared much older than when he'd left for France more than a year ago. Wrinkles framed his eyes, and pain glowed from their depths. War had changed him.

My hand crept to my throat. Why had my brother shown up unannounced? "Is it Mama?" I whispered. "Is she—?"

Will chuckled a little and shook his head, looking more like the big brother I remembered.

"You always could make things seem worse than they were, Rebekah. No, you silly goose. Mama's fine." He lifted one shoulder, as if in resignation. "She's not in danger, at least. But she wasn't up for big doings, either. So I decided to come celebrate Thanksgiving with you."

My arms dropped to my side. Will had been the stable one, like the thick oak that spread its arms over our house in Downington. He knew his duty and always did it. If he hadn't stayed home for Thanksgiving, something was definitely wrong.

"When did you get home? And why didn't anyone tell me?" I hooked my arm around my brother's. It felt small and frail, as if my touch might break it. My stomach soured.

"I was already on my way home when the armistice was announced."

I stopped, forcing him to stop, too. "Why, Will?"

He stared off into the distance, his eyes narrowing as if he could see all the way to France. "I'm dying, Rebekah. They let me come home to die."

I couldn't move, couldn't breathe. Was my heart still beating? Breath and motion returned with a wave of nausea, but before I could ask more questions, Will's mouth lifted in a sad smile.

"I hear you've become a mother, in a manner of speaking. You'd better introduce me." Taking hold of my arm, he propelled me forward, my feet somehow obeying.

An eerie silence stole over the yard, the house. It seemed fitting, given Will's news, so it took me a moment to realize it wasn't normal. Not for this house. Things were rarely silent, even in the middle of the night.

"Ollie? James? Dan?"

No answer.

"Have you lost them already?" Will's playful grin settled me some.

"I haven't lost them," I sassed back. "At least I don't think I have." I went to the cistern first, always afraid one of the boys would fall in while "just looking." But the lid remained firmly in place and the little stool didn't stand near the edge. Hands on my hips, I called again.

This time a giggle drifted up from somewhere nearby. I stepped off the porch, got down on my knees, and peered into the crawl space beneath the porch.

Eight eyes twinkled back at me.

"If you don't get out from under there, that old possum's gonna come and eat you up."

Squeals of delighted fear accompanied their scramble from their hiding place. They were filthy, of course. I opened my mouth to scold them, but the scent of something burning stung my nose. I sniffed the air again.

"My pies!" I flew into the kitchen and opened the oven. Black smoke poured into the house. I waved it away, coughing, as I covered one hand with a dish towel and pulled the first pie from the oven. Instead of golden brown, the crust looked like dried mud. I dumped it in the wash bucket and pulled the second pie from the oven. Even worse than the first.

"I hope you don't expect me to eat that." Will pointed at my pies, lifted Dan off his shoulders, and sank into a chair. His breath heaved out in gasps. Beads of sweat clung to his temples.

I carted in water to souse the pies. The coffee needed warming, too. That would keep my hands busy and my back turned long enough to compose myself from the frustration of burning pies and the shock of Will's news. I couldn't bring myself to ask what he was dying of. Not yet. I only knew it couldn't be contagious or he wouldn't have come.

The coffee boiled. I pulled it from the heat and poured a cup for Will. The children soon tired of the newness of the visitor and left to chase the last bit of sunshine. All except Janie. She sat in Will's lap, gazing up at him in wonder. I think she thought Will was her daddy—some vague baby intuition none of us could quite comprehend.

Will didn't seem to mind. He held her, stroked her hair, planted little kisses on her nose.

The daughter he'd never have. My shoulders sagged at the thought, but I forced them to straighten again. I had to start new pies. Besides, it helped to have something to do, something to think about. And while I worked, Will talked. About home. About his friends. About everything but himself. Or the war.

"Are you fighting off beaus with a stick?" Will asked, bouncing Janie on his knee.

I winced as his words unknowingly probed my wound. "No."

"That's not what I hear."

My head whipped around. "What kind of 'beaus' do you think I have? I'm here with these children all the day long."

"And a fine mess you're making of it, too." His eyes twinkled and teased.

I wanted to hit him over the head with my rolling pin.

"So, you're getting married soon? Do tell."

I slammed the rolling pin on the pie dough. "Did Mama tell you that?"

"Yes. She seemed to think it a sure thing. Some junior ace from around here, or something. Of course, she hasn't given up on 'dear Mr. Graves,' either."

"I'm not marrying either one of them." I marched the cooled, soggy pies to the door and tossed them into the slop barrel before rolling the new piecrusts into the still-warm pie plates. I prayed I had enough pumpkin left in the pot to fill two more pies. If not, I guessed I could whip up chess pie instead.

"Oh. You have other plans, then?" He sipped his coffee, set it down, and pushed it away from Janie's reach.

I scraped the remaining pumpkin into the piecrusts. "Yes, I have plans. Mama doesn't know everything."

He looked as if he didn't believe that any more than I did.

***

Brother Latham gave a prayer of thanksgiving before dishes clanked, voices chattered, and food disappeared much more quickly than it had been prepared. Will ate well and joined in the conversation. But I didn't. I couldn't seem to get my mind off the facts that my brother was dying and all my other plans had vanished like ashes in a strong wind.

The men and children drifted outside once they'd eaten their fill. Irene instructed her older girls to wash dishes. She and I dried and sorted them.

"Want to tell me what's happened?" Irene's eyes brimmed with sympathy, no trace of aggravation. She handed me a platter, clean and dry.

I stared at the dish as if I had no idea what to do with it. Then I breathed the kitchen air, tainted with the scent of stale food and soap. "My brother's dying."

Irene took the plate from my hands, gently prying loose my fingers. Her head shook as she set it aside. "I'm so sorry, honey." She put her arm around my waist and led me to the door. "You go on and visit with your brother. We'll finish up here." Her voice was as gentle as a mama with her newborn babe.

I obeyed, wandering first into the backyard and then around toward the front of the house. Brother Latham had pulled a chair onto the porch. Will and Sheriff Jeffries sat in the rocking chairs while the gaggle of children frolicked on the lawn. Will looked tired, yet one corner of his mouth lifted as he watched the children laugh and play.

I settled myself on the porch step in front of the men, hands clasped around my knees, eyes fixed on the children, ears strained to catch the low concert of voices behind me.

"I just hope it's what they say. A war to end all wars." Will's raspy voice. "I wouldn't want any of those little guys to have to go through what we did."

Silence followed. Then Brother Latham rumbled indistinct words.

A rocker creaked in its motion. Will coughed, deep and long and rattling in his chest, like Aunt Adabelle. A shiver traveled down my back as he composed himself.

"Not sure which was worse—watching those poor souls suffocate in an instant, or having to waste away by inches, like me. Those gases did their damage in so many different ways."

157

Poison gases. I'd read of them in the newspapers. Were the gases responsible for Will's demise? I turned slightly, hoping Will's words wouldn't stop. Instead, he seemed to speak more clearly, as if he wanted me to know without having to tell me directly.

"Maybe I didn't get my mask on in time. Maybe some of those gases lingered in the air after I thought it safe to unmask. Either way, they got into my lungs. And when they don't kill you right away, they cause other things that kill you. Like cancer."

My throat tightened. Cancer ate away at a person, sometimes for months, sometimes for years. I wondered which it would be for my brother.

"I figure if I've got to meet my Maker soon, I might as well go out living instead of lying around waiting to die."

Maybe he'd come to the right place. These kids teemed with life and energy.

"I don't suppose you've given any thought to taking my sister away from all this?" Will's teasing voice caused my head to whip in his direction, just as his gaze settled on the sheriff.

"Well . . ." Sheriff Jeffries drawled.

I tossed them both a grin as sweet as white sugar. "I'll thank you very much to leave my life be, big brother."

Laughter thundered from deep within Brother Latham's chest. Sheriff Jeffries stared at his hat in his hands. Will's mouth curled into a smile, hilarity bubbling out of lungs damaged by warfare, infected with disease. He looked young again. Full of life.

And my heart cried.

In the quiet of the early-morning chores, I told Will about Arthur, letting my silent tears soak into Ol' Bob's side. Will didn't say much, but I could tell his hands itched to pummel the man who'd hurt his sister. So I set him to splitting wood instead.

158

"Should I tell Mama?" I asked.

Down came the axe with a thud. He threw the pieces into the pile and picked up another short log. He leaned on the axe handle and looked at me. "I wouldn't just yet. She doesn't need . . . disappointment right now." He hesitated another moment. "She did ask me to bring you back home, though."

"Oh? And are you going to try?"

He hefted his weapon and brought it down again. The wood fell into halves. He shook his head. "No. Right now these kids need you more than she does. Anyone can see that."

I let out a long breath as Will worked. It felt good to have my brother on my side.

When Will couldn't lift his arms overhead one more time, I set the axe in the shed and our slow steps returned to the house. While he lay recovering on the sofa, he regaled us all with stories of aerial battles and ocean crossings and encounters with British soldiers and their funny ways of saying things.

At sunset, with supper warming on the stove, I wandered out to the porch and stood behind Will's chair, resting my hands on his shoulders. He reached up and covered my fingers with his. I smiled.

"I have to leave in the morning," he said. "I'll tell Mama how well you took care of me."

I threw my arms around his neck, my cheek pressed against his. "Do you have to go? Stay here. I'll take care of you."

"I couldn't do that to Mama. You know that."

I squeezed him again before I nodded, pulled away, and knelt beside his chair, my hand clasping his. "How is Mama, Will? Really?"

"Don't worry, Rebekah. She's just . . . weak." He patted my hand. "You know I won't be staying there, either. I have things I want to see before I can't. Like the Grand Canyon. And the Pacific Ocean. A buddy of mine from the war is going with me."

"But can't—"

His fingers squeezed mine. "I want you to remember me like this, Rebekah. And I want to remember you in this place. Don't worry. You'll get what you want one of these days. Just be patient."

I drew in a sharp breath. How did he know what I wanted? And how did he know I'd get it? Did God give the dying special messages?

"How do you know?" The words blurted out on the breath I'd been holding.

"Because I've watched you. I can see in your every action that you were made for this."

"This?" I huffed.

"It suits you. A house. A farm. Children. The husband who will give it all to you."

I rocked back on my heels and stood. "That's not what I want, Will." I backed away from his startled look, my hands fidgeting with each other. "I'm going to the city. I don't know how or when, but I won't be tied to the seasons and the sun. Don't get me wrong: I want a husband and a child or two of my own. But this . . . ?" I nodded toward the yard beyond the house, to the hog now in its pen, the chickens, the cow and the mules, even the fields farther beyond. "This is not what I want. I want adventure. I want . . ."

His eyes glazed over a bit. I looked away. The children's joyful shrieks carried on the cool breeze. I wondered if memories of childhood days invaded Will's head as they did mine. Such simple days. Days I'd once wished away, wanting to be grown up, wanting my life to begin. Now that I'd crossed that line, I wished I could go back.

Will cleared his throat, pushed to his feet, and faced me. "I'm sorry, Rebekah," he said. "I hope you get what you want. I really do. But be careful. If France taught me anything, it's that new experiences aren't always what we imagine them to be."

He shoved his hands into his pockets and sauntered down the

steps, leaving me to decide whether or not to throw his advice to the wind.

We all piled into the sheriff's car the next morning and drove to the train station. A few people milled around on the platform as the train chugged into view. A lump swelled in my throat. How could I say good-bye to my brother, knowing I might never see him again?

He tousled the children's hair and tweaked their noses one by one. When he reached for Janie, his ashen face turned slick with sweat in spite of the heatless day. I kept her in my arms and leaned her closer to him so he wouldn't have to strain. His trembling hand caressed her cheek. I handed her to Ollie, put my hand in the crook of my brother's arm, and walked him across the platform to the waiting railway car.

"I'll miss . . ." The tears insisted on flowing.

He pulled out his handkerchief and wiped my face. "Don't cry, little sister. I've made my peace with God. I'm ready."

"But I'm not," I whispered. "If you . . . die . . . I'll be all alone. Just me and Mama and Daddy."

"You'll be fine," he said. "You've always been the strongest of us all."

I had?

He chuckled as he lifted my chin and stared into my eyes. "You have no idea."

A quick hug; then he disappeared into the train. I watched him through the windows as he found a seat away from the platform and stared out the window. The train whistled, groaned, and inched forward. I waved until the caboose pulled past the platform, even though Will never turned to look. Only as the train snaked out of sight did I notice Sheriff Jeffries by my side.

161

CHAPTER
24

December arrived. Would Frank be home in time for Christmas? I guessed no. Besides Will, no soldiers had returned to Prater's Junction, though the newspapers predicted the first of our boys would arrive home before the month ended. I didn't know what to think about Frank coming home. Almost two weeks had passed without a letter from him.

Could he have been injured just before the armistice? Or maybe, like Will, poison gases made him ill—too ill to write or travel.

Then one afternoon I pulled an envelope from the box and Frank's familiar handwriting stared up at me.

Miss Hendricks,

Thank you for your letter telling of my family. For a little while after I heard of Adabelle's passing, I still received her regular letters. And then I figured I'd have nothing. But your note arrived, and with it, I found hope again. Sometimes I wonder if you are an angel

*instead of a woman, to step in and take care of my
kids, my house, with no tie to us other than your aunt's
kindness to our family.*

*She talked about you. Did you know that? She
missed you and your brother, hated the falling out with
her sister, although she never mentioned the cause. I
think she pretended my family was hers. And that was
fine with us, for Clara and I didn't have anyone, either.
I guess she was as close to a grandmother as my children
will ever know. Sorry for rambling on so. Not what you
expect of a letter from a stranger, I imagine.*

*What I really wrote to say is that I'm due to ship out
for the States soon. After a few days of debriefing at a
military base, I'll make my way home. You can bet I'll
be looking for the quickest way. I'd hate to disrupt your
life any longer than necessary.*

> *Sincerely,*
>
> *Frank Gresham*

I scanned a separate page addressed to the children as I wiped the inexplicable wet from my cheeks. Frank was on his way home. The thought thrilled and terrified. Before, his homecoming had meant freedom to go to Arthur. Now I didn't know what it meant. I only knew I had no desire to go back to Downington.

My eyes locked on the date scribbled at the top of the page: November 18, 1918. A quick count of days told me he could arrive anytime. I needed to come up with some kind of plan for my future. And fast.

I read Frank's letter to the children before bed, told them he'd probably already started on his journey home. The boys looked a bit confused, but Ollie's eyes took on the brilliance of stars in the night sky. She sat up with me after the other children lay abed. I leaned my head against the back of the sofa and closed my eyes, my insides wiggling like kittens in a sack.

"Tell me about school today, Ollie." I felt her curl her body into mine. I draped my arm around her, pulled her close.

"Garland Winston carved his initials in a tree with Nola Jean's at recess. She acted mad, but I think she liked it."

I lifted my head and opened my eyes. "Nola Jean's not nearly old enough to concern herself with such things."

Ollie shrugged. "She's mostly grown. Almost fourteen. Mama married Daddy when she wasn't much older than Nola Jean."

Irene had said Clara and Frank married young, but she'd never managed to reveal much of anything else. "Tell me about your mama and your daddy."

Ollie stared into a far corner of the room, squinting, as if to remember. "Mama was fifteen years old when she met Daddy. She said she knew right away she'd marry him. She said something in his eyes told her, something deep down. Something he didn't even know yet. That's what she said."

Something in his eyes. I thought I'd read something in Arthur's eyes, too. Maybe I couldn't judge men as rightly as I imagined I could. And yet I read real friendship in the sheriff's manner, and that had proven true. What would I read in Frank Gresham's eyes?

"Anyway, Mama's house was full of kids and empty of money. That's what she said. So when Daddy asked her to marry him, she did. They left the day she turned sixteen and never went back."

"What did her family say?" I couldn't imagine surviving Mama's wrath if I had done such a thing.

Ollie shrugged. "Her brothers and sisters all went other places, and I think her mama got sick and died. Don't know about her daddy. She never said."

I pondered the history of Clara and Frank, two youngsters

embarking on a life all of their own making. The type of adventure I craved so much. Were they pleased with how their lives turned out?

Ollie slid off the sofa and gave me a small smile. "I think I'll go to sleep now."

I pulled her close, kissed her forehead, and sent her on her way. But it was a long while before I could stir myself to put out the lamp and climb the stairs to bed.

⚜

Late that night, my feet pattered the floor of my bedroom. Back and forth. Back and forth. The heavy braid down my back swung with each movement, like the pendulum on the clock at home, ticking away the time. Every now and then I shivered, even though I wore my flannel gown and the window sash sat firmly against the sill.

Frank might arrive tomorrow. Or next week. Almost surely by next month. I chewed my thumbnail down past the round tip of flesh. I paused to listen to the still night, hoping the audible voice of God suddenly would give me clear direction. But only a whippoorwill called in the distance.

I bit the inside of my cheek, trying to hold back tears of despair. My coming here had been God's doing. I never once doubted that. But now it seemed He'd made a mockery of all my dreams. I'd asked for a fish and He'd given me a snake.

I sank back into my bed, pulling the quilt close around me and wondered what advice Irene would give if I asked. A foolish question, really. I already knew how she'd answer. She'd ask if I'd heard from the Lord on the matter.

Pulling my braid over my shoulder, I stroked the tail end, wrapping and unwrapping the curl of hair around my index finger. She'd likely tell me to be patient, to stay still until I knew which

165

way the Lord said to go. At least that's what I'd heard her tell another woman at church. Another directionless woman—only that one had been widowed by influenza.

I flopped onto my back and yanked the covers over my head, wishing all my problems would just vanish, that the Lord would whisk me away to another place, like He did with Phillip after he'd baptized the Ethiopian eunuch in the book of Acts. I huffed and curled onto my side, pulling my knees to my chest. There was more chance that Arthur would land his plane in the cotton field and take me away than that.

Did I need to search the Scriptures more diligently? Pray more earnestly? I'd done so much thinking and planning, planning and thinking in the past year that maybe Irene was right: Maybe I needed to just be patient and listen.

The words of Frank's first letter to me drifted to mind, his belief that even in something as grievous as death the Lord had a plan for good. I wanted to believe that with more than just my head, but I didn't understand why Aunt Adabelle had to die or why Mama and Will had to get sick or why Arthur didn't keep his promises. But perhaps understanding didn't matter as much as I imagined. Perhaps that was the true definition of faith.

Ollie stood beside me, shaking my shoulder in the sunshine-flooded room. "Rebekah, wake up. I can't find James anywhere."

I wiped the sleep from my eyes and sat up, her words barely making sense to my befuddled brain. Then they crystallized. I stretched my arms over my head, unconcerned.

"I'm sure he's in the privy or in the barn with Ol' Bob. You know he thinks he can milk her all by himself."

Ollie's mouth turned downward. "He's not either of those places. I looked."

My feet hit the floor as I rubbed my face. "I'm sure you just missed him. You went to one place while he was in the other."

"I don't think so."

I patted her hand and stood. "Let me get dressed. I wager he'll turn up when he smells breakfast cooking."

But even the smell of bacon didn't draw him out. Worry tangled itself around my heart like climbing roses on a trellis. Where had that boy gotten to now? I served breakfast to the other three, trying to restrain my concern. Maybe he'd crawled up in the barn loft and fallen asleep. Or maybe he'd gone to the creek. Alone. I sucked in a breath as I let a prayer run through my head. *Please God, let him be safe. Just let him be safe.*

"Ollie, keep Janie here. Dan and I are going to find your brother."

She gave me a wary look as she wiped—or tried to wipe—Janie's gravy-smeared face. "What about school?"

"I'm sure we'll be back by the time you need to leave." I grabbed Dan by the hand. "I think your brother is playing a game of hide-and-seek."

"I could eat up his bacon from breakfast, you know," Dan said.

"I'm sure you could, big boy, but why don't we wait just a while longer. In fact, why don't we go find James now? I'm sure you know all his best hiding places."

"C'mon." He pulled. I stumbled after him, still hanging on to his hand, a smile tugging at my lips. See? No cause to worry. Dan would lead me directly to James.

Two hours later, Dan scratched his head as I tried to rub feeling into my frozen nose.

"Are you sure those are all the good hiding places you know?" I asked for the thousandth time.

"I'm sure." His little face screwed up in concentration.

Worry choked me, but anger started pruning it back. Where was that boy? When I found him, I'd tan his hide for scaring me like this, not to mention wasting a whole morning and keeping Ollie from going to school.

I stared into the distance, wishing I knew which way to go. A half mile to the east and we'd come to the Latham's house. Two miles west and we'd end up in town.

"James!" I called as loud as I could. "James Gresham, you get home this instant!"

What if he was home? My shoulders drooped. No matter which direction we searched next, we'd have to tromp back to the house first and see if he was there.

"Let's go, Dan." This time I pulled him, his feet dragging, his head sagging.

Still no sign of James back at the house. Ollie's big eyes revealed her fright. I took Janie from her, knowing the baby needed a nap, but knowing also that Ollie needed my presence. We'd have to search together now, in spite of the littler ones' exhaustion.

Town would be the best option, I decided. More people to fan out and search if we didn't find him there. But he had to be there. He just had to. Fear and worry wove themselves around each other like two colors of yarn knitted into a blanket.

I picked up three teacakes, one for each child, and changed Janie's diaper before we took off again. The trip seemed to take hours as the sun rose higher in the sky. My anger popped and sizzled like butter in a hot skillet as my stomach rumbled with hunger. I'd send him to his room for a week. Make him do extra chores, even help in the kitchen with the cooking and the dishes. Hold him tight and never let go.

If only I could find him.

CHAPTER
25

Sheriff Jeffries sat on the corner of his desk, two men I didn't know standing near him, hands in their pockets. The conversation stopped when he stood and looked my way.

The moment I saw his face, my mad dissolved into terror. "I need help."

In two strides he stood before me, his lips pressed into a tight line, concern visible in his eyes. He laid gentle hands on my shoulders. "What's wrong?"

"We can't find James anywhere. We've been searching all morning." Desperation streaked each word. Dan hid himself behind my skirt. Ollie and Janie both began to cry. I wanted to join them, but I forced myself to calm.

He nodded once. "Come with me." He took my hand and led us to Mr. Crenshaw's store.

After just a few words from the sheriff, Mr. Crenshaw removed his apron and called into the storeroom. "Ruth? James Gresham has gone missing. I'm going to help search."

Three men in the store volunteered to help before Mrs.

Crenshaw appeared from the back room. "Go on." She lifted Janie out of my arms. "I'll watch the other children."

I chased the men to the end of the sidewalk. And that's when a movement in the churchyard near us drew my attention. I peered across the expanse, trying to sort the immovable gray gravestones from the fleeting shadow that had caught my eye. Sheriff Jeffries corralled the men gathering in the street. Mr. Crenshaw entered the tiny newspaper office. I hurried down the steps, past the knot of men, and over the worn track through tall grasses, my gaze intent on that shadow.

The wraith bent above one of the graves, an older one, the weather having already tamped down the mounded dirt. My hand closed on the small gate. It creaked open. James looked over at me, his face a lump of anguish.

"I had to tell Mama that Daddy would be home soon." His lips twisted, his face puckered. He threw himself at me with the hiccup of a long-held sob.

"Oh, baby." I slid to my knees, my face next to his. His arms curled around my shoulders as I stroked his hair and wept with him.

These little ones had been through so much these past months. Some days I wondered if the younger ones even remembered their mother, or if they only remembered the idea of her. And now the daddy they hadn't seen in over a year would return, bringing yet another change. My presence offered almost the only consistency they remembered in their short lives.

Voices sounded in the distance. I looked up to find a group of men walking in our direction.

"I found him!" I picked up James and waved one arm high in the air. "It's okay. I've found him." I trotted toward them as fast as I could, James lying like a lump against my shoulder, his arms circling my neck. By the time I reached the buildings of town, my breath came in gasps and my side ached.

Sheriff Jeffries pried James from my arms. I rested my hands on my knees and gulped in air. "He was in the churchyard." I glanced sideways at the impish little face. "Visiting his mother." I straightened, my breathing returning to normal. "Thank you for your willingness to help. I'm sorry to have called you away from your work."

Heat crept over my throat as the men tipped their hats and scattered. All but the sheriff. He looked as if he might embrace me, right then and there. Now *I* wanted to run. But I didn't dare. Instead, I reached for James's hand and led him back to Mr. Crenshaw's store. Yet Sheriff Jeffries didn't leave my side.

A bell jangled above the door as we entered. Dan threw himself into his big brother's arms the way James had thrown himself in mine.

"Safe and sound, I see." Mrs. Crenshaw smiled from where the bolts of cloth lined the shelves, farther down.

"Yes, ma'am." Sheriff Jeffries answered for me, his hat in his hands again. Its spinning made me dizzy.

I glanced around the open room. "Where are my girls?"

Mrs. Crenshaw straightened a confusion of machine-made lace on a large spool. "Back at my house. I didn't know how long you'd be and I've learned from experience that minding a baby and a store at the same time doesn't work real well."

It made sense. Janie wanted to explore everything right now.

"Isn't that sweet?" Mrs. Crenshaw nodded toward the boys, who still clung to one another.

My heart swelled as full as a corncrib after harvest. I didn't think about the sheriff or Mama or Will or Arthur in that moment. I only knew that, for better or worse, these children held a permanent place in my heart, a place that would ache without them nearby. They needed me. And in some funny, confusing, awful way, I'd come to need them.

"I'm sure you'll be glad when Mr. Gresham gets home. I daresay a young, pretty thing like you will be glad to get this brood off your hands and get back to parties and young men." She sighed and rested her chin in her hands, her eyes staring off in the distance. "Of course, I didn't have much of that myself. Spent most of my days planting and hoeing and picking cotton. But Mr. Crenshaw rescued me from all that."

She turned her attention back to me. "Or maybe you're waiting on a Doughboy of your own?" She raised her eyebrows.

My back stiffened. "No." I placed a hand on each boy's shoulder, feeling suddenly protective of them.

Mrs. Crenshaw shrugged. "Just as well. But you'll still be glad to give the children back to their father, I'm sure."

Of course I would be. Wouldn't I? The reality of Frank's homecoming slammed into my chest. He'd snatch the children away from me. I'd lose them just as I'd lost so many others I loved.

Tears spilling from my eyes, I pushed past Sheriff Jeffries and ran from the store. Past the churchyard where Aunt Adabelle lay. Past the schoolyard where James had fallen in the old well. I ran until my boot caught on a clod of dirt and I fell to the earth, my tears mingling with the dead grass and the dust. Angry tears. Relieved tears. Jealous tears. Tears of exhaustion and confusion and grief and disappointment.

"Why? Why did You make me love them?" I flung the words toward heaven.

But it was Irene's voice that answered back in my head. *"A man's heart deviseth his way, but the Lord directeth his steps,'"* she'd said. *"Sometimes the Lord directs us away from our own plans and towards His."*

I thought of Aunt Adabelle's plans. And Will's. Even Frank's and Clara's. None of their plans for life had worked out as they'd expected. Will had accepted that. He'd chosen to live the last of his days as best he could. What would Frank do? Would he want me gone the minute he arrived, with no warning, no time to adjust?

Would he cling to his children or hold them at a distance? Would he muddle along alone or begin searching for a new wife right away? And if he did marry, would she love her instant family?

"Oh, God. Help me know what to do." Then all I knew were sobs, my heart crying out prayers my mouth didn't know how to utter.

A buzzing sounded from above. I lifted my head. An airplane whizzed across the cloudless expanse, its wings suspended on nothing but air. I drew my knees close to my chest and watched it soar. When Arthur's airplane rose into the sky, how did he know it would stay up there and not come crashing down?

He didn't. He simply trusted that the airplane would work the way it had been designed. Is that what God wanted from me? Just to trust that He'd hold me up, take me where He wanted me to go?

I kept my eyes on the heavens. "I want to go Your way, Lord—whatever that means, wherever You lead."

CHAPTER
26

*T*wo days later, a host of noises from the yard sent me flying to the frosted window. I rubbed a spot clear. Two men in overalls disappeared behind the storage shed near the hog's enclosure.

"What in heaven's name?" Who was roaming our property without speaking to me first? My fury rose like bread dough in a hot kitchen as I charged into the barnyard.

I rounded the corner of the shed and slammed into a body. Wet sloshed down the front of my dress. The overall-clad man stepped back and raised his head.

"Sheriff!" I'd never seen him in anything but a suit before. My mouth gaped, but I managed to shut it. Then I noticed the almost full milk bucket hanging from his hand.

He handed me the pail and stuck his hands in his pockets, leaving a ratty hat firmly atop his head. "There's your morning milk. And I brought some help to butcher your hog."

I swallowed down a yelp as I turned to see the large black pot sitting beside a smoldering fire. I looked back at the sheriff. All I'd ever done at butchering time was make dinner for all those who came to lend a hand. I'd never made headcheese or cracklings or put up lard or readied meat for the smokehouse. Mama did that herself.

Another man in work clothes stood beside us now. "Miss Hendricks"—the sheriff turned formal all of a sudden—"meet Elias Tate. His brother is over yonder, sharpening the knives."

I nodded at the Mr. Tate. He tucked his fingers around the straps of his overalls and rocked back on his heels.

Sheriff Jeffries pulled me aside. "The Lathams will arrive soon, as well. Give each family a few pieces of meat for their trouble and they'll be mighty grateful."

He must have read the panic in my eyes then, for he laughed. "The women will take care of everything. You just need to feed everyone."

I sighed. That I knew how to do.

At the end of the day, the sheriff lingered behind the others, making sure, he said, that the fire had been completely doused. I stood with him, shivering beneath my coat, my breath visible puffs of white in the moon-dimmed dark.

"Thank you." I hated feeling indebted to him, but I took great comfort in the hams and bacon slabs soaking in the curing syrup.

He shrugged. "Nothing one neighbor wouldn't do for another."

"I think you are more neighborly than most."

He poked a stick into the cooling ash. "It isn't hard to want to help you."

I sucked in the smoky night air, its cold stinging my nose and chest. Though that night with Arthur on the front steps of the schoolhouse in Downington hadn't been cold, suddenly it seemed too similar to this one. All alone. In the dark. Words that could mean so many different things.

"Thank you," I said.

His shoulder raised and lowered as he stared into the distance. I wondered what his life was like, a single man in this small town. No family to speak of. Prater's Junction didn't seem to have many girls of an age for him to be interested in. So why didn't he go elsewhere? Nothing held him here that I could see.

He threw the stick on top of the fire pit. "I did it."

I pulled my coat closer around me. "Did what?"

"Asked to be considered for a Texas Ranger."

I shoved my hands into the pockets of my coat. "Congratulations. I hope they accept you."

He stepped closer, so close that I could see every inch of his face, in spite of the cloak of night. "I'd never have dared, but for you."

With a hard swallow, I stepped away. Away from the reach of his arms, his lips. I had no intention of falling for a man I didn't really know. Not again. Besides, though the sheriff had endearing qualities, my heart didn't leap at his nearness.

"Rebekah?" Ollie's voice, from the house.

Sheriff Jeffries touched his hat, stepped back, and nodded. "See you at church on Sunday, Rebekah."

I watched him walk away, this sheriff dressed as a farmer. Was he the reason God had brought me here? Was I missing His plan? Out of sight, the engine of the sheriff's car roared to life and his door slammed shut. He might be on his way to a bigger place, maybe even one filled with the adventure I longed for, but could my heart come to love him?

Only after hearing the gears grind into place and the tires spew earth did I take myself into the warmth of the house.

A blue norther swooped in the next day. Not just cold. Frigid. With the wind howling around the windows as if seeking refuge from itself. I had plenty of time to ponder my future as I huddled under quilts in front of the parlor fireplace, playing games with the children, reading from newspapers and magazines.

Then I heard something that didn't sound like the wind. Untangling myself from the quilt tucked around my knees, I peered through the dingy glass. A large automobile sat in front of the gate, its occupant bundled into obscurity behind the windscreen.

The engine coughed itself still. The driver climbed from the seat.

"Wait here," I told the children as I hurried to let the stranger in out of the biting wind. Icy air swirled in with his stamping feet.

"Arthur." His name came out in a whisper, a breath I'd been afraid to breathe for weeks. My hand searched behind me for the banister, something solid to anchor me upright.

"Hello, Rebekah." Arthur removed his hat, his gloves. Unbuttoned his coat. Gas fumes and cigarette smoke wafted from his outerwear. The smell of leaving and staying all mixed up together.

As he arranged his things on the small table opposite the stairs, his gaze darted around the hall, searching, it seemed, for whoever else might be privy to our conversation. "I'm sorry," he said finally. His eyes hadn't landed on mine in spite of the fact that I stared directly at his face.

I tried to swallow moisture into my mouth. "Where's your fiancée?"

"I don't know."

James stomped into the hall, fists clenched, face blotched with fury. "Rebekah! Dan's cheating!"

Arthur's eyes locked on mine. I sensed his fear. Fear in the fearless aviator.

"I taught them to play checkers." I trilled the words as if we bantered the light conversation of a social gathering. But I wondered at his manner. Did children in general frighten him—or just these, at this moment?

I put my hand on James's shoulder but didn't look down. "Go put the game away now, James."

"But I don't want to. I'm winning."

I pursed my lips and counted to five. "You and Dan can put on your coats and go outside and swing."

"It's too cold outside," came the whining reply.

Sensing Arthur's impatience, I leaned near James's ear, words hissing out of my almost closed lips. "Then find something to do, but don't fight with your brother."

I tried to make my voice sound normal as my hand pinched James's shoulder. "Now, James, I need to talk with my . . . a friend of mine. In the kitchen. You and Dan behave."

James sulked his way back into the parlor, but at least he went. I swept past Arthur and heard him follow. I moved the coffeepot to the hot front burner and tried to think of a way to fill the awkward silence.

Arthur stood by the table. I motioned him to sit. When the coffee had warmed, I filled two cups. "Do you still take cream?"

He nodded. I added a dollop of Ol' Bob's offering and sat across from him, preparing myself to hear what he had to say.

He swallowed down half his coffee before he spoke. "I came to see if we had any chance of starting over."

I flinched and caught my breath, his audacity slapping me with the force of an open hand.

"Start over?" I felt Mama's face fit over mine like a mask. That haughty look she reserved for those who addressed her in a manner less than respectful. "A fiancée ends things quite thoroughly." And yet my heart lurched at the thought that he wanted me again.

He leaned back in his chair, a tad more confident, it seemed. More like the Arthur I'd fallen in love with. "She and I were thrown together during the quarantine. It wasn't like I went looking for another woman." He shrugged. "Besides, with the war over, I'll be discharged. We can be together much sooner than we thought possible."

"Be together? As in, get married?" Something in his manner alarmed me. I wasn't sure what. The return of his arrogance, perhaps?

Again his gaze skittered away. "Eventually."

The word barbed at my heart. "But you were going to marry her right away, weren't you? You told me you were engaged."

He stared at the door that led outside. "She didn't have any reason to wait. You have—" He swatted his hand toward the front of the house, where the children remained quiet.

I stiffened. "I have responsibilities at the moment, yes."

"We'd have to wait, then. Until you get rid of them."

My eyebrows lifted. "Get rid of them? What do you mean? Are you saying you don't want children? Or that you don't want these children?"

"We have our own life to lead, Rebekah. Children would . . . complicate things. Their daddy will be home soon, right? And then you'll be free. Besides, I don't remember you being eager for babies before."

I chewed the edge of my fingernail as I considered how to reply. "You're right. I wasn't. But things have changed. My mother has been ill. My brother is dying. I haven't heard back from Fra—the children's father. But it's more than that."

My mouth proclaimed words I hadn't even thought through completely, words that popped from the soil of my heart like green beans on a hot summer day.

His mouth opened and shut, smooth words slithering from his grasp. That handsome face. Those deep blue eyes. They'd roped me in like a naïve calf. But I wasn't as childlike as I'd once been.

I stood up, raised my chin, and gave him Mama's disapproving look. "I think you'd better leave now."

His eyes narrowed. Weighing his options, I guessed. Wondering how much fight I had in me. After what seemed like an eternity, he pushed back from the table. "Yes. I have to get back."

I handed him his hat and gloves and tapped my foot as he shrugged into his coat. I didn't bother to walk him to his car or even watch him out the gate. I slammed the front door behind him as soon as his feet cleared the threshold.

I found Dan and James pouting on opposite ends of the sofa in the parlor. The smile on my face felt like it rose up all the way from my toes. "C'mon boys. Let's make some hot cocoa."

They leapt to their feet, each grabbing one of my hands. I glanced back at the window. The car Arthur had arrived in had disappeared from sight.

I drew myself a bath that night. I didn't care that it was bitter cold outside or that it wasn't Saturday. I'd not taken very good care of myself since that trip to Dallas. But now I resolved to put Arthur completely behind me. To move forward—even if I remained unsure of my destination.

I leaned my head back until it hung over the side of the tin tub, the warm water like velvet on my dry skin. A bucket of rainwater sat nearby for my hair, but I didn't relish the coolness it would bring to my bath. Not yet.

With a bar of lavender-scented store-bought soap, I scrubbed the grime from my body. And with sheer determination, I scrubbed Arthur from my mind.

CHAPTER
27

$\mathcal{I}$ made it easy for the kids to count down the days until Christmas by hanging a length of rope on the banister, one knot tied for each day until December 25. Just before bed each night, we released a gnarled knot and let it flow loose.

Each day the rope trailed longer, I felt worse for the children. Not only would it be the first Christmas without their mother, it seemed unlikely their father would make it home, either. Their questions plagued me, not the least of which were the queries about Santa Claus. How would Frank want me to answer?

And with each passing day my heart fluttered ever more at the thought of Frank's sudden arrival into our little world. I wanted him to take over the care of his children and leave me free to pursue my dreams.

Didn't I?

The last Saturday before Christmas, I hitched Dandy to the buggy myself and drove us into town. Turning up the collar of my coat, I directed our steps to the brick building on the corner. Our bit of cash had evaporated like a pond in summer, in spite of my efforts to buy only necessities after the Dallas fiasco. But I was determined that the children would have Christmas, even if their father couldn't be with them. I'd make sure he provided presents all the same.

I couldn't ask the Lathams to help. They struggled just to put food on the table for their family of ten. I didn't imagine Christmas at their house consisted of much more than some fruit and candy. But Frank had to have money in the bank, didn't he? His crops had been harvested in the fall.

A fierce wind held the heavy door fast, but I pried it open far enough for us to slip inside. Warmth cocooned me as the smell of wood polish and coal smoke mingled with the sharpness of the winter air. I pulled off my gloves, took a deep breath, and approached the barred window.

"May I help you?" The gentleman behind the bars craned his neck to look past me, looking for my husband or my father, I suspected.

"I need some money from Frank Gresham's account."

The man's cheek twitched as he smoothed the edge of his moustache. "This is quite irregular, Miss . . . ?"

I pulled back my shoulders. "Rebekah Hendricks. I've been caring for the Gresham children since my aunt, Adabelle Williams"— my stiffness softened a bit—"since October."

"Please wait here a moment."

I sat the children on the floor, their backs against the amber wood that ran the length of the room. I didn't figure this to take a long time. But the moments stretched. I peered into the space behind the iron bars but couldn't see the teller I'd spoken with. Only the big silver door of the vault, closed tight.

"Miss Hendricks?"

I reeled around and found myself face-to-face with a man

whose eyes danced in a jolly sort of way. "I'd be pleased to speak with you in my office." He motioned for me to walk ahead. I gave the children a look that I hoped said "Stay put" before I followed.

Seated in the chair that faced his desk, my heart threatened to bounce from my chest as his smooth fingers closed around each other and settled calmly on his desk. Hands that counted money instead of clawing the dirt to make crops grow.

"I understand you have questions about Mr. Gresham's account?"

I glanced at the children through the plate-glass window. "Actually, I need to withdraw some money. It's nearly Christmas. I want it to be special for the children."

He pulled a stack of papers toward him and settled a pair of spectacles on his pudgy nose. "I understand, Miss Hendricks. Unfortunately, Mr. Gresham maintains only a nominal amount of money in an account in our bank. Next to nothing, really."

My stomach soured. Frank had nothing in the bank? But in one letter I'd read, he'd told Aunt Adabelle to divide the crop money as usual. Divide it how? Put it where?

I stared at my purse, fingering the clasp. Frank's letters had been detailed and specific. He seemed to prefer his house and farm kept in similar fashion. Like my daddy. And Daddy always kept money saved in the bank.

"Hasn't he sent home his army pay?" the banker asked.

"I found a little money in . . . the house." My face burned as I thought again of what I'd wasted on my trip to Dallas.

The man cleared his throat, obviously ill at ease. "Given Frank Gresham's reputation, I'm sure Mr. Crenshaw will accommodate you."

My back straightened. Reputation for what? For spending money he didn't have or making good on the debt he owed?

"Thank you." I stood, shook his hand. If Frank hadn't provided anything for his children, I'd have to take care of them myself.

If only Daddy's instructions never to buy on credit didn't sound so loud in my head.

With only three knots left in our rope, we scampered through a sparse clump of trees near the creek in search of a small pine. We found one—barely more than a stick, really. But given that James and I had to cut and carry it, it was perfect.

Beads threaded on a string adorned its branches and a few store-bought decorations that had been wrapped in paper and stored in Aunt Adabelle's dresser drawer bowed the limbs.

"Can we bake a cinnamon cake for breakfast?" Ollie asked.

I hesitated.

"Mama and Miss Ada always did," she whispered.

"Of course we can." But even while I smiled, I wondered if the recipe would show itself in one of my aunt's books or if I'd have to make it up as I went along. A quick search of the kitchen turned up a newspaper clipping pasted on the flyleaf of another cookbook.

So we baked and worked all that night and most of the next day—Christmas Eve. Finally, we hung their socks on the mantel and crept to our beds.

"Will I hear Santa Claus when he comes?" Dan asked.

I tucked the covers around him and kissed his cheek. "I don't think so. He won't come until he knows you are asleep." I tweaked his nose.

He laughed and squeezed his eyes shut. "Tell him to come now, Bekah. I'm asleep."

Their whispers drifted through the thin wall until long past midnight, but even after they quieted, I couldn't sleep. I'd done the right thing buying them gifts, hadn't I? I tossed and turned and prayed, begging God to at least let Daddy cover the amount if Frank protested. Just about the time my eyelids drooped in sleep, four children scrambled into my bed, jarring me awake.

"Let me go down first," I said, inching out from under the covers. "I'll get the fire going and call you."

"Don't take our presents!" The look on Dan's face told me he sincerely feared I would.

I brushed the hair from his forehead. "I wouldn't dare."

Throwing a shawl over my shoulders and socks on my feet, I hurried to the parlor. My hands shook as I lit the kindling beneath the fat logs laid just for this morning. Smoke billowed before the flame caught. I lit two lamps, bowing back the dim darkness of early morning. On the mantel, each sock bulged with an orange and a peppermint stick, a special toy peeking from the top.

The pitter-patter of feet on the stairs didn't give me time for reflection.

"Merry Christmas!" I grinned and joined their frenzy of excitement in spite of the question pounding in my head. Would Frank have the money to cover his children's presents? Would he approve of what I'd purchased? Ollie cradled her new doll. Dan tried to make words with the alphabet blocks, and James connected the sticks and wheels of the Tinkertoys. Janie stared at the teddy bear, occasionally putting out a pudgy hand to stroke the fur. Yet all I could see was the page in Mr. Crenshaw's ledger book.

Frank Gresham. Five dollars and forty-three cents.

Five dollars that could have bought material to replace the clothes the children were fast outgrowing. Or buy a few canned goods to supplement our meals. Or patent medicines to keep us well.

I pressed my hands to either side of my head, trying to stop the furor of my thoughts. But it didn't help. I thought of shoes and doctor bills and kerosene and candles, of soap and staple goods and seeds and—

I needed fresh air. I opened the front door and stepped outside, each breath swirling white in front of my face. Smoked puffed from our chimney, filling my nose with the sharp smell of burnt wood. I walked the length of the porch, my hands wrapping around each other, my thoughts racing off in directions I had no desire for them to go. To Arthur. Will. Mama. Frank.

I don't know how long I stood there. Long enough to lose feeling in my fingers and toes.

Only after I sat in the parlor, a wool shawl around my shoulders, a cup of hot tea in my hands, did I realized that Irene had rescued me yet again.

"I had a Holy Spirit moment this morning," she told me as we sat alone on the sofa, the children upstairs donning their visiting clothes. "While we were reading from Luke, the Lord told me there was another child, wretched and cold, who needed me this Christmas morning. But I didn't imagine He meant it so literally."

I tried to smile with her, but my cheeks remained still as icicles.

She laid her hand on my knee. "You miss your mama as much as they miss theirs."

I nodded and took a sip of the honey-sweetened tea. Chamomile, if I had to guess. "I had a letter from her a few days ago, chiding me for not coming home for Christmas. I hate to disappoint Mama, but I know it's right that I stay, even if she doesn't understand." I took another sip of tea. "I just didn't think growing up would be so confusing."

Irene patted my knee. "George and I didn't think straight, what with putting up little presents for all the children. It slipped our mind that you'd be needing someone to be your family. Can you forgive us?"

I balanced the cup on my knees, still cradling its warmth with my hands, grateful tears sprouting in my eyes.

She eased the teacup from my hands and wrapped her arms around me. "I'll listen if you want to talk."

I didn't think I could, but I poured out the sad tale of Arthur, of trying to be still and listen to the Lord's direction, of my confusion over the sheriff's words and Frank's imminent homecoming. I'd left home believing I had the Lord's blessing to follow my dreams. Now I didn't know if I had any dreams to follow, let alone any direction from the Lord.

Irene's head tilted as if she listened for or to something far away. Maybe she heard the children's ruckus overhead. Maybe she heard the voice of God. "I know it's hard for a young woman like you to believe, but I once dreamed of a very different life for myself than the one I live."

Although she'd listened to my story without expression, I knew my shock at her statement showed clearly on my face.

Irene chuckled. "You wouldn't know it to look at me now, but in my younger days, I had a beau for every day of the week."

I smiled.

She laughed harder, her round girth shaking like the bowl of Jell-O I'd eaten at Arthur's aunt's house. "It's true. I didn't give George Latham a second look back then, with his droopy eyes and his never-ending piety. Good gracious. I had intended to marry someone handsome and wealthy. Someone who would lavish me with fine things. Someone fun!"

Her eyes took on a faraway look. "I wanted . . . I don't really know what I wanted. I just knew it wasn't him. But life has a way of surprising you sometimes." A dreamy smile appeared on her face.

"And?" I prompted.

She looked surprised, as if she'd forgotten anyone else shared the room. "It took time. You see, he had to wait for me to find real faith in the Lord, not just an It's-expected-of-me Sunday attendance."

My back stiffened.

"My favorite sister died of tuberculosis. Her death devastated me. Other beaus either came and petted me and told me everything would be fine or they stayed away, not knowing what to do. Only George offered me real hope. The Jesus kind. And he didn't just say the words. He showed me by his actions. Then he showed me where to find the words in the Bible. The more I read, the more I understood that God wanted my whole life. Everything. Even my plans and dreams."

"So God told you to marry Brother Latham?"

"In a roundabout way, yes. But I couldn't fall in love with George until I'd fallen in love with Jesus."

"But I already know the Lord. So what does that mean for me?"

Irene's eyes held mine. "It means when your life belongs to God it doesn't belong to you anymore. It means sometimes life turns out different than you plan. He will guide your paths, as it says in the Proverbs. But you have to trust that He has your good in mind and follow where He leads."

"He led me to Arthur."

"Perhaps. Or maybe He has something different in mind for you."

"But I'm not like you and Aunt Adabelle and Mama. I can't bear the thought of living out my life on a farm. I need people and adventure. That's what I was made for. I know it is."

Irene didn't reply. Janie's cry broke the tension of silence.

Irene stood. "Follow the path that the Lord has laid out before you. If you listen for His voice and obey it, everything will turn out fine—in the end. Now, let's go celebrate Christmas."

As the children bounded into the room clutching their gifts, I realized that God had not forgotten or abandoned me. He'd shown that by sending Irene—His special Christmas gift just for me.

CHAPTER
28

$\mathcal{A}$s it often did back in Oklahoma, the weather warmed the week after Christmas. I sat in a rocker on the porch, the sewing basket dormant at my side, unspoken anticipation of the new year filling my heart. Nothing could be as bad as the past months we'd endured. Between the Kaiser, the Spanish flu, and the loss of so many of our soldiers, everyone had waged war against an enemy.

I leaned my head back and closed my eyes, soaking up the sun and the sound of the children playing. Ollie skipped rope, chanting a rhyme she'd brought home from school.

"I had a little bird; its name was Enza. I opened the window and in flew en—" Her voice and the thump of rope stopped.

"Who's that?" James whispered next to my ear.

I looked. Only a shadow of a figure really, far away down the road. I closed my eyes again.

"Daddy!" Ollie's shriek lifted me from my seat. She left her rope and bounded down the road. I clutched the porch post as I watched the man's bag fall to the ground. He ran to meet her, swinging her up into his arms and holding her close.

James rushed down the steps and then stopped, turned back to me.

"Go on." I shooed him away, as if it didn't matter. In truth, my stomach clenched. Dan's tentative steps toward his brother nearly drove the last bit of breath from my body. How would I leave these children? Would Frank send me away this minute? Should I begin collecting my things and saying good-bye?

Then I thought of all Frank had lost, of how little this resembled the family he'd wanted to return to. He and I shared one bond, at least—loss.

The boys wandered past the front gate—first James, then Dan, the two of them much more shy about meeting their stranger-Daddy.

I lifted Janie, who was eager to be included. Tears slid down my face, though I told myself I had no reason to cry. Frank would take care of his children, and I'd be free to move to any city I wanted.

He knelt on the ground now, hugging his boys to him. Then he looked up. In spite of the fact that I couldn't see his face distinctly, I saw the longing in his gaze. I held my breath, afraid to shatter the moment, yet afraid the moment would shatter me.

Straightening my shoulders, I carried Janie past the gate. We stood in the road, the little family walking toward us. Dan clung to one of his daddy's hands, Ollie to the other. James danced back and forth in front of them.

"It's Daddy, Bekah. It's Daddy!" He sang the words over and over again while I listened to the suck, suck, suck of Janie's thumb in her mouth. I shifted Janie's weight to my other hip.

Emotion flickered across Frank's face, twitching his lips and tightening his jaw. "You must be Miss Hendricks." Eyes the color of a storm-darkened sky, and just as intense, held me mute.

"Rebekah," James corrected. "That's what she told us to call her."

I couldn't read Frank's expression. Was he displeased with

me? Wary? Grateful? Maybe just exhausted and sorrowful. His gaze slid over to Janie. He held out his hands. She jerked away, her arms tight around my neck, her mouth filled with whimpers.

"I'm sorry." I tried to smile.

His arms dropped to his sides. Ollie and the boys grabbed at his hands. Janie turned for another peek at the man she didn't recognize, thumb in her mouth, eyes big as saucers.

"Don't be scared of your daddy, Janie." I jiggled her as I wrinkled my nose in her direction. She unplugged her mouth and laughed, just as I'd intended. I took a deep breath and stepped toward Frank. He reached for her again. She clung to me. I peeled her off, handed her into his calloused hands.

She stared at him for a moment before Ollie pressed close to her daddy and smiled into her sister's face. "It's Daddy, Janie. Daddy."

Janie reached out baby fingers and touched Frank's face, gently, timidly. Then the grin we all knew so well broke out like sunshine on a gray day. Moisture rose in Frank's eyes. I turned away.

"I imagine you're hungry," I said, staring off toward the beginnings of sunset.

He cleared his throat. "That I am, Rebekah. That I am."

My hands refused to be steady. Frank had come home—and I had no idea what that meant for any of us. Part of me reveled in the elation that Janie had wanted me, not her daddy. But in the next moment, I felt guilty. How awful for your own child to not know you. I glanced at Janie, content on the ground near my feet.

The high pitch of the children's voices and the deep rumble of a man's reply drifted in through the kitchen door, but I couldn't discern the words. I cut lard into the last of the flour for biscuits while bacon sizzled in one big skillet and gravy bubbled in a smaller pot. After I slipped the biscuits into the oven, I stood back and surveyed my work. Hot and filling. I was becoming a pretty good cook.

I dragged Janie with me to the back porch cistern for a bucket of water while my heart pulsed an unsteady rhythm. At the kitchen door, Frank lifted the heavy bucket from my hand.

"Thank you," I gasped as he set the bucket on the table without a word. It seemed a familiar gesture, not the exaggerated kindness one extended to a stranger.

The smell of bacon and biscuits hung thick in the small room. I handed Janie to her sister, wrapped a dishtowel around my hand, and pulled the biscuits from the oven. The clatter behind me intensified as everyone took their places at the table. Ollie doled out forks and cups as Frank's laughter filled the room. Real laughter, birthed from joy. My skin tingled in spite of the warmth. Any man who could laugh like that couldn't be cruel. Maybe he'd let me stay. At least until I figured things out.

"Ollie, grab the butter from the cooler." I heaped Frank's plate with food and soon heard the small butter plate clink onto the tabletop. Frank's voice died away. The others quieted, too.

I whipped around. "What's wrong?"

Frank sat perfectly still, his fist gripping his fork and holding it upright, a napkin tucked beneath his chin. Only his jaw moved, tightening and loosening. I followed his gaze to the newly churned butter. The fancy G pressed into the top remained undisturbed.

I remembered Mama telling me how Daddy had carved her a butter mold the first year they were married. Had Frank done the same? It was such a small thing, really. Why hadn't seeing the children or the house stirred that same kind of emotion in him? They were much more of his history with his wife than a carved butter mold. Yet maybe that mold represented more than I knew.

I reached across the table and picked up the butter dish before filling a second plate. Frank blinked a few times before noticing the food in front of him. Then the moment passed. With my own plate in hand, I took the chair opposite Frank. He bowed his head. We all did the same.

"Great and gracious God—" His voice caught and silenced.

I peeked from under my lashes. The children's heads raised, their eyes squinting open, first at their daddy, then at each other, finally at me. I laid a finger over my lips and bowed my head again, praying they'd do the same.

We waited. I wondered if Frank had fallen asleep. Too much longer and all the food would be cold. Then he took a deep breath. "Thank you, Lord, for this food, and bless the hands that have prepared it. Amen."

It was as if he'd held his own conversation with God—privately—and then let us in on the last bit. Or had he just needed time to compose himself? If nothing else, the man intrigued me.

Through supper, the children chattered on about Ol' Bob and the chickens, the sheriff and the Lathams, the doings in town, church, and school. Aunt Adabelle and their mother hovered over the conversation unmentioned. We didn't speak of the influenza, either. It was as if we'd all made a pact to forget it, to act as if it hadn't changed everything—not just for us, but for so many others, too.

I cleaned up the dishes while Frank carried the children to bed. After I dumped the dishwater on the flower beds and spread the damp cup towel across the bushes to dry, I settled myself in the parlor, wondering if Frank would join me there.

He seemed unsure as he walked into the room, hesitant as he eased into a chair. Like a guest in an unfamiliar home.

"Here're your newspapers." I handed him those I hadn't yet used to make fires, hoping to put him at ease. I picked up one of my aunt's magazines for myself. Pages rustled, turned, quieted as we avoided each other's gaze. The mantel clock counted off minutes with loud ticks.

When Frank cleared his throat, I looked up in expectation.

After a stiff smile, he lowered his eyes to the newspaper again. When the clock chimed the hour, we both stopped reading. Nine o'clock.

He rose to his feet. "Thank you, Rebekah."

I looked at the floor and shrugged one shoulder. It wasn't often I couldn't find something to say, but all the words in my head seemed to tangle together like the yarn in my knitting basket.

He blew out a long breath and set his hands on his hips. "When I heard—" He cleared his throat, let the silence settle between us again before he continued. "My children appear to be happy. You can't know what a comfort that is."

He seemed to have more to say, but he stopped. Was he trying to tell me to leave? I didn't even have money to purchase a train ticket—to anywhere. But how could I say that to him?

He shouldered his bag lying near the sofa. Heat crawled up from my toes as I watched his eyes dart toward the bedroom on the other side of the wall. I hadn't considered sleeping arrangements. Even if he slept downstairs and I slept upstairs, it seemed scandalous.

"I'll bunk with Ol' Bob. Good night." He nodded once before his boots clomped across the floor and the back door eased shut.

I wondered how long he'd be content with that arrangement.

CHAPTER
29

Wriggling into my shirtwaist and skirt the next morning, I listened for any indication of the children stirring in the room next to mine. All remained quiet except for the small sounds rising from below. I knelt next to my bed and asked the Lord for wisdom. Then I made my way downstairs.

I found Frank cracking fresh eggs into a skillet. Not a sight I'd seen often—or ever. Daddy and Will only came into the kitchen to eat. I tied an apron around my waist, wishing I'd been out of bed earlier. "I can do that."

He moved out of the way, carrying the coffeepot to the table.

"I'm sure it feels good to be home." I'd felt terrible crawling into bed last night, knowing Frank slept on prickly hay with stinky livestock. I hadn't even bothered to make sure he had bedding.

"That barn beat all my billets in France." He sipped his coffee, seeming to savor it.

It made me wonder what he had experienced over there, what my brother had experienced, too. "Was it terrible? The war, I mean."

Frank stared at the rim of his cup. "I didn't see the worst of it. I helped build bridges, mostly. Those boys in the trenches had it hard, though."

"My brother was in the trenches." I slid the eggs onto a plate and laid strips of bacon in the skillet as I thought about Will. I'd heard nothing from or about him since he'd left.

"Is he back yet?" Frank sipped more coffee, then tipped the pot to fill his cup again.

I set a full plate on the table in front of him. "Yes." I couldn't say any more than that. I'd already begun to grieve my brother. I turned back to the stove and swiped away the moisture beneath my lashes.

I heard a blanket drag along the floor and the padding of little feet. Dan. As I turned, he stared up at Frank for a short moment before rubbing his eyes. "Daddy?"

Frank lifted his son into his lap. "Did you think you'd dreamed me?"

Dan nodded. Frank hugged his little boy against his chest.

The others arrived, as tentative as Dan. But it didn't take them long to warm up again. Even Janie hesitated only a moment before diving from Ollie's arms to her daddy's.

"Y'all ready for church today?" he asked.

I whirled around, hands covering my cheeks. "Oh my stars, I forgot it was Sunday!"

The children giggled. All except James. He put his six-year-old hand in mine. "It's okay, Bekah. We won't leave you behind."

"Thank you, James." I busied myself at the stove, trying to hide my laughter. Frank didn't try to hide his. It burst into all four corners of the room.

As the echoes died away, his words filled the silence. "George Latham wrote that he's been stopping by for y'all most Sundays."

"Yes." I doled out breakfast to the children, taking in the information that George Latham had written to Frank about us.

"Except when they shut down church because of influenza." I winced, wishing my mouth wouldn't run ahead of my thoughts.

He pushed up from his chair and pulled the tin tub from the corner. "I think I'll get cleaned up first, if you don't mind helping the children."

"Oh no, I don't mind." I watched as he scooped hot water from the reservoir into the tub. By the time he reached the barn the water would be tepid. But he didn't complain. He simply walked out the door as if living in his own barn were the most normal thing in his world.

Rain slashed at the window long before Frank pulled the buggy up outside the back gate. I met Frank on the porch. A few wrinkles creased his pants and jacket. Had they been in his bag, or had he retrieved them from his bedroom in the house?

I shoved an umbrella into his hands. "I thought you might need this."

A smile spread across his face. I didn't know whether to be flattered or annoyed. Did he think I lacked the common courtesy to realize an umbrella would be helpful in the rain?

He cocked his head like Ollie often did. "Can you handle a horse, Rebekah?"

"Of course." I must have had a curious expression on my face, for his gaze slid to the floor.

"I thought maybe you were used to automobiles instead of old-fashioned contraptions like this."

"Oh, no. Mama won't let Daddy get an automobile. She says horses and buggies have been just fine for her family, and she isn't about to be the one to get uppity."

Frank's lips twitched as he turned away, and I found myself wishing we could laugh at Mama together.

"We goin'?" Dan swaggered out to the porch, his shirt buttoned askew.

"Mind if I help?" I knelt down, refastened his shirt, straightened his knickers.

"Ready?" Frank held the umbrella over my head.

"What about the—"

James and Dan dashed past me, scrambling into the buggy. Ollie wasn't far behind, Janie filling her arms. I sighed contentedly as we stepped into the blustery day.

It had felt funny to have a man sitting in my kitchen this morning. Well, not *my* kitchen. Maybe it felt funny for me to be in a man's kitchen. Whatever it was, I decided that having somewhere to go would be a good thing for us all.

By the time we reached the church, the yard held several buggies and a few automobiles. We hurried inside. Frank led us up the aisle, the children following their father, me bringing up the rear of our little parade. Every few steps Frank stopped to exchange greetings with someone. At the third pew from the pulpit, he stopped again, this time pointing us into the empty row.

Ollie scooted down the long bench. The boys followed. Frank stood aside, obviously waiting for me to sit first. I felt the stares around us. Did he feel them, too? We looked like a family, all together like this. Especially with Frank treating me like a lady and not as another child. As he sat down, I nestled Janie on the seat between us. No sense causing tongues to wag.

I glanced at Frank. He looked strained, his muscles taut-to-bursting. I bit my lip. Everything would remind him of her. Every place. Every song. Every person. How did he bear it? With great effort, I forced my attention to the service. At least I tried to. But Brother Latham's words couldn't hold my attention that day. Frank's face kept drawing my gaze instead.

The little lines around his eyes weren't as tan as the rest of his face, as if he'd squinted into the sun for hours and kept the little folds hidden and white. In spite of delicate features, strength showed in his face. No gray streaked hair the color of the scorched stump near the creek. His eyes sparkled blue when he laughed and rested gray when he didn't.

He was still a young man. And quite handsome, I thought. I wondered if any widows had already pinned their hopes on him. I scanned the congregation. But if any women were smitten with Frank, I couldn't discern it. My gaze stopped at Sheriff Jeffries. He stared back at me. I returned a timid smile.

Then I noticed Frank frowning in my direction. Heat burst into my cheeks as his concentration returned to Brother Latham. I studied my hands, feeling reproved. But why should I? The sheriff and I had a friendship that deserved acknowledgment. Maybe I'd misjudged Frank from his letters. Maybe he was more rigid in his views of acceptable behavior. More like Mama.

The service ended before I could unravel Frank's nature. He stood but didn't move. Janie fussed, so I picked her up as Frank stared out the windows opposite, the ones that overlooked the small cemetery.

The sun had dried its tears, so the older children ran out into the churchyard with the others. Frank remained transfixed. My hand felt as heavy as a full kettle as I placed it on his arm.

"Go on," I whispered.

The tortured look in his eyes wrenched my heart.

"Please go," I said again.

With an almost palpable grief, he stepped into the aisle, toward the door near the organ that led directly to the graveyard. A hand touched my arm. I turned. Sheriff Jeffries's grin sparked one of my own.

This man had plans to be somebody. To live the life of a Ranger, far beyond the homes and fields of this tiny town. I could learn to love him, couldn't I?

He took Janie from my arms and escorted us out the door. At the very least, I would try.

When Frank returned to the crowd of lingerers, his face reminded me of James's the day I'd found him at his mother's grave. That same look of somber acceptance, of grief smoothed just below the surface. That same wild joy at seeing other loved ones living and breathing.

He lifted Janie, his gaze drinking her in as if he had but this one moment to memorize her for all time. Ollie, Dan, and James huddled around their father's legs, afraid, I guessed, that he'd leave them again.

"Frank looks good." Irene's voice at my ear. "When did he get home?"

"Yesterday."

"And?"

I glanced at the sheriff, who still hovered beside me. I forced a smile to my face. "Everything's fine. We'll get things figured out soon. He was exhausted last night. We all went to bed early."

Blood rushed into my face. "Of course he slept in the barn, and . . ."

Irene's head tipped back as she laughed. Sheriff Jeffries's mouth twisted into a scowl. From across the yard, Frank's gaze locked on mine. He raised his eyebrows and nodded toward the buggy.

"Good-bye, Irene." I gave her a quick hug, wondering if I would see her again before Frank sent me home. Then I turned to the sheriff. Instead of a good-bye, he held his elbow crooked in my direction.

"I'd be happy to escort you to the house." Sheriff Jeffries's eyes begged me to say yes.

And I knew I ought to oblige. But I found myself wanting to

be with my kids again. I didn't know how much longer I'd have with them. I didn't want to miss a moment.

My mind whirled like the sheriff's hat. "Thank you, I . . ." Frank had the older kids in the buggy now. He turned toward me with a look of expectancy. "I think I'd better help with the children."

His smile faded a bit, although he seemed to work to make it stay. He walked me to the buggy as if my words hadn't disappointed him and helped me up to the seat. "Good to have you back, Frank."

Frank nodded. The sheriff touched the brim of his hat and backed away, his gaze undistracted from my face. But Frank's hard-set jaw and narrowed eyes broke into my line of vision as he plopped Janie in my lap.

"If you're done socializing, we can get on home." He stalked to the other side of the buggy and hopped up on the seat.

I stared at his profile, that rugged face on which I'd seen such vulnerable emotions. But I'd also seen his look of disapproval in church. Now he appeared haughty, almost condescending. My eyes narrowed. What cause did he have to chastise me?

My arms tightened around Janie. She leaned her head on my chest. One corner of my mouth lifted. Janie loved me. And I didn't think Sheriff Jeffries's feelings lagged far behind.

Maybe, like Aunt Adabelle had said, the Lord had brought me to this place for a reason, but it was one slightly different than I'd imagined. A better one, I felt sure. For Henry Jeffries would never break a girl's heart.

I cleaned the dinner dishes, wondering if I should pack my things that afternoon. Although our first interactions had been favorable, Frank obviously didn't approve of me.

James ran into the yard as I tossed out the dishwater. "C'mon, Bekah. We're going to help with the horse."

"I don't think so, honey." Frank wouldn't appreciate my presence. I feared his gratitude didn't extend as far as friendship.

"Please?" James grabbed my hand and pulled. "Please?"

How could I disappoint that pleading face? So I gave in. He dragged me after him to the barn, the sudden shade causing my skin to prickle with goose pimples. My eyes adjusted to the dim light. The boys and Ollie chased each other through the shadows. Apparently "helping with the horse" simply meant being somewhere nearby.

Frank brushed Dandy's raven-colored coat. I leaned my arms on the half-wall of the stall and watched. His face didn't have that hard look now. His love for his horse showed in his eyes, in every tender yet firm stroke down Dandy's side.

I wondered what Frank's face would have revealed if I could have seen him look at his wife. They'd married young, according to Ollie and Irene, but given that he'd hired Aunt Adabelle to take care of things, I suspected he recognized his wife's frailty early on. But had he expected to lose her this soon?

"I bought Dandy just before the war started." His voice startled me. "Before that, Clara and I had an old nag for the buggy, the first horse I'd ever saved enough money to buy. I never dreamed I'd own a horse like Dandy."

"He is handsome." I reached out and slid my hand down the horse's flank. Frank stood on my side of the horse now, so close I could hear him breathe. He smelled of earth and hard work, reminding me of Daddy.

I couldn't see his face now, but he kept talking anyway. "I think Clara loved this horse about as much as I do. She said he reminded her of me, each of us with our night-sky hair and our determination to be the one in charge of every moment." The brush stopped midstroke, but only for a moment. He moved to the front of the horse, caressing Dandy's nose and talking softly to him.

When he turned his face to me again, a moist sheen covered

his eyes. He blinked it away as he laid aside the brush, so quickly I almost wondered if I'd imagined the tears. In the next moment, he captured Dan from behind, threw him into the air, and caught him again.

Dan cackled. "Again, Daddy. Again!"

James jumped at his daddy's arm. "Me next. Do me!"

Frank's deep laughter filled the barn, but it blanketed his sorrow as inadequately as a thin layer of snow over brown grass. His world had been turned topsy-turvy, like mine. I think both of us wondered what would happen next. Turmoil bubbled inside me, twisting my heart first one way and then the other. But the emotion didn't feel like it'd felt earlier in the day. This time it felt like compassion.

I found Frank in the parlor that evening, feet propped on a small stool, head resting on the chair back, eyes closed. The wind whistled through the treetops outside, and I shuddered at the thought of its icy fingers poking through the cracks in the barn walls. Frank probably wanted me to leave—if only so he could have his house back.

His head lifted and his eyes opened. Both the judgment and the grief seemed to have abated. He set his feet flat on the floor and straightened in his chair.

"I guess the barn wasn't as comfortable as you made it out to be." I settled on the sofa, my hands linked in my lap.

"It's not a problem."

The fire crackled and popped. The wind rattled the glass in the windows. And still we sat silent.

"I scolded Ollie for not helping with the dishes tonight."

I shrugged. "She's a little girl who has lost her mama and is very glad to see her daddy."

"Yes." He poked at the fire, rearranging the logs until the flame blazed higher.

"When I arrived, she was taking care of everything all by herself, so I think I can manage awhile without her help." *Awhile.* What exactly did I mean by that? I flapped a magazine to cool my face.

He nodded but kept studying the fire.

I drew in a deep breath. "When do you want me to leave, Frank?"

His head whipped around. "Leave?" He seemed panicked. And yet today he'd been . . . Well, he'd been confusing.

"I just thought . . ."

He clasped his hands behind his back. "Of course. You need to go. I understand. We can manage." He crisscrossed the room, stopped to finger the clock on the mantel. "But the children seem to have taken to you. I'd hate for them to have another loss right now."

I hopped up from my place, suddenly eager to make him understand. "It's fine if I stay for a while. It really is. I . . ." The words died in my throat. I couldn't explain.

Relief seemed to flood his face, calming the flutters in my chest. I'd told God I'd wait right here until He showed me what to do next. And I intended to do just that—if Frank would let me.

"I don't want to impose. I know you've been here three months already." His face mirrored James's again as he ran a hand through his dark hair and blew out a long breath. "I'm not sure I can manage it all on my own. Not yet. But if you can stay for a while longer, maybe until after spring planting, I'd be mighty grateful."

I tried to keep my smile prim, not jump at the offer too quickly. So I let him know with a nod. And I prayed the Lord could convince my heart to care for the sheriff before Frank sent me on my way.

CHAPTER
30

On Monday, the sheriff stopped by for a moment to deliver the mail, saying Mr. Culpepper was down in his back. On Tuesday, Sheriff Jeffries found me in Mr. Crenshaw's store as I shopped for supplies with the money Frank had brought home. And then on Wednesday, the sheriff's car chugged up the lane with no other aim but my company. Or so he said.

I wouldn't again make the mistake of assuming more than was said. For now, I'd spend time with the sheriff and trust the Lord to guide me. Like watching plums turn purple in summer, waiting until that perfect moment of squishy-sweet to pluck them from the tree and pop them in my mouth. And Mama would approve, I felt certain.

Ollie finished the dishes as I changed into my Sunday best. When I walked into the kitchen, Sheriff Jeffries's hat danced in his hands as a strained smile played at his lips.

Frank, on the other hand, stared at me as if I were no more than a scarecrow in a cornfield. No matter. I buttoned my coat and gave the sheriff my full attention. "Shall we drive, Mr. Jeffries?"

He returned his hat to his head and held out his arm to escort me. "You needn't wait up," I called back. "I can see myself in." I didn't wait for an answer.

⚜

We bumped over rutted roads, down paths meant for cows, seeing little as the gray evening slipped on its inky cloak. The sheriff talked of Prater's Junction, of the Texas Rangers, of his dreams for a home and a family. My stomach churned as he talked, wanting him to offer to take me with him into adventure yet wishing he wouldn't declare his intentions just yet.

"You know, Rebekah, from the first moment—"

"Do you think you could teach me to drive?"

His foot hit the brake. We jerked to a stop. He stared at me, his face illuminated by the rising moon and the backwash of the headlamps. "What?"

"Drive a car. Do you think you could teach me?"

He scratched the back of his head, tipping his hat over his eyes. "I'm not sure it's a good idea for a girl—"

"I'm not a girl, Sheriff. I'm a woman. And women drive, too. At least some do. I've seen it in magazines."

"Still . . ." He shook his head.

I leaned closer. "Please?"

He frowned as he pushed his hat back into its rightful place. "All right. But just this once."

With a squeal, I changed places with him, setting my hands on the steering wheel, listening closely to his instructions. With the car in gear I eased off the brake and opened the throttle. We inched forward. I laughed, eyes on the strip of light showing the road ahead. The braver I got, the faster we went, bumping along in the dirt, sometimes on the worn track, sometimes into the unmarked grass.

206

For the first time in my life, I felt free. I held the wheel. I decided our course. I wanted to go on and on and never stop. Filled with glee, I glanced at the sheriff. He remained thin-lipped, but he'd get used to this, I felt sure. He planned to be a Texas Ranger, after all. He could understand my desire for adventure.

But before I knew it, Frank Gresham's house loomed in the dark. And I knew that pursuing adventure with the sheriff meant leaving the Greshams behind. The thought pinched my heart like shoes too tight. How could I survive without James's sweet face and Dan's rambunctious four-year-old antics, Ollie's shy smile, and Janie's teeth emerging into her joyful grin?

We motored toward the fence, my mind still lost in anguished thoughts.

"Slow down." Sheriff Jeffries put a hand on the steering wheel.

"I can do it." I yanked in the opposite direction. White pickets glowing beneath the full moon appeared closer and larger. My foot missed the brake. Wood splintered. A headlamp went dark. The engine died without a sputter.

Sheriff Jeffries practically sat in the same seat with me now, his foot hard on the brake.

I looked up. A shadowy figure rose from a chair on the porch and walked toward us.

Frank.

I pushed open my door and stood on shaky legs, straightening my hat. The sheriff inspected his car. Frank kept his eyes on me. I refused to turn from his reproachful gaze.

"I'm so sorry, Sheriff. I hope I didn't hurt anything."

"Only my fence," Frank grumbled.

I gave him my most coquettish smile. "Nothing that can't be repaired, right?"

The sheriff cleared his throat. I turned to him. "I do thank you for the ride." When did I start sounding so much like Mama?

"My . . . pleasure. I'll see you on Sunday?"

I looked to Frank, then back to the sheriff. "Of course. And I am sorry about your car."

"No harm done. At least, not much." He cranked the engine and backed out of the yard. Down the road it rattled. I winced. I didn't remember that sound from before. Thankfully, the noise faded, leaving only the serenade of night—and Frank's huffing.

"What were you doing?" Frank asked into the darkness.

"Driving a car. What did it look like?"

"Mayhem. I'll thank you not to drive near my fences again." He stalked toward the house, then stopped, turned back. "But I'm glad you're not hurt."

I kicked at a tuft of dead grass smashed into the dirt, the corner of my mouth drifting downward of its own accord. Of course he was glad. He needed a nursemaid for his children for a little while longer.

At church that Sunday, I sat between the boys, an arm around each of them. Ollie and Janie flanked their daddy, pink flushing their cheeks at his attention. Worshippers slipped in around us. I craned my neck toward the back, searching for the sheriff. Irene started the opening bars of the hymn on the small organ. Only then did he slip into a back seat and lay his hat in his lap. I turned my attention to the service, satisfied.

After the closing hymn, I buttoned James and Dan into their coats. Frank did the same with the girls. Irene caught my hand, her cheeks glowing red as coals in a stove, her eyes shiny as a clean windowpane.

"I'd like y'all to come for dinner today," she said.

I remembered the smallness of her house and imagined the meagerness of her cupboard. "There's no need—"

"We'd love to—" Frank glared at me as our words overlapped each other.

My back stiffened. How could he be so selfish? They didn't have room for us there. And I'd cooked a chicken potpie for us, its golden dome only wanting to be reheated.

Frank juggled Janie and his big Bible, one in each arm. "Like I said, we'd love to partake of a meal with you and your family."

I glanced toward the back of the room. The sheriff spoke with the Crenshaw family.

"I've invited the sheriff, too," Irene said.

I pressed my lips into a smile as Irene's gaze moved from Frank to me to Frank again.

"Come on directly. I have a ham all ready." Irene gathered her hymnal and Bible and pocketbook.

I sighed and shooed the boys out the door. It wasn't that I didn't appreciate the invitation. Or the inclusion of the sheriff. Truth be told, I had no idea why her words stirred my dissatisfaction—other than the fact that my heart refused to follow what my head deemed the most prudent course.

Climbing into the buggy, settling Janie on my lap, I thought of Mama again, of her constant requests that I return home. I imagined Mama would encourage me to stay if she knew of the sheriff and his attentions. But did I want her to know yet?

Frank's deep voice rumbled in answer to one of the boys' questions.

No, I couldn't tell her about any of it. Not yet.

I lowered my head until my cheek pressed against Janie's. I prayed again that the Lord would show me His way. Not Mama's. Not mine. Not Irene's. His.

A terrifying thought. And yet one that stirred the same feeling of freedom I'd felt when I'd steered the sheriff's car behind the line of light piercing the darkness.

CHAPTER
31

$\mathcal{I}$rene's house proved as cramped as I'd imagined it would be, but she didn't seem daunted. She directed her girls to set the table while she finished cooking. "We'll serve the children their dinner on the porch," she told me.

"I'll make sure they get their coats on, then." But that task didn't prove as simple as it sounded.

"I don't want my coat." Dan crossed his arms.

"But it's cold outside."

"I'm not cold." He stamped his foot as if to punctuate his sentence.

I took a deep breath. "You will wear your coat or you won't eat." I crossed my arms, too.

Frank sauntered in from the porch. "Is there a problem?"

I held out Dan's coat. "He has to put this on to go outside and eat dinner."

"Why?"

Now I wanted to stamp *my* foot. "Because it's cold out there."

Frank's shoulder raised and lowered. "If he gets cold, he'll come put his coat on." Frank took the coat from my hand and swatted his son gently on the behind. "Go on, now, Dan."

The boy scampered away, but not before I spied the mocking grin on his face. My fists clenched at my side. "How dare you!" I hissed.

"What?" Frank truly looked confused.

I pulled my shoulders back a bit. Perhaps I didn't know much about the care of small children, but I knew I didn't want to care for a passel of sick ones. "I don't want them to catch cold."

He grinned as if I'd told a joke instead of put forth my serious opinion on the subject. "They'll be fine, Rebekah."

"And I suppose you'll take care of them if they aren't?" From the corner of my eye, I spied Sheriff Jeffries and Brother Latham walk through the door. The sheriff's eyebrows lowered.

"They'll be fine. They aren't frail like—" His face crumpled and he turned away.

Like Clara, he'd almost said. Her children. And his. Part of me wanted to wrap my arms around him. But the other part—

With great effort, I lowered my voice, kept it calm and even. "The children have been my responsibility, and I think I have some say in what happens to them." I spun around to leave the room, my anger boiling like a kettle left too long on the fire.

"... only a child herself." Frank's mumbled words sent me flying back.

"We were doing just fine before you came home."

His eyebrows shot up and his mouth dropped open. I didn't wait to measure his response beyond shock. My skirt swirled around my legs as I turned away.

His tone softened, and his words stopped my flight. "I think you need to trust me in this, Rebekah. I wouldn't suggest anything that would harm my children."

I knew that. I really did. I pressed my lips together, determined to keep tears from falling. Only then did I notice Ollie in the corner, her bottom lip trembling. She bit it still.

My heart seemed to sink into my toes. Why did caring so much seem to bring out the worst in me?

Sheriff Jeffries slapped his hat on his head and put his hand on my elbow. "Why don't we take a quick walk before dinner?"

I nodded and let him lead me away. Ollie's lips puckered and her face flushed as I passed by, stinging me like a slap of wet rain on a cold day. Sheriff Jeffries urged me forward. I stumbled. He righted me. Again. Like on the train platform the day I arrived. Always right where I needed him. So why couldn't my heart leap in his direction?

We walked all the way to the shallow creek, without our coats. Frank had been right. The afternoon had warmed more than I'd thought. This time I talked. And Sheriff Jeffries listened. But instead of recounting my dreams of adventure, I found myself rattling on about the children.

He didn't seem to mind. The very antithesis of Arthur. In fact, if Frank had wanted to find a new wife and leave his children with me, I was pretty sure the sheriff wouldn't object. So I smiled up at him as we walked, trying to make myself feel the wild ecstasy I'd always felt in Arthur's presence. But my heart didn't pound harder, and my chest didn't ache with longing for his touch.

As we neared the house again, I noticed his gun belt peeking out from beneath his suit coat. "Do you always wear your guns?" I asked.

"Mostly. You never know what will happen."

"You might have to run down a bank robber or cattle rustler?"

He grinned. "Something like that."

I'd read a story once about Pearl Hart, the famous lady stage-coach robber. How would it feel to wear the heavy pistols slung low on the hips?

"May I try it on?"

212

"My gun belt?"

I nodded, Christmas morning excitement bursting through me.

"Well, I guess it'd be all right." He unbuckled his belt and handed it to me. "Be careful, though."

More weight than I expected filled my hands, but not more than I could handle. A lifetime of wielding cast-iron pots and pans made a girl's arms strong. I strapped the belt around my waist, undecided as to whether I imagined myself a bandit or a law enforcer.

"I see you've found your way back." Frank's clipped words.

I ducked my head to hide my smirk, wondering why annoying this man brought such delight. Was it because he seemed to think he had some kind of authority over me? Maybe I wanted him to know I didn't need another mother.

"Dinner's on," Irene called from the porch.

I unbuckled the holster that crushed against the pleats in my dress. Sheriff Jeffries took it from my hands and strapped it on his waist, his cheeks pink as a summer sunset as we made our way inside.

Seated around the dining table, the sheriff to my right, Frank across from us, I relaxed as Nola Jean asked unending questions about Oklahoma.

"You mean there's no cotton?"

"Yes, there's cotton. But we don't grow any. Daddy grows mostly corn."

She looked sideways at her mother. "Corn's easier to harvest than cotton."

"I expect so," I said, "although I've never picked cotton myself. I can see y'all grow a lot of it around here."

Nola Jean snorted, then apologized. "Too much, if you ask me."

"Be thankful for cotton crops, Nola Jean." Irene slid her knife into the butter and slathered it on a square of cornbread. "They clothe and shelter you."

Nola Jean sighed. "If only it wasn't so much work."

Frank ducked his head to hide a smile.

"Maybe you won't always live on a cotton farm, Nola Jean." I stared at Frank as I said it. I didn't know why. Maybe because I couldn't look at the sheriff, since he sat beside me. Maybe because I wanted Frank to know I didn't intend to stay here forever. Maybe I just wanted to say it out loud, to remind myself. "You could marry a man who will take you somewhere else. Somewhere new and exciting."

Nola Jean pushed potatoes around her plate with her fork. "That don't seem likely, Miss Rebekah."

"What brought y'all to this place, anyway?" I directed the question to Irene, but I knew the answer would come from Brother Latham. And maybe Frank would reveal a bit of his history on that, as well.

Brother Latham took another bite of ham and chewed it down before he answered. "Blackland Prairie's good for growing things. Especially cotton."

"Blackland? Because of that awful black mud?"

He chuckled. "Pretty much. But it's fertile ground. Hard on man and mule, but you have to take the hard with the pleasant in this life. We don't live in the Garden of Eden any longer."

The contrast struck me funny—the Garden of Eden compared to the Blackland Prairie. One lush and green and full. One flat and almost barren, and so far as I'd seen, almost colorless. Was that why Clara and Aunt Adabelle had cultivated such a profusion of flowers around the house? To bring a reminder of Eden?

"My family's been on this land since the War Between the States," Brother Latham said. "Frank here is a regular newcomer. Brought his bride, worked for the railroad, and then bought his land."

"Railroad?" My gaze landed on Frank. I'd heard nothing of this before. Frank pushed his empty plate away, his jaw tightening as Janie's wail wandered through the house.

He wiped his mouth and stood. "Thank you for another mighty fine meal, Irene, but we best be on our way."

Sheriff Jeffries leapt to his feet, too. "I can bring Rebekah home, if you don't mind."

Frank stopped. He glanced at me, then looked away. "I'm guessing you should ask her that question, not me."

Sheriff Jeffries put his hand on the back of my chair. "Rebekah?"

Irene folded her hands and propped them beneath her chin. My gaze searched hers, begging her to tell me what to do and not wanting her advice, all at the same time.

"Of course." I pushed away from the table and dabbed at the corners of my mouth. "But I'll help clean up first."

Irene waved her hand toward me, as if shooing off a fly. "Don't you bother about that. You go on."

So Frank, the children, the sheriff, and I made our way outside. I helped the children into the buggy with Frank, gave them instructions to hold Janie and to be good. Dandy trotted off, trying to drag my heart along behind him.

"May I drive again?" I asked as I watched them disappear down the road.

"I don't think that's a good idea." Sheriff Jeffries pulled at my arm, leading me toward the car.

"Why not?" I walked backward in front of him now, trying to read his face. "I'll be more careful this time. And besides, it's daylight."

He shook his head, opened the passenger-side door for me. "I don't like it. I'd rather you ride here."

I started to protest but climbed inside. When he got behind the wheel, I yelled over the engine's roar. "So do you prefer I don't drive, or women in general?"

He didn't answer, just steered us over the road, arms stiff, eyes straight ahead. I wanted to force him to look at me, talk to me. Instead, I folded my arms and stared out the window. Maybe this wasn't the man God meant for me, after all.

CHAPTER
32

James, I need your help." Authority oozed from Frank's voice the next afternoon, but James didn't budge.

"I want to stay with Bekah and Janie." He slumped his shoulders and stuck out his bottom lip.

"They don't need you in their way. Now, c'mon." The growl in Frank's voice grew deeper. James fled from the room. Frank started to follow, then stopped, hands on his hips, chest heaving.

His eyes didn't meet mine. He just took Dan by the hand and marched out the door. I smiled a bit. I couldn't help it. If he'd asked me, I could have persuaded James to join them. But he didn't. He didn't think I knew how to handle his children. At least not the way he wanted them handled. Yet I suspected that my way was more like his wife's or Aunt Adabelle's.

The look on James's face had told me what I felt was true. He, more than the others it seemed, deeply felt his mama's absence. And in some small way I had filled her place for him.

Janie sat on my hip as I climbed the stairs to find my little man. I'd show Frank I knew how to deal with the children.

"James?"

Head and shoulders jutted out from under the bed. I sat down on the floor, Janie in my lap. "You staying under there all day?"

"No." He scooted back a bit, leaving only his head exposed. "But I wanna stay here with you."

"You're such a good helper." I held his chin in my hand.

He inched forward.

"But your daddy needs a helper, too."

"He has Dan."

"Yes, he does. But Dan's still little. He can't do as much as a big six-year-old. Let me see how strong you are."

He slid from beneath the bed and hopped to his feet. He lifted a large trunk just a smidgen off the floor and let it drop again. Dust scattered into my eyes and nose.

"See what I mean? They need your help with the heavy work."

"But I could help you."

"That's true. But I could call for you when I needed your help."

His nose crinkled, and his head turned toward the window.

"It's such a sunshiny day. I wish I could do my work outside," I said, trying to push him over into the decision I wanted him to make.

"Well, okay. If you think you won't need me right away."

I stood up, Janie in my arms again. "We'll be fine. You run along and find your daddy and your brother."

He dashed away, his face split into a grin. I might not have spent much time around mothers and their children, studying their ways, recognizing their feelings, but I knew what would have motivated me. And it was exactly the opposite of what Mama and Frank would have done.

Satisfied, I let Janie walk the stairs in front of me, her hands above her head, her fingers secure in mine. As we tidied the house, little boy laughter carried through the open windows. James with his daddy, just where he needed to be. But what would happen

217

to my little man when I left him alone with Frank? Or worse yet, with a new mother?

I couldn't think about that. So I laid Janie in her crib and took the short walk to the mailbox. Inside, the newspaper—and a letter.

I cringed as Mama's handwriting met my gaze. I'd chosen not to write her of Frank's homecoming. Not yet. She'd insist I come home immediately. And right this minute, that was the last place I wanted to go. She still thought of me as a child to be shielded from life, even while considering me grown up enough to marry off to Barney Graves.

Bracing myself with a strong cup of coffee, I opened the letter, thankful that Mama remained a day's train ride away. Two pages of nothing, mostly. Until her usual cajoling for me to return home.

> *The boys are coming home from France daily now. When that man arrives, you just pack up and come on home. I expect Mr. Samson will visit soon enough. Someone else can take on those children now.*

As her words meandered through my head, sermons I'd heard during my growing-up years hailed down on me, words about giving a cup of cold water in Jesus' name, of suffering the little children to come to Him. I couldn't quite feel the rightness of Mama's directive, in spite of the fact that she'd offered an escape from Frank's enigmatic nature.

I curled my hands around my coffee cup, wishing I could see through the walls of the house to where the boys and their daddy worked. I imagined Frank's big hands taking his sons' smaller ones, teaching them, training them. I couldn't envision him barking orders or sitting idly by watching his sons struggle.

"Bekah! Bekah! Come quick! Dan fell out of the hayloft, and he's cryin' for you."

Coffee ran in a river across Mama's letter as my chair thumped to the floor. "Stay here and listen for Janie," I called to James as I ran out the door.

Please, Lord, not Dan. I raced through the barn door and dropped to my knees, hovering above the four-year-old's tear-streaked face. I pushed his hair away from his eyes.

"Hush, baby. Tell me where you hurt. Tell Bekah."

No words. Just sobs.

My gaze flew from one end of the barn to the other, frantic anger wrestling with fear. Where was Frank? Where was he?

I slid one arm beneath Dan's knees, the other beneath his neck and lifted him into my lap, his body pressed next to mine. He cried out. I loosened my grip.

"Frank!" My scream echoed through the cavernous building. "Frank!"

I tried to stand, but Dan's limp weight threw me off balance. "Frank!"

"What?" The barn door framed him as he barked the word.

"We have to help him." I stumbled to my feet this time, lurching toward the wild-eyed man.

"What do you think I've been doing? The buggy's hitched. I'm taking him to Doc."

I blinked into the sunlight. "But you left him all alone."

Frank held out his arms, his face paler than I remembered. "Give him to me so I can get him to town." Measured words through rigid lips.

He stalked away, Dan crying more loudly with the jostle of every step. I hurried behind them. "You can't drive and hold him at the same time."

Frank mashed his lips together as Dan screamed louder.

I scrambled into the buggy and reached for Dan. "Let's go."

"Someone has to stay with the others."

"Ollie will be home soon. They'll be fine. Now give him to me."

He laid his son in my arms and leapt onto the seat beside us.

"Stop at the house and we'll tell James."

Frank's jaw tensed, but he did as I suggested. Then he slapped the reins on Dandy's back and we took off toward town.

I refused to look at him as we traveled. Instead, I wiped Dan's face and whispered in his ear until his crying quieted. When we pulled up in front of Doc Risinger's house, I handed Dan to his father and watched them disappear inside.

My hands shook in my lap as I begged God to heal Dan—and to be with Frank, too. For when he'd taken Dan from my arms, the look of utter despair on the man's face had swept every strand of frustration from my body. I might doubt that he'd ever approve of me, but I could never question how much he loved his children.

We returned home hours later, my stomach in knots over the state of the other children and the house. The last thing I needed was an "I told you so" from Frank. I held my breath as we neared the yard. The buggy stopped. Dan's feet hit the ground with eagerness to display his latest badge of courage—a tight sling to keep his sprained arm still. Doc seemed to think he would be fine in no time.

I refused to wait for Frank to help me down from the buggy, although my steps weren't as energetic as Dan's. I lingered on the porch, listening to the children's banter from inside while Frank took the buggy to the barn to unhitch. Just as he strode into the yard, the screen door creaked open.

"Supper's ready." Ollie let the door slap shut again.

Frank sighed. "You were right. Ollie has everything under control."

"She's an amazing girl, really." I managed a weary smile as I read in his eyes the apology he didn't speak.

With the dishes finished and the children settled in bed, I eased down on the porch steps near the kitchen door. The aching tired of a crisis survived had seeped into my very bones. I leaned back on my elbows and looked into the evening sky. Had it been only a month since Arthur's visit? Two months since he'd shattered all my dreams?

Orange and pink melted into the darkening blue of twilight. What did a sunset look like from an airplane? Were the colors more intense or less noticeable? Maybe the whole thing could only be appreciated with your feet planted firmly on the ground.

Frank's footfalls sounded across the dirt, stopping just inside the house yard, a pail of milk in his hand. I shivered and started to rise.

"Don't get up," he said.

I sat back down. He set the milk pail on the porch.

"I've missed this." He eased down on the wide stair beneath me, hands folded, elbows resting on his knees. "Clara and I used to sit out here most nights, except the cold ones, after the babies were abed. Just sit and enjoy." His voice cracked on the last word.

I twirled my shoelace, not sure how he felt about me witnessing his grief. I squinted into the waning day and contemplated the rock-edged path that led to the barnyard and outbuildings.

The crickets chirped. A few chickens squawked before calming. Ol' Bob let out a plaintive moo. The pungent scent of manure wafted on the gentle breeze.

Frank shifted on the step, cleared his throat.

I made the effort of conversation. "Y'all certainly made a nice place here."

He took a deep breath and nodded. "It's all Clara and I ever dreamed of. Growing livestock and crops and children. Hard work, but honest. I can't imagine a better life than this one."

221

"But Brother Latham said something about railroad money." I bit my lip as I remembered the strain between us that day, dining with the Lathams.

He pulled a weed and stripped the leaves from its stalk as he spoke. "I hired on at the railroad shortly after we married. Found I caught on quick about how things worked, how best to build. And where." He shrugged. "It paid for this farm. We didn't want to buy it on credit."

My cheeks warmed. He hadn't yet mentioned the five dollars on account at Crenshaw's store. Did he know?

"It was why the army needed me," he said.

Needed him? He hadn't run off searching for adventure or wanting a reprieve from responsibility. He'd been asked to go. And in doing so, he'd missed a final good-bye to his wife. My throat tightened, imagining the agony of such a decision. "So what will you do now?"

"Keep on. God gives us dreams of what our lives will be, but He doesn't guarantee them. Just asks us to trust Him with the changes." Frank rose, extending his hand to help me to my feet, the lopsided grin on his face making him look no older than I. "Besides, I have you to help take care of things for a while."

My fingers rested against his calloused ones for only a moment, but tingles raced all the way to my toes. I ducked my head and hurried into the kitchen. On the table, I spied Mama's soggy letter.

No, she didn't need to know Frank had come home. Not yet.

CHAPTER
33

Wondered if you'd like a little company." Sheriff Jeffries stood in the kitchen doorway, his hat in its usual place—his hands. Interesting how he arrived just minutes after Frank left to help a neighbor repair some fencing.

I pushed back a strand of hair with my wrist, hoping the flour coating my hands didn't dust my face in the process. "I just put a pie in the oven. You're welcome to stay."

Sheriff Jeffries slid into a seat at the kitchen table, laying his hat on his knee. I turned to the wash bucket and plunged my hands into the tepid water. The part of me that desperately needed a friend thrilled to see the sheriff. But the part that pondered my future trembled. Did I dare do as Frank and trust God to work out the changes to my dreams?

I dried my hands on a towel and pushed away thoughts of city lights and evenings at the theater and purchasing my own automobile. I had enough to occupy the present. The pie would take the greater part of an hour to cook. After that, it would need to cool. And in the meantime, the sheriff and I could share some friendly conversation.

"So what brings you out our way today?" I counted scoops of coffee into the pot before resting it on the hot stove.

"Nothing special. Helped pull a touring car from a ditch. Someone from over in Terrell." He recounted the story, making me laugh. My spirit settled into comfortable as we talked of everyday things, neither of us mentioning the awkwardness of the past Sunday.

As I poured each of us another cup of coffee, the kitchen door swung wide.

"Smells good, Bekah." James plopped himself on the bench at the table, his little legs swinging, his chin resting in his upturned hands. Dan's actions mirrored his brother's.

I couldn't help but laugh. "Would you boys like a glass of milk?"

They both nodded. Then I heard Janie's babble from upstairs. When I returned with her, the sheriff sat chatting with the boys and Ollie, just home from school.

"Pie'll come out of the oven soon." I set Janie's feet on the floor, her hands banging on the bench seat. "We can all have a small piece now and still have some for after supper."

Dan threw a wary look my direction. "Even Janie? She's awful little."

We all looked at the baby. She moved her feet until her hands gripped the spindles that formed the back of the sheriff's chair. Two new teeth gleaming white in the midst of pink gums; she laughed as if she knew we spoke of her.

Then her fingers flew free of their grip. She tottered two steps and fell on her behind.

For a moment, no one said a word. Then Dan busted out laughing. "Janie walked."

Ollie squealed and ran to her little sister. "Janie! You walked!"

Pride swelled my chest as I joined the celebration around the baby.

"What's all the commotion?" Frank stood in the doorway, his face weary, his clothes dusty, but his eyes lit with our joy, even without knowing the source.

"Daddy! Janie walked! All by herself! Watch!" Ollie coaxed her sister into two more steps. I clapped my hands. Then I looked at Frank. The grief covering his face killed the laughter on my lips.

He walked from the room without a word.

By the time I pulled the custard pie from the oven, Frank had returned. But in spite of his efforts, I read the sorrow behind his eyes. The wishing that he could share the moment with Janie's mother, not me. Not Sheriff Jeffries.

"Any news from home lately?" The sheriff sat beside me now, his question drawing me away from the family commotion around the table.

"Not much." I ran my fork through my pie, lifted a bit to my mouth as I watched Frank interact with his children. "Mama seems on the mend. Will has gone off in his car to see the country."

Sheriff Jeffries nodded. He glanced at Frank before turning back to me. "So you aren't headed home anytime soon?"

"No." My stomach twisted. I set down my fork and pushed my plate to the side.

"You done with that, Bekah?" James asked. "'Cause I could finish it for you."

Frank looked at my plate. At me. At Sheriff Jeffries.

I avoided his eyes. "Share it with your brother. More coffee, anyone?" On my feet again, I smiled at both men and turned to get the coffeepot. I wanted to be sick, and I had no idea why. Instead, I played the perfect hostess, filling cups and chatting until finally the sheriff rose to leave.

We walked to his automobile, leaving the clatter of the kitchen far behind. Strings of clouds drifted near the horizon, like tufts of cotton ready to be spun into thread.

"May I come visit again? Saturday evening?" He glanced back toward the house.

"Visit? Us?"

"You, Rebekah. I want to visit *you*."

A Saturday night visit. My mouth felt dry as dust, and my heart pumped faster. Should I commit to more than friendship?

I couldn't let myself think too hard, so I stared straight into his face and answered. "That would be nice . . . Henry." Why did I feel like a traitor as I spoke his name? "I'll make another pie. Or a cake. Or something."

A grin stretched across his face as he slapped his hat on his head. "I'd like that."

He cranked the engine and waved as he climbed behind the wheel. I waved back. When he motored out of sight, I sighed and turned.

And ran smack-dab into Frank.

Hands on my arms, he steadied and dizzied me all at the same time. "Is he coming again?"

I nodded. "Saturday night." I hesitated. "Is that okay?" I couldn't look him in the face.

"If it's what you want." He nodded toward the retreating automobile, something wistful in his voice lifting my heart.

I raised my eyebrows, but my gaze skittered to the house behind me. Shy and uncertain, I longed for retreat, so I stepped around him. "I'll start supper. That is, if anyone's hungry."

⚜

That night, I lay in bed sorting through the photographs in my mind. Barney Graves. Arthur. Sheriff Jeffries. Frank. The children. I spun out stories of the way things might go, but each ending soured with an unsettling regret, almost as if I'd baked a perfect cobbler but forgotten to sweeten the filling.

I pulled the covers over my shoulder and faced the wall. Mama would say to take the sure thing—but was anything in life a sure thing? Irene would say be careful not to overlook what appeared to be the less exciting choice. Yet right now, every path open to me appeared tainted with the mundane.

I wiggled onto my other side, facing the dark room. *What, Lord? What do You want me to do?*

Silence, as usual. No direction. Not a niggling thought. Not a feeling. I could simply go ahead and make my own choice, but thus far my choices hadn't exactly worked out. I imagined again Arthur's golden hair lifted by a breeze, the hurtful words of his engagement spilling from his lips. Why, in spite of it all, did the thought of him still thrill my heart?

I tossed back the covers and shivered in the cold night. I hadn't thrown out the last of the coffee. Maybe a cup would distract my thoughts. My socked feet muted my footsteps as I groped my way to the parlor and threw a quilt around my shoulders, holding it closed in front. Then I padded my way to the kitchen. I found the lamp, but my fingers resisted striking the match. A sliver of moon shone through the window. It would be enough.

A new piece of wood and a fraction of rearranging brought a flame to life in the stove. I reached into the cooler to pull out the last piece of pie, larger than I would normally eat, but comforting all the same.

Pie plate and fork resting in the center of the table, I touched the coffeepot. Almost ready. The door behind me creaked. I whipped around, my hand pressed against my hammering heart.

"I guess we had the same idea." Frank's voice loomed from the shadowed doorway.

"I guess we did." I pulled the quilt closer to my body, thinking I ought to leave yet wanting to stay. "C'mon in. Coffee's almost ready."

I heard Frank step inside. He sat in the chair at the opposite end of the table.

"You willing to share?" He nudged the pie plate in my direction.

"Split it down the middle. There's plenty for both of us." I pushed it toward him, heard the scrape of metal against metal before the plate slid back in my direction. I could make out the glint of the fork resting against its side. Then the smell and steam of coffee curled around my nose, and I realized a cup sat in front of me.

"Thank you." My fork slid through the creamy custard. A sip of coffee melted the sweetness in my mouth before mingling it down my throat.

"I'm sorry. About earlier."

I took another bite. Another sip. "You've nothing to be sorry for." Yet I wondered what he meant. Three quick bites and my pie disappeared, my fork clattering into the empty pan.

"It's not any of my business what you do with your life."

"No, it isn't." I wrapped one hand around my warm cup and lifted it to my lips.

"But do you mind if I ask what you intend to do with it?"

Uncertainty colored his voice. Was he afraid to hear my answer or afraid he couldn't restrain comment on it? I cleared my throat, uncomfortable now, even with the cover of night over our faces. Yet something in me needed to talk. And Frank might understand. He'd lost his love, even if part of his dream remained intact.

"I'm not sure, exactly. I thought God had made it very plain. Now I don't know."

Quiet filled the room. Then his chair creaked.

I took a deep breath. "I've lived on a farm my whole life. But I've always wanted to live somewhere else. Somewhere big, with lots going on. My brother, Will, he got to see the world, to do something important. Like you did. I want the same opportunity."

More silence.

"The world is changing so fast. I don't want to miss it."

His boots shuffled against the floor. "I can see how you'd feel that way. But I guess it depends on how you define 'important.'"

I shrugged. "Same as everyone, I guess. Something big. Something lasting."

His shadow leaned against the Wilson cabinet now. "I think tending my farm and raising my children are the most worthwhile things I can do. So did Clara. That's why we agreed I should go to France. To make the world a safer place for them."

My insides jiggled. Perhaps a late-night snack hadn't been such a good idea. I pushed back my chair. "I'd better get some sleep. The children will be up early."

"I'll be praying for you, Rebekah." His voice rumbled from nearby. I could feel the heat from his body, smell the scent of fresh hay on his clothes. He took the dishes from my hand. "I'll clean up."

I nodded, even though I doubted he could see my response. Then I fled up the stairs and dove into bed, pulling the quilts over my head. Daylight couldn't come soon enough.

CHAPTER
34

*M*ama's account of Will's death arrived the Monday after the sheriff's and my awkward Saturday night visit in Frank's parlor. After a quiet Sunday with Frank and the children.

Tears streamed down my cheeks as I read the letter. Not that Mama had any real details to relay. He'd died as he wanted—in the midst of living. His friend had written that a woman in the Montana town they'd been visiting nursed him as his strength waned. They'd buried him at the foot of a mountain, near a stream.

Will, who had left Downington and seen the world. At least seen more of it than I had. Would I trade his short life of experience for a long one of familiarity? Just a few months ago, I'd have said yes. Now I wasn't so sure.

"What's wrong?" Irene stood in front of me, her voice full of sympathy.

I lifted the corner of my apron to dry my face. "It's Will. He's . . . gone."

"Oh, honey." Irene led me to the sofa and pulled my head to her shoulder. "You go on and cry now. It'll do you good to grieve."

Her words broke something inside me, like an overfull barrel busting out its bands. Tears flowed. Chest heaved. Head and eyes ached. But I couldn't stop crying. She left me for a little while. I curled on the sofa and sobbed alone.

Shoes scraped into the room and left again. I smelled Janie's freshly washed hair as she laid her cheek next to mine. Held her until she wriggled free.

"It's hard to say good-bye." Irene handed me a warm cup of tea, its sweetness teasing my nose. "I do know how you feel. Remember?"

Her sad smile hurt so much I had to look away. But I did remember. Her sister. Tuberculosis. I reached for Irene's hand and gripped it tight. "Thank you."

"I'll be praying for you, Rebekah—and your mama and daddy. But I just ran in for a minute. I have to get home. Do you want me to send Nola Jean to help take care of things?"

I shook my head. "I'm fine. It'll just take some getting used to, that's all."

Irene glanced toward the barnyard. "Remember, it's taking him some getting used to, as well."

I took a deep breath, my eyes meeting hers. "He loved his wife."

She laid a hand on my damp cheek, then sighed and moved away. "It was hard on him, watching her suffer."

"So he went away."

"Not like you think. He went because he was needed, even knowing it could likely leave his children orphaned. But that man trusts God more deeply than most. And he knew he had to go."

Her words echoed the ones he'd spoken to me on the same subject. And I remembered his first letter to me, about God knowing best, even in light of all the death in his life, in his children's lives. His faith shamed me.

Irene took her leave but turned back halfway down the walk. "You know I'm here, if you need me."

I nodded, thankful, again, that the Lord had sent me such a friend.

Not an hour later, Ollie raced into the kitchen, threw her arms around my waist, and squeezed tight. Then she looked up at me, eyes swimming with tears. "Daddy told me," she said. "I'll miss Will, too, Rebekah."

My breath caught. Frank told her? Should he have done that? Hadn't she experienced enough sorrow without having to shoulder mine, too?

"Irene found me on her way home." Frank leaned against the doorjamb, blocking the afternoon sun. "I'm so sorry." The lines in his face looked deeper now, as if he'd aged six years in sixty minutes. Yet another reminder of his own grief. Emotion flickered across his face too quickly for me to decipher.

"Thank you." I didn't know what else to say.

"I can do that, if you want me to." He nodded toward supper warming on the range, his gaze steady on my face. My stomach somersaulted, and my cheeks warmed.

"Rebekah." Sheriff Jeffries broke the spell. He crossed the room and took my hands in his. "I'm so sorry about Will." A quick glance to Frank. "Why don't you come for a drive? It'll do you good."

Frank wouldn't meet my eyes now. He simply took my place by the stove. "Go on."

I pulled the apron from over my dress, smoothed back my hair. But something in me didn't want to leave Frank behind. Not now.

Yet Henry Jeffries's eyes implored me. And it didn't feel right to decline. I bit my lip, looking back at Frank one last time, wanting him to read the "I'm sorry" in my eyes. But he didn't turn from his task.

He'd thought my being here would help him, but maybe I just brought more pain into his life.

Two days later, the *ah-ooga* of a car horn hit my ears long before a topless automobile came into sight. I ran to the fence, eager for normal conversation.

Frank and I had avoided each other since I'd learned of Will's death, each cocooned in our own grief. Janie toddled after me, finally grabbing at my skirt to steady her new steps.

Mr. Culpepper pulled back his goggles and grinned. "Decided to give my horse a rest. What do you think?"

I ran my hand along the edge of the door. "I think it's fine, Mr. Culpepper. Your mail route won't take half the time now, will it?"

His belly shook with laughter. "Don't know about that, but it sure makes for a fun ride." He reached into the pocket of his jacket. "Telegram for you, Miss Rebekah."

Excitement leaked away as my hands covered my churning stomach. My tongue passed over my lips as I tried to reach for the envelope. Finally my fingers obeyed.

"Thank you, Mr. Culpepper." Our eyes met. His turned away first.

"Howdy-do, Frank," he called over me. "Bring those little ones over here to see my new toy."

Frank's gaze met mine, compassion spilling from the deep blue depths. I blew out a big breath and stumbled around to the back side of a pecan tree. With its trunk for support, I slit open the envelope and pulled out the sheet of paper.

Mama misses you. We arrive tomorrow. Daddy.

I breathed a prayer of thanks. Mama was all right. Then Daddy's words hit me. They would be here tomorrow! I pushed away from the sturdy tree and stumbled forward.

A hand caught my elbow. I cried out and looked up. Concern wrinkled Frank's face, clear as the ticker tape on my telegram.

"What's wrong?" His forehead creased as his eyebrows drew together.

"It's Mama." I croaked the words like an old bullfrog.

His face crunched into deeper solicitude.

I sucked in a deep breath of thick, cold air and blew it out again, long and slow. "She and Daddy arrive tomorrow."

"Your parents are coming?"

"That's what it says." I read the telegram again. "Mama misses me, I guess."

"Did you ask them to come?" He said it like an accusation.

"No." And yet, why shouldn't I have? We'd just lost my brother. Would it have been so terrible of me to ask them to visit?

Frank paced in front of me, murmuring, raking his hands through his hair. "It's just . . . It feels a bit . . . awkward. I mean, the two of us, here, and . . ." He shrugged.

I shoved my fists on my hips. "That hasn't seemed to bother you until now. Besides, it isn't as if either of us have any intentions toward the other." Even if his touch did ignite a lightning bolt inside me.

"No, no intentions." He stood still now, not even a twitch of movement. "I just didn't want them to misconstrue our current arrangement."

"Are you suggesting they're coming to pressure you into marrying me?" I snorted out a laugh. "Don't worry. I have very different plans for my life."

"Yes. You've made that very clear." He towered over me, our eyes locked in silent battle.

If only we were fighting on the same side.

"But I don't wanna go to bed, Bekah." The whine in Dan's voice brought a pucker to my lips, as if I'd sipped lemonade with no sugar.

Frank and James hadn't returned from milking Ol' Bob yet. Ollie stood in the kitchen drying dishes. Janie already slept peacefully in her crib upstairs.

"Let's go, little man."

"I'm not your little man. And you can't make me." His eyebrows scrunched down over his eyes, and his fingers curled into fists.

"Oh yes, I can." I lifted him off the floor, his feet kicking out behind me.

"What are you doing to him?" Ollie blocked my way out of the kitchen.

"I'm taking him to bed."

Her eyes narrowed. "You're not his mother, you know."

How many times had I said those words to her over the past few weeks? And she dared throw them back at me now?

"Neither are you." I set Dan on the ground but kept his hand imprisoned in mine.

Ollie's eyes flashed. "When are you goin' home, Rebekah?"

"Ollie Elizabeth!" Frank stood at the kitchen door, James at his side.

Ollie's face paled. "But, Daddy, she—"

"Get on up to bed. We'll talk about this in the morning."

Ollie darted from the room, dragging Dan with her. James tugged at my hand. I knelt down in front of him.

"You're not going anywhere, are you?" His bottom lip trembled.

"No." I ran my hand through his blond curls. "I won't leave you, sweet boy. I promise."

He lurched into my arms, nearly knocking me to the ground. Tears gruffed my voice as I whispered, "Let's get you tucked in, too."

His head nodded against my shoulder. I carried him from the room without so much as a glance at his daddy. My heart couldn't bear to know whose side Frank had taken—Ollie's or James's.

CHAPTER
35

"Will your mama like me?" James distracted me for the hundredth time.

While I swept the floor, I assured him, again, that she would, although my heart fluttered in my chest every time I said it. Who knew what Mama would think? My stomach roiled, and my breath heaved. And so I worked harder.

By late afternoon, I paced the front walk, twisting my good lace handkerchief beyond recognition. Frank remained in the fields, well beyond my sight. "Bedding up" for planting, he'd told me. And already more than a month behind.

What would Mama say when she saw him here? And what would Frank say when he realized I hadn't told my parents he'd come home? I ripped my thoughts from that conundrum and focused again on the children. If only the boys would stay clean until Mama arrived. She needed to see them at their best, right off.

The *chug-a-lug* of a car drifted on the breeze. I leaned over the fence. Dan held open the small gate with his body. Ollie slipped her hand into mine as James whispered, "They're here. They're here."

The same excited terror that tremored his voice accelerated my heart. I drank in fresh air and pasted a smile on my face. I had no idea what Mama would look like after her debilitating bout with the Spanish flu, but I prepared myself for the worst.

Mr. Culpepper had hardly stopped the automobile when Daddy jumped out. He reached for Mama's hand. She set a tentative foot on the brown grass at the edge of the road.

Mama. Paler. Thinner. Softer, somehow. What had done that to her—the influenza or losing her firstborn?

She opened her arms, and I ran into them, our tears mingling on pressed-together cheeks. Then she held me away from her. "Let me look at my baby."

I wore a real smile now, pulling back my shoulders so I wouldn't be scolded to stand up straight.

"You look fine." She cocked her head to the right. "More grown up, I think." She sighed and looked away.

Daddy stood on the porch, an old valise hanging from his hand. "The air's cooling off fast. Let's get her inside."

James tugged on Mama's sleeve. Her eyebrows raised in a look I knew meant disapproval. James crooked his arm like a gentleman, ready to escort her up the walk. I held my breath. Mama's expression didn't change right away, but then her censure melted. With a prim smile, she wrapped her hand around James's small elbow. I closed my eyes and breathed a quick prayer of relief.

One down, three to go.

Daddy kissed my cheek as I walked past.

Mama stepped through the door behind me. "What a charming little house."

Little house? I wanted to laugh. This house wasn't any smaller than ours in Downington. But I let the comment pass.

"And now, Rebekah, why don't you introduce me to the welcoming party?"

I placed my hand on James's head. "You've met James."

Mama tilted her head in acknowledgement.

"This is Dan." I nudged him forward.

"I'm four." He held up five fingers, then folded down his thumb with his opposite hand.

Ollie fidgeted, her hands on Janie's shoulders in front of her. I laid my hand on Ollie's head. "This is Ollie Elizabeth. And little Janie."

"Beautiful girls." Mama's words sounded strangled and stilted, and the look on her face, now the color of ash, made my stomach tumble. She put her hand on Daddy's arm.

"You've had a long day, Mama. Do you want to rest before supper?"

Mama waved her hand. "Of course we'll eat your good supper. We're about starved. You can't eat a bite while the train's moving all around like that."

Daddy grimaced. He looked older than I remembered. And thinner.

"James, take the suitcases to your mama's bedroom. Ollie, help me put dinner on the table. Dan, take care of Janie."

I looked to see if Mama approved of how I handled the children, but she didn't seem to notice. Instead, she fussed with her handbag and frowned.

Oh well. She was tired. Besides, I didn't need her to tell me I'd done well. I knew I had. In the kitchen, I opened the oven door, intensifying the sweet smell of the sugar-crusted ham. Potatoes sat soft in the water, ready to be beaten and buttered and salt 'n' peppered. The biscuits went into the oven as soon as I removed the ham.

"Rebekah?" Mama's voice nearby.

Then the click of the kitchen door.

238

I whipped around. Mama and Frank stared at each other, red rising in both of their faces.

"Who's this?" Mama's voice, barely more than a whisper.

Frank's features turned hard, as if carved from stone. "Frank Gresham." He glanced at me, then back to Mama. "I assume you are Mrs. Hendricks?"

Mama turned fiery eyes in my direction. "I see you know who I am, but I haven't been given the same consideration."

I backed away, not wanting to be caught in the middle of the twister I'd created.

"Ahhhhh!" Hot metal seared my skin. I grabbed my hand, doubled over. Mama and Frank beside me, one voice in each ear, pain blinding my sight.

"Margaret? Rebekah?" Daddy.

I felt Mama and Frank move back. Daddy led me to the table as my scream drifted away.

"We'll need eggs and some clean cotton." Mama taking charge, as usual.

"I have butter and flour right here." Frank.

"We aren't making a cake; we're dressing a burn."

"I realize that. Butter, then flour. My mother swore by it."

"It really hurts." I leaned my head into Daddy's shoulder.

"I know, baby. Let me see." He eased open my hand and studied the raised red splotch on my palm.

Frank arrived at the table first. He cradled my hand in his. I whimpered.

"Hush now." A gentle whisper.

"Let me do that." Mama pressed her fingers into the pristine "G" atop the newly pressed butter and lathered it on my skin.

"Go on now. Let me do my work." Mama scooted beside me. Daddy led Frank from the room as Mama wrapped a clean rag around my greasy hand and tied the ends together.

"Thank you, Mama." I reached up and kissed her cheek.

Moments later, Daddy was there, leading her away. "Let's rest awhile, Margaret." He looked back at me. "Supper will wait."

I nodded. Then Frank stood over me, his eyes more gray than blue.

"I'm sorry." I fiddled with the end of the bandage.

His face crumpled in confusion. "Why? You didn't mean to burn yourself."

"No." I smoothed the folds of the rag around my hand. "Not that. I'm sorry I didn't tell Mama you were home."

"You what?" His voice rose but then fell, as if he remembered the need for quiet.

"Mama didn't know you'd come home." My teeth held my bottom lip as I watched him jump up and cross the room, his hands combing through his hair before resting atop his head.

He blew out a long breath, his gaze pinning me still. "And just when were you going to inform her of my presence—in my own house, I might add?"

"I hadn't quite figured that out yet. But she knows now." On my feet, I swayed a bit. He reached my side in an instant, that little-boy look softening his face.

I pressed my lips together, holding in the sudden urge to laugh. "I imagine we need to get supper finished."

He shook his head and led me to the stove. As hard as he tried to hide it, I spied the corners of his mouth fighting to hold a frown.

　　　　　　　　　　✦❦✦

While Daddy blessed the food, I prayed in my head, asking God to help me be patient with Mama—and she with me. Then voices quieted while dishes clinked and clanked. I filled and re-filled glasses with water and milk and coffee.

A while later, Daddy sat back and patted his stomach. "That

was what I call larrupin' good, baby girl." Daddy's Texas roots always came out that way after a meal he enjoyed.

I glanced at Frank. Had he thought I'd done well, too? I couldn't read his expression.

Mama dabbed her napkin at the corners of her mouth. I noticed she'd only picked at the food on her plate, and yet she'd claimed she hadn't eaten much on the journey. I tried to catch Daddy's eye, to ask him my silent question, but he didn't—or wouldn't—look my way.

"Shouldn't these children be running off to bed?" Mama said.

Frank's fingers tightened around his fork, and his chest puffed out.

"I think they can stay up awhile longer, Mama." I kept my tone light. "The sun's hardly gone to bed itself. And anyway, this is a special occasion."

Mama's eyebrows rose, first at Frank, then at me. I pretended not to notice and hoped Frank would do the same.

"James and Ollie, scrape the plates into the slop barrel." I said it low, hoping to avoid Mama's ears.

But very little escaped Mama, even in her somewhat altered state. "You mean to let these children handle this fine china by themselves?"

Their mama's china, I wanted to answer back. Something they held near sacred. But I swallowed down my temper. "They'll be careful." I turned to them. "Won't you?"

They nodded back, all eyes.

"Mama, why don't you let Daddy take you to the parlor? We'll get some of this put away and join you in a few minutes. Won't we, Frank?"

Never before had I suggested a course of action to Mama. She always did the "suggesting." I held my breath, waiting to see what she would do. And if Frank would respond.

Daddy didn't give Mama a chance to react. He took her arm and led her from the room.

Frank picked up two plates. "You managed that nicely."

"Thank you." I picked up a half-full pitcher of milk with my uninjured hand.

He cleared his throat. "Your mother is a bit . . ."

"Overbearing?" I carried the milk into the kitchen, set it in the cooler.

He followed behind. "You'll have to let me in on your secret if we're all to survive her visit."

"Survive whose visit?" James piped up.

Frank looked like he'd been caught eating dessert before dinner. "You and Ollie bring the rest of the dishes."

The two of them scampered from the room.

I burst out laughing and covered my mouth with my unbound hand.

Frank looked stricken. Then he grinned and handed me a dish towel. "I'll wash. You dry. We'll get this cleaned up in no time."

We fell to work, side by side. And it felt so right.

CHAPTER
36

*N*ever in my life had I imagined one person could cause so much disruption to a household. Whatever the influenza had done to weaken Mama's body, it hadn't affected her tongue.

"You should let down Ollie's dress. It's too short."

Janie whined at my skirt. I lifted her into my arms.

"You're spoiling that child. Let her cry. She's big enough to know better."

She's not even a year old, Mama. And her mama's dead. I think I can hold her when she cries. I shouted the words in my head. And even though Mama couldn't hear, it felt good to answer back.

I put on the sweetest smile I could muster. Janie watched my face and did the same. "Why don't you stay out here on the porch and enjoy this nice morning, Mama?"

Mama pulled her shawl closer around her shoulders. "It's too cold out here. We'd best get inside."

I wanted to walk around to the back door, to enjoy just a few minutes away from her. But one look at the front steps and I knew she'd have trouble with them on her own. I reached her side in a few strides, steadying her as she lifted her foot to the first riser.

243

"I can do it," she snapped.

I pulled my hand away but didn't leave. She teetered just a bit. Then she clutched at my arm before taking the next step up. Without a word, she shuffled across the porch, into the hall, and past the parlor. Letting go of my arm, she entered the bedroom and closed the door behind her.

No thanks. No apology.

At least the boys and men got to leave the house.

I bounced Janie on my hip. "Let's find Daddy. I'll bet he's down with Ol' Bob." Janie didn't care if I meant her daddy or mine.

The barn smelled of horse and mules and manure. Dust twirled in the weak streams of winter sunshine slithering through the cracks between the wall planks. My heart jumped and twirled as well, but settled fast when Frank didn't appear. Had he needed to go farther than the barn for some peace?

Daddy stood up from beneath Ol' Bob. His arms stretched toward the roof of the barn as his back curved into a long arch.

"Thank you, Daddy." I kissed him on the cheek. He grunted in reply and patted Ol' Bob's rump before he shut the stall and handed me the bucket of warm milk. But I wasn't ready to return to the house yet. I leaned against the barn door, watching Daddy work. He drew the boys into each task. Janie, too. His big finger tickled her beneath her chin and brushed one of her golden curls from her chubby face.

"Daddy?" I put the milk pail on a nearby stool.

He faced me, more pain in his eyes than I'd ever seen there before.

"Tell me what's really wrong, Daddy."

His jaw clenched, visible even in the half-light. Over the course of my life, I'd never had an intimate conversation with my father. But I'd always felt closer to him than to Mama. Maybe I didn't feel the need to try so hard to please him. I wasn't sure. All I knew was that I needed him to talk to me now.

244

He slipped his hands into his pockets. "It's been difficult for your mother, you know. It hurt her for your brother to go off like that. She wanted to be with him at the end, as hard as it would have been. You know she hasn't been strong since . . . October." He glanced in the direction of the children, but they paid us no mind, running and shrieking from corner to corner.

"Losing her sister was grievous for her, too."

I hadn't expected him to say that. I slipped my thumbnail between my teeth and clamped down until it snapped. I brushed it away and picked up one of the barn cats, a striped one, and stroked until it purred. Mama wouldn't even come help her sister, so how could her death have brought grief? "But Mama never even talked to her. Or at least, not for a long time."

Daddy rubbed the back of his neck. "When Adabelle left Downington, your mama hurt real bad. She didn't know much about the man her little sister married, and she'd felt responsible for her after their father left."

Janie toddled toward the barn door, squealing with delight. I captured her, swung her up into the air. She giggled in my arms. I smacked a kiss on her lips and directed her tottering steps toward the back wall instead.

"What do you mean? I never heard anything about her daddy leaving."

"No, you wouldn't have." He picked up a rake and started to spread fresh hay in Dandy's empty stall. Frank must have taken the horse out. "His leaving shamed her. Adabelle running away with a stranger did the same thing. Then we got news her husband had died. And Adabelle went to work caring for other people's houses, other people's families, instead of coming home to her own."

His hands rested one on top of the other as he leaned into the rake handle. "Your mama's a good woman, Rebekah, but a proud one. She doesn't like to show when she's hurt." His eyes found mine. "It might look like anger, but it's really hurt."

He resumed his work. "Now her boy's gone, too."

I put my hand on his arm. "But he was your boy, too. Are you saying it doesn't feel the same to you?"

The agony that colored his smile pierced my heart like a needle through silk.

"You raise your kids how you see fit and hope for the best. But you can't know what's going to happen. And you can't change it when it does. It's painful, but life goes on."

It was the most I'd heard my daddy say at one time. I chewed on his words, understanding them far better now than I would have before. Poor Mama. She didn't like having those she loved grow up and make their own decisions, live their own lives.

Even Will, who'd done almost everything she wanted him to, disappointed her in the end. Maybe I could be more patient with her, now that I understood.

"Want milk in your tea, Mama?"

She'd told me long ago it was how the English took their tea. I don't know how she knew, but she let me drink it that way when I was just a girl, when Santa Claus brought me a tea set for Christmas—a real china pot with matching cups and saucers, but tiny. Mama sat with me that afternoon, her hands trading work for play. I hoped my words would spark some remembrance of that time.

"Are you making cornbread again?"

Yesterday's resolve to be patient wilted like a morning glory in afternoon heat. I set the cup of tea in front of her and glanced at the almost flat sack of flour in the corner, next to the fat sack filled with cornmeal. "Yes, ma'am, I am."

"The batch this morning was too dry. Add more milk this time."

I slammed a pot onto the range top and waited for her to scold. But she didn't.

246

"Is that an automobile I hear?" She hurried to the window, as if the car held her dearest friend.

Over her head I could see a cloud of dust surrounding a familiar Model T. I waited for my heart to leap into my throat. Instead, my stomach dropped to the floor. Would Mama latch on to him or freeze him with her silent stare? Either prospect rattled me.

I blew out a long breath. "It's Sheriff Jeffries."

"The sheriff!" Horror colored her words. "What's he doing here?"

I dusted off my hands, removed my apron. "He's a friend, that's all."

She whirled around, eyes narrowed. "That man's friend, or yours?"

Before I could answer, the sheriff stood in the doorway, hat twirling in his hands.

"Rebekah."

Mama's lips twisted into the kind of encouragement I'd come to dread.

"Sheriff Jeffries." I cringed at the disappointment on his face. After all, just last week I'd called him Henry. "Please meet my mama, Margaret Hendricks."

"How do you do, Mrs. Hendricks?" His hat whirled faster. I grabbed it and set it on the table.

His hands fumbled for some other occupation. "I'm sorry for your loss, Mrs. Hendricks. Y'all have been in our prayers."

Mama's lips flattened. I noticed tight lines at their edges. I'd been waiting for her to mention Will, but she hadn't. I guessed she didn't want to discuss her grief. Either that or Frank's presence had distracted her from it.

"What brings you by today, Sheriff?" I prayed he'd say business of some kind.

A flush crept up his neck. "I came to see if you wanted to go for a drive, Rebekah." His gaze skittered to Mama now, as if seeking her approval.

Her face brightened. "Dinner's almost ready, Sheriff. Why don't you stay and eat? After dinner, we'd love to take a drive."

I wanted to sink through the floor. "Yes, please stay."

Dinner and the drive took ages. Or at least it seemed ages. The sun was on its way down when the sheriff left Mama and me back at the front gate.

"Thank you for dinner, ma'am." He tipped his hat to Mama, even though I was the one who had prepared the meal. Then his hungry eyes swept over me before he cranked the engine once more.

"We'll look forward to seeing you at church, Sheriff." Mama raised her arm to wave.

I stepped back to avoid the dust. Poor Henry. He didn't deserve to be a rope tugged at both ends by Mama and me. As we walked back to the house, I wondered again if he was the man God had planned for me. Mama liked Sheriff Jeffries, even if she didn't yet know that his dreams would carry us even farther from her than Prater's Junction.

And Henry was a sight more interesting than old Barney Graves. But could I sacrifice my own happiness for Mama's? Was that the kind of faith God wanted me to have?

I glanced at Mama. She frowned at James careening into our path, jabbering like a magpie.

"Did ya see me, Bekah? Daddy said I run faster than the Kaiser from Uncle Sam!"

Frank followed close behind, arms filled with his smallest son and daughter, Ollie trotting alongside. My heart surged like a horse in full gallop, and I could find no desire to rein it in.

CHAPTER
37

*M*ama sat rigid in the front seat of the buggy long before Frank and I managed to get the children readied for church and out the door. Daddy sat behind Dandy with a grim smile. His eyes met Frank's in what seemed to be a hesitant handshake. Some sort of agreement not spoken aloud.

I climbed up beside Mama. Frank set Janie in my lap before squeezing in the back with the rest of his children, as if he were a child himself instead of the owner of the conveyance and the master of all he surveyed. He'd put himself in the lower place to avoid unleashing Mama's tongue. Not many men would do so.

Mama's presence on our journey hushed even the smallest voices. I don't think even a bird dared chirp as we passed. And as the buggy wheels devoured each inch of road, another part of me tightened.

The people of Prater's Junction had become my friends. Would Mama turn up her nose at them or would she cultivate their good graces and push me more firmly toward the sheriff's arms? I lifted my thumbnail to my mouth. Mama gently pushed my hand back down.

"I hope your preacher isn't in the habit of spinning long sermons, Mr. Gresham," she said.

Silence answered.

"No, Mama. Brother Latham is always very timely. Not too short. Not too long."

I chewed my bottom lip, hoping my answer would stifle her comments.

"Such a nice man, that sheriff. He's a man a girl could depend on. Don't you agree, Mr. Gresham?"

Help me, Lord. Help me, Lord. I bit the inside of my cheek to keep from screaming. I waited for Frank to say something. Anything.

Mama turned her head. "Don't you agree, Mr.—"

"Look, Mama, there's a redbird."

"Where?" She whipped around like a distracted child.

I breathed out relief as I pointed out the church steeple instead.

I sat between Mama and Daddy in the pew, the children between Daddy and Frank. After the service, I didn't give Mama any choice about being sociable. I took her arm and introduced her to Doc Risinger and Mr. and Mrs. Crenshaw and the Culpepper clan. Each one greeted her not only with kindness but gave her a memory of their time with her sister. Did she realize that Adabelle hadn't, apparently, made their estrangement a topic of conversation amongst her neighbors and friends?

As Daddy took Mama's hand and led her to the buggy, Frank sidled up beside me, sending my heart into a sprint. "I asked the Lathams to dinner. Will we have enough to feed everyone?"

I sighed. "I expect, but I wish you'd have told me sooner."

"I know. I'm sorry. I just couldn't stand another meal . . . I mean, I know she's your mother, but—"

I laid my hand on his arm. "You don't have to explain—or apologize."

He nodded once, his eyes raking over the field of headstones.

Mama hadn't even asked to visit her sister's grave.

⚜

Three chickens, fried crisp. A heaping pot of potatoes, mashed, with butter and salt. Cornbread. And green beans cooked with bacon. Even Mama couldn't find anything to complain about. And because of that, conversation flew amiable and free around the dining room table.

Bellies full, the men sauntered off to the barn.

"Mrs. Hendricks, why don't you rest a bit? It's been a full day, I know." Irene led Mama to the parlor while I washed dishes.

"How are you?" she whispered on her return.

I almost answered "fine," as if reciting a school lesson by rote. But the look on Irene's face told me she knew things I hadn't yet spoken.

"It's all right, honey. I know some about your mother. Your aunt and I were friends, remember? And I had a mother, too." Her eyes twinkled as if she'd read every thought in my head since Mama stepped into this house.

"Some hours are better than others." I dunked a soapy plate beneath the rinse water.

Irene laughed in her usual way. I handed her a dripping plate.

"And what about Frank? How's he doing with all this?" She stacked the dried plate on the table with the others.

I plunged my hands beneath the warm water, seeking another dish to scrub. "As good as can be expected, I suppose."

She sighed as she wiped another dish and set it aside. "Will you go with your parents when they leave?"

My knees threatened to give way. I grabbed the edge of the dish tub. "I can't go home with them, Irene. I just can't."

251

She smiled at me, a weary smile. "Sometimes the Lord asks us to do hard things."

My back stiffened, strength surging back into my legs. "He can't ask me to go home again. He brought me here. I know it." My gaze faltered from her face. "I have to stay. For a while longer, at least."

She lifted the stack of clean dishes. "I'm praying for you, Rebekah. Don't ever forget that."

I dried my hands as Irene disappeared into the dining room. Maybe God would hear her prayers. I certainly didn't feel as if He heard mine.

Just before noon the next day, Frank rode back into the yard. I followed him around to the corral, pulled like kerosene up a dry wick. He swung down, set Dandy loose in the pen. My eyes lit on his, but something dark answered back. I bit my lip and looked away.

"Rebekah?"

"Yes?" I turned back. Too eager?

He led me away from the barn. "I went to town this afternoon."

I held my breath, his face hovering only inches above mine.

"Mr. Crenshaw said you bought the children Christmas presents. On account."

I nodded, afraid to look into his eyes lest their blue turn stormy gray.

He settled his hands on his hips, exasperated-like. "Why in the world didn't you just pay cash?"

I picked at a crust of teacake on the skirt of my dress. "Because there wasn't any to pay with. No cash in your letters. None in the house. None in the bank." I raised my eyes to his, not caring what I'd see. "What would you have had me do? Let them think Santa Claus forgot them?"

Of course there was the two dollars wasted in Dallas, but irritation hid my embarrassment. Daddy would repay Frank his precious money if I asked him to. I glared up at him, expecting wrath. But something new crossed his face. Surprise? Admiration?

His laugh started low and worked itself into a regular guffaw. Heat crawled up my face as he shook his head and wiped his eyes. "I heard about your visit to the bank. You certainly have gumption."

"Is that . . . a good thing?"

He blinked surprise. Then a smile started on his lips and ended in his eyes. "Why, yes, I guess it is."

I couldn't hold back my grin, so I studied the ground.

"Don't worry." He laid a hand on my shoulder. I didn't move away. "I covered it all with Mr. Crenshaw today. I guess Adabelle didn't tell you about the tin box under the floorboard in the bedroom."

Relief washed over me. Money had been there all along.

Dan suddenly tugged at my hand. "C'mon, Bekah. Daddy and Uncle Lloyd are takin' us fishing. Right, Daddy?"

"Uncle Lloyd?" I looked at Frank.

He shrugged. "Your father suggested it."

"You comin' with us, Bekah?" Dan pressed his hands together, as if in prayer. "Please?"

"Please, Rebekah?" Frank seemed as anxious as his son for my answer.

Elation coursed through me, almost raising my feet from the ground. I opened my mouth to say yes.

"Rebekah?" Mama's voice pulled my attention toward the house. "Rebekah Grace, where have you gotten to?"

When my gaze returned to Frank, his sunny expression had darkened to a thundercloud. My hands turned to ice, in spite of unhindered sun.

"I'm sorry," I whispered. I ran toward the house, toward Mama, all the while hating myself for wishing she'd never come.

That night the parlor felt as stifling as a kitchen in August. With the kids in bed, Mama worked at her needlepoint. Daddy read the paper. Frank stared at the almanac, but I never saw him turn a single page.

I, on the other hand, couldn't sit still. I fanned myself with *Better Homes and Gardens* until Mama frowned at me. Then I wandered from one end of the room to the other, finally opening the sash and sticking my head into the cool night air.

"Rebekah, put down that window."

I turned around but didn't comply. Mama's needlepoint dropped into her lap. "Lloyd."

"It's fine, Margaret." He turned the page and kept reading. "It was getting warm in here."

I spied James's good pair of pants in the sewing basket next to the sofa. I ought to mend them before Sunday. Without much enthusiasm, I settled down to work. Mama didn't prattle on about the women's forum or church or gossip from town like she did in the evenings in Downington. Nor did she question Daddy about politics or financial matters. It wasn't like her to be so quiet. The silence pricked at my nerves as painfully as my needle on my thimbleless finger.

The clock chimed nine. Had it only been an hour? Daddy folded the newspaper and cleared his throat. "We'll be heading home tomorrow."

My head jerked up. So did Mama's. Had Daddy's announcement shocked her that much—or not at all? I couldn't tell.

"So soon?" The words came out before I thought. I clamped my lips shut.

Mama rolled up her needlepoint. "And of course you'll be coming with us, Rebekah Grace."

The words I had been waiting for but didn't want to hear.

Frank looked as taut as a laundry line. I shoved James's pants back in the basket, trying to keep my voice steady. "I . . . I hadn't planned to."

"But you can't stay here—alone." Her gaze raced back and forth between Frank's face and mine. "It's unseemly."

Frank clenched his fists, his eyes flashing anger. He looked like a cat ready to pounce. "No one around here seems to think such a thing. Your daughter has cared for my children. I happen to think the Lord sent her here on their behalf."

My head jerked up. Did he really believe that?

Mama stared at Frank as if she'd never seen him before. No color lit her cheeks, but a slight tremor moved her lips. "Yet you've ruined her all the same."

I gasped. "Mama!"

"I don't intend to take advantage of your daughter in any way at all, Mrs. Hendricks." An edge hard as iron encased his words.

I sucked in my breath and held it.

"I guarantee you'll have your daughter home before the end of March."

Almost six weeks. What was he planning to do between now and then? Court a new wife? Hire a new housekeeper? Would he let me be privy to his plans, or did he think I wouldn't need to know what would become of the children?

"Are y'all going to plan my whole life for me? Don't I have any say?" I jammed my fists on my hips, my cheeks burning.

Daddy crossed the room, took Mama by the hand. "You're welcome to come with us, Rebekah, but I'm thinking Frank could use your help."

"But—" Mama bit off her words at Daddy's look.

"We can trust Rebekah to do what is right, Margaret."

"Fine. But if she stays, I'm buying her ticket home myself." She glared at Frank. "You can pick it up at the station on your next trip to town."

In an instant, Frank and I were alone.

I couldn't look at him. I feared he'd read too much in my expression. He'd know I couldn't go back and marry Barney Graves. And he'd see that Sheriff Jeffries didn't stir more than friendship in my soul. He'd recognize that somewhere in the past few weeks, I'd gone and fallen in love with a farmer.

I sat hard on the sofa.

"Are you staying or going?"

His voice made me tremble. I pretended it was the night air and jumped up to close the window. But the sash wouldn't budge.

His arms reached over me, slid the window shut before he sat on the arm of the sofa. "Staying or going?"

I moistened my lips, my gaze falling everywhere but directly on him. He moved to the mantel, poked at the embers. The shadowed skin that circled beneath his eyes taunted me as Mama and Daddy's voices rumbled from the next room, then quieted.

I took a deep breath and steadied my gaze on Frank's face. "I told James I wouldn't leave. Not yet."

Daddy reached into his pocket before he left the next morning and pulled out a fold of paper money. He peeled away five one-dollar bills and handed them to me. "For anything you need, baby girl." He kissed me on the cheek before he helped Mama into the Lathams' buggy.

Tears rose and retreated in my eyes as quickly as shallow puddles after a midsummer rain. I couldn't do what Mama wanted. I'd made a commitment to the Lord to stay here until He made it clear I should leave. If the end of March came and I had no other options, only then would I return to Downington.

I had thirty-nine days to figure out the rest of my life. I'd mark them off on a piece of paper, one by one.

James's hand slipped into mine. His eyes danced. So much like his daddy's, only lighter in color. So clear in speaking their need. How would I ever say good-bye?

Mama did indeed buy my ticket home before she left. Even sent it back to me with Mr. Culpepper instead of waiting for Frank to pick it up. I stared at it later that afternoon, a lump forming in my throat.

I turned to find Frank standing behind me, his eyes also fixed on the ticket. And it seemed from that moment on I couldn't get him out from underfoot.

CHAPTER
38

$\mathcal{I}$ gathered the wrung-out sheet and placed it in the basket to carry to the clothesline. Beside me, Frank fed another sheet through the wringer and fished in the wash pot for more.

"So did you often help Aunt Adabelle with the laundry?" I tapped my foot against the hard dirt.

The surprise on his face told me all I needed to know. He nodded toward the basket at my feet. "You ready to hang those?"

"Yes." I tilted my head. "Do you want to help?"

"I can." He wiped his hands on his jeans. "Let me douse the coals of this fire first."

I picked up the basket and headed for the clothesline, calling to the boys and Janie, who played far from the fire and the clothes wringer. They appeared for a moment, cheeks brightened by the cool air. I sent them into the house to warm up a bit, even as I considered shedding my own coat.

Then I trudged around to the side of the house, set the basket on the ground, and pulled the clothespins near. Maybe if I got this all done quickly, Frank would leave me alone. Not that I didn't enjoy his nearness. I enjoyed it far too much. And that made it harder to push him from my mind. I jammed a clothespin over a fold of cloth on the line.

Help me, Lord. Help me to trust Your plans.

Halfway through my task, Frank appeared again, his easy grin spinning my stomach and thumping my heart. His hand brushed mine, tingling the skin all the way up my arm.

"I guess you haven't had any driving adventures lately." He picked up one of Janie's dresses, so small in his hands. He frowned at it. Turned it upside down, then right side up.

"Let me help." I took the dress from him, shook it out, hung the shoulders over the line, and pinned them in place. Then I shook out one of Ollie's dresses. "No. No driving lately."

"Did you tell your mother about that adventure?" He chuckled as he pinned one of Dan's small shirts to the line.

"No!" I laughed, reaching for another piece of clothing. "She'd never understand that."

"I imagine not." He sidled an amused glance in my direction. "But you'd do it again, wouldn't you?"

I stopped working, faced him full on. "Yes, I would. I'd like to drive more. All by myself." A smile tugged at the corner of my lips. "Of course, I'd do my best not to knock down your fence again."

His eyes shone with held-in laughter. "And I'd thank you for that."

Pulling my gaze from his, I reached for another item from the basket. "Do you . . . Have you ever thought about buying a car? My brother had one. A Model T. He bought it before he left for France. Mama mentioned he took it with him on his last adventure. Maybe he sold it to pay for—" The words stuck in my throat, but I imagined Frank would understand.

"Tell me about your home."

"My home?" It took me a moment to realize he didn't mean here. When had I come to think of this place as home? I shook away my shock. "Downington."

He nodded and kept working.

"It's not much different than Prater's Junction, really."

"I guess you miss your friends there."

"Friends?"

He'd edged closer to me now, the basket resting at the far end of the line.

I scooted toward the porch, eased down on the step, leaving him to hang the last few things. "I didn't have any close friends there."

"Really? I imagined you to be in the center of the social whirlwind."

"That would be Mama. Not me." I sighed. "I thought maybe if I were in a bigger place, with more to do, more people to meet, life would be more exciting. Without Mama to direct everything. But it's likely that's not meant to be."

"I'm sure you're appreciated wherever you are." His gaze captured mine, held it even as he picked up the empty basket.

Dan tromped onto the porch. "We're all hungry, Bekah. Is it dinner soon?"

I pushed to my feet. "Yes, it's dinner soon."

Frank stepped between his son and me. "But first Dan is going to ask nicely. Aren't you, Dan?"

The child sighed with his whole body—arms and shoulders and head heaving up, then shrugging down. "Yes, sir." He turned to me. "Bekah, could we please have dinner soon? My belly is growling something awful."

I bypassed Frank and lifted Dan so he and I could see each other face-to-face. "Let's heat up some coffee for your daddy while we get dinner on the table."

Dan grinned. Warmth spread from my fingertips to my toes. If only I could convince myself it was lit by Dan's grin alone and not by his father's nearness.

Other chores called Frank from the house more often than not for the next few days. At first I felt more comfortable. But loneliness crept in right behind. And fear. I wondered when, exactly, Frank planned to tell the children I'd be leaving. I felt sure he had some plan.

Weather more like spring than winter arrived as February continued. Thirty-four days remained on my makeshift calendar.

I wiped an arm across my forehead, drying the perspiration sparked by the blazing stove. Janie whined in the corner, her face pink with heat. The boys and Frank would be warm out in the fields, too. And thirsty. Water would cool them. But then I spied two lemons Frank had picked up at Crenshaw's store. He'd had a hankering for lemonade, he'd said. I'd laughed. Lemonade in February? But it didn't seem so outrageous on a day like today.

It wouldn't take long. And the water from the cistern would be cool enough without ice. I mixed it up in a jiffy, then lifted Janie onto my hip, securing her with one arm, carrying the bucket of lemonade with the other, a ladle for dipping it out hanging from the pocket of my apron.

Janie clapped her hands and laughed as we walked through the barnyard and toward the fields. Almost one year old and still no discernable word.

"Birdie? See the birdie, Janie?"

"Ba, ba, ba." She pointed and babbled something else I pretended to understand.

"Daddy. We're going to see your daddy."

Nothing. She just bounced in my arm, nearly knocking me off balance. I held the bucket a bit higher, determined to steady it, to arrive without spilling a drop.

The fields did indeed look ready for something. Not like when I'd first seen them, with their crops newly harvested. My stomach clenched at the reminder spread out before me. Frank was a farmer. He led a farmer's life. A life I longed to escape.

I set Janie on the ground but kept hold of her hand. Frank and the boys huddled farther off, their backs to us, bent toward the ground, intent on something. I lifted my chin and marched forward. Frank had no intentions toward me. He'd said that before my parents arrived and again during their visit.

Frank turned, straightened. His slow smile made me want to turn and run. I wouldn't be tethered to the land. I would find a life that mattered, a life with an open door to adventure, to change.

"What have we here?" Frank lifted his daughter high in the air. Her laughter cackled through the clear air, twisting my heart.

If Frank didn't want me, I wouldn't have these children, either.

I thrust my bucket into the space between us, lemonade sloshing onto the dirt beneath. "I thought you'd all like something cool to drink."

He set Janie on his shoulders, letting her pound his hat farther down on his head. I handed him the dipper. He drank, eyes widening. Then he handed a half-full ladle to James. "Lemonade. Boy howdy, does it taste good!"

The boys slurped down their share, as did Janie. When my bucket grew light, I reached for Janie's tiny hand. "We best get back and get dinner ready."

Frank nodded—that lopsided, little-boy grin never leaving his face. I bit my lip and stared at the dirt, begging my heart to be still, to be reasonable, to understand that I couldn't want him, couldn't want this. But like an unruly child, it refused to obey. And like an exasperated mother, my irritation flowered into anger.

By the time we'd finished dinner and Frank and the boys left the house again, I had to calm my agitation. And I knew a surefire way to do that: scrubbing floors.

❦

Ollie arrived home from school, dropped her books in the hall, and shuffled slowly into the parlor.

"Ollie?"

No answer. I didn't have the energy to fight her. I left the books where they lay and moved into the far corner of the dining room. The final room. I returned to my knees, scouring away the dirt even though my shoulders and back and arms ached. But the exhaustion kept my mind off other things. Like the man who loved this farm and his children.

I sat back on my heels, wondering how I'd find the energy to cook supper. Maybe Ollie could help out.

Dan held on to the wall, his head poking through the doorway. My heart danced at the sight of him, even in my tiredness. He seemed so much more grown up than when I'd come four months ago. Was that possible? I tiptoed across the dining room and pulled him to me. The scar on his head couldn't be seen anymore unless you searched for it.

"Ollie's shiverin', Bekah."

"Shivering?" I hadn't noticed it grow colder, but I'd worked myself into a sweat.

He wiggled free of my grasp. "Shiverin' under three quilts!" He shoved three pudgy fingers in my face.

I rubbed my forehead. Thank goodness the Spanish influenza was no longer a threat. I would isolate her from the others and slather the Vicks VapoRub on her chest. I wished I still had a lemon to squeeze into hot water with some honey.

My teeth searched for some scrap of thumbnail to gnaw on.

"Where's your daddy, Dan?"

He shrugged. "Said he and Brother Latham had to go somewhere, but he'd be back afore supper."

Just when I did need Frank, he wasn't here. No matter. I'd make Ollie rest, and she'd be better in no time. "You and James take Janie to the kitchen and play patty-cake with her. After I take care of Ollie, we'll fix supper."

Dan nodded with the solemnity of an old man before darting off, yelling for James and Janie.

I found Ollie under a mountain of quilts in the parlor, her

dull eyes staring through me. I pressed my hands against her cheeks. Her skin flamed hotter than a smithy's forge, setting my stomach to quivering. Quilts and all, I managed to get her into her mother's bedroom.

As I pulled back the clean sheets, her eyes widened. "Am I dying?"

I sat beside her on the bed, scolding myself for scaring her.

"No, honey." I stroked back the little hairs that curled around her face as I pulled the sheet over her shaking form. "I just wanted you someplace warm and easy to get to. And away from the others. We don't want them getting sick, too, do we?"

She shook her head and shut her eyes.

"I'm going to brew you some tea, and then you're going to sleep. You'll be fine. I promise."

Her weak smile ripped at my heart as she curled into herself and turned away.

✴ ❦ ✴

"Where's Ollie?" Frank eased into the chair at the head of the kitchen table. I turned from the stove and set the pot of beans on the table, ready to spoon them onto plates.

"She's not feeling well. If you'd been here earlier, you'd know that." Where had that come from? Even I hadn't paid Ollie much attention at all until Dan had alarmed me. But I wouldn't tell Frank that. "I put her in the downstairs bedroom."

His chair scraped against the floor before his feet thumped across the hall. The bedroom door creaked open and clicked shut. Even though I couldn't see his face in that moment, I imagined it all too well.

When he returned to the table, his silence prickled the hairs on my arms. Had I missed something? Was Ollie worse off than I'd imagined? The cornbread seemed to lodge in my throat, cutting off my breath. I carried my half-full plate to the slop bucket and scraped it in. I didn't care if Mama said waste was a sin. Another mouthful and I feared it would all come back up anyway.

I wiped my hands on my apron. "I'll check on Ollie." Before Frank could answer, I'd left the room, my insides as agitated as cream in a churn. But Ollie seemed some better when I reached her side—not quite as hot to the touch, or as restless. I sank into the chair near the bed, the same one from which I'd watched Aunt Adabelle die.

The thought lifted me to my feet. I splashed water on my face and pinched color into my cheeks before I forced my feet to keep moving, across the floor, around the bed. My nerves might be frayed to the edge, but I refused to let Frank see that.

Frank. My hand ran over the top of the combination bookcase, across the front of the pull-down desk where I'd first read his letters. A sudden chill washed over me. I tried to rub warmth into my arms, but by the time Frank entered the room, my teeth chattered as loudly as Ollie's.

He looked from me to Ollie and back again before pulling a quilt from a trunk in the corner of the room. To my surprise, he laid it around my shoulders. "Cold's moving back in. I'll stir up the fire in the next room. It'll help warm this one."

I let myself relax into the chair. But then he stood in the open doorway, struggling to control the concern on his face. "Should I go for someone?"

I shook my head, reveling in the fact that he'd asked my advice instead of taking over. "Not yet. I think she'll be fine. She already seems better. I'll sit with her through the night, just to be sure."

He didn't want to leave his daughter. I could tell. But he didn't want to stay in that room, either. I could see the anguish in his eyes, as if he imagined his wife's final moments in that same bed.

"You take care of the others. I'll watch over her."

He finally complied. But even after the house quieted, it was deep into the night before I heard his footsteps crunch over the dead grass on his way to the barn.

CHAPTER
39

A heavy cough shook Ollie's body as the scythe-shaped moon cut the inky sky with a slash of brightness. It reminded me all too well of the wet rattle of Aunt Adabelle's final moments. If the cough turned deeper I'd have to boil some water and make her breathe the steam. At least I remembered that much from my own childhood bouts of coughing.

Night crawled toward day. My head nodded toward my chest in spite of my concern. I knew a night in the chair wouldn't make for a good morning, so I curled myself on the far corner of the bed.

Next thing I knew, I startled awake, heart racing like a train at full speed. The windows remained dark. No noise invaded the house or its environs. I listened for a little while, on alert for whatever had disturbed my slumber. Finally I eased my head back down, my eyes closing of their own accord.

Then Ollie moaned. I crawled up beside her, felt the heat of her body even through the covers.

"It's okay, honey. Bekah's here." Hands shaking, I fumbled for a match to light the lamp. The flame threw its brightness into the room, illuminating Ollie's face, afire with fever.

A smidgen of cold slippery-elm tea remained in the cup by the bed. I held her head and forced the liquid between her lips. After opening the top of her gown, I dipped my fingers in the Vicks and smeared it over her chest. The sharp menthol smell cleared the last dregs of dreamland from my head.

"I'll be right back, honey." Shivering, I stirred the coals in the stove, brewed more tea, took down the bottle of cough medicine, and prayed. I would not panic. And I wouldn't call for help, either. Nights were hardest in the sickroom. Patients almost always looked better by the light of day.

I returned to Ollie with the fresh tea and a spoonful of medicine. She'd fallen asleep again. I hated to wake her, but after a gentle shake, her eyes opened enough to take both. I sat on the edge of the bed and stroked her wheat-colored hair. She snuggled into me, as a sick child does to her mama. My breath caught in my throat.

"It's okay, baby." My arm cradled around her as I whispered the words. I leaned back against the iron headboard and lifted my legs to the mattress. Slowly, gently, I spread the quilt over us. Then I closed my eyes and fell fast asleep.

"Who's fixin' breakfast?" James whizzed into the bedroom.

I'd hardly opened my eyes before Ollie moaned. "I hurt all over, Bekah."

"Janie's awake!" Dan yelled from the top of the stairs.

I put my hand on my head, trying to figure out what to focus on first.

"How is she?" Frank downed the cup of coffee in his hands—cold, I felt sure—and sat in the chair I'd vacated long ago.

"Who's gettin' Janie?" Dan called again. Then I heard Janie's mad cry.

Frank's face looked as haggard as mine felt. Had he slept at all last night? My socked feet hit the chilled floor.

"Bekah!" Dan again.

"Make Ollie drink some of that tea." And I was off. A quick breakfast. Something to feed Ollie. A cold noon dinner. More tea. And coffee. One minute in the kitchen, the next in the bedroom, forgetting in one place what I meant to do in the other. Frank appeared oblivious to the chaos. He had eyes only for Ollie now.

She labored to breathe, even with Vicks on her chest and steam in her face. She barely managed to lift her head from the pillow to drink down the broth I'd made from a scrawny chicken. Frank bathed his daughter's face as tenderly as any nurse.

I took the rag from his hand sometime that afternoon. "Go romp with the boys awhile. They need you, too."

He blinked up at me, confused. As if he'd forgotten he had other children. Then his eyes cleared. "You're right. You'll stay with her, won't you?"

I pushed him toward the hall. "Yes. Now go handle the boys and Janie. I'll watch Ollie."

Worry pecked at me while the boys whooped their excitement at their daddy coming to play. We couldn't endure a worse night than the last. I feared she needed the doctor. But while Doc Risinger had indeed recovered from his tangle with the Spanish Lady, he'd slowed his workload and had sent inquiries for another doctor to come to Prater's Junction. Irene said he hadn't found anyone yet because most of the younger doctors hadn't returned from France.

The sun dipped closer to the earth. Daylight would disappear in a few hours.

"Frank?" I hoped he would hear my call over the boys' squabbling.

He did. In fact, he came dragging each boy by the shirt collar.

I kept my voice calm, though I wanted to shriek. "I think we need to get the doctor—and maybe Irene."

Frank's fingers unclenched, leaving the boys free. Without a word, he charged into the pinking light. I watched from the window until I couldn't see even a speck of him in the distance.

Ollie groaned out my name. I returned to the little mound in the middle of the big bed. "James, take the little ones to the parlor and keep them there."

"Okay. But the fire's 'most died away."

Of course. I hurried in, poked the logs, and fanned the flame. The moment I returned to Ollie's side, my knees hit the floor by the bed, fingers clutching at one another, squeezing until the pressure cramped my hands.

Please, please, dear Jesus. I grabbed fistfuls of the quilt now, and lowered my face against their colored patches. *We can't put her in the ground, too.*

The boys and Janie made more noise than a pack of dogs treeing a coon. I hushed them, managing to get more tea and medicine into Ollie before she drifted to sleep once more. Building blocks still banged from the next room, but at least they tried to keep their voices quiet. And still the sun lit the window.

It seemed like it'd been forever since Frank disappeared from my sight. And yet it also felt like only a moment. I wondered if God had stopped the sun in the sky as He had for Joshua and the children of Israel. But just as the thought entered my mind, the sun dropped behind the horizon and the earth fell into shadow.

I needed light to fight off the darkness. But for the lamps to burn again I had to trim the wicks, and I hadn't made the time. Truth be told, Ollie often did that job. But now my little helper lay too weak to rise from her bed.

I poured kerosene into the clear bowl, trimmed the wick, and touched it with a burning match. Light glowed brighter as I replaced the chimney.

Dan appeared at my side. "I think Janie's scared of the dark."

As I picked up the lamp and plunged into the hall, the darkness peeled back, giving way to light. James and Dan herded Janie to the kitchen while I remembered all the sermons I'd heard about Jesus being a light in the darkness, showing us the way.

Stumbling through the hall and into the kitchen, I brightened another lamp, dispelling the dark within its reach. Had I let Jesus illuminate my path—or had I tried to make my own light? I refused to let myself dwell on the subject, but it loomed up in the gloaming, forcing a confrontation.

Had I mistaken my own light for God's leading? Maybe. It seemed I'd completely misread God's plan for me. My heart had yearned toward the wrong thing. And now it pined for what I insisted it didn't want.

But still, Aunt Adabelle had believed—and said with her dying breath—that God had brought me here. To this very place.

I poured milk, cut cornbread. Janie whined, her hands pulling at my skirt. I lifted her into my arms. Her shape shimmered before me as I heard Irene's voice in my head. *"Life has a way of surprising you sometimes."*

My heart swelled, pushing tears into my eyes. I beckoned Dan and James to my side, pulled them in, held them tight.

Dan wriggled away first. "When will Daddy get back? He said we'd build a tower of blocks afore bed."

"Soon, Dan. He'll be back soon." *Please, God, let him come back soon.*

As if in immediate answer to my prayer, the kitchen door banged open against the wall. Frank hung his hat on a peg, but it fell to the floor. He yanked the gloves from his hands, his bare fingers reaching for mine. "Irene's coming."

"What did she say?" I gripped his hand more tightly, surprised at his touch, greedy for his strength.

"She's not far behind, in the wagon. I came through the field. It was faster."

I poured out hot coffee and handed him a cup. He savored that

first drink, and then his eyes found mine. "They had a visitor—
didn't wait to find out who. He took Brother Latham to get the
doc."

Doc Risinger. Fever, cough, chills. The nightmare had returned.
But at least this time I didn't have to face it alone.

⚜

Irene, Frank, and I watched and prayed and nursed Ollie half
the night before Doc Risinger arrived. His skin looked thin as
paper in the lamplight as he leaned across the bed and examined
Ollie.

He gathered the rest of us in one corner of the room. "I'd hoped
the scourge had passed over us, but I was wrong."

My skin prickled. "What do you mean?"

His wiry hair, whiter now than when we'd first met, stuck
out from all ends. "Spanish flu. I've seen enough of it now to
recognize it."

I shook my head and backed toward the wall. "She can't have
that." My hand crept to my throat, my whispers resounding until
they ceased being whispers at all. "It's gone. No one in these parts
has it anymore."

"Rebekah." Frank took my shoulders in his hands. "Doc's here.
Just let him—"

"He doesn't know. He's just a doddering old man. Can't you
see? She needs a real doctor!"

Ollie moaned. I pushed past Frank and rushed to the bedside.
"Do something! Help her!" My shrieks filled the room before
Irene slapped me right across the face.

I stared at her in silent shock, just as she'd intended. Then her
voice broke through, calm and gentle as an April dawn. "You have
to be strong, Rebekah."

She glanced quickly at Frank's pale face before raising her

271

eyebrows at me. Then she put her arm around my waist. "Why don't you go upstairs and rest? We'll take care of Ollie."

I whimpered like a kicked puppy, but one look at Frank's red-rimmed eyes composed me. He looked as if a stout wind would blow him over. "I'll be quiet. I promise."

"Good girl." Irene nodded as I sank down next to the bed, folded my hands, and begged God to give me the flu instead of Ollie.

For two straight nights I fell asleep on my knees, my head resting on the mattress. When I woke the third day, a yellow streak of sun streamed in through the window and fell across Ollie's body. Doc Risinger and Irene had cautioned me that we might not know the severity of the illness for several days. But as long as the purple spots didn't appear, there was hope.

I studied Ollie's thin face. Pale, from forehead to chin. But no darkening tones. I forced my legs to straighten and my head to change direction. I staggered to the kitchen. Irene and Frank sat at the table drinking coffee. Irene poured me a cup, as well. I sipped it, plain black.

Irene laid her hand on mine. "She's holding her own."

I tried to smile, but my lips refused to obey.

Ah-ooga. Ah-ooga.

Before the others could move, I bolted for the porch, waving my hands for the visitor to cease his noise. One of the older Latham boys hopped from the running board of Mr. Culpepper's automobile.

"Tell Mama to come quick. Beulah's sick. So's Daddy."

Irene must have been standing behind me. She bustled down the walk, the hurry in her step the only indication of crisis. She even managed to remember to wave good-bye as she climbed in beside Mr. Culpepper.

Little Beulah. I licked moisture into my lips as I reached for the column holding the porch roof overhead. But my hand landed on Frank instead. His arms closed around me. I buried my head in his chest.

All I could think was that I'd sent Ollie to school carrying the Spanish flu.

CHAPTER
40

After Frank's arms, I knew nothing, until I found myself in bed alternately hot and cold, throat parched, chest tight. But I needed to be with Ollie. I threw back the covers, or I thought I did. They barely fluttered. I groaned, closed my burning eyes.

Then cool covered my forehead. A wet cloth. I tried to reach for it, but it hurt to move, so I succumbed to sleep. I dreamt strange vignettes of Mama and Will and Daddy and Aunt Adabelle. Arthur and Sheriff Jeffries even made appearances. And those sweet children. Far off in the distance I recognized Frank. I never saw his face, only his back, but somehow I knew him.

Finally, my eyes opened to darkness. I sat up, head pounding with pain.

"I'm here, Rebekah."

"Who?"

"Frank." An arm cradled my back. "Drink this." Tart liquid dribbled into my mouth. "Sleep now."

"But Ollie—"

"Shh." A hand stroked my hair. "Just get yourself well."

I tried to focus on his face, but my eyes wouldn't cooperate. So I returned my head to the pillow, drifting again into a crowded slumber.

People I loved, and who loved me, jumbled together, saying things I knew they'd never say. I walked among them in confusion, no one speaking to me directly. I asked everyone what I should do, where I should go. But not one head turned in my direction. I could only listen.

I woke again, every bone alive with aching. Daylight now, eyes focusing more clearly. No one sat in the chair by my bed. I pushed myself up, reached for a cup of water on the table next to me.

"Let me help." The cup lifted, held to my lips by hands much stronger than mine.

"Thank you." Hot tears slid down hot cheeks, stealing the clarity of my vision.

"Don't cry, Rebekah. Please don't cry." It sounded like Frank. Yet would he be so solicitous toward me? Another apparition, I imagined. I eased back down to sleep, anxious to shut out the pain that filled my chest with every breath.

More tumultuous dreams. Then my brain registered the birds outside my window, my eyes recognized the sunshine streaming through the window. I shifted beneath the covers and spied Sheriff Jeffries dozing in the chair by my bed.

I sat up too fast, spinning the world around me. My shaky hand went to my head, trying to still the motion. The sheriff hovered over me, touching my cheeks, my forehead. Without permission or embarrassment.

He closed his eyes and fell back into his chair. "You gave us quite a scare, Rebekah. You've been in bed two days."

I attempted to pull threads of thought from a tangled ball of memory. "Ollie?"

"She's been asking for you."

I swung my feet over the side of the bed, noticing a rumpled skirt covering my knees instead of my nightdress. At least I had that much dignity left.

The sheriff helped me stand, his shoulder and arm bearing my weight. "I'll take you to her."

I wanted to voice my thanks, but I couldn't manage the words. I had to concentrate on the steps. I had to get to Ollie.

Frank slept in the chair beside Ollie's bed, his elbow propped on a table, his hand holding his head somewhat upright. As we entered the room, he leapt to his feet.

His confused gaze searched my face, and then his eyes narrowed at the sheriff. "Should she be out of bed?" Gravelly words.

"Fever's broke." A clipped response.

I looked from one man to the other, trying to comprehend the antagonism that crackled the air between them. A shiver swayed me. Each man's face softened, but I disregarded their concern. I needed to know about Ollie.

She looked so tiny in the middle of her parents' bed. A slick, almost bloodless face. My stomach clutched. Was she dead? Then I realized that no spots shadowed her eyes or her cheeks. Her body shook with a deep cough. I winced, trying to suppress the answering one creeping up my own throat. Frank reached across the bed and felt her face and the back of her neck.

He dropped back into the chair. "She's still fine."

I wavered. Frank jumped up, caught hold of my arm, and kept me upright. He led me to the bed and urged me to lie beside Ollie.

As the fog in my head cleared further, fear pounced at me like a threatened bobcat. "Where are the boys? And Janie? Tell me." I gripped Frank's shirtsleeves.

"They're fine. They're at the Crenshaws. Under the weather, but not the flu. Definitely not the flu."

I looked to the sheriff. He nodded. Once.

"Truly?" My gaze held Frank's. He wouldn't lie to me. He couldn't. "I promise."

I let out my breath and relaxed into the pillow propped behind me. Then I remembered Irene—the news of Beulah and her hasty exit.

"Irene?"

Now Frank refused to look anywhere but Ollie's face. I held my breath. *Not Irene. Please, God, not Irene.*

A fit of coughing shook me. Frank's tortured eyes found mine, but it was Sheriff Jeffries who found a cup of water. I sipped until the wracking calmed. I lifted my eyes to the sheriff. If Frank wouldn't tell me about my friend, he'd have to.

"Doc's there." The sheriff refused to hold my gaze.

I pushed up from the bed, clung to his arm. "I have to go." In spite of my dry eyes, my voice sounded gruff and full of moisture. "Please. Take me to her."

His gaze slipped to the floor.

"Please . . . Henry."

His head rose. I hadn't expected to see quite so much antici-pation in his eyes, but I pushed my uneasiness aside. I had to be with my friend, as she had been with me.

The corner of his mouth lifted. "You might want to change clothes."

If I'd had the strength, I'd have thrown my arms around his neck.

Frank pushed past us. "She's not going anywhere until she eats something." Watching him retreat into the kitchen, I wondered why I couldn't restrain the upward twitch of my lips.

By the time I'd consumed some oatmeal and coffee, given myself a bird bath and changed my clothes, the sun had risen to full height and I had to lie down again. "Go for me, Henry. Please. I have to know."

He finally agreed. After he climbed into his car and chugged away, I sat at Ollie's bedside and watched Frank coax broth between his daughter's lips.

Seven precious days had slipped away as Ollie, then I, fought off the Spanish Lady that claimed Aunt Adabelle. Days I could never regain. I figured up just over three weeks remained until I must board the train and leave this family behind.

"No more, Daddy. No more." Ollie's rasp rent my heart.

Frank dabbed her lips with a damp cloth, and her eyes closed in restful sleep.

I straightened the top of the quilt near Ollie's chin. A rush of tears dammed behind my eyes, my nose, my cheeks. I took a deep breath, pushed Ollie's hair from her face as I'd done for my aunt, and laid my hand on her cheek, thankful for the coolness.

The horror of my vigil over Aunt Adabelle returned as a knot in my chest. Did Irene share that experience now or was she in the oblivion of fever, as Ollie and I had been? And Mama. She couldn't fight off the ravages of the flu a second time. And what if Daddy should fall ill? She certainly didn't have the strength to nurse him.

"What are you thinking?" Frank's words came so soft I wasn't sure I'd heard them.

I tried to smile, to break the sorrow that stretched between us. "Thinking about Mama. And Will. And Adabelle."

Clara's unspoken name shouted itself into the silence. My eyes sought his face. "Irene won't die, too, will she?"

"We can pray." He bowed his head, his voice booming now as he implored the God of the universe to spare the life of his friend. Although tears rolled down my cheeks, I smiled as I watched him pray. Deep faith, strong character, and a love for others. Could there be a finer man?

"Thank you," I said when he finished. I wondered if I imagined the tremble in his hand as he straightened the covers over his daughter.

278

"Irene's not any worse, but the baby . . ." Sheriff Jeffries's hat spun between his hands.

I stood, in spite of the wooziness in my head. "I have to go to her."

Henry took my hand, led me back to the sofa. "She'll need you more later, I think."

My hands dropped limp into my lap as Frank came into the parlor and sprawled in a chair. His stubbled chin and shadowed eyes sank into my understanding. He hadn't rested in days, what with nursing Ollie.

"Please, Frank. Get some rest. I'll watch her. I promise." I glanced at the sheriff. He didn't look nearly as haggard as Frank. "Sheriff Jeff—Henry will stay a while longer and help."

Frank didn't protest as I'd expected. Instead, he trudged from the room, bent like an old man with a lifetime of burdens. My throat ached with longing. But I knew he didn't want me. He considered me only a blessed help in his time of trouble. Nothing more.

I held out my hand to the sheriff, forced my dry lips to smile. "Come help me take care of my girl."

CHAPTER
41

$\mathcal{T}$hree days after my feet steadied on the ground again, I stood in the graveyard by the church, a cold wind whipping my skirt around my legs and snaking up my stocking-clad legs. A pale-faced Brother Latham stood over the gaping hole, eyes raw with grief.

Irene's bundled shoulders shook as she wept silently. I laced my arm through hers, but liquid fear dotted my forehead. What if she swooned? I didn't think I could hold her up.

But even as the thought crossed my mind, Frank reached over and anchored her from the opposite side. I smiled my thanks, but his face remained blank, as if he grieved a loved one, instead of Irene.

And maybe he did. Maybe this burial made his wife's more real.

Brother Latham paused several times during the service, but he made it through, prayed a final prayer, and dropped the first handful of dirt on Beulah's child-sized box below. I winced as the hard clods banged on the soft wood. So different from the squish and plop of Aunt Adabelle's final farewell.

I squeezed my fingers around Irene's arm as she bent forward to do what her husband had done. I turned away as the earth flew from her hand, trying to mute the sound. Then, at Brother

Latham's direction, I led Irene toward the church. She needed to sit, to rest. As did I.

Doc Risinger took my arm as Frank gave Irene his full strength to lean on. We climbed the steps, and then Frank slipped back to the grave site. Inside, I unwrapped Irene's shawl, unbuttoned her coat, led her to the back pew. She bowed her head. Doc Risinger found us there, pulled me just out of earshot.

"She needs time to recover, body and soul."

I nodded. "I'll do whatever I can to help."

His moustache twitched. "And what about the others that need yer care?"

"Frank can handle them."

"He's who I was meanin'. He's walking on the edge of illness himself, what with nursing ye and Ollie both."

"Nursing us . . . both?"

His bushy eyebrows inched up and down like caterpillars across a sidewalk. "Aye, girl. Didn't ye know?"

"But Sheriff Jeffries . . ." The fog in my brain vaguely remembered Frank by my bed, soothing words, gentle hands. But hadn't I dreamed that?

Doc shook his head. "Sheriff didn't come until the last. He took the little ones to the Crenshaws', but he had other things to tend."

My mouth gaped as my head whirled in confusion. Frank took care of me? Me and Ollie? "But he . . . How could he manage us both?"

"Blamed if I know. But he did. Better than most, I might add. Went without sleep. Without food." Doc shook his head. "Couldn't bear to lose ye, either one."

Either one? My throat tightened, and tears blurred my vision. Could it be true?

"Rebekah?" Irene's voice croaked like an old woman's, clawing at my heart.

"I'm here." I knelt beside her.

She closed her hand over mine as she hauled in a bucketful of air. "Thank you. I don't know what I'd have done without you. Nola Jean's a good girl, but she doesn't understand. Not like another mother."

Another mother? Did she really think of me like that? I felt so young. So inadequate in the face of her grief. I'd never birthed my own child, let alone buried one. But after watching Ollie suffer, I guessed I had more understanding than a schoolgirl would.

She squeezed my hand and forced another smile, all at the same time. "The Lord gives and the Lord takes away. I still choose to bless the name of the Lord."

I pressed my lips together. If she could believe those words in light of the death of her child, I determined I could, too, even if every desire of my heart ended in destruction.

I stayed over at the Lathams' the next day to help, though Nola Jean took care of things. I sat with Irene, letting her talk about whatever came to mind. When the silence stifled, I asked her questions, forcing her to think beyond her pain.

"Tell me about Frank and the sheriff. They don't seem to be friends, exactly."

"Oh, honey, that's an old tale now, but neither one of them can seem to forget. Clara used to laugh at them both. Like two dogs circling a carcass picked clean, Adabelle used to say."

I laughed. Mama would not have approved of such an expression. "What happened?"

Irene sighed. "It was just after Clara and Frank came here. You know all about that, I expect."

"Ollie told me their story." I wondered if Irene knew about the story Ollie had told me of Nola Jean's young suitor.

As if reading my thoughts, Nola Jean arrived with two cups of tea. Irene held her daughter's hand a long minute before letting go, but Nola Jean didn't linger. Irene sipped at her tea. "Clara and Frank, both of them no more than children, rented a room at the Jeffries's house."

I leaned forward. I hadn't expected that.

"Henry was right about their age, but still in school. Frank went off and worked on the railroad, hoarding money to buy that farm. That left Clara and Henry often in each other's company. Clara invited sympathy, with her frailty. Just the kind men like to champion."

Unlike me. A girl with gumption. Maybe that's why Mama kept trying to arrange things. She feared I'd end up like Aunt Adabelle, far from home, taking care of other people's families. I chewed at my thumbnail. I guessed she had a right to that fear.

Irene set her cup aside and leaned her head on the back of the chair. "Really wasn't anything to tell. Frank came home late one night, found them together in the parlor. Playing checkers, if I remember right. He was young. He hauled off and hit Henry square in the nose. Clara was furious."

"And they never reconciled?"

"Henry and Frank kept an amiable truce, mostly. Then Frank left for the war. Clara and Adabelle needed Henry's help, and he always gave it."

It explained some things—but not what I felt to be a recent deepening of that rift. "I'm glad you told me."

Irene looked right into my eyes, and I felt she could read all the way to the bottom of my heart. "Be careful with them, Rebekah. With both of them."

My stomach twisted; my mouth went dry. I gulped the rest of my tea, wishing I could tell Irene all my uncertainties, my fears. About Henry. About Frank. About my ability to know my own heart. But she had burdens enough to bear at the moment, so I remained silent. As I carried our empty cups to the kitchen, I realized Irene's intimations terrified and excited me all at the same time.

CHAPTER
42

*B*rother Latham preached from the sixth chapter of Matthew the Sunday after we buried his youngest child. I latched on to verse thirty-four: "Take therefore, no thought for the morrow: for the morrow shall take thought for the things of itself. Sufficient unto the day is the evil thereof."

It was easier said than done, for my thoughts constantly drifted toward the dwindling number of days and Frank's continued refusal to discuss telling the children of my upcoming departure. I tried to force my mind away from Frank and Henry and Irene— and how it would rip out my heart to leave Ollie and James and Dan and Janie behind.

My heart swelled as I watched Janie change each day. My baby. At least she felt like mine. And that made the battle over worry even more difficult. Day passed into night. Night into day. Yet each bird with wings outspread reminded me again that God cared for me, that He knew every wind that blew my way and changed my direction. And He knew the days that remained of my welcome in this home.

So when a few days later the chug of an automobile up our road caught my ear, I instructed myself not to worry as I wiped my hands and stepped out onto the side porch. The automobile didn't have the distinctive sound of Sheriff Jeffries's car, but it had to be him. I'd prayed for the Lord to make clear my future. Was this His answer? What would Henry say?

"Be with me, Lord." I picked up Janie, thankful that the boys "helped" Frank in the farthest field from the house.

The engine sputtered and stopped. I pinched color into my cheeks before stepping into the yard, wanting the soft grass to mute my footfalls. Janie clapped her hands and laughed. I hugged her to me as we rounded the front corner of the house.

But I didn't recognize the roadster parked near the fence, nor the young man in the driver's seat. He whistled and pointed at another man, one standing at the front door. That man spun around.

"There you are." Arthur rushed down the steps to where I stood frozen. He looked serious, solemn even. His arms reached out as if to embrace me, then dropped to his side.

"What are you doing here, Arthur?" My voice held a flatness I hardly recognized. And my heart didn't skip a beat.

"I, uh . . ." He glanced back toward his friend in the car before leaning closer to my ear. "We need to talk."

"Then, talk." I shifted Janie's weight to my other hip.

He cleared his throat and shuffled his feet. "Listen, Rebekah, I've been thinking." His gaze moved to Janie, to the ground. "I was too hasty—about the children, about everything. We can work things out. I understand that they need you to take care of them for a while longer." He cocked his head and narrowed his eyes just a bit. "But their daddy will be home soon, right?"

Suspicion raised my eyebrows. "What's happened, Arthur?"

He swiped a hand through his pale hair, grown longer since our last meeting. "I'm being officially discharged. I thought maybe you and I, we could . . . all those things we talked about . . ."

Words I had longed to hear teetered on the edge of his tongue, but I didn't harbor tender feelings for Arthur any longer. I read more in the depths of his eyes than he knew, like I believed Clara had in Frank's. Except she apparently saw good; she saw a future. I, on the other hand, sensed a danger in Arthur I'd overlooked before.

"We could what?" I asked.

He looked perturbed. "Get married, Rebekah. Isn't that what you wanted?"

My head screamed that everything I wanted had changed, but I shut away my unease as I considered the possibilities. At the very least, I had to see if he meant what he said.

I swallowed down my fear. "What happened with your fiancée? You never quite explained that, you know."

He slapped his hat on his head, glanced back at his friend waiting in the car. "Listen, I have to go. Borrowed auto and all. But I'll be back." He planted his lips on my cheek and jogged away. His friend started the engine and they tore off down the road without a backward glance.

I stared after them, shocked. The strangeness of Arthur's behavior niggled at me. Maybe he really meant what he said. Maybe I could learn to love and trust him again. But could I resurrect my passion for the dream now buried beneath my attachment to these children—and their father?

We wandered to the back porch, Janie and I. I tethered her to my chair and poured cream into the churn, letting my uncertainties agitate it to butter. A half-hearted version of "Over There" hummed from my lips. The war might be "over, over there," but a battle as fierce as any those boys ever fought raged inside me now. I'd followed my heart only to have my plans shatter like glass against granite. Not once, but twice. And now Arthur appeared again. Was he God's plan for me?

Yet he'd broken my heart, and he'd never made things clear about his previous engagement. I churned faster, harder.

What would Mama say if I took up with him again? Or Irene? Frank, I felt sure, would be glad to be rid of me. But what about Sheriff Jeffries?

More questions than answers arose from my musings. Questions and a lump of butter beneath my plunger.

∗∘∗

Long after the children drifted to sleep, I sat at Aunt Adabelle's desk chewing the end of the fountain pen. Words didn't come as easily as I'd thought they would. My hand refused to write *Mama, Arthur came back.*

Long ago, as a little girl, I'd dreamt of my wedding day. I'd walk into our little church in Downington on my daddy's arm. I'd leave on my husband's. Mama's roses would adorn my hair, as well as the altar. Afterwards, at home, we'd eat cake and drink lemonade while our neighbors and friends wished us well. That faceless man who stood beside me, holding my hand, would be completely at ease with everyone around him. He'd slip seamlessly into my world, as I would into his.

But I couldn't make Arthur's face fit into the picture anymore, no matter how hard I tried. And the thought of his elusiveness on both occasions since that day at the airfield made me shiver.

Unbidden, Frank's face appeared in my mind. His agony in the graveyard. The love that spilled out of his eyes as he listened to his children around the dinner table. The feel of his hand on my head as I lay ill.

I dropped my pen, trying to keep my thoughts from following trails that led to nowhere. But I still couldn't bring myself completely back to Arthur. As much as it pained me to admit it, I'd allowed my head to be turned by a flattering tongue and a pretty face. I'd thought he was everything good and honorable, but his actions had proven him to be exactly the opposite. I didn't think

I could sacrifice the dream of a good man even for the promise of adventure.

Restless feet carried me to the window. I lifted the sash just enough to let in a swirl of cold air and after-dark sounds. A bird called. Another answered. I spied a bright red wing and knew it was the pair of cardinals nesting between the twisted branches of the roses that crawled along the fence. Were they discussing their home? Their children? They twittered again before turning silent.

With a longing so deep it surprised me, I realized my time to nest had arrived, too, even if it meant setting aside long-held ambitions. Arthur didn't fit into that picture—not anymore. And I knew in my heart Sheriff Jeffries didn't either, though he'd try.

I wandered back to the desk. There in the cubby in front of me sat Frank's letters. The few written to his wife. More to Aunt Adabelle. A couple to me. I pulled out the picture I'd once studied in ignorance. The now-familiar grin made Frank easy to spot, even from a distance. I ran my finger over the colorless image. If I were honest, I'd admit that what I really wanted was what I'd sworn I'd never have.

And if I couldn't have what my heart longed for now with such a fierce and sweet desire, I wouldn't settle for something less. I'd trust the Lord before I jumped at the next handsome face and promise of adventure.

I pulled a sheet of paper to me.

> *Arthur,*
>
>   *We cannot be together. Now or ever. I'm not sure it ever would have worked between us. Please forget we ever met.*
>
> *Rebekah*

I waved the ink dry and read it over again. A bit harsh, maybe, but not undeservedly so. I sealed the envelope and, for the last time, addressed it to Arthur Samson. I only wished that he'd receive it as fast as a telegram so I'd know it was over for good. But a telegram would have been cruel, as well as an unnecessary expense. I could be patient.

Back in the parlor, I picked up the big Bible and read until my head nodded. Then I stumbled up the stairs and knelt beside my bed.

"Help me to be patient, Lord. Help me to trust You." The words stopped. On my knees in the dark silence, I realized that by committing my way to the Lord, I'd accepted a journey into the unknown. Fear tremored my heart.

Maybe I didn't crave adventure as much as I thought I did.

CHAPTER
43

*T*hree days later, Janie screamed in protest as I lowered her into the crib for her afternoon nap. Her arms flailed toward me as if she knew that I had but two weeks left to hold her.

"It's okay, baby." I savored her arms around my neck as she calmed, but when I tried to return her to bed, her hysteria began again. No words yet, just tears. If only she could tell me what was wrong.

But she couldn't. So I climbed into the bed the children shared, Janie still clinging to my neck. "I'll sleep, too, Janie."

She calmed and curled into the crook of my body as if she belonged there. The sun streaked through the closed window, warming the room. After a few minutes, her breathing evened. I relaxed. My eyelids grew heavy.

The bellow of a car horn caught me just before sleep. I eased out of bed, raced downstairs, and threw open the front door, eager to stop the noise and keep Janie napping.

Arthur.

My breath stilled in my chest as fear crawled up my back. Hadn't he received my letter?

He stood beside a large touring car, one hand on the horn, one foot crossed casually over the other. The old Arthur, full of swagger. In a dapper suit instead of an army uniform, hat tipped back on his head, satisfied smile on his face.

"I'm here." He opened his arms.

I shrank back.

"Uncle Sam's through with me for good now." He sauntered up the walk, until he stood with one foot on the porch step. "I'm a real civilian again. Mother is so pleased that I'm getting married, she bought me a new suit and a new car."

"Didn't you—didn't you get my letter?" My fingers gripped one another, twisting like the knot in my stomach.

"Aw, little girl, you didn't think I took that seriously, did you?"

"You should have. I meant every word."

He ambled up the steps. "C'mon. It's Valentine's Day. You know you're my best girl, Rebekah."

I crossed my arms and retreated closer to the door. "I don't know that, Arthur. All I know is you had a fiancée and now you don't. You seem to think you can exchange one girl for another, the same way you change from a uniform to a new suit."

His eyes took on the wariness I'd noticed the last time he'd visited. He inched toward me. "But you have to marry me, Rebekah. What'll Mother say if you don't?"

"That isn't really my concern, is it?"

His eyes narrowed, his expression suddenly menacing. "But she thinks I'm getting married."

I. Not we.

An idea swirled, soft as fresh taffy. I pulled it this way and that. Then I cocked my head and stared straight into his eyes. "Did you tell her about me or about the other girl?" As the thought hardened like cooled sugar, I stepped boldly toward him. "Did your mother make promises about when you married that you want her to keep? Then your fiancée left you. Is that it? Is that why you came running back to me?"

He backed away, eyes wide, mouth gaping. I nodded in the direction of his new car. "Was that part of the deal? And the clothes? Maybe a business proposition, as well? Am I right, Arthur? Am I?"

A movement caught the corner of my eye. Frank rounding the corner of the house, baseball and glove in hand, the boys cavorting around his feet.

"Hello there." Frank stopped just beyond us and handed the ball and glove to a speechless James. "I don't believe we've met."

My lips felt stiff as wooden planks. "This is Arthur Samson. Arthur, meet Frank Gresham."

Arthur's eyes narrowed as Frank came forward, hand extended. Arthur slipped me a sideways glance, his face brightening.

"Ah, the children's father. So nice to meet you, Mr. Gresham." He pumped Frank's hand. "I know Rebekah is glad to have you back." He sidled up to me, planted his arm around my waist, and pinned me to his side. "We've been waiting for you to return. You see, we're engaged to be married."

Frank's smile shifted a bit as his eyes sought mine. "You should have said something when I arrived home, Rebekah. I'd hate to think I made a man wait a minute longer than necessary to take a wife."

I pursed my lips and ripped myself from Arthur's possessive grasp, wishing my glare could consume him like fire. "I am not engaged to this man. I told him we were through. I have no idea why he's come here. He has no business with me."

Frank's blue eyes turned stormy when he looked at Arthur. "Is this true?"

"Well, I . . ." Arthur fidgeted with the lapels on his jacket and straightened his tie. "I didn't think she really meant it." His old grin returned, as if he and Frank had a long history of friendship between them. "Lovers' spat and all."

His arm went possessively around me again. I tried to spin away, but he held me fast, his fingers digging into my side. "You know how women are, always saying one thing and meaning another."

I freed myself from his grasp, fists clenched, chest heaving like an angry bull.

Frank stepped between us, the chiseled muscles in his arms flexing tight beneath his rolled-up shirtsleeves. "I don't believe I know that, son. Seems to me, women generally say what they mean. At least my wife always did. And I haven't known Rebekah to do differently."

I peeked over Frank's shoulder in time to witness the color drain from Arthur's face, leaving his appearance more like an alabaster statue instead of a man. He backed down the dirt walkway, crashing into the fence, feeling behind him for the gate, then for the door of his shiny car. "Yes, sir. Maybe I was wrong, sir."

One corner of my mouth lifted as Arthur inched around the front of the car and reached for the door.

"You need some help with that?" The amusement in Frank's voice made me imagine the twinkle in his eye.

"No, thank you." Arthur sat behind the steering wheel, looking like a little boy caught smoking in the hayloft. The gears growled as he turned the car to head back toward town.

Frank raised his hand. "Sure was nice to meet you."

I stood next to my protector as Arthur's tires kicked up a swirl of dust around us.

"I hope I didn't frighten your young man." Frank stared after the car.

"He's not my young man."

Frank turned slowly, eyebrows raised, as if questioning that I spoke truth. My bravado deflated as quickly as a punctured tire.

"I thought he was, once. But I realized a while ago that I was wrong." I hesitated, suddenly embarrassed by the whole affair.

James pushed between us. "Can we play ball now, Daddy?"

Frank kept his eyes locked on mine for a long moment before he tousled his son's hair. "Anytime you're ready, son."

The next Saturday dawned clear and warm, like spring preening in her new dress. With a light step and a tune on my lips, I worked back and forth from stove to table. Bacon and eggs and biscuits and gravy. Whatever had possessed me to stir up such a breakfast?

Frank rubbed his hands together as he slid into his chair at the head of the table. "Woo-whee. Smells like Christmas."

"Daddy," Ollie scolded. "Christmas smells like cinnamon, not bacon and biscuits."

Frank laughed as he tucked a napkin into his shirt. "So it does, Ollie. So it does. But I'm thinking this breakfast smells mighty fine, too."

Janie squawked and reached for a biscuit. Ollie broke one open and laid it within her sister's reach. I set a new ball of butter on the table and took my seat. Frank blessed our food before he filled his sons' plates.

It felt so right, the six of us around the table enjoying a meal. I set my elbows on the table, rested my chin on my clasped hands, and watched. Frank tipped his head, his question as clear as if he'd spoken. "What?" his gesture said. "Why are you looking at us like that?"

I shrugged my answer, hoping the truth wasn't apparent in my eyes.

He picked up his coffee, washed down his eggs, and cleared his throat. "I thought we'd make a trip into Terrell today."

"All of us?" Ollie nearly shouted.

"That's right, honey. All of us."

Ollie's head whipped in my direction. "Terrell, Rebekah." Her wide eyes told me this was a pleasure she'd experienced before, one she longed for again.

"How does that sound, Rebekah?" Frank's words turned all eyes in my direction. "Think you can get us ready?"

I laid down my fork, breakfast suddenly a rock in my stomach. Did he mean this as my farewell party? Maybe he'd tell the children that two weeks from today I'd board the train and ride back out of their lives.

Frank grinned at me and pushed his plate away.

I let out a long breath and managed an answering smile. "I'll have us ready. Ollie will help."

"Me, too!" The boys' words tangled with each other.

Frank slapped his hands on his legs and stood. "I best get my chores done, then."

As he left the kitchen, I grabbed his empty plate along with my half-empty one. Terrell might not be quite as big as Dallas, but according to the things I'd heard, it had a sight more to offer than either Downington or Prater's Junction. And if I were doomed to live out my days in Downington, I wouldn't let this last opportunity for excitement pass me by.

We rode into Terrell behind a skittish Dandy. We weren't the only ones in a horse and buggy—or horse and wagon—but enough automobiles zipped from street to street that Dandy spooked quite often.

Frank gripped the reins, held Dandy's head more tightly. "Times are changing, aren't they?"

I took a deep breath. "And will you change along with them?"

"When it seems prudent." Frank shrugged. "Some things are

lasting; some are gone in a flash. I'll adapt to the lasting changes, but it might take me some time to figure out what those really are."

I considered his words as the jangle of harnesses and the creak of leather intertwined with the chug of motors, just as the smell of gasoline mingled with that of horseflesh and manure. Before, I might have protested his cautiousness. Now I wondered if it held more wisdom than my desire for everything new and flashy.

"'Course, if this bond election for new roads comes out right, I might be tempted to jump right into the automobile craze."

I shot up a silent prayer for voters on their way to the polls, then reproached myself. I wouldn't be here to enjoy new roads, anyway. Let alone any automobile Frank might be persuaded to purchase.

Dandy walked farther into the heart of the city. My head turned this way and that, craning to see every possible sight Terrell afforded. A large hotel. Several grocers and drug stores. Auto shops and harness makers, almost side by side. The train depot.

"Oh! What's that?" I pointed toward a large building fronted with massive columns.

"Carnegie library," Frank said.

"Mama took me there once," Ollie whispered from the back.

I bit my lip, wishing my comment hadn't elicited that response. And yet that was the truth of the matter. They'd had a mama. One that only Ollie and James and possibly Dan remembered. I swallowed hard and glanced at Frank. His face held no discernable expression.

"What do you remember about it, honey?" I asked Ollie.

"Rows and rows of books. And being shushed. A lot."

I laughed. I couldn't help myself. My mama would have had to shush me, too, I imagined.

We rolled on down Moore Street. Then Frank turned and hitched Dandy to a post and we climbed from the buggy. Frank set Janie on his shoulders. She clapped and grinned. I caught Dan by the hand.

People swarmed before the storefronts. I felt certain I gawked like a country girl as we clomped up and down the board sidewalks, my arm swinging with Dan's. My day in Dallas hadn't been filled with such wonder. Only with expectations—and then disappointment. But today Ollie and James walked beside me, wide-eyed and excited. And I couldn't help but join in their enthusiasm.

We ended our meanderings at the soda fountain. With my handkerchief, I wiped away the dirt that had collected on our sweaty faces before we stepped inside. Frank ordered three sodas. I shared with Janie, Frank with Dan, and Ollie with James. As we rested and laughed, the contentment on each face both freed and squeezed my heart.

James slurped up the remaining drops in his glass and let out a long sigh.

"Good day, son?"

James nodded. "A family day."

I held my breath and let my gaze rest on Frank's face for only an instant before my trembling hands fussed with Janie's dress. He had nothing but smiles for his son. What did it mean? Did he like the idea of us as a family? Maybe just seeing his children's happiness had sparked his own. I beat back hope, reminded myself that it wasn't me he wanted.

He slapped his hands against his knees and stood. "We best be on our way back before the sun decides it's worked long enough and heads to bed."

"Daddy"—Dan grabbed his father's hand—"you know the sun doesn't have a bed."

"Oh." His forehead wrinkled as he gazed into his son's upturned face. "Doesn't it?"

"No. Bekah says it goes to the other side of the world at nighttime."

"Does she now?" His eyebrows rose in my direction. Why in the world did I blush and turn away?

"Well, let's race it home, shall we?"

❦

The children nodded to sleep, one by one, as Dandy's pace steadied us home again. I kept quiet, as did Frank. Had James's comment disturbed us both? The thought made my head hurt, for I couldn't discern the answer. So instead, I wondered about Mama.

I hadn't heard a peep from her since she'd arrived back in Downington. I expected a long letter detailing my youthful foolishness for remaining with Frank's family, but none arrived. Had Daddy stayed her hand or was she simply not speaking to me? And did it matter?

She had plenty of opinions as to what my future should entail. But in spite of her suggestions, I couldn't find the peace I sought. Whether she recognized it or not, I had my own life to live. My own decisions to make. The Lord wanted *me* to hear Him and obey.

But as day passed into day, I found myself afraid to ask for His direction. For more and more I wondered if He'd side with Mama and tell me to be content to go back home.

❦

"I've been praying for you," Irene said after church the next morning. Her face didn't hold the same laughter as it had before Beulah's passing. It had turned serious and searching.

I squirmed in my seat, for the first time uncomfortable with my friend.

She sat beside me. "How are things at the house?"

"Fine." But I couldn't meet her eyes. I smoothed my skirt, crossed my ankles, pulled my handbag closer to my body.

She placed a hand on mine. "I'm still praying."

I nodded without looking up, my gaze stuck on her hand until it moved from view.

Then the sheriff stood at the end of the pew. "Rebekah?"

With a small shake, I tossed off my melancholy and offered him my brightest grin. He returned it, tucking my hand in the crook of his arm and escorting me from the church into the gray day. More winter than spring.

"May I stop by this week?" His eager eyes terrified me. I needed to tell him I'd be leaving soon.

"I . . . Well, I guess that would be fine." What could I say? Please don't ask of me what I can't give? Maybe I imagined the question in his eyes after all. Maybe he just needed a friend. I laid my free hand on his arm. "Please, come. It's always a pleasure."

CHAPTER
44

Sheriff Jeffries knocked at the kitchen door just after supper the next evening, his hat turning in his hands, his tongue swiping across his lips. Frank and the children retreated to the parlor as I poured coffee and sat across the table from Henry, my heart thumping a frantic pace. It had been a long time since I'd felt so uncomfortable in his presence.

"I've been thinking . . ." He stared into his cup as if he could read his next words on the dark, shifting surface.

Frank's low laughter drifted in from the parlor. My feet longed to run to him, to hear what childish antic had brought amusement, but I stayed in my seat.

Henry pulled a paper from the inside pocket of his jacket and slid it across the table.

"What's this?" I unfolded it, and my breath caught at the words. "A Texas Ranger."

He nodded, pride shining in his eyes. "It's all because of you, Rebekah."

"Me?" I bit my lip to hold back the tears. Henry would get to live his dream.

"I'd have never tried if you hadn't encouraged me."

I reached across the table and squeezed his hand before I realized what I'd done. I let go as fast as if I'd touched a frozen water pump handle barehanded.

But he held on. "I love you, Rebekah. I think I have since the moment I caught you on the train platform."

I held my breath, wishing I didn't have to disappoint this man.

"Come with me. Marry me." His eyes radiated hope.

I remembered the driving lesson—and the dinner at Irene's. Henry Jeffries had adventuresome dreams, but he wanted a safe wife. Someone to be coddled and cared for, like Clara Gresham. I wasn't sure I could be that, just as I could never seem to be the docile daughter Mama longed for.

I reclaimed my hand, wishing I could soften the hurtful words. "I can't."

He sat back as if I'd struck at him.

"We aren't right for each other, Henry. We'd come to despise each other, I think. Eventually."

His head shook. "We wouldn't, Rebekah. I'd do whatever you wanted, be whatever you wanted."

Such the opposite of Arthur. Humble. Caring. Saying he loved me. "That's the problem, Henry. You shouldn't have to change for me." Why couldn't I return his affection? Why did the Lord doom my heart to care for those who didn't care for me?

"Everything all right?" Frank poked his head into the kitchen, his eyes meeting mine. Those blue eyes, deep with passion and love for his family.

I pushed away from the table and ran out the door, all the way to the barn. I groped through the dark interior, hearing Dandy and Tom and Huck gallivanting in the corral, Ol' Bob mooing from her stall. I lifted my skirts, charged up the ladder and into the hayloft, and wept, wondering if I'd just turned down my very last chance at love.

I kept myself apart from the family after counting eleven days remaining on my paper. Frank didn't ask any questions. He just grabbed three squares of cornbread and a cup of coffee and returned to the barnyard. Or the fields. He didn't bother to tell me which.

I was glad to escape him, for no matter how I chided my heart, it continued to race in his presence. He'd already made it clear he had no intentions toward me. And now I'd refused two eligible young men who did. Perhaps he thought me young and foolish. Perhaps he wished I would leave. After all, he'd said he wouldn't need me to care for his children forever. Yet I saw no evidence that he intended to take a wife to mother them, either. What was his plan?

My disconcerting thoughts set me to slamming pots and barking orders. Courage stirred until I believed I would spew all my words the minute he walked in the door. But I knew how he'd react: He'd stand there quietly, smiling shyly, as if he didn't want to offend, leaving me to bite my lip and turn away in hopes he wouldn't see the flush creeping up my neck.

A whole week I endured, until I imagined my heart would burst from my chest. Something had to change. And it seemed I needed to be the one to make it happen. Ollie skipped off to school that morning. James and Dan raced out the door close behind.

"Stop!" I called.

Their shoulders hunched and heads hung as they turned back.

"Take Janie with you."

"Why?" James asked.

"Because I said so." I led her to the porch, put her hand in

James's. He huffed his displeasure, but Dan bent low, his hands on his knees, his face near Janie's. "You can be the bad guy, okay?"

I wanted to laugh and cry as they helped her down the steps. But I also wanted this infernal waiting to end. I needed it to end.

They turned the corner, headed for the front yard. I ran in the opposite direction. To the garden behind the house. In the far corner, among the soil Frank had readied for planting, I dropped to my knees and covered my face.

"I've waited so long, Lord. What do You want from me?" My weak and weary heart cried for help as the cool morning warmed, but I didn't move. I prayed, desperate for direction. The Lord had brought me to this place, to this family. Aunt Adabelle had been sure of it. And so had I. Until this moment, I believed He'd asked me to stay, too. But the unwelcome new stirrings inside me couldn't be denied.

I had no desire to torture Henry Jeffries or Frank, one who wanted me and one who didn't. And I had no desire to bring further heartache to the children, either. But they needed me, didn't they? Or did I just wish they did?

The longer I prayed, the more I sensed what had to be. "Why is doing the right thing so hard, Lord?"

He didn't answer back. But He knew all about my struggle. He'd sweat His own blood over the agony of His obedience.

Take no thought for the morrow. I took a deep breath, brushed the dirt from my skirt, walked back into the house, and started dinner.

I knew what I had to do, though it rankled all the same. But fresh air and a stretch of the legs would do me good. I could walk to town at leisure, not in haste like the day Dan cut open his head. I would enjoy the solitude, the exercise, and the last of the winter-scented air. And when I arrived in town, I'd send a Western Union telegram to Mama and Daddy to let them know I was coming home.

I set the pork chops on the kitchen table, but I didn't sit. Instead, I pulled off my apron and donned my hat. "I hope you don't mind, but I have some errands that must be done in town. I won't be long."

Frank and the boys looked stunned but didn't protest. And so I hurried away, enjoying the journey much less than I'd tried to convince myself I would.

The telegram didn't take long to write. *Arriving tomorrow. Rebekah.* No other explanation needed. A man I didn't recognize copied down the telegram. Thankfully, no one else stood by to wonder about my business.

I fumbled for the money in my pocketbook. Daddy's money. Plenty to cover the telegram and any cost to change the train ticket. I ought to offer the rest to Frank, for Dallas and for the Christmas presents. Or maybe I could send it back later.

My bottom lip trembled just a bit. I caught it with my teeth. No one must suspect my agony. Like leaving a limb behind. Or five.

I'd heard whispered stories about men with amputated limbs, how they still hurt long after the appendage was severed and buried. It would be the same with my heart, a lingering ache for Frank and his children, no matter how long they'd been gone from my sight.

Frank could hire another housekeeper—someone like my aunt. He could live in his own house, sleep in his own bed, be with his children day and night. And I supposed I'd survive—even though my heart felt like an old dress Mama had ripped to pieces to make a rag rug. I imagined myself as that dress, once a pretty thing to be admired, now destined to be trampled beneath dirty feet.

"More time," I whispered to myself as the road to the house both pulled and repelled me. "I wish I had more time."

Deep breaths calmed me on the outside. Measured steps took

me to Mr. Crenshaw's store, the remainder of Daddy's money clutched in my hand.

Mr. Crenshaw peered past me as I entered. "Alone today?"

Then I noticed Sheriff Jeffries. He paled, doffed his hat, and scooted past. I watched him go, swallowing down the ache in my throat.

"How can I help you?" Mr. Crenshaw's friendly face brought me back to my task.

"Peppermint sticks, please. And . . ." My gaze swept over the shelves. "Two combs, a lace handkerchief, and a lace bib." I laid Daddy's remaining bills on the counter. Maybe the trinkets would soften the blow.

After Mr. Crenshaw had wrapped my purchases, my dawdling excuses vanished. Heavy steps carried me back toward Frank Gresham's farm. I let my shoulders droop and my feet drag as I traveled the lonely road.

Aunt Adabelle's face intruded into my musings, purplish blotches on a bloodless background. A woman, from all accounts, who loved people—especially this family. In fact, she'd used the last of her earthly breath to commend them to me.

"God sent you." Words that had both sustained and challenged me.

I knew Mama loved me, too, but I dreaded returning to her brand of affection. Yet after these months of caring for the children, I could imagine some of the love behind Mama's actions. And I wondered if in this experience came my chance to be different. To let go of the ones I loved in spite of my longing to keep them close. To trust all our futures to the Lord, not to my own plans.

The farmhouse appeared as I rounded the bend. No longer unfamiliar. Now every porch and window and square of yard held a memory. My chest ached, but my will stood firm. Come morning, I'd announce my plan to catch the train home. It would be easier that way. No time for the children to work themselves into a tizzy. No time for anyone to try to change my mind.

I'd make my good-byes in my own way, like Will had. Remembering the last days with my brother, his grace in the midst of his own personal tragedy, made me proud. I wanted to be as strong as him.

I circled around to the back gate and pasted on a carefree smile before gliding through the kitchen door. "I'm home—and I brought presents!"

Feet pounded the floor, little faces lit with contagious excitement. Frank presided over them with a smile as bright as the sun.

And oh, how I wished this could be my real life.

I packed by the light of the moon. An owl hooted far away. A whippoorwill answered. Kneeling beside the narrow windowsill, I laid my cheek against the cool pane of glass. If I'd known what would happen—that a stranger's children would weave their way into my heart and change everything—would I have come? Being a farmer's wife and a mother hadn't been the dream of my heart. How could I have known it would become what I wanted? What I needed?

That October night before I left home seemed years ago. I'd been a different girl then. But if I truly believed God cared for every detail of my life—and I did—I had to believe He preferred this me to the old one.

After one last pleading look into the heavens, I slipped into bed, closed my eyes, and let dreams come as they would. I didn't have the heart to conjure them up anymore.

CHAPTER
45

*L*ong before the sun showed itself above the horizon, I threw a few short planks into the range's firebox and made myself a cup of tea instead of coffee. I'm going home, I told myself, trying to believe it was a good thing. Everyone in Downington would make a fuss over me, like they did over anyone returning from a long visit.

The hot, honey-laced tea coated my throat and kept back the tears that hovered so near. I'd make a big breakfast, and would leave dinner cooking, too. The last time I'd make dinner for them all.

I squeezed my eyes shut and banished all thoughts of *last times*. I'd caress those memories on the train, with the world whizzing past. Strangers would watch my tears and wonder, but not ask. By the time I reached Downington, I'd put on my happy mask. Forever.

"Is it morning already?" Ollie slumped at the table, rubbing her eyes.

"Yes, but very early morning," I said. "I'm sorry if I woke you."

"You didn't. James kicked me. I don't think I can sleep with those boys anymore. I'm too big, and they're too rowdy!"

I slid a pan of biscuits into the oven before giving the gravy a stir and moving it to a place away from the heat. "Don't worry, honey. You won't have to put up with them much longer."

I wanted to clap my hand over my mouth, but I held still, hoping she wouldn't take any meaning from my words.

But she did. Her mouth dropped open. "You mean I can move into your room, with you?"

I turned to the stove and whipped the gravy round and round with a fork. I needed to tell her the truth, but I wasn't yet ready. The fork slowed. I gathered my thoughts, measured my words. "Yes, honey, you can move into my room soon."

She squealed. I shushed her. She threw her arms around my waist and laid her cheek against my back.

"What's got you so excited, Ollie girl?" Frank's cheerful words punched me in the stomach.

Ollie let go, her feet tearing across the floor. "Oh, Daddy. Rebekah says I can move into her room. I don't have to sleep in that big bed with the boys anymore."

"Did she now?"

I could tell Frank wanted me to look at him, wanted to ask questions with his eyes. But I dared not turn. He'd read what I intended to do, and I wasn't quite ready for that.

My fork whirled faster. Maybe my agitation would mean lumpless gravy.

"What's goin' on?" Dan, with James close at his heels.

And quick as butter melting on a hot stove, life moved forward.

I cooked and served and ate, soaking in each voice, each laugh, each turn of the head, saving them up for when I'd need them most. But I didn't speak. I didn't look Frank in the face, either.

Dishwashing brought relief. I could gaze out the window instead of at the family, but my hands fumbled with the familiar task. A tin plate clattered to the floor before I could plunge it beneath the dishwater. I stooped to pick it up.

Ollie glanced at me as she clinked another clean cup on the shelf.

"I sure am clumsy this morning." I tried to laugh, but it came out more as a nervous twitter. I had to tell Frank before Ollie left for school. It wouldn't do to say no good-bye at all. I just couldn't bear a long one. "Go on now. Get your books together."

She jumped off the small stool and hurried away. I dried my hands and took a deep breath. Nothing to be nervous about, I told myself.

"Oh, Lord Jesus." It was as close to a prayer as I could manage without falling to pieces. The Lord knew what I needed. Strength. Courage. Faith that He had some future for me that would assuage the current pain in my heart.

I walked the familiar path to the barn, stopped in the doorway, squinted into the darker center of the building. Ol' Bob mooed. I took it as her good-bye.

"May I speak with you for a minute, Frank?"

He stopped working. "James, Dan. Keep Janie out of trouble."

"Yes, sir." Both boys gave a salute.

Frank's long legs consumed the expanse, and he met me in the bright sunlight. We rounded the corner of the barn and moved away from its wall, closer to the pigpen.

"Is there a problem?" He bent slightly, resting his arms on the top of the rail fence surrounding the sty, one foot propped up on the lower slat.

I picked at the jagged edge of a fingernail and cleared my throat. "I'm going home."

"I know." He looked almost . . . stricken. But it passed. Worried about not having made arrangement yet for the children, I imagined. He cleared his throat, kicked at a clod of dirt. "At the end of the month."

"This morning, actually. I have my train ticket."

Only his jaw moved, the muscle tightening and loosening and tightening again.

I paced behind him, reached the other side of the small enclosure, chewed my lip, waited for him to say something. Anything. But the silence closed in around me. I had to get free of it.

"I've been here long enough. I know that now. You need to be with your family, Frank. You need to sleep in your own bed, be among your own things. The children are comfortable with you again. Besides"—I grabbed the top rail of the pen to hold me steady—"I have my own life to live."

I stared off into the distance, hoping he thought I gazed happily into the life I desired.

The quiet boiled between us until his words spat out like a flash of lightning. "Just like that, you'd abandon us?"

I whirled to face him. "Just a few days earlier than you promised to send me home, remember?"

He shoved his hands into the pockets of his overalls and looked me over as if I were a possum in the bedroom. "They've lost their mother. And Adabelle. Now they'll lose you, too. You don't think they'll feel that?"

I shook my head, my heart breaking into tiny shards. "They're young. They'll take to whoever you bring in as quickly as they took to me."

His face reddened. He stalked toward the barn, then turned and came back, pointing his finger in my face. "Let's get this straight. I've not asked you to leave. You've taken this on yourself."

"It's for the best, Frank. It really is. But . . ." I hesitated. The intensity of his anger made me unsure of my final request. My voice shrank to nearly a whisper. "Will you tell them for me?"

His eyebrows arched. He threw back his head and belched a derisive laugh. "You want to leave? Fine. I can't stop you. But I'm not going to be the one to tell them. You are."

He stomped to the barn. I fumed back to the house. "Coward," I muttered under my breath.

I wasn't sure if I meant him or me.

I knew I had to tell Ollie before she left for school. It would be a quick pain, like pulling the dressing from a wound. I had to say it now, before I lost my nerve.

"Ollie!" I called up the stairs.

"Yes, ma'am?"

"Are you ready to leave?"

Instead of answering, she skipped down the stairs, jumping over the last two steps into my unsuspecting arms. I caught her, but barely.

"Oh my. You're too big for me to catch you like that."

She grinned up at me. "I know, but sometimes I wish I was little again."

I hugged her to me for a long moment, then held her away. I retied the ribbons on the bottoms of her braids. "You look adorable, Ollie Elizabeth."

I took her hand and led her out the front door. "You be good at school today." My courage waned, but the words had to be said. I took a deep breath. "I won't be here this afternoon, Ollie. I'm going home to Oklahoma, to my mama and daddy."

She cocked her head, a quizzical expression on her face. "When are you coming back?"

"I'm not. I mean, I'm not coming back to live here. I'll come to visit, maybe. And you can come and visit me."

Her hand separated from mine. She stared at me, her mouth hanging open. "But we need you, Rebekah."

I shook my head. "No, you don't. Your daddy will take care of you, I promise."

"You can't go." Tears dripped down her pale cheeks, her voice escalating into hysteria. "You can't leave us!"

Then I noticed the back door standing open, James and Dan gaping at their sister, confusion screwing up their faces. Frank stood behind them, Janie in his arms. I wanted to crawl in a hole. It wasn't supposed to go like this. My lips trembled, looking for words to comfort them. To comfort me.

James bolted through the hallway and wrapped his arms around Ollie, buried his head in her chest. I squatted down in front of them, determined to hold back my emotions but sensing them rising out of my control. The children weren't supposed to care as much as I did.

I laid my hand on the back of James's head as if giving him a blessing. "Good-bye, little man. I'll miss you."

"Me, too?" Dan bowled into me now, Janie toddling behind.

"You, too, Dan." I wrapped my arm around him, my nose near the scruffy skin of his neck. I breathed in the peculiar little-boy scent, like a wet dog in a closed room. Then I lifted Janie and kissed her nose before setting her back on the floor.

I retrieved my suitcase from where I'd stashed it in the dining room and raised a hand to Frank. He didn't return my farewell. I wasn't sure he even saw it. He just stared at me with a look of terror.

I dashed out the door, down the walk, and out the gate.

A collective howl rose up behind me. I wanted to run but turned back, in spite of myself. The four children stood near the road now, bawling and squalling, faces mottled red, words pleading. A torrent of tears rushed toward release as I forced my leaden feet toward town.

Then Janie's baby voice rose above the din. "Ma-ma!"

My steps halted. So did my heart. The plaintive cry filled every crevice of my being.

"Ma-ma!"

The caterwauling ceased. I turned. Ollie's horror-stricken face told me I'd heard right. Gripping the handle of my suitcase and clenching my teeth, I tried to hold in my own keening.

Janie dropped to her pudgy knees in the middle of the road. "Ma-ma!" She fell on her face in the dirt and sobbed.

My gaze rose past her to Frank, who stood at the top of the steps. His horror seemed to mirror my own. I'd thought by leaving I'd alleviate his suffering, but it seemed I'd only deepened it.

He made his way across the yard, his eyes fixed on mine. He passed his frozen children as if they were merely trees in a human forest and stopped in front of me, so close I could smell Ol' Bob on his shirt. I tilted my head back, looked into his face.

My heart bumped against my chest, though I'd felt sure it had stopped beating altogether. His arms reached for me, then fell back to his side. "Please, Rebekah. Please stay. They need you. I told you that."

"I can't." My vision blurred as I shook my head.

His thumb caught a tear on my cheek, wiped it dry. I glanced at Janie, still lying heartbroken in the dirt. I ached to go to her, but I didn't want to make things worse. Ollie seemed to read my thoughts. She picked up her sister, but her attention remained on me.

I looked back at Frank. "Can't you see? I'm giving you your life back. Your whole life. Your house. Your family." I tasted the salt of my tears.

He grabbed my shoulders. "But don't you understand, Rebekah? I can't have my whole life back. When I left for the war, I knew nothing would ever be the same. And it isn't. Clara is gone. I have to make a new life now." He sucked in a deep breath. "And I want to make it with you."

"Me? Are you saying . . ." I held my breath, holding the words inside me, afraid they'd meet the air and burst like a soap bubble.

His lips curled into a smile that chased every trace of gray from his eyes. "Marry me?"

A screech overhead drew my gaze to the sky. A hawk soared lazy circles far above me. Ollie's rope-skipping rhyme from school chanted in my head.

> *I had a little bird,*
> *its name was Enza.*
> *I opened the window*
> *and in flew Enza.*

Influenza had swooped down like a hawk on a field mouse and changed the entire direction of my life. But she'd also ripped the veil from my eyes. I suddenly saw my heart clearly, like my reflection in a mirror instead of the surface of a pond. Before, my dreams involved moving away from what I didn't want, instead of moving toward a true desire. Away from the mundane. Away from Mama's directives.

Now I could see what my heart wanted all along: a family to love and cherish, a simple home to call my own. A life lived fully every moment. A savoring of joy, even a relishing of pain, because it proved my existence on this earth, not some flight above it.

Ollie took a step toward us, Janie filling her arms.

Frank loosened his grip on my shoulders, his eyes searching mine. "I came home afraid of being alone. But I wasn't alone. You were here."

He put his hands on his hips, laughed, shook his head. "You exasperated me sometimes, Rebekah. No doubt about that. But you made me feel alive. And you taught my heart to love again. I never expected it to happen so soon."

My suitcase dropped to the ground with a thud, but my mouth refused to move. He laid his hand on my cheek. I leaned into it, eyes closed. A breeze swept past me, scented with the promise of spring. But this time I had no desire to fly on its fickle path. This time, my feet remained contently atop solid ground.

"We'll never be rich or modern, but we have lots of love to give." He moved closer, his body almost touching mine.

My eyes flew open as joy curled up from my toes, lifting my mouth into a smile. "I can't think of anything more I could ask for." Then a giggle rose up through my tears. I bit my lip, but it refused to stay inside. "Except maybe an automobile of our own."

Frank's laughter rang out across the Blackland Prairie. "I'll even teach you to drive it. I promise."

His arms circled me, pulled me close. The children danced around us, cheering happily. And the moment Frank's lips touched mine, I knew that in this seemingly ordinary life I'd encounter nothing less than one adventure after another.

ACKNOWLEDGMENTS

When Spanish influenza swept the country in the autumn of 1918 and, to a lesser extent, in the winter of 1919, it did more than close schools and churches and fill cemeteries; it changed families forever. Two of my great-grandmothers succumbed to the illness, leaving husbands and children behind. In one of those families, a niece came to care for four children (my grandmother being the oldest girl) while their father fought in France. And she married him after he came home! However, beyond those similar circumstances, the characters in *Wings of a Dream* are entirely fictional.

In the process of writing a novel, many hands have a part, sometimes over the course of many, many years.

Thank you to the sponsors of the 9th Annual Legacies Dallas History Conference, where Melissa Prycer's presentation on women during WWI and Dr. Erik D. Carlson's on WWI pilot training at Love Field gave focus to my story. I am also indebted to Lolisa Laenger and Hal Simon at the Heritage Farmstead

Museum in Plano, Texas, and to various docents at Dallas Heritage Village for taking time to answer my questions.

Charlene Patterson, thank you for believing in and championing this book, even in its rougher drafts. Your input has made me a better writer and made this story more than I ever imagined it could be.

Bethany House staff, you are awesome! Thank you for being so good at what you do and for being such a pleasure to work with.

Cherryl, Cheryl, Mary, Leslie, Beth, Becky, Jill, Andrea, Paula, Mom, Dad, Debra and Kirby, Dan and Jen, Dawn and Billy, your prayers mean more to me than you will ever know. May the Lord abundantly bless you for your faithful encouragement.

Mary DeMuth and Leslie Wilson, you strengthen my stories and my faith. I'm so glad we journey this writing road together.

Robin and Bill, thank you for always pointing me to Jesus. You are more than friends. You are family.

I so appreciate my parents, Ann and Don Delp. How do I say thank you for never laughing at my dream, for making sure I had good books to read, and for shouting my accomplishments to the world? And of course for birthing me into a family full of such interesting characters!

Elizabeth, Aaron, and Nathan, I am so honored that the Lord let me be your mom. The three of you mean more to me than all the books in the world. (And you know that's saying a lot!) Thanks for putting up with the writing days, the research days, and all the craziness in between.

Jeff, our journey together has taken so many twists and turns we didn't expect, but I wouldn't want to experience this life with anyone but you. I love you. (And you are an awesome agent, too!)

Finally, to my sweet Savior. I will boast in You alone. May You never be ashamed that I call You my God.

ABOUT THE AUTHOR

*A*fter a lifetime of penning short stories and the beginnings of novels, Anne Mateer completed her first full-length novel in 2001, thanks to the NaNoWriMo (National Novel Writing Month) challenge to write 50,000 words in a month. From that point forward, she studied the craft of writing, attended writers conferences, joined a critique group, and practiced, practiced, practiced. She completed four more novels. Three times she received the encouragement of being named a finalist in ACFW's Genesis Contest before receiving a contract for *Wings of a Dream.*

Anne has a passion for history and historical fiction, a passion that often rears its head during family vacations. Thankfully, her husband shares and indulges her love of the past. Anne and her husband live near Dallas, Texas, and are the parents of three young adults.

Find out more about Anne at *www.annemateer.com*

If You Enjoyed *Wings of a Dream,* You May Also Like…